Praise For

CROSSING THE BRONX

"*Crossing the Bronx* is about family, betrayal, and the emotions that compel brothers to cross each other in ways that are hard to forget and even harder to forgive. David Hirshberg is a master storyteller who compels you to turn the page to see what happens next. His characters come alive with colorful language that is believable regardless of differing cultural roots, economic status, generations, even neighborhoods that change from street to street. What is fascinating is the descriptions and dialogue of the women in the story. Whether you've ever been in therapy or not, you'll appreciate Dr. Silverman's razor-sharp questions and astute comments to Jay's memories. They are spot on. Likewise, Jay's mother, a Bukharan mountain Jew, is depicted with great empathy as the salt-of-the-earth grounding force for her family. Francesca, Jay's girlfriend, is a funny, street-smart woman who masterminds much of Jay's plan to save the neighborhood. She helps him without ever being overbearing. Last, but not least, is *Nonna Ebrea*, Francesca's grandmother, also known as the "Queen of Tremont." *Nonna Ebrea* may (or may not) be a converso who clings to real or imagined Jewish roots. What is beautiful about David Hirshberg's women is that they are so three-dimensional, so believable, and written with empathy and love, which is remarkable given that the author is a man."

—HAYA MOLNAR,
author of *Under a Red Sky: Memoir of a Childhood in Communist Romania*

"*Crossing the Bronx* is a gritty, darkly funny, and deeply human tale of family, crime, and survival in mid-century New York. With sharp wit and unflinching honesty, it follows Jay deVenezia, the Italian-Jewish son of a larger-than-life Bronx cop tangled with mobsters, politicians, and power brokers. From stolen childhood secrets to courtroom showdowns, Jay's story slices through memory, myth, and mayhem to reveal how loyalty, betrayal, and the lure of easy money shape lives and neighborhoods. A riveting journey through the city's underbelly—and the fractured heart of a family—that leaves you asking: Who really pays when the game is rigged?"

—ABIGAIL POGREBIN,
co-author of *It Takes Two to Torah*,
and author of *My Jewish Year* as well as *Stars of David*

"The third in David Hirshberg's groundbreaking trilogy of characters caught in the riptides of mid-twentieth-century America, *Crossing the Bronx* is a gritty, raucous look into the forces—both righteous and unsavory—that have determined the very nature of New York City. Hirshberg has reinvented the story of Jacob and Esau, revealing new complexities in this classic tale of brothers at odds—and added to the mix some strong female characters, raw encounters, and delightfully nostalgic settings (like a record shop with listening booths). Hirshberg asks us to consider when and where allegiance to family must end so that something bigger can be served. This is a witty, compelling book—a perfect completion to Hirshberg's other two novels, *My Mother's Son* and *Jacobo's Rainbow*."

—BARBARA JOSSELSOHN,
author of *The Secret Orphanage*

"*Crossing the Bronx*, the smartly titled new period novel of New York by David Hirshberg—and named for the famous expressway built in 1955—speeds along in many lanes simultaneously. Hirshberg brings alive an epoch of New York history that has echoes of such period cinematic classics as *Chinatown* (the rich screwing the poor in major land and construction deals) and *A Bronx Tale* (fathers and sons involved with cops and robbers), and builds toward the perfect exit ramp."

—JEFF WALLACH,
author of *Mr. Wizard* and
Everyone Here Is From Somewhere Else

"A lost piece of New York history brought to life in this vivid novel of intrigue, crime, romance, and redemption, Hirshberg reminds us of what the Bronx once was, and why corruption—and a little thing called the Cross Bronx Expressway—changed the face of a neighborhood and the fortunes of its inhabitants in so profound a way. For anyone who loves New York, this is a must read."

—MICHAEL LAVIGNE,
author of *Not Me*, *The Wanting*,
and the upcoming *A Song at the Edge of World*

"*Crossing the Bronx* is a novel for the ages—both for its pinpoint ability to bring to life New York City in the 1950s and its rendering of the urban political conflicts that often result in the rich and powerful grinding down the poor and middle class, no matter the consequences. The grit of the borough is all here, with tough-guy talk, bloodlust, extreme greed, and the raw emotions of families struggling to survive in a town that forgives and forgets nothing. This is a Jacob and Esau story, transported to a modern city that's on the move, with a vengeance. Despite all the pressure Hirshberg neatly applies in *Crossing the Bronx*, he ultimately offers us hope—in family and the fighting spirit to take on overwhelming political forces. This novel is a carnival, a circus, a rich coloring of the Bronx that was."

—MICHAEL GOLD,
author of *Horror House Detective*

CROSSING THE BRONX

ALSO BY DAVID HIRSHBERG

Author's website:
www.DavidHirshberg.com

Crossing the Bronx completes David Hirshberg's Mid-Century Trilogy, following *My Mother's Son* and *Jacobo's Rainbow*. Hirshberg's works illuminate the 1950s and '60s, a time framed by World War II and the Vietnam War, when Jews began to shed their outsider status and integrate into the fabric of American society, cloaked with both its goodness and strife.

CROSSING THE BRONX

A NOVEL

DAVID HIRSHBERG

BEDFORD, NEW YORK

Copyright © 2026 by David Hirshberg
All rights reserved.

Published in the United States
by Fig Tree Books LLC, Bedford, New York

Jacket design by Asha Hossain Design, LLC
Interior design by Beth Kessler, Neuwirth & Associates, Inc.
Cover photo: Courtesy of the Lehman College Leonard Lief Library (CUNY)
Author photograph by Alison Sheehy Photography

Library of Congress Cataloging-in-Publication Data Available Upon Request

Hardcover ISBN 978-1-941493-40-3
Paperback ISBN 978-1-941493-39-7
eBook ISBN 978-1-941493-41-0

Printed in the United States
First edition

1 3 5 7 9 10 8 6 4 2

To Ann

CONTENTS

1	You be the judge.	1
2	Some *cojones* . . .	16
3	. . . the *mishegas* that eventually ended up with me in jail.	22
4	I'm telling you, this is batshit crazy stuff	27
5	Newsflash: He's not a Jew anymore.	41
6	They play race music at Spins?	53
7	Tremont's gonna take it up the ass . . .	57
8	I guess it's the same shit as Jones Beach . . .	67
9	So what are you suggesting?	74
10	Little lies, white lies, half-truths, they're all okay.	77
11	I knew it had to be big, otherwise you wouldn't have come in person.	80
12	How'd Bootsie pull that Mickey Rooney line out of his ass?	84
13	. . . the time I called his cat up for a practice *Aliyah* . . .	93
14	You could've led with that, Ike.	103
15	Did she ever say anything to you about the money?	122
16	We'll noodle it out	132
17	You've got to admire their *chutzpah*.	140
18	That *bastardo* is freelancing.	148
19	Just like the cash I collected in 1942	157
20	Back off, schmack off	168
21	He died with his boots on.	179
22	There's still a little left in Alanphant	192

23	Let bygones be bygones.	199
24	It must've been someone else who looked like me	203
25	It hit me like a ton of bricks	208
26	I had so many misgivings.	218
27	I might've been the reason he became a punk.	221
28	What are you, backwards Nostradamus?	233
29	You *schmuck*, you just got convicted by a different court.	242
30	I tried my best to give it all in chronological order	251
31	She became sullen within a short period of time	257
32	. . . he couldn't pick him out of a lineup	259
33	I'd like to meet the guy sometime, to show him my gratitude	265
34	Yeah, I got a brother.	280

Acknowledgments — 289
Author's Note — 291
About the Author — 293

1

YOU BE THE JUDGE.

It was reported in the *New York Mirror* that a City cop had stopped his car when he saw a woman trying to change a tire on the other side of the road, yelled over the top of the partially opened window that he was going to give her assistance, opened the door, swiveled his body out and then, well, was crushed by a car that sped by, ripping the door clear off the hinges and dragging him underneath; when I heard the news, I mouthed, *Say good fucking farewell to Ike deVenezia.*

He'd been driving at night in a violent rainstorm on Crotona Avenue. He'd just gone through the park, and ironically was approaching 176th Street in the Tremont section of The Bronx.

"The Good Samaritan," Dr. Silverman—my court-appointed shrink—said hopefully.

"The ironies of appearances," I said.

"Acknowledging a charitable act doesn't imply succumbing to praise for someone whom you otherwise disdain," she said. "You didn't feel *any* compassion when he was killed? Especially under the circumstances?"

"Did I wish that the man I'd called my father for twenty-three years would die or suffer? Of course not. Look, let's just say that we wore different uniforms."

He was laid to rest at Mount Judah Cemetery in Ridgewood, Queens, on a very chilly December 27th in 1955.

After the graveside ceremony, we went back to his house in Tremont. This was only the second time in my life I'd seen my brother formally dressed; it was an outfit so inconsistent with his station in life—a dark blue, double-breasted suit with a thin pinstripe, a white-on-white button-down shirt, and red challis tie—he stood out more because of this costume than he did as the older son of the deceased.

We couldn't fit more than a dozen inside his place, so the cops and my father's cronies from the social club on Arthur Avenue gathered in the front yard, in the street, or in the narrow, cracked cement driveway between the houses, blowing on their hands, rubbing their opposite arms. They snaked their way in to pay respects to my mother, who nodded formally as each one passed. She never took any of their hands. Swirls of blue uniforms and black suits rippled through the house, then cascaded down the front stoop, flushed away, never to be seen again.

Ike had been 6'2" and weighed 220 or 230. He was imposing without being handsome. But I have to be honest, he wasn't ugly either. Just a normal-looking guy. His presence, however, was larger than life. With his height and his muscles fitting the uniform like the perfect silhouette of a mannequin, people would shy away from him, and when he entered a store or a room, things got quiet. Mr. Amodio was convinced that the guys stealing stuff from his grocery store would unload their pockets and re-deposit the pinched goods back on the shelves if they caught a glimpse of my father walking down an aisle. What my mother had seen in him was beyond me until I got older and realized that a steady paycheck and respect in the community wasn't a bad bargain; although, if she'd been brought up in a different era, she might've pulled up stakes and taken me upstate and changed our names so he couldn't find us. But who knows if that's true—it's like speculating on what presidents would've done if they hadn't died in office or what movies Hollywood stars would've made had they been able to stay off the bottle.

Dr. Silverman wanted to know more about the relationship between my parents.

"My mother could never penetrate the walls that he constructed; frankly, I don't know if any woman could've. Under the circumstances, she held up pretty well considering she'd suffered through the catastrophe of finding out what he'd been involved with all those years. They said in the papers that she must've known—you can't live with someone embroiled in those kinds of shenanigans and not be aware—but I can tell you, flat out, that until it all started to unravel after he died, it was news to her. Oh, for sure she knew he was what they call a *nogoodnik* judging by the guys he hung around with—you saw them, hiding their faces behind papers or fedoras, pulled down low over their foreheads as they went into court. She suspected he was more of a Willie Sutton kind of guy. You know the story: he robbed banks with guns that weren't loaded because he didn't want to hurt anyone, as opposed to Pretty Boy Floyd, who not only robbed banks but also machine-gunned cops to death. So, she assumed the late nights with his drinking pals at the Italian clubs on Arthur Avenue and the poker games in the back of Irish pubs might've included a little dice game, some betting on races, playing pool and darts, drinking contests, that kind of thing. She told my grandmother that he likely fixed a ticket here and there, clubbed the occasional hoodlum a little too hard during an arrest, and threatened a few witnesses—standard things in the force. She knew he wasn't on the take, that's for sure, given how we'd lived. There was this thing with girls, however. Women. There was one a few years after they were married that apparently went on for a while. A couple of years anyway. After that, my mother figured it was just a series of one-night stands. She could usually tell: the alcohol and the too-elaborate excuses for his lateness or forgetfulness. I have to say, through it all, she never fell apart."

"Until you were charged."

Dr. S. had a point.

She'd seen the transcript of what I wrote and read to the judge, the allocution prior to sentencing, after all the evidence had been presented.

The truth is, as you know, I turned myself in. I am guilty of everything you have been told, but it was not for glory, revenge, or reward.

I did not benefit in any way. You may ask if there had been another way to handle it. An anonymous tip, perhaps? What if I had just kept my mouth shut? Was I being a martyr? These are legitimate questions worth considering. What it all boils down to is that I did what I thought was right. I did not think about the consequences, and I have no regrets. I will live with what I did. I only request that when you take everything under advisement, please ask yourself who the guilty party is here, who is really responsible for all of this mayhem, and how we—those of us here in this courtroom and the others who will read about it on the subway or watch it on the news—are going to make sure the things that caused me to do this do not happen again. That is the crux of the issue. That is what is at stake. Your Honor, although there will be some who revel in my downfall, those are the same people who will triumph if the merry-go-round stops with me and fails to bring the real culprits to justice. Thank you."

I resisted the suggestion of my lawyer to ask for forgiveness or otherwise bring God into it. "The judge is Irish Catholic," he said, "and a little repentance may be very beneficial to you; it'd be easier for him to give absolution."

That wasn't exactly the means to get me to come around to his way of thinking.

After my deal, there was another plea arrangement followed by a trial that dominated the headlines of the New York tabloids for weeks.

I pleaded guilty to a Class A misdemeanor, but the judge refrained from making any scathing remarks during the sentencing. He stuck primarily to '*the law is the law.*' My attorney told me later that, privately, the judge wished me well. I wasn't surprised, considering I'd been sentenced to only three to six months at Alden, twenty miles east of Buffalo, with the proviso that upon release I begin regular visits with a therapist, in addition to reporting to a parole officer. They let me out after three months for exemplary behavior.

No one in Alden thought of himself as a criminal. Technically, we all were, as we'd each broken some law or another, but this was the place where they sent the misfits who'd been too stupid to come clean about what they knew of some criminal enterprise or another, or were there for convictions such as conspiracy, perjury, bribery, or embezzlement. Nothing violent. Many of these guys would sit around in the common room or dining hall and commiserate with each other, telling stories that showed them in the best possible light, and occasionally plotting revenge on those who'd testified against them, knowing full well that this was all false bravado. They'd return to their homes and families, reeking of contrition, embarrassment weighing down on them so heavily that they'd appear to physically shrink in front of friends and relatives.

We had room to walk around, there were places where we could play ping pong and watch TV, and radios were played softly in our cells, purposefully kept low to avoid annoying anyone else. We got used to our lives having been reduced to occupying undersized spaces, which for me, wasn't so different from where I'd grown up. Our place in Tremont was small, about 1,000 square feet, with the three postage-stamp-sized bedrooms on the second floor. Eric and I shared what was called a Jack and Jill bathroom, but through high school it was mine, as my brother (only my mother and I called him by his real name, everyone else called him Bud) was older and out of the house at seventeen when he finished school. We had a screened porch in the back that was an illegal add-on, my father's pals having been enlisted to help. The floor planks warped, the screens never quite sealed correctly, and the cement posts cracked—things I noticed only when I left the house for good. The backyard was a misnomer, as there was little grass. It was mostly dirt and hardscrabble wild bushes that thrive in urban areas where sunlight is intermittent and water is brackish, containing oil, diesel, and other debris from the nearby tracks. Separating the yard from the railroad bed was a six-foot-high, chain-link, fenced-in area closed off with a bicycle lock attached to a gate. Inside this area was junk that other cops brought over—the detritus from storerooms that they couldn't pawn but wouldn't give up on either.

The noise from the New York Central was ever-present, and when the diesels were hauling freight at night, the fumes permeated the house and rattled the floorboards incessantly. Occasionally, I'd hoist myself up through a movable cover in the ceiling in the bathroom, which led to a crawl space from which the previous tenant had punched through to the roof. Once, when I was nine, on an oppressively hot night, I scrambled up to the roof and was about to go to sleep when I heard some muffled noises in the back yard. Peering over the edge of the roof, I saw two men unlock the gate on the fence, dig near an old refrigerator, place a duffel bag into the hole, cover it up with dirt and stones, and leave after relocking the gate, having not spoken a word. I was tempted to go outside and check on what I'd witnessed but thought better of it in case the men returned with another load to hide. I said nothing to anyone. For the next two nights, I resolved to dig up what had been buried there. Then I'd chicken out, settling for daydreams about what treasures might be found. On the third night, my curiosity overwhelmed my good sensibility. I scaled the fence and dug carefully into the ground, trying to make as little disruption as possible to the surface. The grave was shallow. After digging only a foot or so, I felt the duffel bag, undid the zipper, peered in, and saw that the blue bag was filled to the brim with bills—tens, twenties, and hundreds. None of the bills were banded or paperclipped. It was all loose. I stuck my arm into the bag as far as it could go and still didn't reach the other end. I couldn't imagine how much money was inside. I looked around. I was alone. My first instinct was to zip it, cover it up, and go back inside. After a minute, I did precisely that, but only after scooping as many hundreds and twenties into my underpants as I could. I walked gingerly to the fence, then realized that the money would fall out when I climbed it, so I threaded the bills through the openings of the fence, scaled the fence again, and ran inside to get something big enough to hold my haul. The laundry bag was big enough, but my mother would find it in the morning. A shoebox that held my stamps was too small, and anyway, where would I put the stamps? I started to panic. Then I thought of the perfect hiding place. I retrieved Alanphant from the chair where he'd kept a watchful eye on me since I was six years old. I kissed him, and told him it was all being done for a good cause. I took out my Swiss Army knife from a drawer, sliced into the stuffed animal's back, removed most of the padding, and replaced it with the money I'd stolen from the hole out back. I reminded myself to stitch up Alanphant in the morning. Then I went to sleep.

IN 1939, MY MOTHER TOOK ME and my grandmother to the World's Fair in Flushing Meadows Park in Queens. They were most interested in gawking at the 600-foot-high Trylon, the extraordinarily huge Perisphere, and the nearly 1000-foot-long Helicline, a staircase that connected these monumental structures: the three centerpieces of The World of Tomorrow. I, on the other hand, was mesmerized by the cows on the automatic rotating milking machine platform and was especially excited to see Elsie herself, in the flesh, a symbol that hooked me to Borden's milk for the rest of my childhood. The Futurama exhibit contained a 1/3-mile ride suspended over a future America, where you could look down upon many thousands of models of what life would be like in 1960. Being six, I was particularly enchanted by the hawkers of games of chance and food, the barkers who'd offer free eats and prizes—inducements to lighten adults' wallets for their kids. Passing by one of these stations, I was struck by the sight of an enormous stuffed animal, almost my height—a mass of gray fabric with a long stringy tail, giant floppy ears, an elongated snout, and two immense tusks jutting out from its lips. I stopped in my tracks. I had to have it. Even at that young age, I knew not to make demands or to carry on in such a way as to annoy my mother. I made a beeline to grandma. I pointed to the animal and suggested that it would be a nice gift for my brother, who was at school and couldn't join us.

"Which one?" Grandma asked, seeing right through my ruse.

I pointed.

"The big gray elephant?" Grandma asked.

"Yes, the Ellenphant!" I exclaimed.

My mother and grandma looked at me to see if I was making a joke.

"Now, how can you refuse a kid who's in love with an Ellenphant?" said the man behind the counter.

Needless to say, they bought it for me. After caressing it for the hour and a half it took to get home via the Flushing Line, the 42nd Street Shuttle, and the Number 5, I placed Ellenphant on my bed. When I showed my new prized possession to my brother, he said, "It's not Ellenphant, you dipshit. It's Alanphant." At least that's the way I heard it. Even when I eventually learned the correct pronunciation, he was Alanphant to me—my steadfast friend who never divulged the secret he kept inside for years:

That I was a thief.

OCCASIONALLY, I'D GO UP on the roof with my brother during the day. One time, the landlord spotted us and shouted at us to get the hell down. Eric configured his right hand into a gun, pointed it at the dumpy guy and said, "Go fuck yourself." To me, he said, "I'm not afraid of a *guinea* named Pappalardo who owns a beauty parlor."

My brother had nicknames for his friends: "Nappy" Nate, "Paddy" Sean, and "Caramba" Carlos. Having said this, I can tell you that Eric wasn't a bigot. He got as well as he gave from these very same guys: sometimes "ric-dick" or "e-prick"; he took no offense. Actually, I kind of think he was proud of it, as he was the ringleader of these swells who all grew up around us and whose ambition was first to apprentice to the *goombahs*, *hooligans*, and *gamberros* who controlled the streets and then to replace them. In our neighborhood, we called hoods *rocks*, and Eric was the most polished stone in the community. He was the spitting image of our old man by the time he was eighteen. They had the same coal-brown eyes. Eric was just a little bit shorter, but his muscular arms and thick neck advertised his toughness. Coupled with black hair exaggeratedly swirled into a giant curl that hung down between his eyebrows, he wasn't someone to challenge; you didn't talk back to him. He bought a 1937 brown Dodge coupe with his craps winnings when he was sixteen and drove it around Tremont with the radio blaring to enhance his stature with friends and foes alike. The rumble of the muffler served as a magnet, attracting the sisters and female friends of wannabe hoods. Driving around our neighborhood with a cutie nestled up against him got nods and winks from the old men on their stoops, who undoubtedly fantasized that they could've taken Eric's place back in the day, regardless of how unlikely that would've been. I've noticed that the older a guy gets, the greater his proclivity to see himself in a magnified role when he revisits his past—a harmless invention that helps him get through a day of chronic physical aches and mental anguishes.

MY BROTHER WOULD YELL at me for the most inconsequential things despite my mother's protestations. He'd respond by laughing, swiping something she'd made in the kitchen, and stomping out, shoveling whatever he'd grabbed into his mouth and continuing his rant until the front door slammed and he was drowned out by the sounds of cars or the train. It could've been dead of winter, but my mother's face would be on fire, reflecting an anger that couldn't ever be suppressed.

Eric was a bully. And a jerk. He'd trip me, knock me off my bicycle, break my pencils, hide my scrapbooks, steal my stamps, short sheet my bed, take my change, spill ink on my homework, give me noogies, and embarrass me in front of my friends by revealing intimacies. It was endless. I lived in fear. There wasn't much I could do except stew about it. And tell my mother. As I got older, I didn't run to her as often. The very last time I did, it was with a specific purpose. It was winter. All the kids on the block would have snowball fights, and although I was always on my brother's side, I had the urge to cold-cock him with one when he wasn't looking. But I never did. Eric's specialty was to create two kinds of snowballs: small, hard-packed ones dosed with a coating of water which turned them into ice balls and ones shaped around a stone.

I was walking home from my Hebrew lessons on one of the coldest days of the year, in a snowstorm, after the sun was down, the only light coming from the occasional bulb over a front door, when I saw a group of more than a dozen boys engaged in what I can only describe as a snowball fight that simulated a street brawl. It was intense. I didn't want to get involved, so I circumvented the attack zone, walking behind the house adjacent to ours to sneak up to our back door. Next to the milk box, I noticed Eric's stash of snowballs—the ones with the stones inside of them. It was time. I picked one up and walked back around the house, peeking out from behind the corner that faced the street. I saw Eric. He didn't see me. I let loose with the hardest throw I'd ever attempted. It missed Eric but slammed into the face of a kid he was fighting, who went down as if he'd been hit by an uppercut from Rocky Marciano. He screamed. I withdrew to the back of the house, unseen, opened the side door, and showed my mother Eric's stack of stone-filled snowballs.

The upshot? The kid was taken to the hospital with a broken nose and two busted teeth. Eric was booked as a juvenile delinquent the next day and taken to Juvie Hall, where he spent the rest of the school year. The parents of the injured kid spread the word in the neighborhood that they'd seek retribution but were persuaded otherwise after a woman named Donatella delivered a cash-fat envelope to their house. My father's version of discipline to Eric was to instruct him never to make snowballs with stones inside of them again. My mother was so frustrated with both of them that she packed me up and went to her mother's house in Pelham Bay, where we stayed until the end of the Christmas vacation.

That was my revenge. I never hesitated in betraying my brother and tricking my mother. I succeeded in getting my brother punished for something he didn't do. I was a liar and a manipulator in addition to being a thief. I had no guilt. None. My mother praised me for showing her the evidence that allowed her to turn in my own brother. She gave me a hug, rubbed my back, and cooed, "You're such a good, honest boy."

Alanphant and snowballs were the most memorable things I could recall from my childhood.

When I mentioned these things to Dr. S., she said, "You know, Jay, some memories can take on a different characteristic each time they're recalled."

I was thinking: *She has a point here—pay attention.*

She continued. "Details can be subjected to a withering cross on the witness stand of memory, and you can't be expected to provide an identical answer to multiple questioners because you can be probed under very different sets of circumstances and at times far removed from the event."

I couldn't tell if this was her fancy, clinical way of saying she didn't always believe every word of my stories but was with me in gist.

"It's said that our memories play tricks on us as if they're distinct from us—a second party that's been granted a dispensation from our primary remembrances with no recriminations or ill will. So, do we suffer a penalty if we're flagged with a minor memory infraction even if there's no harm to third parties? Does it matter if we paraphrase what someone said even though we report it in quotes as if it were a verbatim transcription? What if we leave things out by omission or commission? Aren't we then editorializing instead of reporting? And what do we make of diaries or other notes written down immediately after an event? Aren't we a little too eager to accept these words as actual records instead of critically assessing them while keeping in mind the author's slant, which may put him or her in a more favorable light than otherwise might've been the case?" She ruffled through her notes. "In your situation, though, the details you shared with the police, your attorney, your friends, and me have always been essentially the same."

Yes, I had experience on the wrong side of a cross examination, so I knew what she was talking about. As I sat there listening to her, my mind wandered back to the plea agreement that was the root cause of why I was in her office. When the DA and my attorney gave their summations to the judge, they gave slightly different versions of what I'd done, but both statements stuck to basically the same set of facts. I didn't dispute the events or the timeline. My attorney argued that the *intent* of what I'd done wasn't criminal and that, in fact, I'd been trying to prevent a crime from taking place.

Dr. Silverman was right. Recalling my day in court, I saw the judge, prosecutor, and those in the peanut gallery—especially the stringers and photographers from the papers. Their sensational headlines would compete for attention at the newsstands, promising a main course of murder with a side dish of corruption of the high muckety-mucks. The reporters would seize on any seeming inconsistency in my testimony to paint me in an unfavorable light, thereby casting doubt on the guilt of the defendants.

"I'm doing my best to tell it all to you exactly as it happened," I said to Dr. S.

"I appreciate that, because I only know what I've read in the papers or seen on the news."

"What good would it do me to lie to you now? I've done my time. The facts are the facts. But you're right; if I were to tell you the same set of facts six months from now, I might not use the same words, and I might tell them with a different style or add a little color here and there, but the substance would be the same, that I can tell you for sure, one hundred percent," I replied with satisfaction.

"It's as if you're writing a memoir with me, Jay, a fusion of memory and imagination, thematic reflection and good old-fashioned storytelling that details pivotal events and emotional incidents into scenes."

In just a couple of minutes, she'd managed to help me rebuild the feeling of confidence that had been lost to me since before this whole episode began. I left her office with the same feeling I had when I'd walk into Coogan's and notice a woman stealing a glance at me, careful not to let her date notice. I'm taller than my old man and my brother and don't have their Charles Atlas physiques, but at forty pounds lighter, I cut a pretty svelte figure. I have my mother's slim build and light blue eyes that mesh well with what she likes to call my thick, ginger hair. I keep it short, with a beard of equal length, having cut both after my maternal grandmother remarked to all at a Thanksgiving dinner that I looked like a golem, as if she'd seen one herself, so there was no need to deny her certitude.

Dr. Leah Silverman was a babe, pure and simple. I could tell from the diplomas on the wall that she was ten years older than I, but if I hadn't seen the dates, I would've assumed she was my age. She was about 5'6" and had short, black hair cut in the Audrey Hepburn style, as opposed to the Lauren Bacall look, which was all the rage with the girls from The Bronx, who admired the queen of film noir even more, knowing she'd grown up in our neighborhood as Betty Joan Perske.

Despite the fact that she got paid a pittance by the state to deal with ex-cons like me, she gave it her all as if I were one of her posh clients. I'd occasionally see them in the lobby of her building, pretending they were there waiting for a friend instead of biding their time before spinning jaded versions of events to their shrink—about issues that guys like me would find trivial or absurd. I mean, if I told any of those nervous Nellies *my* stories, they'd dump a brick and would run out without wiping themselves.

I have to tell you, Dr. S. was the part of the judge's requirement that I liked. I had to see her once a week for three months after I was released, so I arranged for it to immediately follow the visit with my parole officer, a good-enough, chain-smoking, near-to-retirement Irish guy with a brogue so thick I had to follow his lips to make sure I got what he was saying. He was as bored with his job as I was with the repetitive nature of the checklist of questions he asked. I always showed up on time and didn't give him any crap. The last thing I wanted was for him to send in a report that might trigger the judge to send me back to the can. The word that had me shit-scared was *recidivism*, which had been pounded into me by my lawyer, who'd taken the case as a favor to a rich, Jewish client who arranged for him to defend me on account of my being a fellow member of the tribe.

Yeah, I'm a Bronx Jew from a working-class family. I'd go with my mother to Kabbalat Shabbat services on Friday nights (I can't remember my father or brother ever going with us). She bought me books on Jews and Jewish history for my birthdays. I even had a mezuzah on my bedroom door. I studied with Rabbi Leviev, the furthest thing from a caricature of a Hebrew teacher you could imagine. He was smart, had a wonderful sense of humor, and told stories of Bible figures, assuming their identities as a way to make this unfamiliar language understandable. I don't shy away from saying that I looked forward to Hebrew school.

My father was a *dago*-Jew, more Italian than Heeb. deVenezia, from the original ghetto. Orphaned, which may explain his lust for acceptance by those in power and his rage when he beat the shit out of me. Or maybe not. Let's face it, I'm not the shrink. He was the only Jew in the orphanage with a hundred Catholic kids, and it was his good fortune that he had the physical characteristics to stand up for himself. At twelve, he pried a crucifix off one of the walls and used it to pound the daylights out of a kid four years older who'd taunted him in front of the others on account of his circumcised dick. That night, so he said, he got rid of Isaac and became Ike—the self-described Ike the Kike. How's that for balls?

How my mother put up with him is beyond me. Her family came from Krasnaiya Sloboda in Azerbaijan, one of the so-called Mountain Jews of whom it was said that they'd stopped at the base of the mountain, gazed up, and prayed to God that they wouldn't have to climb it. Instead, they endured passage on a horse-drawn cart that took weeks to get to Odessa, where they got on a tramp steamer that eventually took them to the Promised Land: The Bronx, New York.

Here's how they met: My old man had just graduated from the academy and was a patrolman in the 44th precinct in The Bronx, close to Yankee Stadium on 161st Street. He was initially assigned to look out for fare jumpers on the platform of the Number 4 train at 167th Street and then to position himself near the pizza shops and bars on the blocks next to the Stadium to be within earshot of some owner who'd rush into the street after someone who'd skipped out on his tab. One look at Ike the Kike and the jig was usually up. He'd stand there, stropping his billy club, and if that didn't deter the guy, my father would holler at the top of his lungs that a slice wasn't worth a bullet in the back, which would always get the guy to stop. Invariably, this would result in Ike getting a lifetime pass for food and beer, no questions asked. It was after witnessing one of these events that my maternal Uncle Mikhail (known as Mickey) introduced Ike to his sister. For the record, although Mickey said he was a witness, it's also possible, probably even likely, that he was the *schmuck* who stole the pie. At any rate, my mother and father first met outside the six-story limestone and brick apartment where my grandparents had escaped to freedom, surrounded by their Bukhori-speaking neighbors in Pelham Bay, gratified that they could melt in peace into the American pot. Or so they thought.

IT'S EASY TO UNDERSTAND how my father was attracted to my mother. With lightly colored olive skin, luminescent hair that seemed to catch the light and encompass her head like a faint halo, deep set blue eyes, high cheekbones, and a smile that beckoned both men and women, she was most frequently characterized as exotic, a descriptive that was a conversation starter, especially for those who'd never encountered anyone who didn't have conventional looks.

When my father wanted to put on the charm, he could do so with the best of them, and that he did to woo my mother. She was shy with those she didn't know well, but on the dance floor, she imagined herself in a Busby Berkeley dance routine from the musical *A Connecticut Yankee*, wearing an elaborate costume when she and Ike would whirl around at a Sunday afternoon synagogue dance. After my father's funeral, she told me that those hours when they danced were the happiest of her life, when Ike shed both his cop clothes and demeanor to simply enjoy her presence. They married in 1928. Eric was born the next year. They moved to the house in Tremont that overlooked the train tracks, six blocks east of the Grand Concourse and a few blocks west of Tremont Park. There, during the day, women with their children roamed the playground, fields, and rock outcroppings. The night belonged to the Italian men who played chess and checkers, smoked cigars, drank high-alcohol Marsala wine, and started speaking in dialect when a stranger entered the park.

It was rumored that Vincent Impellitteri, the future mayor, would meet at night in the park with Tommy Lucchese, the boss of his namesake crime family, and stroll among the players, dispensing goodwill in the form of twenty dollar bills—deposits that would pay loyalty interest in the form of votes and *omertà*. The echoes of those meetings were heard all the way up to the sidewalk tables outside of the *pasticcerias* and the *panetterias* on Arthur Avenue, where the *vecchios* would sit, sip, and snarl the days away. Only later did I find out that the park was also the place where my father and brother had a rendezvous in the middle of the night with Robert Moses, who wielded the most power in New York despite never having held an elected office. You could say that it was inevitable that this park where I used a Spaldeen to play stickball, handball, punchball, and a version of stoopball against the rocks was where all the narratives of my origin story really converged. For better or for worse.

You be the judge.

2

SOME COJONES...

Giaquinto Brothers started out the way most immigrant construction businesses did in the early 1890s—with a horse-drawn cart that carried wreckage away from building sites—cracked bricks, broken pieces of concrete, rusted iron supports, twisted window frames, clogged pipes, and assorted undocumented rubble. Manhattan was transitioning to higher rises to accommodate its growth as the engine of trade for the forty-four states. The mass of new construction was constrained only by the speed and efficiency of the carting companies that could make the trash disappear. Powerful draft horses pulled the debris uptown to be deposited in barges that would offload the contents onto shorelines of the Spuyten Dyuvill Creek that extended the landmass of The Bronx, as well as to the east side of the Hudson River, where new docks were being built at a furious pace to enable goods to be transported to and from Europe and the Orient. By the turn of the century, Giaquinto Brothers had a dozen carriages and, in 1904, they invested in a Manhattan truck made by Mack Brothers Motor Car Company, which soon supplanted the horse-drawn carriages.

The brothers insinuated themselves into political clubs throughout the City. Substantial contributions enabled them to exercise undue influence with the powers to be in Tammany Hall, quite an achievement in the Irish Catholic dominated organization. Richard "Boss" Croker had a Giaquinto daughter as a mistress, and this opened up the way for the company to be awarded lucrative, no-bid contracts to build bridge approaches, parking garages, apartments, sanitation facilities, and firehouses. They had no prior experience in creating these kinds of structures, but with sky-high fees they had enough c-notes to bring in the best tradesmen, kick back to the members of the Hall, and create a gorilla squad to patrol properties at night to prevent theft of materials, which could fetch disproportionately high amounts of cash from another builder short on limited supply items.

Prosperity allowed them to build in and occupy houses on the Grand Concourse, the elegant avenue that connected Van Cortlandt Park to the north with the Madison Avenue Bridge in the south, which spanned the Harlem River and connected The Bronx to Manhattan Island. The arrival of the second oldest brother—Alberto "2-Cig" Giaquinto—to a four-story mansion at the corner of the Grand Concourse and 188th Street set the stage for my father being a cop, my brother being a punk, and me being a turncoat.

Alberto usurped the leadership role in his generation after convincing his younger siblings that their syphilitic oldest brother was a liability to their newfound status. The brother's near blindness, uncoordinated movements, and emerging dementia were the subject of ridicule in the Hall and the mayor's office, where the distribution of contracts depended not only on *la bustarella* but also on the perception that these second-generation immigrants had rid themselves of the trappings of the first. When it became embarrassing for the family to sit with him on Sundays at Our Lady of Good Counsel Parish on Park just south of 178th Street, the time had come for Alberto to act. He told his younger brothers that the eldest had been sent away to a sanitarium near Lake Placid; no one either questioned Alberto about the decision or asked for the address upstate. They wouldn't have found him if they'd looked.

Alberto was of average height with above average girth. His moustache, eyebrows, nose, and ears looked like they were removable parts on the Mr. Potato Head doll I got for my Uncle Mickey's daughter when she turned eight in 1952. He constantly smacked his lips and pushed his tongue against the side of his mouth, which made it appear his jowls could also be disassembled. He lived large, as they say. His appetite was big for all things: food, clothes, women, cars, and the day-to-day accoutrements of life, which included partying with the boys at the social club on Arthur Avenue. It was there that he'd celebrate a new contract, a new car, a new babe, or a photo in a broadsheet—each acquisition being the excuse for him to hand out a cigar to the first bootlicker who'd wish him well, whereupon he'd take out one for himself and light both with a ten-dollar bill. It was okay for these sycophants to call him "2-Cig," but heaven forbid anyone else did so; it would set off repercussions no one wanted to know about.

One day when he was outside the club sipping espresso with his cronies, a tall, bulky kid of about sixteen wandered up. He bent over and picked up a money clip by the cast-iron chair and, addressing 2-Cig as "sir," inquired if the clip was his. He placed the clip next to Alberto's empty espresso cup, tipped his cap, and then withdrew immediately, resuming his walk down the street. Alberto Giaquinto bellowed out, "Hey kid, com'ere, come back here, com'over here, I want to meet ya, formal-like." The kid looked back, and without hesitation not only returned but grabbed an empty seat at the table and offered his hand to 2-Cig, who guffawed. This elicited nervous laughter from the minions who took their cues from the guy to whom even the priests would defer. "Some *cojones*," Alberto said to the others. He turned and noted to the kid, "That's balls in spic talk, in case ya didn't know."

"*Testicoli*," the kid said, then raised himself a few inches, grabbed his nuts with his right hand, and jutted his chin forward in a nodding fashion.

This prompted Alberto to stand, which caused his audience to gasp, anticipating a beat down, but instead, he smiled, gestured for the kid to make himself comfortable, and asked him his name.

"deVenezia," he said by way of introduction, and that's how my father met the Giaquinto family in the summer of 1918—one of those serendipitous occurrences that can have profound repercussions no one can anticipate. For the first few years that Ike the Kike worked for 2-Cig, he never told anyone his first name. They didn't know he was a Jew. He was just another wop from Venice who spoke an Italian that was somewhat understandable to the Sicilians who worked in the construction company and frequented the social club on Arthur Avenue. He started out as a night watchman, guarding the sites for the jobs the Giaquintos were working. He'd been provided a heavy flashlight, thick, steel-toe boots, bib overalls, and a flat cap that he could pull down over his ears on cold nights. And in an easily accessible buttoned pocket on the left front of the overalls, he kept a razor-sharp shiv. When I was little, Eric told me about this. Then he pretended to come at me while making a stabbing motion. I flinched and told him to get off it, which enraged my brother into continuing to do it. Eventually, after exhausting his moment of superiority, he took up some other activity as if the pretend assault had never taken place. Given the fear of my father from the earliest days, I always assumed that Eric was acting out a real event our father had told him about.

"DID IT EVER OCCUR TO YOU that Eric fabricated this story as a means of having you live in fear of him as you did of your father?" Dr. S. asked during one of our first sessions.

"Sure, but all it did was reinforce my apprehension about being alone with Eric," I replied.

"Did he ever overtly threaten you?"

"You mean come at me with a knife or make a motion as if he were going to push me off the roof?"

"Yes."

"Let's put it this way: I was wary and used every excuse to have someone else around, even my mother."

She couldn't actually protect me if it came to blows, but her very presence had an impact on him and kept him at bay. It got be like a play where everyone knew his or her lines, and we were choreographed by our knowledge that if we stepped off of our marks, something really bad could happen. Dr. S. told me that by acting in this way, my mother and I deflected the anger and intimidation from both my brother and father, who nonetheless thought us weak and inconsequential—a tradeoff that we agreed to with alacrity.

✦

ON A SUNDAY IN 1919, my old man took the Third Avenue El from 177th Street in The Bronx to 42nd Street in Manhattan, paying a nickel to escape to a place where his anonymity would allow him to meet up with a girl on 10th Avenue. This adventure was made all the more sweet by being able to use his winnings from the back room of a joint where they served alcohol for religious purposes, which was permitted under the Volstead Act. They celebrated by exclaiming "Jesus Christ!" after each winning hand, with my father substituting "For the love of God!" which was equally acclaimed. On this particular day, he meandered around midtown, reveling in his good fortune, and found himself north of Grand Central Terminal, eyeing the great expanse of railroad tracks stretching from Lexington Avenue on the east to Vanderbilt Avenue on the west. From 42nd Street to 56th Street, the rail yard cut a gash through midtown, and he observed two ways that people navigated through it. Most adults used the iron catwalks suspended over the tracks, an unpleasant but indispensable choice to avoid an arduous detour, but which necessitated being in the midst of smoke and ash from the trains below and holding on for dear life as the massive trains caused these pedestrian bridges to vibrate, sometimes violently. But the kids and young adults oftentimes played chicken, waiting for the precise time that one train would pass, enabling them to cross a track and then repeat the process up to forty times to get to the other side of town.

On his way back home on the El, my old man came up with an idea that he presented to 2-Cig the next day. Sitting at the same table outside of the social club where they'd met two years earlier, Ike suggested that Giaquinto Brothers should ask the City for permission to put up chain-link fencing on both sides of the tracks to prevent injuries and deaths from track jumping. It would also have the added benefit of keeping the trains on time, since they wouldn't have to stop or slow down to avoid hitting someone. And, he added seriously, the company should offer to do this for free. Instantly, 2-Cig saw the brilliance of this suggestion and put in a call to the big boys at Tammany Hall, who arranged a meeting the very next day with William Wilgus, the chief engineer of the New York Central. As it turns out, at that very time, he was working on plans to bury the rail tracks underground and to lay Park Avenue on top of the tunnel that would take the trains in and out of Grand Central. The offer of the chain-link fence was instantly accepted, and the goodwill that was created was paid back within days when Giaquinto Brothers was rewarded with the contract to construct all the scaffolding for the tunnel and the roof, as well as to provide security after the workday was over. The relationship with Wilgus paid additional dividends in the future as the Giaquinto firm was designated the construction manager of choice when any other firm was dismissed from the job for poor performance.

Ike was rewarded with a promotion to security manager and entrée to 2-Cig's deliberations with his favorite boys at the social club.

When they were celebrating the outcome of the meeting with Wilgus, 2-Cig told them that the bigger benefit was in the form of the introduction to the New York State Parks Commissioner, whose disdain for the inconveniences that Manhattanites would have to put up with during the massive tunnel construction project was uttered in such a matter-of-fact manner that even Wilgus was taken aback. In his well-tailored, double-breasted suit, Robert Moses's presence at the meeting was to insist that both the eastern and westernmost sections of what would be the new Park Avenue would actually have north-south parks running parallel to the tracks—objections of politicians and local residents whose apartments were to be demolished be damned. In the end, it was the power of James Joseph Hines, the most influential player at Tammany Hall, who convinced Mayor Jimmy (Beau James) Walker to reject Moses's plan after telling him that the majority of those who'd be displaced were Irish.

My old man surrounded himself with goons of every persuasion, never hesitating to hire those who 2-Cig called coloreds, and he wasn't shy about using a little force to make sure the construction site wasn't compromised. And it never was. His success prompted a call to come to the social club on the fourth anniversary of his working for Giaquinto Brothers. There he was met by the Giaquinto Brothers' attorney who informed Ike that he'd passed the exam to be a police officer, which surprised Ike, since he hadn't taken the test. 2-Cig handed him a cigar, struck a match to a ten dollar bill, lighted both, then waved to the fellas to join in the festivities, who all laughed as they drank the "cider" that was trucked in at night in large barrels and stored behind a false wall in the basement.

3

... THE *MISHEGAS* THAT EVENTUALLY ENDED UP WITH ME IN JAIL.

Once at the academy, Ike understood the significance of the move to the police force. He'd have access to patrol plans, street assignments, stakeouts, and information on who was a stool pigeon, who was on the take, and who was vulnerable to a bribe—including who had entrée up the line. Within a year, he knew the score of every guy in the precinct and turned over a list of names to 2-Cig that was appreciated with a couple of hundred-dollar bills, a not inconsiderable sum for a twenty-year-old whose modest pay was augmented by free meals at local eateries and reduced rent from the landlord of the small building on Tremont Avenue who knew the benefit of having a cop occupy the ground floor apartment. Ike wasn't as popular in the neighborhood as the middle-aged Irish patrolman who'd amble down the sidewalk, playing tricks with his baton to amuse the kids, whistle at a pretty girl, and tip his cap at his elders, who'd smile and engage him in some innocent conversation about the weather, his family, or the church. Ike's status was based on deference and respect, both of which sprang from fear. No kid would risk stealing something from a store, no guy would take a swipe at his girl, no driver would risk not putting a nickel into a meter when Ike was on the street. No one presumed an intimacy—he wasn't called Ike or cursed at in Italian.

MY FATHER'S VALUE TO THE GIAQUINTOS increased immeasurably the day they found out he was a Jew. It happened this way: there was an altercation at a haberdashery on 176th Street when a nephew of one of the Giaquinto brothers got into an argument with one of the owners, who'd informed the young man that the store wouldn't be opened on Monday, September 28, 1925, as it was Yom Kippur. This didn't sit well with the customer. He threatened the owner so loudly that passersby thought there was a robbery taking place. Word spread quickly down the street to where my old man was patrolling. Entering the store and sizing up the situation through the angry shouts, he cuffed the young man across the back of his head, which sent him sprawling to the floor. Standing directly over the kid, Ike hollered at him to show some respect. From the ground, the kid muttered that his uncle would give payback for this; my father leaned down to within a few inches of his face and hissed, "Just tell anyone who wants revenge to set a time and place with Ike the Kike and we'll go head-to-head."

2-Cig took my old man into Tremont Park that night. Walking past the men playing chess and checkers, he told him that while the Giaquintos could navigate through the Irish clubs, wards, businesses, and the police and fire departments with ease, they had less entrée to establishments that the Jews ran and that Ike could serve as a liaison—an envoy—a person who could speak the language, as they say.

"*Capisce?*" he asked.

"*Capisce*," my father answered. 2-Cig slipped an envelope into Ike's hand and patted it as if to cement an arrangement where no written contract was ever to be negotiated.

"Ya know," 2-Cig said, directing Ike to a bench up against a rock wall where he could survey the comings and goings without having to look behind him, "the idea of a *dago* Jew is kinda funny, don't ya think?"

Ike knew not to respond as this was not really a question but just the manner in which 2-Cig started his conversations.

"Some combination, kid, huh? I mean, look, ya cross a *guinea* who knows how ta use his knuckles with a Heeb who can pick ya pocket and what've ya got? A winning ticket, my young friend, that can be cashed in for big moolah. I'll drink to that." With that, he raised his hand as if it included a glass that he mimed clicking with Ike's, then he inhaled deeply on his stogie, creating a pronounced glow that served as a stop sign for anyone hovering in the park who might've wanted to approach the head of the family. "Cheroot is French," he said authoritatively, admiring his cigar, then continued, "I'll give 'em that, but no *culattone's* ever gonna work for me, nosiree." He looked at my old man, a signal for Ike to nod in agreement. That's what you always did if you wanted to stay on the good side of 2-Cig. That or call one of his enemies a *stugots*.

IT WAS YEARS LATER on that same spot that 2-Cig revealed his latest plan to my old man: "So's the thing of it is, I got word that Moses is gonna make a highway connectin' the George Washington Bridge ta the Sound," by which he meant Long Island Sound. My father instinctively knew that the reference to Moses was not to the Prophet, but to Robert Moses, a man who would barely tolerate a description of him as "of Jewish origin," a carefully selected phrase that allowed him to still be ingratiated with the rich German Jews of Temple Emanu-El, whose influence in the financial community was omnipresent. At the same time, it enabled his entrée into the WASPiest clubs and salons in Manhattan, whose members would deign to interact with someone who'd consigned his birth religion to a distant memory heap. "Now we's got ourselves an opportunity," 2-Cig continued, "ta make some big dough. Eleven miles of road—excavatin', clearin', under-beddin', concrete, not even countin' the overpasses and exits. It's like buildin' the Pyramids. Too bad we can't use slaves, ha, ha, but that's okay; we got *guineas*, spics, polacks, micks, and coloreds by the hunerts who'll work for piss-ass wages," he said, then inhaled his cigar for an extra deep draw. "Big money, Ike, but ya know what? As much as that is? It's only fifty percent of what it could be. Ya got that? Not that fifty ain't bad, it's nothin' to sneeze at, nosiree. But twice as much is ten times better, am I right?"

My father nodded, knowing 2-Cig well enough to know that his stories may be roundabout and sometimes seemingly nonsensical, but if you waited until he was done, kaput, you'd realize that he always had a point to make so you needed to pay attention.

"It's gonna be built. They gotta give jobs ta the boys who're back from the War, but the thing is, they ain't sure where. My cronies downtown" (by that he meant in the Department of Buildings) "tell me there's two routes up for grabs, and ya could say it don't mean a damn thing ta me which one they pick. Who cares? It's gonna be the same amount of work, and there's prob'ly not a dime's worth of difference in terms of what I'll bid and whatnot. But here's the but, and where ya come in, handy and all, if ya get what I'm sayin'. If we knew in advance which route they's gonna select, we could make a fuckin' killin' by buying out the shopkeepers and the apartment houses. These dumb *schmucks*—that's a Yid word, no?—heh heh—don't know shit, so we give'm cash. Ya can see them smiles when we unfold the wads of hunerts. Clear 'em out, bye bye, see ya, get your asses outta here. Ya know the City pays a shitload to get people out, they can force 'em, ya know, they say, whaddya call it? Eminence domain? The fancy word the lawyers use. Ya can look it up. Anyhows, so's we get in there first, those *paesans* don't know crap about how City Hall works, and we'll get 'em ta sell ta us. Low ball. Then, we own the places and'll hold out like pricks for the big dough the City'll pay. We'll organize phony tenants groups, march in the streets, hold a meetin', ya know how it goes. Protest how they's not payin' us enough. The *New York Mirror* and the others, they'll think it's the little guys gettin' screwed, so we'll make headlines. Someone'll stuff a few bills into Nicky Shark's pockets—ya know the Inquisitive Foto guy for the *New York Mirror*? Front-page shit. No kiddin'. Then, just before the mayor's finally had it, and he threatens ta go ta the other route anyways, we'll fold like card tables and walk away with big bucks. Sell high. Ya know, I think we can make more on this than on the road, I'm tellin' ya."

2-Cig paused to let it all sink in. Finally, my father said, "So you want me to go to Moses, Jew-to-Jew like, and tell him what's in it for him if he goes to the Department of Buildings and insists on a particular route? For whatever reason. Something he'll have to make up that's convincing. I don't know what, but that's what he's gonna get paid for."

"Smart boy. Jews take care of ya own, so make sure he knows. Now here's the catch. Once he agrees on our route, he's gotta work it so that the Department of Buildings guys won't just roll over on day one. We're gonna need some time ta buy the buildings and the leases along the route and then ta organize the protests. Otherwise, it don't do us no good. We're shit outta luck if word leaks out and we don't own nothin' along the route."

"He's gonna know I'm not doing this on my own. I'm just a shit-ass patrol cop."

"Let'm think you're doing this for a Heeb builder, like Levitt, for chrissakes—or better yet, for one of them church-goin' Jews on Wall Street, the guys with Yid names who've got the red-haired, green-eyed mick wives. That's ya job, come up with somethin' that makes sense ta him, but no names, just hints. Be secretive, okay? Got it?"

"Yeah, I got it, but why's he gonna take a meeting with me?"

"Okay, so remember the Nicky Shark guy, with the camera who takes pictures I was talkin' about? He ain't just got man-on-the-street photos of nobodies asking 'em about how shitty the Number 6 local is. See, he's become a big shot. Every dickhead wants ta make sure he shows up for some ribbon-cutting ceremony or have 'im there at a swanky restaurant on Madison taking shots of his wife for her birthday, crap like that which'll get inta the paper. He's taken so many pictures of folks at the Polo Grounds for Giants' games, Horace Stoneham has a regular seat for him in the owner's box. No shit. He's like a made man for the social set, okay? And here's where it gets interesting and ya come in. This guy's got pictures of fellas comin' outta apartments where they've been diddlin' some chick, and others of pencil pushers who work at City Hall, and even judges taking envelopes and stuffing them inta their inside jacket pockets. Can ya fuckin' believe it?"

Ike knew what this meant: Nicky Shark was on the Giaquinto payroll, and 2-Cig had something on people who could be squeezed.

"So, my young friend," 2-Cig continued, "ya just wait for me to tell ya where and when ta show up, and Moses'll be there, waitin' for ya."

And that's how it all played out. The start of the *mishegas* that eventually ended up with me in jail.

4

I'M TELLING YOU,
THIS IS BATSHIT CRAZY STUFF

Robert Moses wore his hubris like a morning coat, as a kind of plumage, and was supremely confident that he could get the better of anyone—you know, Skull and Bones and all that. The cumulative effect of his constant string of construction victories created a persona so intimidating to others that they'd refrain from speaking up when it was in opposition to what he might be thinking, which would result in unctuous toadying that reinforced his behavior. How one guy could've amassed so much power for such a long period of time without ever having been elected to anything was the stuff of legends and doctoral dissertations.

The engineers at the Department of Buildings analyzed the best route for the proposed Cross Bronx Expressway by studying the concentration of apartment buildings and stores, the neighborhood flow of pedestrian and vehicular traffic, the expense of exercising eminent domain, the community ambiance, as well as the cost of construction. It was a tour de force—a three-hundred-page study that they presented to their boss, Billy O'Boyle. He staked his reputation on it and hoped it would be the impetus for a promotion. When he presented the plan that called for the construction to go along Crotona Park East to the top management of the Department of

Buildings, he got a perfunctory, albeit pleasant reception, but no decision was taken. He was informed that Robert Moses was thinking of a route two blocks to the north of what the engineers had recommended, which didn't make sense from an economic or community point of view in that it was twice as expensive and would result in turmoil for the lives of the people who worked and lived there.

But Robert Moses was Robert Moses.

IT JUST SO HAPPENED that one of the junior engineers from the Department of Buildings lived uptown, in Manhattan, on West 157th Street, a block away from Coogan's, and stopped in to throw a few down after work on a day when a young, attractive woman named Francesca was there with a few friends. It was probably just an excuse to be seen by some guys who'd flirt and buy them drinks, which is how they became known as the Coogan Teasers Club, in polite company anyway. Francesca was the ringleader, proud to have rarely spent a dime and had never, no way, left with one of the guys. It was the usual storytelling about work—all of the gals had administrative jobs at Presbyterian Hospital—about so-and-so messing up the carbon paper or not ordering the right kind of bandages, that sort of thing, when this guy from the Department of Buildings came over after recognizing one of Francesca's co-workers from the neighborhood. They invited him to sit—why not?—another round of drinks for free, and he had a lot of stories to tell about powerful men downtown who were shaping the very fabric of the City. He was funny, down-to-earth, and knew how to tell a tale. He'd begin by lowering his head and voice conspiratorially and shoot them the rapid back-and-forth eye movements like those featured in Saturday morning animal cartoons at the movies. Then came the setup, where he'd lay out the facts, sometimes with funny asides, saying "I'll drink to that, I will," his Irish lilt enchanting the girls. And then to the finale, a satisfying conclusion that wrapped up all the loose ends, prompting one of the girls to say, "I was just going to ask about that!" an exclamation point that was the instigation of more laughter and a signal for another round.

After an opening act of a few funny, short anecdotes about what went on at the Department of Buildings and a couple of beer chasers following shots of whiskey that would've had any of the girls three sheets to the wind, this guy, Liam Sweeney, started down a narrow path from which he wouldn't be able to return. The jokes subsided, the tangential narratives weren't to be found, and his sing-song tone was replaced by a furtive whisper, an unconscious acknowledgment that he was divulging a secret that, were it to get out, his livelihood would be taken from him, and where would that leave him or his family?

"SOMETIMES, WE CAN'T HELP ourselves," Dr. S. said when I recounted all this to her. "It's a risk we take, and it can happen even if we're not inebriated or otherwise compromised. Our consciences have powerful needs that can override our sensibilities. Usually, we see this when a defendant in a heinous criminal trial—think murder—suddenly ups and acknowledges his guilt, not necessarily to get a reduced sentence, although sometimes that plays a part. It's because the admission enables him to finally live at peace by shedding his fraudulent mask, giving him a sense of normalcy and alleviating the terror and fear that he's been living with."

LIAM SWEENEY began to recall the information in the report he and his colleagues had prepared for his boss, the facts spilling out rat-a-tat-tat.

"Here's the thing," he said *sotto voce*, making eye contact with each of them, a gaze designed to capture their confidentiality, the absurdity of this having been lost on him. "There's this section of The Bronx—East Tremont—where Robert Moses wants to put the new expressway. It's a vibrant community, and he'd have to knock down more than 150 buildings—apartments and stores—where thousands of people live. They'd all have to find new places to live, but it's more, you know, the entire community would be destroyed, a neighborhood gone, families no longer living together, shopping and walking and riding bikes with each other, *poof!* It'd be vanished just like that. *Janey mac*! And what makes this crazy," he said, his eyes reflecting his choice of the word, "is that there's another route, our plan, a couple of blocks south, where there are just a few buildings and less than fifty people. Okay, bad for them but Jesus, Mary, Mother of God, a whole shitload less than what'll happen if Moses gets his way.

"I mean, something's up, you know, not up like on the up-and-up. It makes no sense. It smells, and when something stinks like that, you know it's rotten, it is."

Francesca was stunned. No one said anything for a while. She didn't say that *she* was from Tremont. One of her friends suddenly said she had to go to the ladies' room. The other two girls went with her as well, leaving Francesca alone with Sweeney.

"You're talking down by the park? The way you guys planned?" Francesca asked, her voice uncharacteristically unsteady.

"Yeah, Crotona Park. You know, the one with the lake. Fishy, no?" he said. He motioned to the waitress to bring another beer, and as he was staring at her, all but forgetting he was with another person, came out with, "It's got to be some Moses Jew thing. That's all I can think."

Francesca slid around the banquette, thanked Liam Sweeney for the drinks, and fended off his protests that she stay. She managed a smile, then met up with her friends before bidding them farewell.

FRANCESCA WAS QUITE TALL, 5'10" or so and slender, which accented her height. With heels, she could've been caricatured as an exclamation point, an image that drew me to her when I saw her standing at the bar at Coogan's, clamoring for the bartender's attention and succeeding despite others' remonstrations at being ignored. Rather unobtrusively, I made my way next to her, supposedly to order a drink, but in reality to see if there would be an opening for me to start a conversation. After a few seconds, I heard a soft, "Jay, is that you? Jay deVenezia?" and when I turned, a girl was smiling at me, lifting her beer bottle up, as if to reinforce her greeting. I was flabbergasted. How did she know my name?

"Francesca Casterella . . . you don't remember me, do you?"

"I'm sorry, I don't. Wait—"

She interrupted me, "I know what you're thinking. No, this isn't someone putting me up to pretending. That'd be funny, wouldn't it? Uh uh, no. I saw you many times, basketball games, at Tremont High. Hard not to remember a six-foot, five-inch Italian Jew!"

"You couldn't have been in my grade. I would've known you."

"A year ahead of you."

"Do you still live in Tremont? Work around here?"

"No and yes. What I mean is, I'm in the neighborhood, down the block, on Edgecombe across from the Polo Grounds. But the family's still in Tremont, including my *nonna*. I'm there every Sunday for dinner. And yes, my office is on 165th Street, Presbyterian, the hospital at Columbia. I'm in the purchasing department. And you?"

"I work at the record store on Broadway."

"Spins?"

"That's the one. Sometimes I think I live there, too, I work so late sometimes. I live only a few blocks south, also on Broadway, a small place, fourth floor, no elevator."

"Spins is an amazing place. All the music pumping out, kids dancing in the aisles, a lot of fun. I haven't been there since high school. Now I'll have an excuse to go back."

One of the benefits of having a beard is that the area of your face that blushes is less visible.

SPINS STARTED out selling records, books, and games but shed the books and games when the demand for three-minute 45s went off the charts after the War. That's when the store was revamped to make it teenager-friendly—a place where kids could hang out, especially after hearing one of the new "disc jockeys" play a song on the radio the night before. Gavriel Yudakov, the owner, placed small turntables next to the record stacks, and while at the outset it was a good inducement to buy records, the cacophony of mixed sounds became so intense, the kids complained they couldn't hear their record and started to come less often. While driving back to the City from upstate paying at toll booths on the Hutchinson River Parkway, Mr. Yudakov came up with the idea of constructing small soundproof booths where kids could play records without disturbing others in the store. They were so popular that sales of records exploded, prompting him to take over the stores on both sides of Spins and eventually installing eighteen glass-enclosed booths. In the back of the store, past the storeroom where he kept inventory, he built another room with a conference table and chairs.

What I didn't tell Francesca then is how I got the job managing the record store. After high school I enlisted in the army. I went through basic training at Fort Dix in New Jersey and spent my first year in the engineering corps—a fancy term for the group that builds bridges and tunnels, which would prepare me for nothing other than joining a Giaquinto construction crew upon discharge. I was never disciplined for talking back or cursing, as I'd show my displeasure by speaking Italian, which my noncommissioned officers didn't understand. One day, hearing me express annoyance using the colorful term *merda santa* (holy shit), a *guinea* Lieutenant passing by culled me from the group (*merda santa*) and marched me to an office where he introduced me to a captain who'd been looking for someone to handle an unfilled job: teaching English to orphaned Italian boys who'd been allowed to emigrate to the US after the War on the condition of serving with Uncle Sam's finest. Although being fluent in Italian got me out of a dirty, back-breaking job, it required me to spend all day around young, wild, ill-educated *mamalukes* (idiots) who only wanted me to translate curse words, such as *ffangul* (go fuck yourself).

I mustered out in 1955, in some ways a different person from the grunt who showed up at the camp on the first day. The most obvious manifestation of change was in my physical appearance: the scrawny teenage string bean could now be described as a trim sinewy young adult. But strength wasn't just measured in appearance. Having been promoted to corporal, I was a non-commissioned officer who had responsibility to ensure that the management of my group of wannabe Americans would be successful, so I emulated the techniques of those sergeants whose discipline was meted out with helpfulness and encouragement. I gained confidence when my suggestions were accepted and learned how to compromise when superiors amended some of my recommendations. In a word, I became a grownup.

On the first Sunday after my discharge, my mother, father, brother, and I were invited to a welcome home party for me at my maternal grandparents' home, which we called Little Azerbaijan. Uncle Mickey was there, along with my mother's cousin, a well-dressed, middle-aged man whose command of English belied the fact that he was born in the Caucasus. He was tall with a shock of prematurely white hair, which didn't make him look older than he was, perhaps because his thick, full beard was still mostly black. His blue eyes twinkled. Mine changed to alternative hues of blue depending on what I was wearing. What impressed me was that he also could speak enough Italian to get on with my father, brother, and me, who sometimes looked like *mamalukes* to the rest of the family when they were speaking Bukhori, which my mother would translate for us. Although I suspected that she intentionally left out some words or even sentences that likely were critical of my father and brother.

This was fairly typical. I found out later that my mother was selective in what she told me when missing pieces filled in holes that I hadn't known existed. Her motivation was protection, and it was representative of the times. Later generations shared everything with their kids in an effort to be transparent, but their lack of life experience didn't provide them with the context to process it correctly. That's why I wasn't exposed to the drumbeats that rippled through the Jews of New York as to what was happening in Germany, save for the generic comments about how Jews were being "mistreated" by the Nazis in the thirties and early forties. I only heard the word genocide in 1944, my mother having referred to what the Ottomans had done to the Armenians. She'd suffered through two holocausts, she said, the first as a witness and the second as an observer. The distinction was that in 1915, her family left Azerbaijan on a trek to a better place, residing temporarily in Constantinople, while the second took place when they were in New York. They were among the last families to get to the US before the Immigration Act of 1924 shut off the spigot of the wretched refuse sailing past the Statue of Liberty.

"We knew what was happening to the Armenians," she said. "Soldiers would come back to the City and told—sometimes bragged—about the massacres in gruesome detail, perhaps as a warning to us Jews to remain subservient. We never knew if the atrocities would pivot from the Christians to the Jews. We were both *dhimmi*, members of a sub-class that could go about our daily businesses and activities but had to be ever watchful of someone stepping out of bounds, so we kept a keen eye and a tight rein on those we suspected could annoy the authorities or the masses, either one of which was capable of bringing down terror on us."

I knew so little about what was happening to the Jews of Europe during the first half of the forties. I picked up snippets of things at my grandmother's home, an occasional word or sentence in English that instantly became Bukhori when they thought I'd overheard something, so I never got the full flavor of what they were talking about. I once asked my mother if she could teach the language to me. Her response was, "It's enough that you know Italian and are learning Hebrew, both of which you can use, but Bukhori is only for gossip and telling old stories, neither of which is of concern to you." Italian was, of course, the lingua franca of the street, the parks, and the stores, where it could get you an extra topping or scoop for free, a motivator to keep up with the most colloquial expressions as it related to curse words and girls. It was different with Hebrew. Because I only heard it at school, twice a week after 3:00 p.m., and on Saturday mornings at 9:00 a.m., it was harder to learn, constant immersion being the easiest way to speak another language. I'd never had a class in Italian, yet I had the same vocabulary and accent as my father and brother. Eventually, I could read Hebrew pretty well; understanding what I was reading was another story.

Eric refused to go to Hebrew school. My mother was furious. I can still recall a screamfest practically verbatim that she had with my father.

"Jesus Christ, Rebekah, the boy doesn't want to go. It's better that way, he can't embarrass your family by starting and then dropping out."

"Who gives a God damn about embarrassment, Ike. Always my family. It's bad enough you don't follow any traditions. Would it be so terrible for you to hang around to light candles on shabbat? Why's that asking so much? Your *goombah* pals wouldn't approve?"

"What a load. I don't deny being a Jew. You've no right to pin that on me. They all know. They could care less. And it's not my business to rub it in their faces. They don't bring up Jesus stuff to me. It's off limits, and I've turned out all right. I married a Jew, so you carry on the tradition; wear those pants if you must." With that, he made a dramatic exit. Up in our room, Eric laughed, mimicked the boom sound of the door slamming, turned to me and said, "*Nostro padre, che bravo ragazzo.*" I didn't think Ike was a good guy at all, showing disrespect, even contempt for my mother.

♦

IKE WAS INVARIABLY charming at these family get togethers, a behavior that annoyed me no end. I wanted the family to witness his outbursts and cruelty so that later, if I'd report them, they'd say, *Of course, none of this is news to us, we saw that all the time.*

"But it never worked out that way," I said to Dr. S. "He was cunning enough to know that his denials could only be nullified if others came forth to testify. He was devious, but I had to give him credit, he was a grand master at playing intra-family chess."

"Give me a better feel for him when you were younger, growing up. Put me there with you," she said.

I needed to tell her what it was really like, yet I didn't want to embellish. It's a trap we often fall into, which, in the end, invariably comes back to haunt us, as a third party will pounce on an inconsistency or implausibly exaggerated tale to make the point that what had been said was hyperbolic and therefore invalidated everything that came before. I closed my eyes and took a deep breath.

I opened my eyes to see her staring at me, notepad and pen resting on her lap. She told me to start without saying a word.

"He was all business when handing out corporal punishment. His face would become flushed and taut, his eyes would fix upon the target—me—and then his arms and legs would whirl like a windmill, powered by the gears of rage. It was only during these episodes that I received his undivided attention. While he was good with physical punishment, he was outstanding in his capability to crush my spirit with an attack upon my character, my performance, or my demeanor. Most of the time this was done at the time of a triumph, like when I'd win at ringolevio or stoopball.

"He had no shame. He'd explode when some hidden fuse would ignite, and if it happened to be when a friend was around, it didn't seem to have an effect on him. I used to wish that mirrors filled every inch of our walls and that when he'd catch a glimpse of himself in one of his rages he'd stop abruptly and approach the mirror with that look of curiosity, doubt, and consternation that animals do when they see their own image."

I couldn't stop.

"One time, when my mother and I were with him at a restaurant, Ike aligned his chair in such a way as to be in the direct line of sight of a kid at another table, and he made faces, hand signals, laughed, and cooed, all the while ignoring me completely. By the end of the meal, his chair was turned completely away from us as he basked in the compliments and smiles from the other children and their parents. On their way out, they stopped by our table to tell me how lucky I was to have such a father.

"I thought I'd puke.

"Get this: after playing stickball out on 178th Street—I must've been, say, nine or ten—the mother of one of my Irish friends asked me a lot of questions designed to tease out if my father's behavior was typical or aberrant with '*your people*,' the delicate phrase she used that had no meaning to me at that time. Perhaps this was designed to be the start of an intervention dance; if it was, it had no second step.

"I had this recurring dream: that after one of his punishments, instead of sulking and feeling sorry for myself, I'd stand up slowly with my head down to catch him completely off guard, then explode with a sharp jab from my left hand to his gut, followed by a roundhouse right with all my might that'd smash his nose. He'd tumble down from the force of the blow, astonished by my reaction, blood pouring out, and in that instant of physical superiority, I'd seize the moment to lean over him and tell him, in a surprisingly clear and confident voice, that if he ever, ever, did anything like that to me again, I'd make him pay for it forever.

"How's *that* for balls."

"A dream wouldn't stop the physicality or the threat, but I'm sure it calmed you down," Dr. S. said. "After all, that's why we do it. Dream."

"I still do," I said.

"We all do," she said, revealing an intimacy, staring at her notepad. There was an awkward silence that I didn't know how to interrupt. After a few seconds, she looked up and asked me when he stopped the beatings.

"When I was a freshman in high school, which made life a bit more bearable. All I had to anticipate were the verbal thrusts. I had no ammunition to counter these, except to leave, something I thought about every day—either moving away from home or joining the army, which is what I did at eighteen."

"Did you ever know the why of it all? Have you wondered if it was the result of him being an orphan? Or growing up as the only Jew around? Do you know of some trauma?" Dr. S. asked.

"Honestly, I didn't have any idea at that time. I worried that it was like alcohol addiction that you get from your parents, that kind of thing."

We were both quiet for a full twenty seconds. Then I started up again, feeling the urgency to complete my thoughts.

"As I think about it now, upon reflection, despite the physical and mental abuse, despite never having heard a kind or loving comment from him—"

"Really? Never?"

"Never a squeeze, not even a touch from him, honestly." I paused. Then I finished my thought. "I was, in a strange way, more fortunate than most."

Dr. S. looked shocked.

"Oh, I didn't think so when I was a kid," I added quickly. "But I have a different perspective now. Don't get me wrong, I'm not saying I wish other kids had a father like him. God no. But if you look at it through a prism that breaks down life into its component parts, then I had the opportunity, starting at a very young age, to understand what *not* to do, how *not* to behave, how to steel myself against disappointments, how to stop and think about something and make sure that I'd do the opposite of what he'd have done. It was an unusual gift I got, and I've made sure that it's one that'll never be returned."

AT ONE POINT during the "Welcome-Home-from-the-Army" party, my mother's cousin and my father left the house to go for a walk, likely to enjoy a cigar. They were gone for an hour. In the car on the way back to the house in Tremont, my father told me that there was an opening for a store manager on Broadway in uptown Manhattan near the Polo Grounds, and he thought I should go meet the owner at the store the next day around closing time. I didn't know what I was going to encounter, so I put on my best clothes and asked my brother if I could borrow his 1937 brown Dodge coupe. I expected to be rebuffed but was pleasantly surprised when he agreed, flipping the key to me and not admonishing me to drive carefully so it wouldn't get even a small scratch. On Monday, I walked in to see a grinning Gavriel Yudakov, who welcomed me as the new weekday manager of Spins. "You're a cousin, so call me Gavi," he said, in English, in Italian, and finally in Bukhori. Then he lightly pinched both of my cheeks.

Yes, I blushed when Francesca remembered me and said she'd then have an excuse to come back to Coogan's. I had to confess, it made me feel somewhat inebriated, which is what happens when the cocktail of excitement mixed with nervousness overwhelms insecurities.

As Francesca and I moved away from the bar, scouting out a small café table next to the far wall, several regulars slapped me on the back, winked, gave me a thumbs up, or called out to me: "Hey, Joogan."

I smiled and began to regain my composure.

When we got to the table, Francesca asked, "Did those guys call you a Jew or something?"

"No, no, I know those guys. I kind of have a nickname here, that's all. Joogan, spelled J-o-o-g-a-n, not J-e-w-g-a-n. But it might as well be, since it's a combination of Jew and Coogan."

"You're okay with that?"

"Yeah, look, it's an Irish pub, and practically everyone who comes in is Irish—or Catholic anyway, like you. I'm one of the few Jews. Someone said it one night, a bit smashed, when we were playing eight-ball. That's what we do most of the time. He didn't mean anything bad by it. It just came out; kind of funny. Anyway, that's what they call me. Not sure if many of them know my real name. I actually kind of like it."

"It's better than the nicknames the Italian guys have, you know," she said, "like 'Four-finger Frankie,' 'Columbo the cut man,' 'Loose-lips Lorenzo,' I could go on and on. I sometimes believe that these names are made up by the headline writers at the papers. I mean, you think these guys make this shit up about themselves?"

It occurred to me that I was starting to moon over "Francesca the *favolosa*."

We relived a bit about high school, she doing much of the talking about incidents and people who weren't well-known to me, yet she drew me in. Her way of telling a story was like a comedian who'd set you up, then pivot to what you thought was a tangent, only to rope you right back to the beginning, coming full circle, something you weren't prepared for, yet it all came together almost as a set piece, leaving you both satisfied and hungry for more.

"I had no interest in college," she said. "Enough of school, and anyway, if I could earn a salary, that would help with making ends meet for the family. All of us. Did you know either of my brothers? Or my sister?" I shook my head. "There are four of us, and we all work, which helps out Mom and Dad a lot. We all stayed at home, but after a few years, it became . . . oppressive. Don't get me wrong, we're close, but eventually we all had to leave, otherwise we'd end up at each other's throats, you get the picture."

I did.

"I work at Presbyterian. It's a great hospital. I've met good friends, the girls I usually come with. We stop by for a beer, it's free you know . . ." I was startled. "If you're a girl, that is." She winked, her way of putting me on notice that the bill would come my way. "We're kind of regulars—not lushes or anything—mostly a bottle or two, sometimes a game of pool. We can nurse a beer for half the evening. But I have to tell you, we haven't been by for a while. We didn't want to run into this guy we met a month ago. He got drunk and started to tell tales out of school, kind of creeped us out. I took a chance tonight, by myself . . . and am glad I did," she said, clicking her bottle to mine.

I gave her the lowdown on my brother, making his behavior seem more comedic than calculating. The time was geared for introductions, not deconstruction.

Then, turning from banter, I asked, "What about the guy you mentioned?"

"Oh yeah, his name's Liam something . . . Sweeney, Liam Sweeney, works in Buildings in Manhattan. Gave us the whole story of some plan to build a highway from the Bridge, across Manhattan and The Bronx. I mean really, what boring crap, and not exactly what we come here to listen to. My girlfriends cut out and went to the powder room. I didn't want to be rude, so I stayed. I mean, I wasn't even making eye contact with him. I was looking all around the room, practically wearing a neon sign blinking *Get me the fuck outta here*. You would've thought he'd get my drift. As bad as it was, I stayed. That is, until he came out with some nasty Jew stuff about someone named Moses, not Moses the Bible guy, some bigwig I guess who's in charge of the road. I've got tell you, Jay, not because you're a Jew, I don't stand for that shit. And not because my *nonna* says she's a Jew. Really. Thinks she is. Says it all the time because she's got a Spanish name, Daniela, with one l. In Italian it has two. It's from the Old Testament, she says, and it means *God is my judge*, so she thinks she's one of the—what do you call them when they became Catholic to get out of the way of the Inquisition?"

"*Conversos*. You know, from having converted."

"Got it, easy to remember. Anyway, she says she's one. We tell her it was a mistake, they probably meant to write Daniella with two l's on the birth certificate, but she gets all upset. I think she wants the attention. So we refer to her as *Ebrea. Nonna Ebrea*. It's become a family tradition."

Was "Grandma the Jew" just a funny nickname, or did it have an edge to it?

"We say it with a chuckle, but I have to tell you, she does some strange things."

"Like what?"

"I'm telling you, this is batshit crazy stuff—she kisses two fingers on her right hand and then touches the inside of the doorframe each time she enters a room. She says she's just imitating her mother. And when the sun goes down on Saturday night, she wishes us a good week. She tells us that she used to wear Halloween costumes in March. Sounds loony to me. Look, for all anyone knows, she does come from a converso family, but that's not the point. This Sweeney guy was out of line."

I told her what I thought her grandmother's gestures represented—vestigial leftovers from a prior age that had no meaning to her but did to practicing Jews today, and that the dressing up in costumes might have been for a Purim carnival, which does usually come in March. I was polite, but wanted to get to the Sweeney stuff, because whenever there was something that had to do with a big construction project in the City, I figured 2-Cig was involved, and *that* was going to be interesting.

5

NEWSFLASH: HE'S NOT A JEW ANYMORE.

"I spent a lot time late at night at Alden—it was so quiet—thinking of how so many things that were unknown to me had affected my life," I said to Dr. S. "*If only* was a constant refrain at the start of a conversation I'd have with myself. *If only*: I'd known, or understood, or sensed. *If only*: this event hadn't happened, or took place in a manner in which I could've changed the outcome. *If only*: the circumstances had been different."

"For the most part, life doesn't work that way, Jay," she said in a manner that was neither dismissive nor condescending. "We're not omniscient. And maybe that's better. We're constantly challenged by having imperfect information and needing to figure out how best to proceed within certain limitations. At least you have the luxury of knowing now about so many things that went on in a parallel universe. Many people are forever in the dark."

She was right. I had to learn to be grateful for what I know now and not wallow in the could-have-beens. What I can say, is that through guilt and acrimony, I did eventually find out about almost everything that went on with my father from my brother. Here's how it all started:

They found a parking spot near the corner of 175th Street and Third Avenue in Tremont. At first, they thought they should be inconspicuous, in casual clothes, the better to just blend in, until Ike realized that by wearing his cop uniform, he might actually stand out less and gain more information from those who lived and worked in the area. "*Counterintuitive,*" proudly remembering a word from a class at the police academy, he told his older son, who was also dressed as a patrol officer, wearing an older uniform from Ike's closet. Eric even got the hang of playing with his billy club, placing his hands at various parts of the circular leather strap and flipping the wooden handle in patterns, which always ended up firmly in his grip. No one would've suspected he was just a punk.

Their mission was simple: canvas both sides of East 176th street from Arthur Avenue to West Farms Road, a distance of about eight-tenths of a mile, and make notes about every building. They were to go into each store, chat up the proprietor, find out if he was the owner, if not, learn who the owner was, where he lived, how long he'd been there, that kind of thing.

"If they ask ya, tell 'em ya helpin' out with a census, they'll blab their guts out," 2-Cig told Ike, and that's exactly what they came prepared to do, with little spiral pads and pens at the ready.

As it was a little after nine in the morning, there were no customers at Pirozzi's Pizza, a small restaurant with an even smaller bar adorned with photos of men, women, and children in the streets and hanging out of windows in a small Italian town. Ike was struck by the similarities of scenes right there in Tremont, where children played in the streets and adults sat in flimsy, webbed chairs on rickety old fire escapes, paying attention to nothing other than the ebb and flow of daily life. He imagined that the shouts, car horns, tire screeches, and radio shows blaring from open windows in the photos were the same as he was used to in this neighborhood just a few blocks south of where he lived.

A simple *Yo!* from Eric was received in kind with a smile by Paulo Pirozzi, who extended his hand for them to sample a calzone just out of the brick oven. Paulo's shortness when standing near Ike and Eric was the basis for a smirk from his wife, who was placing different kinds of pies in the heating trays on the counter of the bar. When Paulo got close enough to read deVenezia on Ike's ID, he smiled, let out a *Paesan!*, and pumped his hand like a jack raises a car. Ike finally extracted his hand to introduce his son. They talked pleasantries in Italian. Eric's notice of Paulo's habit of running the four fingers of his right hand against his hair above his ear caused him to knock his knee against his father's under the table when Paulo put the calzone on a plate in front of them.

Over espresso made by Paulo's wife—who didn't touch the rim of the cup as far as Eric could determine—Ike began to go over the list of questions for the census. Within a few minutes, he'd wheedled out of Paulo the kinds of facts that 2-Cig needed, an occurrence that'd be repeated each time they engaged a proprietor or superintendent.

Next door, at Scattennato's Cleaning and Tailoring, they'd barely walked through the door when Rocco Scattennato noticed a small stain on Eric's sleeve, took out a bottle of fluid, gently rubbed it on the shirt, and told him he could bring the uniform in before ten any morning and have his son Alfredo deliver it by bicycle that same afternoon. Rocco spoke pidgin English, so Ike once again conducted the interview in Italian. Rocco surprised my father with a question about the census, indicating that he knew the next one was scheduled for 1960 and that the questions—which he answered freely and congenially—seemed premature to him. Taken somewhat aback, Eric jumped in to indicate that the concern was that Italian Americans had been undercounted in the previous census—something he made up on the spot that seemed to mollify the tailor and pleased Ike no end.

Across the street, they knocked on the superintendent's first floor door, which was opened by Mrs. DeLucia, who informed them that they could find her husband in the basement attending the boiler. Down an unstable staircase, working in oppressive heat, they talked to Emiliano about the census but got little more than monosyllabic grunts that signaled they were interfering with his work. He had all his tools spread out on the cement floor and was kneeling on an oil-soaked blanket as he used his wrench to loosen nuts, huffing and puffing, perspiration streaking down his face, which became blackened as he used his wrist to keep it out of his eyes. He never made eye contact with them. However, they did manage to get the key piece of information they wanted: that there were eight apartments on each of the six floors, all of them rented, including a small room next to the boiler where the handyman lived.

My father and brother crisscrossed the street, engaging mostly with middle-aged men with women and older folks occasionally chiming in, which usually got a flicking of the wrist or eye roll that was intended to send a message to Ike and Eric that whatever was being said in the background would only count if it agreed with what the man was telling them.

The hierarchy consistently on display in this community was different from what I'd observed in my Mountain Jew grandmother's home, where the king of the castle was a titular title, and the only throne he could sit on was in the bathroom.

It was also dissimilar from what they encountered when they strode into Benjamins, a store that faced 176th Street with four plate glass windows, each containing mannequins draped with articles of clothing selected by one of the four Benjamin wives. Their husbands were Irving, Sidney, Mendy, and Harry, and their features and mannerisms were so similar that some thought they were quadruplets. In fact, there were nine years between the oldest (Sidney) and the youngest (Harry). The family started out in the needle trades on the Lower East Side of Manhattan but moved to The Bronx after the Triangle Shirtwaist Factory Fire of 1911. Their first store catered to men who needed to wear uniforms—coveralls for construction workers and janitors, suits for elevator operators and doormen, and expanded to an additional store next door when they added uniforms for women such as nurses, domestics, cooks, and even Catholic school students. After the world war and the flu pandemic, they met the demands of the newly emerging middle class who flocked to The Bronx, the closest suburb to Manhattan, by offering clothes for businessmen and casual attire for both men and women.

"Well, for goodness sakes, it's Bud," exclaimed one of the Mrs. Benjamins, who came bouncing out from behind the counter to greet him with arms extended. "Look, Sidney, it's Bud, Ike's son, the cop, you remember when he came to your aid . . . oh, it must've been thirty years ago! And here he is in the flesh," she said to the others, now noticing Ike, who'd come in after my brother. She gave Bud a hug, explaining to all that her daughter Judith had gone to the prom with him when they were seniors in high school. "Look at you now, so handsome in your officer's uniform."

"Auxiliary police," he lied, to Ike's satisfaction. "Just helping my dad. We're here to talk about the census. How's Judith doing?"

With that, Eric learned an important conversation lesson—to make sure that the last item in a string of comments is the one that you want to discuss. Otherwise, you might get lost in an exchange that could take you to Jersey and, once there, it's extremely difficult to find your way back. Five full minutes on, he was reminded of why he broke up with Judith: stunningly beautiful, but the queen of nonsense and trivial stories that went nowhere.

"The census," one of the Mr. Benjamins finally broke in, his exasperation mirroring what Eric was feeling. "You're here about the census? We're Jews, eight of us, the four couples live in apartments upstairs, all the kids gone with the wind. Good thing we all get along," he said, seemingly meaning it, "otherwise, we'd end up killing each other."

"Please don't talk like that, Sidney, it breaks my heart."

There was an uncomfortable silence for a few seconds, then Sidney said to his wife, "It was a figure of speech, honey. I'm sorry, truly. Very sorry." He turned to Ike and Eric. "My wife's family was murdered. In Poland. During the war. She'd been sent here right after the armistice in '18, the only one. All the others wanted to stay." He kissed his wife on the top of her head. One of his brothers adeptly changed the subject.

"What's it like to be a Jew on the force? They're almost all Irish, aren't they? Do they let you drive the paddy wagon? I can't believe they call it that themselves."

"They treat me fine, really," Ike said. "Maybe because of my name, they think I'm a wop. Could be. Most of the guys, I'm pretty sure, don't give me any guff behind my back."

"Yeah," said Irving, "not surprising, you're the biggest Goddamned Jew I've ever met."

Everyone enjoyed that.

It was the perfect time for Ike to get down to business. "Say, do you own the place, the whole building, or do you rent? Just asking because they want us to find out these kinds of things."

"For the census," Sidney said.

"The Bronx always get screwed," Eric interjected. "Undercounted, you know? And that could mean they take away a post office or a train stop on the Central. They do that, all based on how many people there are, if the buildings aren't owner-occupied, things like that."

"We own this place and the RKO next door, lock, stock, and barrel," Harry said. "No mortgages. No debts. Free and clear."

"So no one can take them away from us," Judith's mother said quietly, having regained her composure. "Like those *gonifs* who raise the rents so high that the widows have to move in with their children."

"And the *goombahs* who threaten us with the racket of protection insurance so the store and the movie house won't be burned down," Mendy said. "As if we're poor *schmucks* who don't know who'll kick the can of gasoline through our window and follow it up with the torch."

"When you first came in," Harry said, "and before my sister-in-law recognized your son, that's what I thought this was all about. A shakedown. That you were a couple of *mamzers* looking for a *cockamamie* payoff. But now that I find out you're a couple of *Yiddishe* boys on the force, I'll flush that notion down the toilet and even offer both of you full credit, 100 percent, for a jacket or slacks or shoes of your choosing . . . of course with the agreement of my family," he said. His eyes swept the room and were met with acknowledgment manifested in smiles and head bobs.

"You're too kind," Ike said, recognizing the irony of this expression, knowing full well that he and my brother were indeed a couple of *mamzers* whose patrons were planning on doing the same kind of damage as the guys with torches, only they'd do it with pieces of paper backed by the votes of the powerful men on the councils and commissions of the City.

They took their leave with hugs and handshakes all around.

"Good people," Ike said to Eric, showing no signs of remorse for what was coming their way.

Walking back to their car, they were startled by the rumble of a mufflerless 1941 Mercury sedan as it approached the edge of the sidewalk, nearly side-swiping them. Eric yelled out, "Jesus fucking Christ. Hey asshole, watch where the fuck you're going. You could've killed us."

A guy got out and says, "Eric, hey, amigo, *lo siento.*"

"Carlos, Carlos, Carlos, c'mon, man," Eric said.

"You know this schmuck?" Ike said.

Carlos Colón. He's Bootsie's Bootsie.

"I should write you a ticket and shove it up where the sun don't shine, but since you're a friend of my son's, and a Puerto Rican to boot . . ." Ike said.

"What's it to ya?" Carlos interjected, absentmindedly fingering his gold chain with boxing pendants hanging around his neck.

"Calm down, Carlos. We're not in the ring here," Eric said.

Ike said, "Let's just say I'll forget about the reckless driving if you help us out. Are you with me, Tonto?"

"Sure thing, *kemo sabe*," Carlos said.

"Back from where you were driving, say over towards Bryant, there's a number of Puerto Rican stores over there, right? Like *bodegas*," Ike said.

"People gotta eat," Carlos said.

Ike said," A lot of your people down there?"

"Yeah, man."

"I'll give you a hundred bucks, Carlos, if you do us a favor," Ike said.

"*Si, capitán*."

Carlos opened his trunk, and pointed to a set of sharp pointy tools and a few guns, including a derringer.

Eric said, "No, Carlos, no. Those aren't the things we'll need. Graph paper and pencils is all we're gonna use. *¿Tú entiendes?* By the way, that's about half of what I know in Spanish."

"*¿Es una broma o lo dices en serio?*"

Ike said, "English."

"Is this a joke or are you serious?" Carlos asked.

"No joke, deadly serious," Eric responded. "Let's start now."

"Half down, man."

Ike handed him fifty bucks.

And that's how Eric recruited Carlos to accompany him, with and without Ike, to get the information about the Puerto Rican stores and apartments that 2-Cig needed.

IKE AND ERIC CALCULATED that it would take about ten days to complete their assignment, as they had about ten blocks to cover, with an average of eight establishments on each side of the street, for a total of more than 150 places they had to go to. Given that they had only two days a week to canvass—Sunday and Wednesday, which were Ike's off days from the force—they figured they would finish in about five weeks. After each day they went out, Eric would take all the information from the spiral bound notebooks and organize the data on graph paper. When my mother inquired what this was all about, Eric simply said he was helping his father gather information on crimes in the area, which would be turned over to his father's superiors, who were deciding whether to increase patrols in Tremont or even place a new station house in the area—another response that endeared Eric to Ike.

My mother never fell for it. "The two of them are cooking something up," she said to me after my father's funeral, having kept her skepticism in check. "Especially with your brother in a uniform. A couple of *nogoodniks*. I was right."

WHEN 2-CIG SAW Ike and Eric approaching his table outside of the social club on Arthur Avenue, he nodded to one of the men cradling dice who then disappeared through the door and returned quickly with a tray and cups of espresso.

"Whaddya got for me, kid?" 2-Cig asked. Eric handed him the graph paper with all the information they'd collected: for the apartments, the number of rooms in each and the monthly rent; for the stores, the square footage, the number of windows facing the street, and the monthly rent or how much they paid when they bought. 2-Cig ran a finger down each of the eight pages, occasionally nodding, sometimes mumbling, and once in a while tapping a particular name and smiling.

"Ya did the PRs, too, I see," he said, calling out a few Spanish names that were familiar to him.

"Carlos," Eric said.

"Ah, *caramba,* our own *gamberro,*" 2-Cig responded, catching Eric off guard, not knowing that 2-Cig was aware of Eric's nickname for his friend.

2-Cig then nodded approvingly, and looked over to his hangers on, a tic that they knew meant to come over and see the graph papers.

"He's an apple," 2-Cig said to Ike. "He dint fall far from the tree." Ike responded by putting his arm around my brother with a little pressure, the signal to take a seat at the table.

On their way back to the house, Eric said, "2-Cig doesn't talk so much, you know. He moves his head an inch, or raises his eyebrow, makes a kind of face, changes his position in his chair, taps a finger, gives certain look, and it's as if each of the guys there knows precisely what to do. Get a cuppa coffee, fetch this or that, sit down, stand up, whatever. It's like they were all deaf and they learned that hand signal stuff—what do you call it?"

"You thinking of sign language?"

"Yeah, a special kinda sign language for hoods. I gotta learn that crap."

"Well, learn this: we gave him enough stuff, so he can now call Nicky Shark."

"Who?"

"The guy that's gonna get us to Moses."

"No shit?"

"Not that Moses," Ike said.

NICKY SHARK NEVER TOOK A PHOTO of 2-Cig. That was the rule. No cameras when 2-Cig was around. Period. It was easy for Nicky to agree. After all, 2-Cig was one of his largest benefactors. Nicky was the quintessential New Yorker; you could tell by the way he changed his diction, vocabulary, and mannerisms depending upon the crowd he was with. Want to capture the Italian daughter of the consigliere throwing the bouquet at her wedding? Wear a zoot suit, bring an envelope to slip into the inside jacket pocket of the girl's father, and make a comment about some *batchagaloop* that he knew in advance would get a laugh, a pat on the back, and a shout out to others, "You gotta hear this c'mere." Have to get a shot of the newlyweds hoisted up on chairs over the crowd at a Jewish ceremony where the groom's father handles the books for the mob? Wear a *kippa* and make a donation to B'nai B'rith. Need to attend the baptism of the grandson of the guy who heads up the longshoreman's union? Go down to the docks in coveralls, find the guy who gives the orders and decides who works and who doesn't, and drop some bills into an upside-down green Saint Paddy's hat with a shamrock on it that sits on his desk.

Yeah, sure, a New Yorker through and through. Except that Nicky Shark was born Nikoloos Sharkis in 1893 in Beirut, came to the US as a kid, no-speakity-ingy, went to an Ivy League college, and ended up hobnobbing with the elites of the social and political castes as well as the heads of the underworlds. Only in America.

He was a chameleon, as much at home with the Park Avenue bluebloods who went to church with the Rockefellers as he was with the *guapos* and everyday stiffs who took the subway to work. So how did he gain access to anyone and everyone? It started out simply enough. He showed up at the Metropolitan Desk of the *New York Mirror* with his camera and a piece of paper that said, "*Should a wife believe the things she hears her husband say in his sleep?*" The editor was about to throw him out on his ass when Nicky showed him a photo of a well-known businessman coming out of an apartment house that wasn't his own in the act of greasing the doorman with a twenty at two in the morning. "You got more?" was answered by a trove of other compromising photos, and he was hired on the spot at eight bucks a day. How he got these scoops was a matter of conjecture. It became a parlor game first in the newsroom, then rapidly spread to board rooms and the offices at City Hall. The roar of the 1920s included political, corporate, and private mischiefs, all of which provided the fodder for his increasing fame as his pictures became accompanied by stories in which he got a second fiddle byline credit. Later in life, he started the rumor that Fellini based his character Paparazzo in the film *La Dolce Vita* on himself—a fabrication that no one believed to be true, yet it was written up in *Who's Who* as part of his official biography.

Payday was dwarfed by what he got from folks who gave him hush money and from others, like 2-Cig, who wanted him on call for special assignments.

When he started out, no one knew what he looked like. The *New York Mirror* used a cartoon-like silhouette next to his name, and you couldn't find a Nicky Shark in the phonebook. It wasn't that he didn't have a phone. His voice on the other end would be enough for the other person to gulp down some Pepto-Bismol, knowing that a shakedown was coming. His anonymity allowed him to secret himself into places where no one suspected he'd be. In addition, he was one of the first to print up business cards with phony names, companies, and titles, which gained him entrée into places at a time when few people questioned credentials.

Nicky Shark. Made in America.

NICKY AGREED TO MEET 2-Cig at Tremont Park around eleven at night, when there'd be no kids around. 2-Cig got there early, lit his stogie, held it in his hand, and moved it up and down, the pre-arranged signal to allow Nicky to find him in the pitch-dark park. Watching the dimly lit street, 2-Cig saw only an old man, walking slowly, wearing a dark fedora, gabardine pants, and a silk shirt, scuffling his wing tips along the sidewalk. *What's a* vecchio uomo *doing out this late*, he thought, and almost came out to greet him and point him north along Arthur Avenue, where he'd find comradery with others of his ilk at one of the social clubs. Instead of continuing on the street, the old man shuffled into the park, approached 2-Cig, straightened up, extended his right hand, and simultaneously lifted his hat so that 2-Cig could see that it was none other than Nicky Shark.

2-Cig got right to the point. "Whaddya got on Moses, anythin'?" he asked.

Nicky looked at him as if he were unhinged. "Robert, Robert Moses, for Chrissakes. He keeps his dick in his pants. That's what they say."

"That's what we all say, ha ha. Listen, ya remember the Northern State Parkway shit?"

"The bribe? Sure, but that was more than twenty years ago," Nicky said. "Ancient history."

"Listen to me. If it happened once . . . ya get where I'm goin'?"

"You got something in mind?"

"The expressway, here, in Tremont."

"Yeah, so what? It's set to go along Crotona Park."

"That's the thing," 2-Cig said. "It ain't gonna go there, no fuckin' way."

"You know that for sure?"

"If it was for sure, ya wouldn't be here, my friend. We gotta make it happen ta go along 176th Street, not Crotona Park. See, the land along the park is owned by the mick Hibernians, and they don't want this Goddamned highway going right up their asses, so they'll come up with some dough to give ta the Jew."

"Newsflash: Moses isn't a Jew anymore."

"Ya missin' my point. Jew, not Jew, who gives a shit? We gotta get him ta change his plan."

"Can they come up with enough to do that?"

"Jesus fuckin' Christ, why the fuck do ya think I'm talkin' to ya? They'll get the money, if I have anythin' to do with it. The thing is, we gotta get it ta Moses, and ya gotta know about it, that's all. Got it?"

"I get twenty five, not a cent less. Half down."

They shook hands.

That set everything in motion: A bulky envelope with no return address was sent to Nicky's apartment; Nicky paid a visit to the head of the Department of Buildings; Nicky arranged a meeting at the home of Robert Moses; 2-Cig called on the head of the Ancient Order of Hibernians; 2-Cig told Ike where and when to meet with Robert Moses; Ike told Eric he could come along for the ride.

At the same time, Francesca invited me to dinner with her family.

6

THEY PLAY RACE MUSIC AT SPINS?

The Casterellas lived above the hardware store in Tremont that the family had owned since they moved uptown from the crowded streets of lower Manhattan. Originally, Francesca's paternal grandfather, Alessandro, eked out a living selling handmade tools out of his knapsack and saved enough to rent—then buy—a pushcart that became popular in Little Italy for special items such as brass knuckles, beanbags filled with chips of paving stones, and metal files to which he added wooden handles so they could be used as weapons. For those who couldn't pay cash, he extended credit, and within a few years had made enough from both the retail and usury businesses that he sold the pushcart, moved to The Bronx, and opened a hardware store. He brought some of the more unsavory inventory with him, which was sold to a few favorite thugs out the backdoor where his family wouldn't see what was going on. Or so he thought. After the war, he added propane tanks to his inventory—grills had become popular not only for the tiny neighborhood backyards but also for balconies and fire escapes. He originally stored them in the small lot next to the detached garage then moved them to the basement after several thefts.

He married Maria Ferrara, who, at five feet seven inches tall, was the same height as her husband, so she never wore heels and most of the time while working at the store eschewed shoes as well, preferring stockings. She had a way of gliding and bouncing around, an endearing trait that resulted in her nickname of *Signora Ballerina*, which outsiders assumed was her real surname. She died in the flu pandemic of 1919, so *Nonna Ebrea* was the only grandmother that Francesca knew.

Alessandro Casterella Sr. died in 1943, holding out until Italy switched sides in World War II. *Nonna Ebrea*'s husband, Antonio, died on April 12, 1945, the same day as FDR—a double mourning at Francesca's home. She moved in with her daughter and son-in-law shortly after the funeral.

I was seated across from Sophia, Francesca's mother, the better she could see my whole face. Her two brothers and sister were friendly; I was pretty sure I recognized her younger brother Enzo as someone who'd show up regularly for basketball games. Her father couldn't get over my height, constantly making references to it as a substitute for conversation. It was *Nonna Ebrea* who assumed the responsibility of welcoming the stranger. She looked at Francesca and asked in Italian if he, meaning me, understood any Italian.

"I do," I said in Italian, "better than Hebrew," which was my not-so-subtle way of getting my heritage out on the table at the outset. *Nonna Ebrea* was beside herself. She actually took her cloth napkin and started to fan her face in a dramatic fashion worthy of someone taking a screen test.

"Aha, an Italian Jew. A converso? From Venice, I assume," she said. "The ghetto, yes?"

"Not a converso, Mrs. Lagana. Truth be told, I was born at Bronx Maternity Hospital, but my father was born in Venice, yes. He doesn't know much about the past; you see, his parents moved here when he was an infant. He was orphaned at three and has little memory of his folks."

"Such a tragedy," she said. Her gaze met the eyes of everyone in her family in a sweeping fashion and ended with me. She nodded her head slowly, muttering, "poor man."

She should only know, I didn't say.

"And your mother, she's an Italian Jew too?"

"No, ma'am. Her family's from Azerbaijan, north of Persia. They're called Mountain Jews, although I doubt her family ever climbed a mountain. She doesn't speak much Italian, a word here and there, you know, at the grocers or the cleaners, enough to get by. Besides English, she speaks a dialect of Persian called Bukhori, like nothing you've ever heard of. I hardly know a word."

"You know Francesca from before?" she asked.

"Well, kind of, yes, but not so much. Maybe passing acquaintances in the hall at school. We were in different grades."

"And now?" she asked, the kind of awkward question for which there might be no right answer—the kind you had to sidestep carefully or risk being deported just when you thought you had a visa to stay.

"We got re-acquainted at Coogan's, the bar across the river near the Polo Grounds."

"Joogan works nearby," Francesca added, "at a record store not far from the hospital."

"Spins?" her older brother asked.

"Jewgan? What kind of a name is that?" her mother asked. "I thought his name was Jay," she said to Francesca, as if I were invisible.

"It's a great place," her brother said.

"Coogan's or Spins?" her sister Kara asked.

"Both. Look, I can't believe I haven't run into you there," her older brother said to me.

"Coogan's or Spins?" Kara added, laughing so hard she had difficulty getting the words out.

All of us kids laughed.

"What's so funny?" their mother asked.

We couldn't stop.

"And what about Jewgan?" Sophia asked again, this time looking directly at me.

"It's a nickname, that's all. I got it at Coogan's."

"How's it spelled?" Sophia asked. "J-e-w? Insulting, no?"

Nonna Ebrea looked like she wasn't going to be able to get a new breath.

"No, Mrs. Casterella, it's J-o-o, the J for the first letter of my name, J-a-y, that's all. My friends think it's funny."

"They give you a nickname there too?" she asked her oldest son Leo. "Like the one you got at Fordham, Mister Big Shot? Huh?"

"No, Ma."

"So why's it so great, Leo, this place, Coogan's," she asked him.

"There's music, you can play pool, pinball, some people dance. Coogan's is always hopping, that's all. It's a place where we can hang out, you know, after we drop off the kids at Spins."

"That's where they go to listen to records, Ma," Francesca said.

"They stay for an hour, so we go to Coogan's," Leo said. "We have a beer or two, see some friends, then go back to pick 'em up at Spins. Everybody has a good time."

"They play race music at Spins?" Sophia asked.

"Yeah, Ma, and hillbilly stuff, and the new folk music, and all the songs on *The Hit Parade*, like Perry Como, Vaughn Monroe, the Andrews Sisters, and Dinah Shore."

"Dinah Shore's a Jew," *Nonna Ebrea* said to no one in particular.

Francesca told me later what she wanted to say to change the subject: *Jesus H. Christ, Ma, stop with the big fuckin' deal about listening to some colored guy sing*, but opted instead for a more diplomatic interjection to divert her mother from going off on "the coloreds."

"You want to know something's that more important than nicknames and race music, Ma? Huh? Well listen to this: they're going to knock all the buildings down on this street. Your street. Right here. Both sides of 176th street to make way for the new highway. Everything. Apartment houses, homes, stores, you name it, it's all coming down. You're going to be shit outta luck, that's all I can say."

"Watch your mouth, young lady," her father said.

Francesca gave him a look that, decoded, said, *That's what you're concerned about? Me saying 'shit' when I'm telling you your life's about to come crashing down on you?*

This was the Liam Sweeney stuff that she'd mentioned to me the first time we met at Coogan's.

Dinner broke up shortly thereafter.

"Call me tomorrow if you get a chance. Any time. I'd like to talk about the highway," I said to Francesca on the front steps. I thanked her for the dinner. She gave me kiss on my cheek. While that was nice, it was the squeeze on the arm that I savored as I got into the 1938 two-door Ford Coupe that Gavi let me use and for which he only docked five dollars a week from my paycheck.

7

TREMONT'S GONNA TAKE IT UP THE ASS . . .

"At this point, you still didn't have the whole picture, did you?" Dr. S. asked, a few weeks into our sessions.

"Because of what this guy Sweeney told Francesca—and I believed that she got it right, by the way, no misinterpretation—I knew something was up and that it must involve 2-Cig since it was a big construction project. But it wasn't until I went to visit my mother a few days after the dinner that I began to discover pieces of the puzzle."

"You're not saying you mother was involved, are you?"

"No, no, God no, nothing like that. When I went upstairs to my old bedroom, I passed Eric's. His closet door was open, and I thought I saw my father's uniform hanging there. That was strange. So I went in. I could tell it was an old one, one that Ike didn't wear anymore. It was faded and missing his ID badge. What was it doing in my brother's room? So I asked my mother. 'I don't know,' she says. 'Sometimes he wears it when he comes over to see your father. At first, I thought he'd signed up, you know, taken the exam and was a new recruit, but if that was the case, he'd have it at his place and would be wearing it every day. He's up to something is what I think. I don't bother asking about it as I'd never get a straight answer. As long as there isn't any blood on it, I gave up questioning him.' That was the end of it as far as she was concerned."

"She knew her limits," Dr. S. said, "something that's hard for anyone, let alone a parent, to acknowledge. Part of it is natural. When you get older, parents recede, appropriately. They allow their kids to make their own decisions and suffer the corresponding consequences. It's the learning process. There does come a time when it stops—parenting that is—and it sounds like your mother knew where the boundaries were and honored them. Not, I assume, that it wasn't killing her inside, especially when she had another son who was still open with her and sought out her advice as a parent, and as someone who's simply had more life experiences and could offer comfort and counsel."

She nailed it.

"That was the first thing, the uniform. Then it was Eric showing up at Spins. He'd come in, either alone or with one of his pals, usually Nate, occasionally Sean and Carlos. They never caused any trouble. In fact, it was the opposite: the kids thought they were cool.

"Carlos Colón was one of the few Puerto Ricans who ventured north from the South Bronx to interact with the Italians, Irish, and Jews in Tremont. My brother met him when he stumbled upon a mumblety-peg game for cash, in which Carlos took on all comers and won big, without once having the pocketknife cut into his patent leather shoes. He was a sight to see: high-waisted tight jeans held a short-sleeved multi-colored bowling shirt in place, cinched by a garrison belt with USA embossed in the gold buckle. He usually wore what Eric described as a Robinhood hat, although it didn't sport a feather. While it was a cartoonish look, no one snickered at Carlos, the Golden Gloves winner who could punch above his weight. He attributed his boxing prowess to the agility to prance around the ring, bobbing and weaving, skipping over an imaginary rope, keeping his opponents off-guard and frustrated, which generally allowed Carlos to look for that momentary opening when he could snap a jab or a hook right to the guy's chin. It was this facility that he used to his advantage at Spins, grabbing a girl's hand and leading her around the record stacks in what appeared to us to be a well-choreographed dance, but to Carlos, it was an extemporaneous expression of joy, especially when it was to the beat of a tango such as "*Hernando's Hideaway*."

"As popular as he was, his stature was enhanced when his sister would come in with him. Graciela the Gorgeous was what she was known as by Eric, Sean, and Nate and for good reason. She reminded everyone of Lena Horne, with smooth light-brown skin that today would be described in the manner of a paint swatch as *wheat* or *biscuit*. And her legs! She showed them off not by short skirts, but by longer ones that hung loosely and seemed to float to mid-thigh when someone passed by, the currents lifting them for a brief moment, revealing a perfect shape, causing Sean to utter an 'Ooo la la.'"

Dr. S. smiled and gave a silent laugh. I was enjoying myself and couldn't stop.

"Sean McMennamin tried to emulate the James Dean look from *Rebel Without a Cause*, his hair kept long on the sides, as if it were a foundation that upheld the bird's nest bouffant that perched on top, which I worried was a potential landing spot for pigeons. He always wore tight-fitting T-shirts, usually white, underneath a red loose-fitting jacket with a stiffly starched collar that hid a gruesome purplish scar, the result, he'd say, of, 'Something I'm not gonna tell you about, so don't ask . . . but if I was gonna, let's just say you don't want to hear about the other lad, may God have mercy on his soul.' The younger kids envisioned some sort of knife fight which enhanced his standing, while I assumed it was the result of a metal-working accident from his father's machine shop where he was known to horse around and ignore common safety precautions. In any event, he was a hood who stuck close to Eric, occasionally doing jobs for the boys at the social club, including roughing up some poor shmoes who didn't give enough deference to the guys who ruled Arthur Avenue.

"To me, he was a harmless character, cracking his gum, snapping his fingers, blowing smoke rings, winking at girls, sprinkling his comments with colorful Irish words like *bowsie, gammy, gobshite, jaykers,* and *sca*, whose meanings we'd glean from the context of his stories. He kept up a constant stream of "yeah, yeahs" no matter what anyone else was saying. He kept the kids entertained, which meant they were in the store longer, the greater the opportunity to buy more records.

"Nate was kind of exotic, the 'colored guy' who wore sharp clothes—lots of bright colors and high-topped Thom McAnn boots, as well as a porkpie hat that tilted on his head at a rakish angle. He knew all the new music, including the 'race stuff' that so annoyed Francesca's mother. Nate would take time to steer the younger kids over to where they could browse the tunes from The Platters, Chuck Berry, Ray Charles, Bo Diddley, and Fats Domino, and he'd delight them with stories and anecdotes that he'd heard from one of the first Black DJs in New York on WLIB. Nate would take center stage mimicking some of the Black singers well, which got the kids jiving. Then he'd pivot to imitate white crooners such as Perry Como, Rosemary Clooney, Eddie Fisher, Doris Day, and Patti Page, which convulsed the kids in spasms of laughter. Oftentimes, when Gavi was around, Nate would make his way to the office in the back and let Gavi know what the kids were most excited about and what was low in inventory in the racks.

"It was good business whenever Carlos, Sean, and Nate came in."

"More than that, you liked these guys, Eric's pals, I can tell, from your body language, and the way you describe them. Yes?"

"There was something about them more than the hood personas, you know. They were characters, all three of them, and when they weren't doing 2-Cig's bidding, they were fun, different, so yes, I did, like them, all three. Especially Nate and Carlos. Not sure if I trusted Sean, just a feeling," I said.

"It's okay to be wary, to be cautious; it helps to keep your guard up when there's a lot of uncertainty," she said.

"Anyway, I was actually stupid enough to think Eric's visits were a way of reaching out to me, you know, to be a better brother without exactly apologizing. He'd never do that, but maybe for once he was realizing that I wasn't a dick or a mama's boy and that I had some redeeming qualities."

"Why were you so skeptical?" Dr. S. asked. "From what you've said, it could've been just that. I can't tell you how many times siblings who were totally estranged find an event or even a word, a single word, or a look that can start the rebirth of a relationship."

"For a while, I did believe it. He'd come in, give me a big 'hello,' even once or twice a kind of clasp, not where both people wrap their arms around one another but a hand around my shoulder, pulling me towards him so that we'd touch. Nice. I could actually see him smile when he'd do this. He'd ask about new releases and take a few into a booth to play. Nothing odd about that. One of the kids who hung out a lot asked me why my brother always took his records into the last booth—number 18. He thought that was funny. 'Habit, I guess,' was what I told the kid and thought nothing of it. Like a lucky charm. Or a ritual, like one of the Giants who used to take the handle of the bat and retrace the batter's box each time he stepped up to the plate. Who knows?"

"A tic. We all have them," she said. "Mostly harmless. This one didn't seem offensive or nasty."

"That's the thing, it was so, ahhh, unobtrusive that I went about my business. It was only later, when Eric grabbed a few 45s and 78s and waited until a kid came out of Booth 18 even though there were several other booths that were free that I thought *This doesn't seem right*. I didn't say or do anything. Maybe the sound was better in that booth, and my brother had figured that out. It was always like that. Eric would wait until number 18 was free. Strange, but hey, no harm. Right? Then one day, the kid who noticed all this Booth 18 business calls out, 'Hey, Joogan'—by that time, even the kids were calling me Joogan—they probably thought it was my name, you know, maybe Dutch or German. Anyway, he says to me, 'Whenever your brother goes into that booth, he sings like everyone else, but it's not to the words of the song.' I thought he was nuts until I stared for a while when Nate was in that booth with him, and I could see that they were having a conversation but not facing each other. They'd talk, gesticulate, then nothing, followed by more lip moving and hands all over the place. You think we Jews are the only ones who talk with our hands? Ha! No monopoly on that. I watched as they finished, opened the door of the booth, and went out. That was the pattern that I saw with Eric and Nate. What was going on? It was bizarre."

"Knowing you, you weren't going to let this go. Cat with a string. It's your pattern, by the way. You don't leave anything alone until you're satisfied that it's done, over.

"You know, a legacy of the army, I think. Whatever you start, you've got to finish. And then report up the ladder."

"Anyway, let's get back to the issue at hand: How did you find out what was going on with your brother and his friend Nate in Booth 18?" Dr. S. asked.

"It's a bit of a story."

"I've got time," she said, not looking at her watch.

"Okay. On Monday evenings—we close the shop at 6:00 p.m.—I have to reconcile the books. Inventory and receivables, the unglamorous part of being a store manager I don't savor. I do this in the back room. It's really quiet in there, no doors and no windows either.

"On the following Monday, I found it strange that there were coffee cups and sandwich wrappers and crumbs scattered on the table and underneath the chairs. At first, I assumed Gavi had been in there to look over the books and have lunch, leaving without telling me he'd been there. I've got to tell you, that made me feel good. He trusted me and didn't see the need to keep an eye on me at all times."

"I can tell there's more string you're about to unravel."

"I'm going to need all my fingers."

We both laughed. She nodded to signal me to start up again.

"I thought about how to find out who was going into that room and when—forget about the why, that comes later. The next Monday, I found myself consciously looking down the hall that led to the back room every couple of minutes and occasionally pretending to go to the bathroom, which was next to it. Around four o'clock the back door opened, and a guy I could swear was Bobby "Bootsie" Albanese, one of 2-Cig's *soldatos* came in. He was part of a crew that came to Ike's fortieth birthday party. They'd tapped a keg in the backyard, and it was the first time I had beer. I remember I threw up. That was a scene."

"Bootsie?" she said.

"Yeah, Bootsie. He supposedly got his name from his penchant for wearing engineer boots to weddings, baptisms, and even funerals. Yet, it was equally likely that he got this nickname because after he whacked some guy, he'd invariably bend down to make sure he wasn't breathing and then would barf all over him."

Dr. S. winced.

"Bootsie went immediately into the room in back. What was he doing at Spins? Did he know Gavi? I returned to the front of the store and was surprised to see Nate enter Booth 18 with a stack of records, none of which he put on a turntable. There it was, what the kid had observed—speaking, listening, and gesticulating. After about ten minutes he left. At the same time, I saw the door to the back close and caught the last part of Bootsie's backside as he slid out. It had to be only one thing."

"A direct connection from the booth to the room in the back," Dr. S. said.

"Bingo. After I closed the store, I went into Booth 18 with a flashlight and a stool. I peered into and then took apart every socket, light fixture, vent, and ceiling panel until I found it."

"Ah, the wire."

"Attached to a tiny speaker and receiver buried in the housing for the light in the ceiling track. I went into the room in the back and searched there too. It took me longer because the room was much bigger, and I also didn't want to leave a trace of particles from where I jimmied a fixture or tile. After about twenty minutes, I found it inside a heating duct. That's how 2-Cig's cronies were getting their messages to the troops without the cops or the feds knowing what was going on. Actually, pretty clever."

"Do you know how it got there?" she asked.

"My guess is that my father tipped 2-Cig off that the cops were watching them at the social club. They needed another place to have private conversations. And it all came to me then: Ike speaking to Gavi at my grandmother's house, me getting the job offer from Gavi, my brother starting to come into Spins and being pleasant. So who put it in? Maybe Eric came in at night and hooked it up. Who knows? But my brother's sudden friendship? It looked to me like bullshit, a hoax. It was all part of a game. The only problem is that I was playing without knowing the rules. I was so naïve; I should've known. They made a sucker, a sap, out of me."

"Betrayal can have the same impact on someone's psyche as severe illness does on their physical health. It can lead to depression and worse. Did you experience any symptoms? Beyond anger? Did they last? How did you cope?" Dr. S. asked.

"I was really pissed off. Strangely, though, not at Eric. He was doing what he'd been told. Was he a phony? Sure. When I told my mother about this, she said, 'So, what else is new?' That I hadn't seen it coming was really annoying to me, I can tell you."

"That's understandable. You were open to re-establish a relationship with Eric. Why wouldn't you embrace what you saw as new behavior? There's some good in all of this that you can take away, however: your natural reaction was positive. Some people are so cynical that they'd have been suspicious right at the start, and who knows how that could've exploded into some kind of confrontation."

"I knew Ike was behind all of this. I zeroed in on him. My mother said she thought I was a volcano about to blow my top, that she could see steam coming out of my ears. We got a laugh out of that. I had to do something. I wasn't going to quit my job. I liked it a lot. I couldn't confront Gavi. For all I knew then, he might not've been aware of what was going on and that he and Spins were being drawn into something that could get him into a lot of trouble. It crossed my mind at that time that maybe he was even part of it. Going to him wouldn't have a good outcome either way, so I went in another direction. I decided two could play this game."

"That's when you decided to record the conversations?"

"Yup. That way, I'd have up-to-date information on what was going on."

"You knew how to do this?" she asked.

"Not at all. That's when I called Leo, Francesca's brother."

"You'd met him at his parents' home. Was there a spark? A connection?"

"There was. I'd been jaded on account of my brother—Leo and Eric were about the same age—but the way he looked, his mannerisms, his openness allowed me to lower my protective shield, the one I used to raise when I met guys for the first time. I've got to tell you, the army helped. You know, we were all thrown together: goofballs, brainiacs, jocks, thugs, you name it. And being Francesca's brother, well, that had a lot to do with my approach. People say you can size someone up pretty quickly and many times you get it right."

"So, what did you see?" Dr. Silverman asked.

"A guy with a warm smile who wasn't embarrassed to give his sisters a peck on the cheek. He included me in conversation without testing me, if you know what I mean."

"I do."

"Although he was only a few years older, he was a grownup. Not stuffy, just mature, I guess. And he looked the part of an up and comer. He dressed well. The only one I knew who wore button-down shirts. Always tucked in. And chinos. And penny loafers. He had that Humphrey Bogart look, you know, the one that shows off self-assurance without putting you off. He had a big job at Westchester Electronics in New Rochelle. A sound engineer. He seemed to know everything about electronics. Since his family would be severely impacted by construction of the Cross Bronx Expressway ripping a hole through Tremont and destroying the street they lived on, I knew he'd be sympathetic to what I wanted to do, especially since hearing his sister blurt out at dinner what she'd learned from Liam Sweeney of the Buildings Department. It took him less than half an hour to rig up the recording device, which he spliced into the wire that connected Booth 18 to the room in the back at Spins. He showed me how to replace tapes and urged me to store them in a safe place, preferably not in my apartment, cautioning me that if I were ever suspected of crossing the guys who were involved in this scheme, they wouldn't think twice about tearing my place apart to look for the tapes before they turned their attention to me."

"So what did you do? With the tapes?"

"I had a better idea. I stored them in Alanphant."

AFTERWARDS, LEO AND I walked towards the Polo Grounds, noticing a group of men on top of an apartment building on Edgecombe Avenue who gathered there frequently to watch games for free. We crossed the street and stood for about fifteen minutes on Coogan's Bluff, where we could see the Giants playing a game against the Boston Braves. "I'll treat," he said impulsively, a suggestion that was met with instant agreement from me. It was a chance for us to take our minds off of the antics that were taking place at Spins. I bought a scorecard for fifteen cents and Leo bought a pair of binoculars for seventy-five, since we were up in the back of the second deck. "The center field fence is even further out than at Yankee Stadium," he said, scanning with his binocs to get a better look at the players and towards other parts of the stands to hunt for good-looking girls. I filled him in on what I knew about what was going on, gave him a little insight into Ike, Eric, and 2-Cig—some tidbits—and asked what he'd do if he were in my place. Keeping his field glasses glued to his eyes and sweeping them from side to side, he stopped and kept them stationary for almost a full minute before speaking to me.

"Holy shit, Joogan. Do you see what I see?" he said. "Look, down there, in the first row on the third-base side: four guys, one with a fedora, another wearing a straw hat, a third guy smoking a cigar, and a fourth without a hat."

"What about it? What's the big deal?" I replied.

"What's the big deal? You've got the mayor next to the owner—Horace Stoneham—and if I'm not mistaken, that's the guy everyone calls 2-Cig, and the fella without a hat is the Moses guy. They're all together, four of them in a row. Now you tell me what's *that* all about?"

I took the binoculars from Leo. There was Robert Wagner, the mayor, sitting in between Horace Stoneham and 2-Cig, puffing away; the guy next to him was indeed Robert Moses.

"Holy shit," I exclaimed.

"There's no way those guys are going to fight among themselves. They're all on the same team. It's gotta be true, what Liam Sweeney told my sister."

"Tremont's gonna take it up the ass," I said.

8

I GUESS IT'S THE SAME SHIT AS JONES BEACH...

Nicky Shark's backstory was the stuff of legends. Spawned by a relentless self-publicity drive, he dropped anecdotes about his life into newspaper stories and in conversations with the socially connected. His embellishments were greeted by a certain amount of skepticism—*charming*, people would say in that special way that belies the word's true meaning—yet were accepted as entertainment because they were unoffensive and harmless. It was rumored that Cole Porter was going to compose the music and lyrics to a Broadway show about a character named Slicky that was thought to be about Nicky Shark, but the odds were strong that this was a fairytale planted by Nicky himself. Not that it would be disbelieved. 2-Cig ate up every yarn that Nicky would spin when he entertained the boys at the social club on Arthur Avenue. On a few occasions, when my father came back from one of those evenings and I was still up, he reveled in repeating the stories Nicky told, even trying to mimic his accent and cadence. These might have been the only times in my childhood when I could recall a fond moment with my father.

And in a strange parallel, I learned about Nicky Shark's recent comings and goings from my brother during the period of time immediately before I was sent to jail.

Eric told me that Nicky always held his nose when he walked to the Department of Buildings. It had nothing to do with what was inside. It was located across the street from the Fulton Street Fish Market. The stink of raw fish entrails rotting in vast barges to be sent back to the very spots where they'd been captured was overpowering. Then, too, the smell of a few hundred men—some in bloodstained aprons, others wearing calf-high boots walking behind large push brooms—carried from the bursts of air that blew in from the East River was enough to make him gag. Coupled with the noise of the fishmongers and vendors, the buyers clamoring for attention to their bids, and the exhaust of the diesel trucks that came and went, he was reminded of his early years in Beirut, waiting in the cart that his father would use to wheel the fish and produce the restaurants relied on. Except back then, it was exciting. The smells, sounds, and sights of trawlers, fishermen, hawkers, and riffraff that populated the shore of the Mediterranean spoke to him with the wonder the innocent take in. He'd not yet experienced the crushing weight of his father's anger and frustration that this was all there was to life. "That's why prisms are as important as mirrors," he used to say after he grew to be a young man in the US, his family having immigrated in 1899, "where the perspectives change depending upon the angle that one views another person or event."

His family was Eastern Orthodox and had a wary but not antagonistic relationship with other Christian groups such as Maronite Catholics, Melkite Catholics, Armenian Orthodox, Armenian Catholics, and Protestants. His mother shopped at the food stores of the Jews, who extended handshakes and credit with equanimity. Young Nicky had little interaction with Muslims, his parents telling him that his family was considered *dhimmi*—tolerated until such time as they weren't.

Nicky grew up in Lower Manhattan within sight of the lady of the harbor. His parents never failed to pay homage to the beacon that had welcomed them as if she were alive. His father walked to the only place he could get a job without knowing much English, and this was, of course, at the fish market. After all, he would be in his milieu. Nicky picked up street English within a few months and proper English at school, where his foreignness was offset by the fluent French that his family spoke at home. He'd never been taught Arabic, a sign that his parents had already made the decision to abandon Lebanon and head west, literally and figuratively. He excelled at school to such an extent that he was able to enroll at Columbia, a finishing school of a sort that gave him the wherewithal to navigate through and around a different class of people—a trait that would serve him well when he became a thread in the fabric of upper-crust New York life. Nicky was as much at home at the fish market, the Arthur Avenue clubs, ball parks, subways, newsstands, and shoe shine parlors as he was at the Fifth Avenue mansions, exclusive clubs on the upper east side, and private offices of the leading Catholic clergy within the five boroughs.

Eric recounted Nicky's description of how the construction scheme unfolded in detail; here's how I remembered what he told me. Nicky entered the office of Billy O'Boyle, the director of the Department of Buildings, despite not having an appointment after being waved in by the secretary once the intercom squawked, "Okay, send him on in." Billy was close to sixty, yet never used William, preferring the name his mother used, an acknowledgment that her youngest was still her little boy. The pleasantries went on for longer than Nicky preferred. He wanted to get down to "*bidnez*," yet he understood that to interrupt Billy would deprive him of the pride he felt being solicited by a personality as famous as Nicky Shark. So, Nicky played the game, remarking on the lovely photos of Billy's family, knowing full well that Billy dipped his stick in Asian sauce, habituating Chinese whorehouses at noon while telling his staff he was going out to get something to eat in Chinatown—a double-entendre that he shared with his drinking buddies. It was through one of them that Nicky first got the tip and then the photos, which was the reason he knew he could always get a meeting with Billy even without having scheduled it in advance.

Nicky signaled to Billy that it was time to talk about buildings issues by making a pretend camera with both of his hands and moving his right index finger up and down to resemble the clicking that would indicate a photo had been taken.

I practically memorized the back and forth between Nicky and Billy that Eric told me, recalling it from how Nicky mentioned it to my father and brother at the social club on Arthur Avenue. It was so vividly described, it allowed me to see it as if it were a play where I was the only one in the audience.

"I understand from reliable sources that you're considering two alternative routes for the new expressway that's going to cut across The Bronx," Nicky said. Eric imagined that by using the word 'cut' Nicky was thinking about how the borough would be bifurcated. Perhaps it was just an expression whose implication wasn't well understood at the time.

"Let me explain, Billy," Nicky continued without waiting for the director to respond. "The powers that be, you know, in the church, well, they're gonna be mighty upset if selecting the route along Crotona Park East means that the Hibernians building will be turned into rubble. You know it? Beautiful building, lovely grounds, many good affairs there. Real pissed off, and I wouldn't put it past the bishop to go to the archbishop. You don't want to be on Francis Cardinal Spellman's shit list, do you?" he asked in a way that was meant to be a declaratory statement. "I'm not saying you'd be excommunicated, but sure as shit you'd be *persona non grata*, I'm telling you. No more Al Smith dinners for you, my friend, and your grandkids will find themselves frozen out of Catholic Youth Organization sports."

It was enlightening for me to hear that the other side used religion to cower the faithful in the same as we did.

"Lookit," Billy replied, "we can go to the City Council, have them pass a law, off the books, you know how they hide shit, no one ever knows, and they give the dough to the Hibernians so they can move to another place. They'll be plenty there, more than what's necessary, you know, that can be spread around, everyone's happy."

"Normally, Billy, we could do that, no problem, but we got a real issue here. Moses is dead set against the Crotona Park route. He wants it to go across 176th Street. He's already made up his mind."

"Jesus Christ, God forgive me, I gotta suck hind tit offa some Heeb-turned-Protestant fancy uptown bigshot? What's his beef? Why not go through the route my guys said is best?" He pointed to the report that was sitting on a credenza that Nicky was sure Billy hadn't read. "I guess it's the same shit as Jones Beach," he mused.

"Jones Beach?" Nicky asked, trying to determine the connection between the beautiful sandy beach on the southern shore of Long Island and the route for the Cross Bronx Expressway.

"Yeah, you know, the parkways, the bridges."

Nicky was smart enough to know when to let others talk. He'd been deposed a number of times and had been well coached by his attorneys, so he encouraged Billy by turning palms up and bringing his fingers forward, which Billy recognized as a signal to *give me more*.

"When they built it, the beach, there was a lot of opposition in the towns on the shore—Freeport, Merrick, places like that—they didn't want no coloreds or spics to use it. I thought you knew about this."

Nicky nodded horizontally.

"Yeah, they couldn't make it a rule, no signs that said it was for whites only. They couldn't get away with that even if they tried, which they didn't, so, you know, they knew that those folks didn't have a lot of cars. That's not how they'd get to the beach; they needed buses from the Port Authority or somewhere in Queens. Yeah, so how do you make it so the buses can't get to the beach?"

"I never thought about that," Nicky said. "How?"

"You make the overpasses on the highways too low for buses, that's how. Pretty fuckin' smart, if you ask me. No buses, no coloreds or spics. Here, I'll show you."

Billy swiveled his chair around, opened a file drawer behind him, pulled out a folder, turned back, and handed it to Nicky without a word spoken. It was a couple of pages from an appendix to an official document authorizing the construction of the overpasses on the Northern State, the Meadowbrook, and the Southern State Parkways to be set at a specific height over the roadways that would preclude buses from using them. There were handwritten notes in pen, which Billy pointed out were from Robert Moses, each page initialed with a fancy RM in script.

"He added this, the appendix, real quiet like, no hearings, nothing." Billy paused for a few seconds then said, "So's what I'm thinkin' here is the same thing. He wants to go north a couple of blocks with the expressway in The Bronx because the people who own fancy places on the park a couple of blocks south—where my guys want to build it—will shit a brick if he puts the road there, and I'm guessing that he doesn't give a crap if he's gotta tear down some old apartments and stores where some more coloreds live, am I right?"

Nicky knew that he had the basics right, but that it was 2-Cig's plan not Robert Moses's and that the people who'd get displaced were mostly Italians and Irish, something Nicky wasn't going to reveal.

"Yeah, that's probably it, Billy. Can I?" he asked, taking a small camera out of his briefcase and pointing to the document.

"Sure, take them in color. You'll get Moses's blue fountain pen initials."

Nicky took a photo of each page, then put the camera back in his bag.

"You know," Billy continued, "sometimes I think we should just let the politicians and their big money pals make all the decisions. To hell with me, with the department, 'cause they don't give a rat's ass about what we do anyway."

"Calm down, Billy, there's an easy way out of this. Go read the report from your department and ask a few questions. Don't say you're against what your guys wrote, just some things like 'on the other hand what if . . .' and 'you've done a great job and all, but you're not saying you're 100 percent sure about everything, so give me some answers to questions that may get asked at the City Council about alternative routes.' That'll set the stage for you to bring in some fat-cat honchos, a group of advisors, folks who'll go along with whatever you say and whatever you give them, if you catch my drift. You've got to give yourself some cover."

"Yeah, I guess so, because if I don't, someone from the Jew York Times is gonna write an article about me and say I'm just some potato-head hack who rolled over because I'm on the take from Moses. Let 'em come see my little saltbox in Hunters Point to see how I'm so rich. Or have 'em follow me on the Number 7 train to work."

"The thing is, Billy, it's all set in stone, and you don't want to kill your career and jeopardize your pension."

"Why don't I just jump out this fuckin' window, give my wife some insurance, which I would, except that I nailed it shut to keep the stink of the fish market outta here. But you know what? The stink inside's just as bad."

"Are we okay?" Nicky asked.

"Yeah, okay, I got it," Billy said, knowing full well that if he didn't get it, the photos of his Chinatown escapades would find their way to the mayor's office.

On the way down the elevator, Nicky's heart started to race. He had to get to Robert Moses to secure his agreement to hold out for the route to go across 176th Street. If he'd presented it to Billy as Moses was *thinking* about it as opposed to having already decided, he wouldn't have gotten the result he'd just achieved. He went to a phone booth and dialed Robert Moses's office and set up an appointment to see him the following day. After hanging up, he wandered over to a newsstand on the corner of Fulton and Williams Street and plunked down a nickel to pick up a copy of the *New York Mirror*. He walked down the steps to take the Number 4 train uptown, found a seat and read about the threat Horace Stoneham had made to move the Giants out of Manhattan, possibly to Los Angeles or San Francisco, unless he could build a stadium in another part of New York City. In the interview, he indicated that the Polo Grounds was no longer a suitable park. What he meant was that it was a dump.

Nicky got off the subway a stop earlier than if he were going to enter his building through the front door. He walked a circuitous route to the building that backed up against his and rang the bell of the superintendent who greeted him without saying a word, then guided him into the basement. He opened a series of rooms with a massive ring of keys and delivered him into the basement of Nicky's building. He accepted a couple of twenties pressed into his hand, the usual fee for allowing Nicky to come and go this way without fear of being spotted. Once inside his apartment, he double locked the door and refrained from turning on a light. He went into the bathroom, quietly closed the door, and felt for the set of tiles on the wall that responded to pressure from his hands. Pushing them revealed a small hidden room that had originally been a linen closet. It was now his darkroom, fitted with a safelight, an enlarger, a few different sized pans, some chemicals, a variety of print papers, and some shelves with folders. After he finished the process that revealed the images from the appendix with Robert Moses's initials, he took the newly developed photos as well as a folder from the shelf, poured a drink—Scotch, neat—sat in his favorite easy chair, and drowsed off, the pictures scattered on the floor in front of him.

9

SO WHAT ARE YOU SUGGESTING?

I knew Eric was impressed with Nicky Shark. The rise from humble beginnings. The ascension to hobnobbing with New York power brokers. Nicky was a player and someone for my brother to emulate. I could sense it in the reverence with which he told of Nicky's meeting with Robert Moses.

Nicky took the eleven steps up to the front door of Robert Moses's brownstone on East 92nd Street with aplomb, knowing how he was going to approach the master builder of New York, a man so powerful that most people were intimidated in his presence. Many had left his office labeled a fool, their careers dead-ended.

He was greeted by a servant who ushered him into a parlor on what was called the first floor but which actually was ten feet over the street, above the servants' quarters that one could access by a door underneath the steps. Nicky was kept waiting—deliberately, he presumed—a tactic designed to create anxiety. None of this mattered to Nicky. He was of a different ilk from those who cowered in front of the likes of Robert Moses. Years of confronting politicians, judges, union heads, corporate executives, and investment bankers when he had the goods on them had left their mark. After a while, Nicky realized that he'd had the intimidation edge even when he had nothing on these guys. They always thought Nicky knew something about their escapades, which told him a lot about how those with power abused their privileges in ways great and small.

The parlor room had a stiff, formal air, with a few unimpressive landscapes that evoked a time and place you were supposed to believe represented a history or tradition that underpinned Robert Moses's station in life. Nicky Shark knew better. He'd seen this before, albeit on a less grand scale. Growing up on the Lower East Side, in a fifth-floor cold water flat, he'd been surrounded by pictures of ancient Greece, from postcards, newspaper clippings, and reproductions on cheap canvases that crinkled from the hot, sticky wafts of air that'd make their way to the top of the building. His father thought they partially compensated for their insufferable circumstances, reminding them that while the nationality stamped on their passports had been Lebanese, their hearts were in Greece, the ancestral home of the Sharkis clan.

Robert Moses made his entry before he turned the corner to enter the parlor, saying, "Please, sit," a command that anticipated his guest would've stood when he heard footsteps in the hall. Nicky had never moved from his chair. Robert Moses was dumbstruck; in that fleeting instant, Nicky knew he'd come out a winner.

With receding hair brushed straight back, deep-set eyes, prominent eyebrows, full lips, and a long nose, it was hard not to envision Robert Moses as the child of *yekkes*—those Jews whose penchant for things German caused them to subvert their heritage, thinking that being Germanophiles would prevent them from being viewed as "the other," a conceit that was destroyed by the Holocaust. He dressed like the lead in a play about those Jews who'd stepped up to the baptismal font of high society: blue-buttoned, double-breasted suit, white-on-white Egyptian cotton shirt, gold collar pin under a perfectly knotted silk tie, and highly polished black wing-tip shoes.

"Thank you for seeing me on such short notice," Nicky said.

Robert Moses nodded. There was no verbal acknowledgment or small talk. Nicky stepped into the momentary breach.

"I'm not going to beat around the bush," Nicky said. "I understand that there are two alternatives for the new Cross Bronx Expressway through Tremont. I know firsthand that the Department of Buildings is recommending that it should go along Crotona Park East, opposite the park, as opposed to the other possibility of 176th Street, two blocks to the north. As you're well aware, I've got no expertise in this area. I can't tell you which is the better route from a traffic or cost point of view. What I can tell you is that the 176th Street proposal is preferred by some people you've done business with in the past, and I can guarantee that this route won't be opposed by the Department of Buildings, whose director is prepared to overrule the plan put forth by his staff."

Nicky could sense that Robert Moses thought he was impertinent and that his monologue was perhaps an affront. Yet, he also theorized, correctly as it turned out, that he wouldn't be shown the door. Moses knew Nicky wasn't flying solo. He was there to deliver a message.

"What's on your mind, Mr. Shark?"

"You can call me Nicky," he replied, willing to bet his offer of informality wouldn't be responded to in kind.

"Nicky."

"Since you've expressed no particular preference for which route is best—please correct me if I'm wrong . . ." Nicky hesitated, and Robert Moses said nothing. "There's a lot of good that can come out of a decision to go with 176th Street. The people on Crotona Park East won't be disturbed, and the *overpasses* on the expressway can be made tall enough for all modes of transportation."

He stopped and let that that sink in.

The Robert Moses stare that was terrifying to those who depended on his approval had no effect on Nicky, who could respond in kind without blinking. After a wordless confrontation of about ten seconds, Robert Moses asked, "So what are you suggesting?" in a monotone that belied it was in the form of a question.

"A walk in the park," Nicky answered.

Robert Moses knew precisely what that meant: 2-Cig's code for a meeting in Tremont Park at night.

"Thursday at eleven," Robert Moses said. And with that, Nicky Shark headed for the door and down the steps with neither a handshake nor a goodbye.

10

LITTLE LIES, WHITE LIES, HALF-TRUTHS, THEY'RE ALL OKAY.

Ike made sure to tell Eric not to wear his chauffer's getup for the meeting in Tremont Park, lest Robert Moses think Ike's uniform was a costume. The street lights were out, courtesy of some of 2-Cig's boys—the better no pictures could be taken in case someone leaked the site of the meeting. Right on time, a car arrived, and Moses got out of the back seat when the driver opened the door.

Jew to Jew, that's what 2-Cig had told Ike. *Come up with something that was believable to Moses without naming names. Just hint.* Ike and Eric had practiced a few things, mostly centered on goodwill that a few 'unnamed, well-placed men of our faith' wanted to tell him, but it seemed so hollow that Ike knew he couldn't pull it off. Moses would automatically think a guy with "deVenezia" on his ID would be a Catholic; to start explaining his origins would get convoluted. Moses would think he was a *schmuck*, certainly not someone to deal with, considering the circles in which he traveled. Ike also knew that Moses had thrown away his Jewish clothes and had cloaked himself in the Episcopalian church. He wouldn't give a shit about a lowly Jew beat cop talking to him as fellow *lantzman*. Ike instinctively knew not to bring up the money angle. 2-Cig would attend to that and, anyway, money talk coming from a guy wearing a uniform with his name on his shirt was, well, fucking unbelievable.

Ike was a guy from the streets—the kid who grew up in a Catholic orphanage, lived with *guineas* whose last names ended in vowels, and micks whose names contained apostrophes. That was his milieu. So he took cues and instincts from his past and offered the following to Robert Moses, the greatest power broker in the US, in a way that was natural and comfortable to him:

"A good friend of mine is named Finn Collins, although he goes by Tom. He's the head of the Ancient Order of Hibernians on Crotona Park East, a couple of blocks south of here. Opposite the park. A regular part of my territory. He tells me that he heard there's a possibility that a new highway—the one from the Bridge to the Sound—is gonna come along the edge of the park, which would mean his clubhouse would be razed. He's all for a highway, got to get the trucks from Jersey off the local streets—progress and all that—but he's thinking that if it went north a couple of blocks, say through 176th Street, well, his building would be saved, that'd sure please the archbishop, and the folks who go there won't have to look for new homes. Have you ever been inside, Mr. Moses? A real nice place. My son Eric here used to play basketball out back; they get kids from all over Tremont. It gets them off the street, out of trouble. Makes for a better life. So anyway, Tom Collins asked me to ask you if there's any way the highway could go north, and if that could be arranged, they'd like to make a donation to a charity in your honor, or not, if you'd prefer to be anonymous."

Neither man moved a muscle. They were like two statues. Robert Moses took Ike's measure. Ike held his breath.

"Are you familiar with Alberto Giaquinto, officer deVenezia?" Robert Moses finally asked.

"2-Cig, yes, sir," Ike exhaled.

"Does he know you are here tonight?"

"Yes, sir."

"And does he know what you were going to say, what you told me?"

"No, sir."

"Why is that, officer?"

"Because what he suggested I say to you would have insulted you, sir."

"So you arranged all this with Mr. Collins on your own?"

"Yes, sir."

Robert Moses stood still for a few seconds, looked at both Ike and Eric, then said, "The charity I'm thinking of has a lot of mouths to feed. Fifty thousand of them."

"I hear you," Ike said.

Robert Moses turned and walked back to the car.

Eric said, "You're up shit's creek without a paddle. You never talked to Collins, did you? What the fuck? And I never played basketball there. I don't even think they have a court; if they did, I'd have known about it."

"Relax. Those are the details no one ever checks up on. Little lies, white lies, half-truths, they're all okay. You can bet that people won't remember any of them. Half of life is made up of all the false crap we tell others—and ourselves. The big lies? Yeah, they're all over that stuff. Notice I told the truth about 2-Cig not knowing what I was going to say. If I lied about that, I could be wearing cement shoes tomorrow. We did our job. 2-Cig only has to come up with fifty Gs. He'll recoup that twenty, fifty, maybe even a hundred times over from the eminent domain payments he's going get from the City."

11

I KNEW IT HAD TO BE BIG, OTHERWISE YOU WOULDN'T HAVE COME IN PERSON.

My father headed to the social club on Arthur Avenue first thing in the morning after he and my brother had met with Robert Moses in Tremont Park.

"What do you think 2-Cig'll say when you tell him you didn't use the Jew stuff and promised Robert Moses fifty grand?" Eric asked.

"Well, I'm going to be dead to him, or he'll give me a kiss if he thinks I got him on the cheap."

"Glad I'm not in your shoes," Eric said.

"Look at me," Ike replied. "As far as 2-Cig is concerned, you and I wear the same pair. Got it?" It was then that Eric realized accompanying his father to the park meant that he'd crossed an invisible boundary that had pushed him into uncharted territory.

At the club, Ike told 2-Cig how he approached Robert Moses, choosing to ignore the tactic 2-Cig had proposed and freelanced on his own. When he finally came to the punch line of the fifty grand that Moses demanded, 2-Cig didn't bat an eye. The other guys sitting at nearby café tables were silent, waiting to see how 2-Cig would react, coiled to spring into action if necessary.

2-Cig inhaled heavily, blew a cloud straight over Ike's head, and jutted his lower lip out. He looked around at all his compadres, tapped the table with the fingers of his left hand, and bounced his head from left to right. Then, quick as a cat, he reached into his right pocket—a move that got the other men to sit or stand straighter, putting pressure on the balls of their feet, the better to launch themselves in Ike's direction. They stood motionless as 2-Cig flipped a cigar towards Ike, who caught it with his right hand, and dropped it into Eric's, a sign meant to show Eric that he wasn't just some stumblebum along for the ride. During the celebration that followed, Ike told 2-Cig of Eric's important contributions during the canvassing of the establishments on 176th Street. "He's fast on the draw," my father explained. 2-Cig turned his right hand into a gun, pointed it at Eric, said, "Bang, bang," and gave an exaggerated laugh. He was joined by a chorus of hyperbolic expressions of approval and amusement from the minions now gathered around my father and brother, including many shouts of *bang, bang*, which Eric feared would become his nickname with this crowd.

After a few more rounds, 2-Cig stood up and announced he was going to see Tom Collins at the Hibernians building on Crotona Park East.

Tom Collins greeted him with an effusive clinch, which to outsiders would appear genuine, yet it was a practiced form of greeting that was the standard repertoire for these men, who falsely believed that a demonstration of civility, even affection, would do them good in a time of need. Tom Collins and 2-Cig were cautious with each other. They'd clashed over the years. Tom Collins's truck drivers were in the Teamsters' Union and had refused to cross picket lines when some of Giaquinto Brothers' workers had gone on strike. Holding up deliveries resulted in some unanticipated losses for 2-Cig. His retaliation took the form of surreptitiously funding independent drivers to underbid and beat Tom Collins out of lucrative contracts. They shared unimaginable success stories and devotion to the Church, yet remained estranged without overt animosity. Once, when a Collins grandson asked a Giaquinto granddaughter to a prom, both grandparents had a sit-down and agreed to keep the kids apart. The only common bond was with Bootsie, 2-Cig's loyal soldier who was Tom Collins's wife's cousin. Frequently, late at night, you could find Bootsie regaling the guys at the Hibernians building with tales of his exploits, his coterie knowing that exaggeration was part of the stories, but it was the very hyperbolic nature of them that made him engaging and funny. Both 2-Cig and Tom Collins used Bootsie to send messages—and sometimes cash—back and forth.

2-Cig walked to the back of the Hibernians building where they sat in the small meeting room that contained a treasury of images of Saint Patrick in various regalia, always looking heroic. The two men were drinking the special cocktail for which Tom got his nickname. Tom Collins's habit of picking tobacco grains from his widely spaced teeth usually annoyed 2-Cig no end, but in this instance, he knew better than to bother his host. He had an important issue to discuss.

2-Cig decided to hit Tom Collins over the head. "Ya know the guys downtown wanna bring the new expressway right through this place. Right up Saint Patrick's cheeks," he said, pointing to all the statues of the Irish missionary.

"I knew it had to be big, otherwise you wouldn't have come in person, would you now."

"A sign of respect, Tom."

"A gentleman always, Alberto, I say."

"We's, you and me, can head this off at the pass, the way those bumble-fucks out west like to say," 2-Cig said.

"So what is it you have in mind, my friend?"

"Here's what we're thinkin': I know a guy—"

"You always know a guy."

"It's all about connegshuns, Tom. Who scratches whose back or who squeezes whose balls."

"I'm going to cross my legs," Tom said, raising his glass and winking.

"Seventy-five Gs is gonna get the job done. They move it ta 176th Street, guaranteed, my lips to Jesus's ear."

"That's a lot of cash, Alberto. We're just a piss-poor chapter of Shanty Irish, donkeys, and narrowbacks. Our guys are in the trades, no big shots. Can I jew you down?"

"I gotcha, Tom," 2-Cig said, knowing Collins was full of shit. There were plenty of lace curtain guys on the roster. "Here's what I'll do for ya, but only 'cause we go way back."

"Way back."

"I'll come up with twenty-five, one-third, my friend, outta my own pocket. For ya building, for Saint Patrick here."

"It's an honor, sir, a blessing indeed," Tom Collins said. He stood up, motioned for 2-Cig to do the same, and grabbed his arms with his hands, shaking them slightly. He stared intently at him, trying to discern if he was seeing a final act of sincerity or an opening curtain to a show of deceit.

"Done," 2-Cig said, extricating himself from the faux embrace. He turned around as he was taking his leave, met Tom Collins's eyes, then tilted his head upwards and uttered one of his pet phrases, "God has granted me happiness."

2-Cig decided to walk back to the social club, proud of himself for getting a $50,000 commitment from Tom Collins, knowing the $25,000 number he threw out as his contribution would never have come out of his own pocket. The fifty Gs would get to Moses in small bills. 2-Cig would also see to it that Billy O'Boyle would wake up in a few days and find a new 2-door, 2-tone Plymouth Belvedere in his driveway. A Cadillac would arouse too much suspicion.

12

HOW'D BOOTSIE PULL THAT MICKEY ROONEY LINE OUT OF HIS ASS?

Eric's job as a chauffeur allowed him the freedom to come and go as he wished, which enabled him to accompany my father or show up at Spins on short notice. He got to drive a four-door Lincoln Cosmopolitan, the kind with the metal visor that made the split front windows look like glasses that locked gazes with you when the car came down the road. He'd hang out at Quinn's on Hoffman Street, a block away from 2-Cig's club. There he'd regale the customers sitting on stools at the counter drinking Knickerbocker or Rheingold beer with tales of his exploits, derived from what he'd heard and overheard from his passengers, exaggerated for effect, which was intended to grab the attention of a girl. Connor Quinn loved having him at the bar; he was entertainment, which he didn't have to pay for. His only concession to my brother was having the phone at the bar on an extension cord so that Eric could answer it—his means of getting information about his next ride.

Eric would show up at Spins wearing his customary outfit: black chinos, a white shirt buttoned at the top without a tie, a black jacket. He'd leave his black cap on the front seat of the Lincoln so that his long, black hair, greased in the duck's ass style with a curl that came down over his forehead, wouldn't be messed up. The first time he walked in when Gavi was there, my mother's cousin whispered to me in all seriousness, "Has Bud become a Satmar?" then broke into an uproarious laugh. It was so infectious that I couldn't stop laughing, knowing that the last thing my brother wanted to look like was a Yiddish-speaking Hasid from Brooklyn. From then on, out of Eric's earshot, Gavi would refer to him as the Hasid. It never got stale.

"What are you laughing about?" Eric asked, and we politely put him off by telling him that what was hilarious to us about some kid at the store wouldn't be funny to him. As we chatted, Nate went to Booth 18, stayed by himself for a few minutes, then rapped on the glass and motioned for Eric to join him. Each took out a piece of paper and a pencil; you could see them writing while they were listening. Their lips hardly moved. To a kid watching them, it appeared that they were writing down the lyrics to a song. I knew they were taking notes from what someone was telling them. They were together for almost ten minutes, stashed the papers into their pants pockets, came out, waved goodbye to us, left the store, and crossed to the other side of the street. They got into Eric's limo and peeled out, leaving rubber, smoke, tire screeches, and looks of wonder from the kids in the store. More than one came up to me with a variant of "Your brother's a cool cat." I made my way to the back and saw Bootsie open the door and exit.

After I locked up and turned all the lights out that evening, I quietly removed the tape from its hiding place and strapped it to the back of my right knee so it could neither be seen nor discovered during a pat down. Paranoia born of legitimate fear allows you to take precautions, something I'd learned from being a part of 2-Cig's world, even by extension. I dialed Leo Casterella's number and asked if he had a tape recorder I could borrow.

"You got a tape?" he asked.

"Yeah. I'm dying to listen."

"Come on over. My sister's coming for dinner."

"I'll pick her up on the way."

I showed up at Francesca's apartment on Edgecombe Avenue, having decided to walk, the better to be able to scurry into an alley if I thought someone was on my tail. She was waiting in the lobby and suggested we go out the backdoor to work our way through the driveways to get to Amsterdam Avenue. I agreed, turned to step to the other side of the building, then felt her hand pull my right arm backward, causing me to turn to face her. "Hey," was all she said before planting a kiss on my lips.

"I guess that's what we'll say from now on when a kiss is next on the agenda."

She smiled.

I said, "Hey." She laughed and moved close to me. I put my arms around her and gave her a kiss, dramatically bending her backwards like the sailor did to a girl on V-J Day in Times Square on August 14, 1945. Francesca laughed so hard she almost fell.

"Let's go," I said. She reached for my hand and didn't let go until she pushed the buzzer at Leo's apartment, nine blocks north, just off Amsterdam.

Leo had what they used to call a bachelor pad. Next to the coat closet at the entrance was his laminated diploma from Fordham as well as a commendation from the university president related to his service running the student newspaper. Both were proudly displayed to show his guests that he wasn't just some dumbass goofball from The Bronx. There was a small kitchen that had enough space for three to sit café style at a round table. He used his dining room table as a gadget center, with transistor, short wave, AM, FM, transoceanic, and VHF radios, car speakers, tape recorders, microphones, batteries of all shapes and sizes, and wires of every configuration. They looked to me like puzzle pieces that were going to be assembled into a device which I couldn't envision on an episode of NBC's *Watch Mr. Wizard*. On the far wall, two wooden rows of shelves were filled to the gills with hundreds of record albums suspended over a credenza that contained a record player with speakers. The adjacent living room had a Davenport with a pull-out bed—often used by his younger brother, Enzo—a seventeen-inch Admiral TV with a set of rabbit ears, a couple of deep-seated, Danish-style easy chairs, and a shag carpet that looked like you could've cut it up into small pieces and sold it as men's wigs. Posters of movies lined the walls, my favorites being Grace Kelly and Cary Grant in *To Catch a Thief*, Jane Russell and Marilyn Monroe in *Gentlemen Prefer Blondes*, and *The Big Bluff* with John Bromfield and Martha Vickers, which included a sexy shot of Martha in a dress hiked up to what my mother would call her *pupik*, one of the Yiddishisms she'd picked up from her Ashkenazi friends. The bedroom had a queen-sized bed, nightstands on which stood lamps with a coiled metal tube such that they could be maneuvered at almost any angle, and a mirror on top of a chest of drawers. His bathroom had both a tub and a shower.

The contrast with my place was startling. It was a railroad flat that looked like it'd been selected by the New York Historical Society as an exhibit to show people how the other half lived at the turn of the century. It was fifteen feet wide and long enough to accommodate three rooms, although it was configured for four in order to be able to advertise it as a two-bedroom apartment. The absence of a hallway meant other people traipsed through my bedroom at will, which allowed me no privacy when they went to the bathroom, which for no good reason was at the end of the second bedroom. My mother, being charitable, called it utilitarian and reminded me it was my first place and that I'd be moving up after a short while—a remarkable statement from a woman who'd stayed in her first barely adequate home for more than thirty years after marrying my father. The only thing that made it special was silent Alanphant, ever-present to greet me when I came home.

LEO TOOK THE TAPE from me as soon as I entered and gently threaded it through the spools of a recorder, looked at me as if he needed permission, then pushed the start button when I gave him a nod.

"Who's this? Nappy Nate?"

I could imagine Nate cringing and giving the finger to the mouthpiece. "Yeah. Bootsie?"

"Who the fuck else do ya think it is? Where's Bud?"

"Outside."

"Tell him to stop jerkin' off and to get his Hebrew ass in there with ya. I ain't gonna tell yuse guys twice."

We heard the glass door to the booth open, which let in a hubbub from the goings-on outside of the booths. After a few seconds, I heard my brother's voice.

"Yo Bootsie, Bud."

"Hear me real good, dipshits. I'm only gonna say this once. Are you listnin'?"

"Yeah, go ahead, Bootsie, we are," my brother replied.

"Okay, take this down. Get a pencil. A week from Sunday, there's gonna be a get-together, important, in Westchester, all day, and yuse two are gonna pick 'em up and take 'em there."

"Who? What time?"

"Stop interruptin', jackass, and listen ta me. Bud, make sure your cumstains are cleaned offa your pants, and Nate, you gotta get a new pair. The tailor, Rocco Scattennato, he'll make it up for ya, but ya gotta get to him quick. Bud, be outside of 39 East 92nd Street to wait for Robert Moses at eight. That's the morning, fuckface, so don't show up at night. Sharp. Then you're gonna drive to Gracie Mansion. You know where that is?"

"Yeah," Bud said. "I pick up the mayor?"

"No, pick up Mickey Rooney and stuff him in the glove box. Jesus. Wagner's guys know about the Lincoln Cosmopolitan. They've got the plate number. Here's where ya gonna take 'em. Both of yuse, same place. You know how to get to the Hutchinson River Parkway?"

"Yeah, I do," Nate said, probably still seething.

"Me, too. I've taken guys to Mount Vernon," my brother said.

"Okay. Get off at Purchase Street and go north. That's left, geniuses. Go five miles. See a driveway between two big stone pillars. There's a gate; the guards'll see ya plates, let ya in. Drive up to the main house. Get out and open the rear doors."

"Thanks for telling me, I wouldn't have known what to do," Bud said sarcastically.

"Good boy," Bootsie said.

"Not your dog, Bootsie," my brother replied.

"Watch your mouth," Bootsie said forcefully.

"Who for me?" Nate asked, choking off the conversation between Bud and Bootsie before it got out of hand.

"Ya gonna have a Cadillac, black, four-door. It'll be on the street in front of the hydrant outside ya building. Don't get your balls in an uproar. Ya ain't gonna get a ticket. Go down ta the Village. Ya know where West Washington is?"

"Yeah, I think so, next to the Square."

"So, this guy with sunglasses, he'll have 'em on even if it's cloudy. He'll be there on a bench in the park, a quarter to eight. In the morning. Check the magazine that'll be on the passenger seat. He's on the cover. So don't pick up some moron who happens to be blind or something, dimwit."

We could hear my brother whisper, "Carmine DeSapio, the big shot."

"The Tammany Hall guy?" Nate inquired.

"Shut the fuck up and listen to me, Nate my boy. Go to the corner of Perry and Greenwich. Get outta the car and lean on the hood. A guy will come outta a brownstone, kinda a fat fuck. He'll probably have a hat down low over his moon face, in case someone's there who could spot him, so close the door real quick and get your ass up the West Side Highway."

"Who is it?" Nate asked.

Quietly to Nate, my brother said, "You'll find out. These guys all talk a blue streak: names, dates, money, who they're porking, all kinds of things. Just don't stare at them in the rearview mirror."

Bootsie continued, "When ya get there, they'll show ya where to park. Ya can go inta the house. Do yourselves a favor: Don't be assholes. I'll be watchin'. Stay, but for chrissakes, don't bother no one. And if anyone asks ya to do somethin', just fuckin' do it. I don't care if it's get 'em a smoke or wipe their hineys. And remember, whatever ya hear, ya didn't hear. Am I clear?"

"Yeah," my brother said.

"Yes, boss," Nate added, in a most unctuous way.

"One more thing. We talk, here, like this, every Monday, noon. Got it?" Bootsie said.

The tape ended.

"HOW'D BOOTSIE PULL that Mickey Rooney line out of his ass? Amazing, huh?" Leo said. "What's this powwow all about?"

Francesca said, "I'll bet dollars to doughnuts it's about the expressway. Big dollars. Why else would they have Robert Moses, Mayor Wagner, and the head of Tammany Hall all in a room together?"

"Especially," I added, "since it's being arranged by 2-Cig."

"Your father's gonna be there," Francesca said. "They wouldn't allow Bud to go unless he was there too."

"Who's the fourth guy?" Leo asked. "Any ideas?"

It struck me: "Leo, at the Giants game, there was the Mayor, Robert Moses, 2-Cig, and the owner. Horace Stoneham. All in his box. He might be the moon-faced guy."

"What's he got to do with the expressway?" Francesca asked.

"I don't know," I said. "But something's going on. If they knock down all the buildings on 176th Street, they could clear out another area for a new ballpark."

"You know the Inquisitive Fotographer, for the News . . . what's his name?" Leo asked.

"Nicky Shark?" Francesca said.

Leo continued, "Yeah, that guy. He's been going around town asking folks about whether the city should do something for the Dodgers, like get them some land or a loan to remake Ebbets Field. You ever been there?"

Francesca and I both nodded negatively.

"It's a dump. And anyway, there's no land in Brooklyn. No place to go. They're not going to tear down Coney Island to make room for the Dodgers," Leo added.

"So what? O'Malley's not going to be at this meeting in Westchester. At least, his name never came up," Francesca said, mentioning the name of the owner of the Dodgers, which impressed me.

"What if, just suppose," I said, my mind racing through possibilities, "that Stoneham also wants a new ballpark for the Giants. He goes to the mayor and says, 'Whatever you do for the Dodgers, you do for me.'"

"Yeah," Leo said, "but there's nothing they can do for the Dodgers, no place to go. So they'll do nothing for Stoneham and the Giants either. They're both shit out of luck".

"Not the way I see it," I said.

"What are you getting at?"

"The mayor's got to do something for at least one of them. If the Dodgers skip town, he'll do anything to keep the Giants. So moon-faced

Horace Stoneham will make a big Goddamned contribution to Wagner's re-election campaign, all hush-hush, under the table," I said, a sense of satisfaction coming over me as I began to see how this could all play out.

"But there's no room next to the Polo Grounds. There's just the river and Coogan's Bluff," Leo said.

I said, "Yeah, no room at the Inn, but what about twenty-five blocks north?"

"There's no big open piece of land up there, Jay. I don't see what you're driving at," Francesca said.

"The new expressway," I said. "They're going to condemn the whole stretch in Tremont. You know that from the guy you met at Coogan's who works at the Department of Buildings."

"Liam Sweeney," Francesca said.

"So, what's to prevent them from condemning a little more land, either in Tremont or any other part of the route for the new expressway? They're willing to knock down a whole neighborhood in Tremont, why not also in Claremont or Mount Hope or Morris Heights? Or even over here in Manhattan, say near Fort Tryon Park, close to the Bridge? I mean, think about it. Stoneham gets his new ballpark for the Giants, DeSapio greases everyone on the City Council to vote for it—his stock goes up in value like the companies on Wall Street—Robert Moses endorses it—you know he doesn't give a crap about crashing through neighborhoods, and the mayor gets re-elected. It's like a game of musical chairs, only in this case, it's money, and when the music stops in this game, there's a chair full of dough for everyone. Nobody loses. And who the hell makes out like a bandit even better than any of those guys?"

"2-Cig," Leo and Francesca said simultaneously.

"You got that right," I said.

"Unbelievable," Francesca said, then quickly added, "What I mean is, it's incredible. It all makes sense. It's actually unbelievably believable," she said, and we all laughed.

"2-Cig does the demolition on the Polo Grounds and wins the bid to build the new stadium. All in addition to what he's going to do with the construction of the expressway. Where do you think his campaign bucks are going to go? I have to say: If this is their plan, it's actually brilliant," I said.

"If you define brilliant as positively screwing thousands more people out of their homes and jobs than we thought was going to happen in Tremont," Francesca said.

13

... THE TIME I CALLED HIS CAT UP FOR A PRACTICE *ALIYAH* ...

Francesca and I walked to my place from her brother's, holding hands, not saying very much. She was wearing a dark blue beret, the kind with a little stalk sticking straight up, which reminded me of the spike in the hair of Alfalfa from the *Little Rascals*. She looked very hip and I told her so.

"It's the Beat look," I said.

"I'm as cool as a cucumber," she replied. "Okay with you, Daddy-o?"

"I dig," I said, and we both laughed at our silly pretensions.

When we got to my place, we put the tape into Alanphant, then sat in my tiny kitchen drinking tea.

"We're like the little people," Francesca said. "Powerless. We can't do anything. Let's face it, we don't have any actual evidence. All we have is 2-Cig's guy—Bootsie—telling your brother and his best friend to be chauffeurs a week from Sunday. Everything else is supposition. They may be cooking something up, but it could be nothing like you imagined. There's so much going on in the City, who knows what they're up to? For all we know, Wagner's going to run for governor or president and this is his way of entertaining guys before squeezing them."

"Could be you're right," I said.

"Yeah, well, I said it to see if I could get a rise out of you, and guess what, I couldn't. I don't believe for a minute what I just said about it being for something else or an innocent get-together. If that were the case, they wouldn't need 2-Cig to set it up or to use your brother and Nate as chauffeurs. It's about the expressway and everyone cashing in on it. Well, everyone but the people who're in the way. We need to find out what the meeting at that estate in Westchester is all about."

"Forget about that. No way that's going to happen," I said.

"I'm not so sure," she said.

"You got an idea in that gorgeous head of yours?"

"Are you coming on to me?" she teased.

"Now why would I do that?"

"Because you're falling in love with me, that's why," she said.

"And how do you know that?"

"Because it takes two to tangle . . . or is it tango? . . . which is right? They both sound okay."

"Two to do something, forget about which word. What are you saying?" I asked.

"I'm saying 'hey' for starters."

I leaned closer to her, careful not to spill either cup of tea, and kissed her on the mouth. After a minute, she looked at me and addressed me as if she were an announcer at a game commenting on the action on the field: "I'm here in my boyfriend's apartment, making out in his kitchen, very excited and wanting to tangle . . . or maybe tango, but whatever it is, I want to go into his bedroom to make love to him and listen to him tell me he loves me."

We'd moved on from "hey" to "tangle."

Around two in the morning, she began to nuzzle, which I thought was a prelude to another round. She disabused me of that notion quickly. "We never finished our conversation in the kitchen," she whispered, something we do even when we know no one can overhear us.

"About what?" I said sleepily.

"When I said I'm not so sure. Not so sure we can't do anything about it."

I rolled over onto an elbow and faced her. "What do you have in mind? I hope it's not that I'll figure out a way to break Nate's leg so he can't drive and then approach Eric and tell him that if he never needs anything . . . like another chauffeur, for instance, hardy har har, I'm your man."

"I hadn't thought of that—a *goombah* approach. It's not so out of the question. Desperate times require desperate solutions. Yeah . . . not my first choice. Here's what I'm thinking."

I sat up like I was back in class giving the teacher my full attention.

"Okay, we get Leo involved. Westchester Electronics. They sell more than just products. They know everything about electronics. Leo will get me his stationery, and I'll create a phony purchase order at my office. It'll be for the house in Westchester where they're all going to meet a week from Sunday. Not for products. For a sweep. You know, the thing where they walk around with contraptions that look like Geiger counters or metal detectors to search for bugs? Hidden, like the tape recorders my brother did for you at Spins."

"How is this going to work?" I asked skeptically.

"Okay, give this a shot: Leo shows up in his company truck at the gate, the guardhouse—"

"Unannounced?" I interrupted.

"It has to be that way. Hear me out. He shows the guy the purchase order. Says he's supposed to look for eavesdropping devices for the big meeting, mentions the date—that kind of detail creates authenticity."

"Is there a signature on the PO?"

"Yeah, we'll do one for 2-Cig."

"But you don't know what his signature looks like," I said.

"Neither will the guard."

"Fair point."

"When the guard sees the name Alberto Giaquinto, he's not going to question that. And if he calls Leo's company, one of Leo's co-workers will cover for him—a guy who owes my brother. For favors. Big time."

"What if he calls in to the main house? For verification?" I asked.

"Let him," Francesca said. "You think when he tells someone on the inside that Alberto Giaquinto wants the place swept clean that anyone's going to argue the point?"

It actually started to sound plausible.

"So Leo gets inside and starts a phony sweep," I said.

"Yeah, but what he's really going to do is plant devices. Think of the irony of it."

"Pretty clever, I admit. It's risky for Leo, no?"

"He'll be done in fifteen, twenty minutes. He'll use a different name, and if they do ever call Westchester Electronics, the name will be covered by his co-worker. I'm even thinking that Leo should have the guard sign the piece of paper on the way out."

"Okay, let's say that all works. How do we get the tapes back? We've got to hear what's on the tapes, otherwise this whole caper is of no use to us."

"Jay, there won't be any tapes."

"What? Wait, am I missing something? The whole idea is to hear what's going on. Isn't that why he's going to plant devices?"

"Yes, devices, but not tape recorders. Bugs directly into the phone."

"You mean taps?"

"Exactly. On all the phones. These big Wall Street honchos got lots of lines," she said.

"So we wouldn't hear anything that's said at the meeting. I don't get it," I said, feeling a little exasperated.

"With tapes, you wouldn't be able to hear anything anyway. You know, with guys talking over each other, mumbling, making noise eating and drinking, speaking to the people who're serving them, coughing, think about it. With taps, now that's a different story."

"But who's to say they pick up a phone, and how do you know it'll be important, not just a 'honey, I'll be late for dinner' kind of call."

"My guess is that every half hour or so, they're going to want to speak to a crony and tell him what's being discussed. To get feedback. Or confirmation. It's in these private moments when you'll really get a feel for what's happening, who's out to get who, that kind of thing. Look, I don't know for sure. It's just human nature. And anyway, what other cards do we have to play? I mean, if you weren't such a pansy, you would've just said you'd bust Nate's legs."

With that, I lunged towards her and went after her legs with my pillow. After we lay back down, I said, "This may be all well and good from our point of view, but how do you know Leo will buy into it? He's got a good job and hasn't ever been mixed up in a crazy deal like this, especially with guys like 2-Cig."

"He'll do it for me because he loves me. Because he knows I love you. And because *Nonna Ebrea* thinks you're the cat's meow."

WE CALLED LEO EARLY to make sure we got a hold of him before he left for work. Francesca was right. He didn't think twice about it. He was in.

"Yo, I can play the streetwise *dago* to a T. Whaddya say, fella, huh?" he said, using a voice and cadence that sounded like Bootsie.

"NOW I KNOW why you were attracted to Francesca," Dr. Silverman said. "Smart and clever. Some cookie. Did you have an inkling that she had this in her?"

"I got a glimpse from the way she conducted herself with her family. To me, she was like a jack-in-the-box, all coiled up, ready to spring. There was simply going to be a person or event that would crank up the music, and out would pop a new version of Francesca that would startle those who'd known her as the modest, good, Italian family girl from Tremont."

"You were that person?" she asked.

"Maybe it took the right circumstances."

Dr. S. looked out the window for a moment and then came back to me. "Would Eisenhower have been Eisenhower if there weren't a D-Day? We could think of other examples. Something to ponder."

We sat for a moment. Pondering, I guess. Then I resumed.

"I admired her relationship with her older brother. I was envious, I have to admit. There's more. She had a streak of independence, unusual for a girl from her kind of family. Second generation Italian. She was adventuresome without going off half-cocked. All of this, put together, made her so distinctive and special. That's why I felt comfortable introducing her to my mother. Also, I wanted her to know that while my father and brother were—how should I say—different . . ."

"That's charitable," Dr. S. said.

"My mother is the salt of the earth. I wanted the two of them to meet."

"You set that up?"

"Yeah. My mother is so formal, old school. She told me how she'd do it, starting in low gear, explaining the plan to invite her over for dinner, giving tidbits of cultural information to Francesca along the way.

"She asked me for Francesca's address and sent a formal invitation to meet in the afternoon to shop together in preparation. Francesca took off early on a Wednesday and met her on the corner of the Grand Concourse and East 187th Street. She waited for Francesca on the sidewalk, greeted her with a hug, and gave her the lay of the land. 'There's a market on the corner, and within a block, you can find a butcher shop, bakery, fish market, and liquor store; all kosher. Come with me. It's a world so close to your home that you never knew existed.' My mother *kibitzed* with the owners, *hondled* where appropriate, explaining the nuances of the Jewish bid and ask to Francesca, and otherwise explained the intricacies of Jewish food and dining customs. This so intrigued my girlfriend that she asked the baker if she could borrow a piece of paper and a pencil. He willingly obliged on the condition that she'd come back to return her loan—a not infrequent occurrence in any setting in which Francesca found herself.

"Dinner was made from scratch: *lagman*, a meat with both noodles and vegetables; *bakhsh*, chicken parts cut into cubes and seasoned with coriander, parsley, and dill; naan, like Indian tandoor bread; and salad made with tomatoes, cucumbers, green onions, cilantro, salt, pepper, lemon juice, and chili peppers. My mother explained that these are favorites of Bukharian Jews, whose very existence was unknown to Francesca, who remarked that the dishes were so distinct from what her European Jewish friends ate, such as raisin kugel, brisket, and *challah*. 'I didn't know that there were so many different kinds of Jewish foods,' she said to my mother. 'You shouldn't be so surprised. After all,' my Mother replied, 'think of the difference between the heavy pastas and beef sauces from Sicily as compared to the lighter chicken, polenta, and risotto meals from Milan.'

"Francesca asked if they could turn on the transistor radio that was on the counter. Within a few minutes, the two of them were jiving to the beat of WABC, a non-choreographed show of foot tapping as an oven was opened, dancing with a partner—the door handle of the refrigerator—using knives and forks as percussion instruments to scrape bowls into the garbage can, taking plates, glasses, and silverware from their cupboards to the table top, and whirling around like dervishes.

"Francesca remarked that their aprons looked like her smock from kindergarten when they finger painted.

"My mother grabbed the bottle of kosher wine and used it as a mock microphone to sing along with Chuck Berry: 'Maybelline, why can't you be true? Oh Maybelline, why can't you be true? You done started doin' the things you used to do.' When Fats Domino's *Ain't That A Shame* came on, Francesca took the mic from my mother and belted out: 'You made me cry when you said goodbye. Ain't that a shame my tears fell like rain. Ain't that a shame.'"

I said to Dr. S., "They were having a great time, singing, dancing, cooking, preparing. They were drunk. Or tipsy, I should say. Women don't get drunk—that's got such a negative connotation. It's usually applied to men, anyway. Strange, isn't it? Certain words carry a label depending on whether they're related to men or women. Blouses and shirts are the same thing, right?"

Dr. S. said, "That's why extemporaneous speaking is a game that few can master. It's one thing when you have the time to prepare, especially in written form, but another when it's *boom, boom, boom*, rapid fire back and forth. You have to be conscious of what you say, the words you select, how you use them, inflections, emphasis, tone. Everything matters, and while you can sometimes fall back on a meaningful apology if something doesn't come out right, the very frequency of those kinds of explanations are indicative of how insincere they really are."

I never got tired of Dr. S.'s insights. I was in her office as part of the court-inflicted punishment, yet it was the opposite of what we had to endure at the penitentiary at Alden. There, a group of guys behind bars were forced to listen to interminable stories from fellow inmates with only an occasional grunt or generic comment from the therapist, whose primary consideration was to check out at precisely forty-five minutes after the session started.

"In the end, how did it go? With the dinner. I'm especially eager to find out what happened when your father was thrown into this mix," Dr. S. said.

"Ah, I should've mentioned. My mother scheduled this on a day when my father had dinner on Arthur Avenue with 2-Cig and his pals."

"Smart move," Dr. S. said.

"Anyway, it couldn't have gone better. Francesca amused us with funny anecdotes about her family, including stories of *Nonna Ebrea*, for which my mother gave me looks that I decoded as: *See, other families have their oddities too.*"

"How did it end?" she asked.

"Oh, that's a funny thing. Around 8:30 or so, I heard someone come up the front steps. I feared it was my father. I got tense. But when there was a knock on the door, I realized it wasn't him. I had no clue who would be coming over to visit that late. My mother got up and welcomed Rabbi Leviev, who apologized when he saw Francesca and me. It appeared that he didn't want to come through the threshold. He handed a book to my mother and started to leave.

"I'd never realized how impressive he looked. Perhaps when you're a kid, you assign a label to someone—in this case 'teacher'—and your image is clouded by that representation. Now, as an adult, I saw a man a little over six feet tall with a beautifully trimmed beard that contained streaks of burnt orange and silver, large, deeply recessed, owl-like blue eyes that looked like they could see in the dark, and more reddish hair than he was entitled to—sculpted in a wave, as if to announce his fastidiousness. In a word, he was handsome.

"At twenty-three, I was still learning from him. Not in the sense that he was teaching from a syllabus, more as a student of how best to speak extemporaneously, to listen to others with an open mind, to notice how those in charge can energize followers with non-verbal cues. In a classroom, he'd taught me some of the intricacies of Hebrew, all the while subconsciously allowing me to understand how to use English in a more sophisticated fashion. I thought of my mother in this regard too. She had a command of the language that far outstripped her modest station in life, something I've noticed among members of the second generation of Jewish immigrants. I remembered how she'd diagram sentences for me, exaggeratedly enunciate each syllable of a new word I'd learned, and would start every day at breakfast with an addition to my vocabulary, using flash cards she created by printing on the inside of the box of a frozen foods package, nesting the word in a sentence that I might actually use. I soaked it up; my brother on the other hand, never paid attention.

"Anyway, my mother insisted Rabbi Leviev come right in and introduced him to Francesca. Then he came towards me with extended arms, which I let him slip around my back. I did the same to him. 'I'm sorry for intruding,' he said, 'I was just coming over to give your mother a text.' He handed a book to my mother, who explained that she was part of a small group of women who studied with the rabbi on Shabbat mornings on the second floor above the bakery on 187th Street. Invited to stay, Rabbi Leviev entertained my mother and Francesca with stories of the preparation I went through for my bar mitzvah, including the time I called his cat up for a practice *aliyah*, draping her in a *tallit* I made out of a napkin. He had endless accounts of how my inadvertent mispronunciations could turn an innocent word into a curse.

"His laughter was contagious. It was interrupted by the phone ringing. Since my mother was pouring another cup of coffee for the rabbi, I picked it up. It was Leo, searching for me. I'd told him about the dinner. He asked if I could stop by when it ended. Francesca had said that she was going to spend the night at her parents' home a few blocks south of my mother's house, so I told him I'd take her there first and then head over to his place in Manhattan. We thanked my mother for a wonderful evening, shook hands with the rabbi, and took our leave.

"Francesca slid over close to the driver's seat and placed her head on my shoulder. In front of the door to her parents' house, she said 'hey,' kissed me, squeezed my arm, then opened the door. Through the partially rolled down window, she leaned in and said, 'She's where you get your goodness from. Don't ever forget that.' Then she blew me a kiss and skipped up the short front walk to the stoop."

"I found out the next day," I said to Dr. S., "that my mother was nothing less than enchanted with Francesca."

"Maybe the daughter she never had," Dr. S. said.

I thought about the relationship my mother had with my grandmother and realized that, despite our closeness, my mother never had the opportunity to experience what her mother had with a daughter.

"On the drive to Leo's place, I wondered if he was having second thoughts about his assignment to place bugs in the house in Westchester in four days."

"Understandable. That was a big ask," Dr. S. said.

"Especially since we didn't have a backup plan. But as soon as I got there, he assuaged my concerns by showing me a new phone he'd installed in his bedroom. He told me to answer it and keep talking; he didn't care if it was gibberish or the Gettysburg Address.

"When I heard him say, 'All clear, you can hang up and come in here,' I went into the kitchen where he had another phone and a tape recorder. He pushed the start button on the tape, and I heard my rendition of Lincoln's famous speech—at least what I'd remembered from the opening and closing lines. It all came through clear as a whistle.

"'You didn't notice the bug, did you?' he asked. 'No,' I replied, 'but I wasn't looking for it. I'm sure one of the guys will, though, no matter that they'll be told about the place being swept clean.' He directed me back into the bedroom. 'Unscrew the piece over the microphone,' Leo said. I did. 'There's no bug here,' I said. 'So how'd you get the recording? I don't get it.' 'Look at the bell,' he said. 'Okay, so what?' 'Looks like an ordinary bell, right?' 'Right.' 'Okay, now watch this.' He put his middle finger and thumb around the bell, tugged gently and showed me a tiny device stuck to the inside. 'No one would ever suspect something *inside* the bell. They'll twist off the cap over the microphone, see that there's no bug, twist it back on and start yapping.' 'Where'd this come from?' I asked. 'What do you think we do all day long at Westchester Electronics? Sit around and jerk off over some Dick Tracy wristwatches? I just had to make sure of three things: that I could insert it into a phone in a few seconds, that no one would notice it, and that the sound quality would be good. Maybe not perfect, but good enough for us.' 'You're a genius,' I said. 'I'll drink to that,' he said, walking back to the kitchen where he poured himself a glass of red wine. 'I may have to use your Davenport,' I said, 'I had a lot at my mother's house tonight.' 'Be my guest,' he said, pointing to the closet where I could get sheets and a blanket."

Dr. S. said, "Your mother may have found a daughter, but it sounds to me like you finally got a brother."

14

YOU COULD'VE LED WITH THAT, IKE.

On the Thursday before the big meeting, Leo drove the Westchester Electronics 1954 Chevy 3800 Panel Van up to Purchase.

"This is how it all went down," he said. "I wore a blue denim work shirt with the company logo on it, just above the spot where I usually pin my name tag. I arrived just before nine, pulled up to the guardhouse, rolled down my window, and handed a clipboard that contained the purchase order for the bug sweep to a guy in a gray uniform.

"'Hiya,'" I said, then looked through the windshield and remarked, 'Whoa, some nice place ya got here.' The *ya* was intentional, to puff up the importance of the guard. 'Me, I work out of a crummy office in New Rochelle near the train station. The only good thing is I get to go to mansions like this in Scarsdale, Rye, and Bedford.'

"I kept up the chatter while the guard was perusing the purchase order. 'How much dough you think a guy's gotta make to get a place like this. Jesus, all that stone. What's he got, his own quarry?' I gave a false chuckle."

Leo impersonated himself with a silly snigger that caused both of us to crack up.

"Okay, no more impressions. I'm no Frank Gorshin, that's for sure," he said to us, in his best imitation of how that comedian would become Burt Lancaster.

"'A SWEEP FOR BUGS?' the guard asked."

"'Kinda,'" I replied, "'but not the insect types. Just kiddin'.'

"'I don't have anything on this,' he says to me. I held my breath for a second then said, 'It's signed and all. Here,' I pointed. 'Alberto Giaquinto.'

"The guard stepped back into the small house and opened a binder. He thumbed a few pages and ran his finger down them. He took his sweet-ass time.

"'You can call my boss,' I said with as much confidence as I could bring to the fore. 'His name's right there, underneath Mr. Giaquinto's. He signed it too. He's a busy guy—the owner's nephew and all that—but I'm sure ya could track him down. Take ya time, no skin offa my ass.' With that, I reached for my coffee and tried to look casual as I pretended to drink from my empty mug.

"'Mr. Giaquinto's on the guest list for Sunday,' the guard finally said to me. 'So I guess if he ordered it, it's okay. Just drive up, but don't park in the circle. There's a spur off to the left. Gravel. Park there. I'll tell them you're coming in.'"

I was impressed: Francesca's bluff had worked.

I said, "I guess the guard didn't want to cast doubt on 2-Cig's signature; it was a risk that could cost him his job."

"So I ended it with a smile and a 'Thanks, Buddy.' Then my heart practically shot out of my chest as the guard said, 'Hey, wait a minute,'" as I was rolling up my window.

"'Yeah?' was all I managed to say.

"'What's your name?' he asked me.

"'Al,' I say to him, then quickly adlibbed, 'Actually Alphonse, but no one calls me that except my *nonna*. Alphonse DeEsso, like the gas stations.'

"At that point, feeling my oats, I asked, 'Hey, can you sign and date it, time and all? They keep close tabs on me, so's I gotta make sure the guys in the office know I'm doin' my job. Especially the boss's nephew. A little kiss-ass goes a long way, am I right?'"

LEO'S RUSE HAD WORKED WELL; I could see that while he'd pushed it right up to the limit, some instinct told him not to overdo it. That happens when actors go off script. Overconfidence can breed reckless behavior.

I'd seen this on more than one occasion at Fort Dix. Guys who were star athletes in high school would take off to lead the platoon in a five mile trek by sprinting through tough terrain with sixty pounds on our backs only to collapse, writhing in pain, retching their insides out, having overestimated their capabilities, which they'd measured against their achievements on a field or a court where they'd been invincible against overmatched opponents. I took this as a yellow-flag warning to myself to make sure I didn't fall into this trap.

I ASKED LEO, "Did the guard sign the purchase order?"

"He did, thank God. So I gave him a two finger tip of the imaginary cap and drove up the driveway to the house. I was met at the front door by a woman in white gloves who didn't extend them to offer a handshake. She was wearing a suit, the hem halfway down her legs but still showing a nice ankle."

"'Mr. DeEsso?'" she said.

"I replied, 'You can call me Al.'

"In a rather formal way, she said, 'I'm Mrs. Donahue, Mr. DeEsso. I understand you are going to inspect every phone.'

"'Yes, ma'am,' I said. 'Some house ya got.'

"She was kind of curt, but I didn't take it personally. I guessed she was always like this. Working for a big shot and all. Anyway, she said, 'Mr. DeEsso, you may start on the first floor, in Mr. Aronheimer's office. Let me show you the way.'

"I marched through the main reception area. It had a twenty-foot ceiling and a staircase to the second floor that looked like a ram's horn in the shape of a capital G. I made sure not to trip over the Persian carpets as I made my way down a long hall. Once in the office, I took out a small cloth bag that held what looked like a miniature cuticle scissor, tweezer, and several kinds of screwdrivers. As I unzipped the bag, I asked Mrs. Donahue if she'd like to observe what I was doing, knowing full well she'd have no interest in this unscheduled, time-consuming event that was taking her away from her planned assignments. She stayed by the door. I have to tell you I congratulated myself on this offer to her, which I hoped would remove any suspicion she might otherwise have had. I made sure to talk out loud to myself, another feint designed to pretend I was checking for a bug while actually secreting one. Ha ha!

"'Okay,' I said, after having unscrewed the cap. 'Nothing here. That's good news. Now to the phone itself.' With my back to Mrs. Donahue, I used my right hand to pull out a bug that had been clipped to the inside of my left sleeve. 'Let's have a look around,' I said as I inserted the bug underneath the bell, where I adhered it securely to the inside of the phone with a dab of silly putty. Can you believe it? Silly putty! I moved my head around as if I was checking inside the mechanicals of the phone, then I stood up, and as I approached her, I held out the small cloth bag with the utensils and showed it to her. 'The tools of the trade!' I said proudly, another part of my act to support the legitimacy of my work. She brought me to other rooms, where I repeated this pretend security check and planted additional bugs. When I was finished, Mrs. Donahue walked me to the front door. I'd been in the house less than half an hour.

"'Thank you, Mrs. Donahue.' I said.

"'Goodbye, Mr. DeEsso,' she said. She didn't say 'you're welcome.'"

"You were a tradesman to her, that's all," I said.

"I wonder where *she* came from," Leo said. "Anyway, I drove slowly back down the driveway, leaned over the passenger seat, cranked down the window, and asked the guard to initial the purchase order at the bottom where it indicated Service Completed. He complied without giving it another look."

"I can't believe you got away with it," I said.

"I've got my sister to thank."

I said, "People are so easily duped."

"You can get away with almost anything, I suppose," Leo said, "if you've got the balls and play the game like you belong."

There was no better example of that, I thought, than Nicky Shark.

"Did you ever think about what you would've done if they'd suspected something?" I asked.

"Nothing specific," Leo replied. "Probably just have mumbled some nonsense and hightailed it out of there. I wasn't thinking about any of that. Just so Goddamned happy I pulled it off without a hitch. But having said that, I was glad it was over. My heart was kind of racing. I turned north onto Purchase Street, pulled over onto the tree-shaded shoulder a half mile down the road, and retrieved four radio receivers from the glove box. I put them on the seat next to me and waited for a call. I needed to make sure that the bugs were live and that the reception was good. After about fifteen minutes, I heard Mrs. Donahue's voice quite clearly on one of them. I resumed driving north with the receivers still on, listening to her speak with someone at a grocery store. I had to determine how far the signal went. I was relieved when I spotted the access road to the Westchester County Airport. I knew that if the signal was still strong at the airport, the parking lot would give us good cover on Sunday."

That was the plan: Francesca and I would join him there in the 1938 two-door Ford Coupe for a parking lot picnic, where our entertainment would consist of listening in on the most private conversations of politicians, business tycoons, and hoods.

"DID YOU EVER CONSIDER that your snooping was unethical? Forget about illegal," Dr. S. wanted to know. "You were going to be privy to intimate conversations that even others in attendance at the meeting weren't going to know about. I get what you were hoping to accomplish, but did you or Francesca or Leo have any qualms about how you were going about it?"

"At the time? Honestly, no. We were caught up in the attempt to get information so that we could find a way—I know this seems implausible—to block Robert Moses and 2-Cig from destroying Tremont. It's not as if we consciously weighed the pros and cons of wiretapping—snooping, eavesdropping, whatever you want to call it—and took a vote to proceed, knowing it violated some moral code. Uh uh."

"How would you feel if someone had access—on a real time basis—to your personal conversations, without your knowledge?"

"I wouldn't approve. I'd be downright pissed off. But there'd be no need to do something like that."

"That doesn't matter. Why didn't you go to the DA at that time?" she asked.

"We didn't have any actual evidence. Nothing to give them. We knew what they were up to—"

She interrupted me. "What you thought you knew was pure supposition."

"From a legal point of view, sure. But we knew what was up."

"I don't doubt that, Jay, but that's not where I'm going. There's a right and a wrong here."

"Yeah, well, 'I was only following orders' was the legal way. Wasn't that their defense? Sometimes the legal way isn't right, just as the illegal way—what we did—isn't wrong. Well, okay, it was wrong I guess . . ."

"You guess?"

"Bad choice of words. It was wrong, period. Are you asking me if I'd do it again?" I said.

"Would you?"

"It depends on the circumstances."

"So here you go again being the arbiter, the judge for your own case. Isn't that what they call a conflict of interest?"

"What do you want me to say? That I'm sorry? I'm not. But okay, what I will cop to is that this was a special case, and it, or something like it, may not present itself again."

"Not good enough. You're trying to worm your way through this."

"You want me to say that it was plain wrong and that, in the future, when I'm faced with a similar set of conditions, I'll let the passion die down, rethink things, and not go ahead with it?"

Dr. S. asked, "Is that such a bad idea?"

"Life's not always black and white. There's a lot of gray. It's hard to say in advance what I'd do without knowing a lot of the details," I replied.

This was so true. I'd be tested later in the year with this very issue.

"In the end," she continued, "this was the incident that got it all started. That ended up with you being sent to jail, required to meet with the parole officer and with me."

"Well," I said with a smile, "at least one of those things wasn't punishment."

WE THREE JUNIOR DETECTIVES spread out a blanket on the grass near the parking lot at the airport on Sunday morning. We were equipped with two beach chairs that I took from Francesca's parents' backyard, a transistor radio, some pillows, a thermos bottle filled with coffee, paper cups, bagels with cream cheese, the four radio receivers, a copy of the *New York Mirror*, and a practiced excuse for why we were there in case someone asked why we were picnicking at the airport when there were so many nicer places at the Kensico Dam nearby.

We took a circuitous route, not wanting to be spotted on the Hutchinson River Parkway or Purchase Street by my brother or Nate as they drove the big chiefs to the powwow. We'd come up Route 22, which took us at least an extra half hour because of the lights, but it allowed us to canvas a diner in North White Plains where one of us could pick up some lunch that afternoon.

It was officially spring, yet early in the morning, there was a chill that caused us to shiver. Unless it was our nerves. I had on a nondescript windbreaker—Francesca had reminded both Leo and me to wear clothes that others would have difficulty describing—and a plain navy blue knit hat. I'd left my Giants' baseball cap in the hall closet after Francesca said "absolutely not" before we left my apartment.

I kidded Leo that he read the newspaper like a Jew, from the back to the front.

"Sports pages first," he said. "I can't take the news of the day until I read the stories of the games and the scores from yesterday. Well, well, the Giants lost to the Braves. So what else is new." A few minutes later, he said, "Hey, get a load of this: You'll never guess today's question in the *New York Mirror* from Nicky Shark, the Inquisitive Fotographer. Are you ready? 'Who do you blame if the Giants and the Dodgers skip town?'"

"You've got to be kidding," Francesca said. "Holy shit, they're setting up the mayor for a fall."

"Probably. But it does seem odd that this is the question, today of all days, when Wagner and Horace Stoneham are here in Purchase, huddling together with Robert Moses, Carmine DeSapio, and God knows who else." I said.

"Your brother, Nate, and Bootsie Albanese, for starters," Leo said.

"*Pishacockers*," I said.

"Pisha-what? What's that mean? You and your *cockamamie* Yiddish expressions," Francesca said, laughing, obviously having picked this word up from my mother."

"People of little significance," I said. "*Shmendricks*. Don't ask. Anyway, 2-Cig for sure, and if my brother's there, my father will be, no question."

"What about the head of the department of Buildings?" Leo asked. "Maybe him too? I mean, at the end of the day, he's going to be in charge."

"On paper," Francesca added. "It's Robert Moses who's going to oversee everything: the construction, the finances, the approvals, the publicity, you name it."

She was right.

"Wouldn't it be great if Nicky Shark is there to ask these guys the questions that we'd really like to hear," Leo said. "Let me see *those* answers in the paper tomorrow. I like the way he shoves a microphone into the face of some straphanger who's got about five seconds to understand the question and then come up with an answer. It's their visceral reactions to probing questions that are most interesting."

"Fat chance," Francesca said. No way they'd have that *pishacocker* there," she said, barely able to get the word out before laughing hysterically.

"You're becoming quite a *Yiddishe* mama," I said. She raised her eyebrows.

"The only person I'm not sure of is the head of the Hibernians chapter from Crotona Park East. Tom Collins. He's got a stake in this with his clubhouse in the way, and I'll bet his members include some high rollers." I said.

Just then, we heard a voice on one of the radio receivers. We stared at it, shushed each other, then realized how idiotic that appeared, realizing that no one could hear us. It was about 10:30 a.m. We stared at each other with scrunched-up faces. It wasn't Mayor Wagner's voice; we heard him on the news every night. It wasn't Horace Stoneham's either; we could tell, from the times he was on the radio speaking about the Giants. Not Carmine DeSapio's; his voice was inflected with the idioms and tone of the streets. It was certainly not Robert Moses, whose imitation patrician voice was more akin to FDRs. *Who else could it be?* I mouthed to the two of them, careful not to make a sound that might obliterate a clue. We had to try to figure it out by context:

"Yeah, it's like I said in your office. They're gonna go the other route, not what your boys want to do. You're gonna have to create that advisory board whose job is to put their stamp on it. Approval. Suck it up, Billy boy. They're gonna take care of you. Believe me." After a pause, we heard the other guy say, "Okay, Nicky, I'll keep the fuckin' window shut, no insurance for my wife, ha ha." The line went dead.

Nicky Shark! We mouthed to each other.

"Maybe he's talking to the guy who heads up the Department of Buildings," Leo said so low we could hardly hear. "The guy Liam, who works at Buildings, the one who took a shot at you at Coogan's," he said to Francesca, "he told you that they were going to overrule the department's recommendation to go through the Hibernians building, two blocks south of 176th Street."

That made sense.

But Nicky Shark? What circumstances would get the Inquisitive Fotographer invited to the Aronheimer mansion with all the big shots of New York?

We sat around on the blanket and waited for the next call. Twenty minutes passed.

"Donatella, it's Alberto."

Leo mouthed, *Who's Donatella?*

2-Cig's niece, Donatella Giaquinto, I mouthed back. Later, I'd fill in the blanks regarding the couple of times when I was a little kid that my father allowed me to traipse along with him on one of his walks up Arthur Avenue to sip espresso with 2-Cig at a café table on the sidewalk. Donatella would pucker her lips or wink or lightly touch my father's arm and shoulder, signs I saw as friendship, now decoded these many years later as having a very different meaning.

Donatella always lined up or sat closest to 2-Cig, while the *goombahs* jockeyed for a position holding up the outside walls of the club or meandering around the sidewalk, hoping against hope for an invitation to sit. Behind her back, they called her *regina della mafia*—mafia queen. She was about forty, with a bouffant hairdo and a great figure, which she used as a magnet to pull the iron will of her uncle's cronies to her side.

"It's all set. deVenezia's promise of fifty Gs got Moses ta lay out the reasons for why the road needs ta go troo 176th Street. Go get the money from Tom Collins. Remember ta tell him it cost seventy-five, and I'm kickin' in twenty-five. But not really."

The two of them laughed.

"They'll keep it under wraps for about four months. We gotta get goin' now. We gotta get ta alla 'em on 176th Street pretty quick like."

"I'll get the graph paper that deVenezia's boy gave you and have a go at it myself," she said.

"No good, sweetheart, you know, the wives."

There was silence for about ten seconds. I envisioned smoke coming out of Donatella's ears as she had to suffer in silence listening to her uncle simply saying "the wives," by which he made it clear that while her speaking to the men would get their full attention—much as my drill sergeant could with just a squint—the women on 176th Street would recoil at what they would perceive as an intrusion that would have to be repelled. A well-crafted tease that allowed a guy to have a peek when she lowered her head or crossed her legs would get an otherwise tough guy to resemble a teenage boy whose hormones are just beginning to kick in.

"Let Bootsie handle it," 2-Cig continued. "Dependin' on the whos and whats, ya know, the size of the store, whether the guy rents or owns it, how many apartments in the building, the number of rooms, all the stuff they got written down. We gotta figure out how much ta offer 'em. Not too generous so's we don't pay 'em too much but also not jewy enough for 'em to say 'no.' We gotta, whaddya say—walk a fine line."

"I'll speak to Ike's kid," Danielle replied, matter-of-factly.

Leo pointed to me and shook his head. Before I could tell him 2-Cig was referring to my brother, 2-Cig said. "Bud's a smart Heeb. Have him fill in the blanks. Like how much he thinks it'll take ta buy 'em all out. Four months.

That's all we got. Light a Roman candle under Bud's ass. We gotta own all this shit before Moses makes an announcement of the new route and Wagner tells everyone that the City will buy 'em out under eminence domain."

"HOLY SHIT," Francesca said after they hung up. "It's not just that they're going to blast through the neighborhood; they're going to dupe everyone into selling out at a cheaper price than what the City will pay."

"Why would they care about owning all the apartment houses and stores? Why would they give a crap about being in the real estate business for, what, a year or so at most?" Leo asked.

"It's gotta be that 2-Cig is going to scare the bejesus out of these people by telling them that the City will pay less under eminent domain in a year than what he's going to offer them in cold, hard cash now. It's a lie. But you know what? A lot of people will believe him, and the lure of cash is hard to ignore, especially for folks who're just making ends meet," I said.

"Which is just about everybody in Tremont," Francesca said.

At that point, Leo opted to go get some lunch for us at the diner on Route 22. As he drove away, Francesca looked at me and said, "Starting tomorrow, we have to get off our dead asses and do something about this."

"Going up against Robert Moses? The mayor? Carmine DeSapio? And don't forget 2-Cig. Are you nuts? What do you think we can do? Don't get me wrong, I'd like to do something, but do you honestly believe we can get them to change the route? No way that's going to happen. Not by us *pishacockers*, anyway," I said, hoping to insert a little levity and realism into the conversation.

"You think I'm a Greek girl trying to push that big rock up the hill?"

"Sisyphus," I said.

"It's the one thing I remembered from ancient history in the eleventh grade," she said. "It stuck with me because it seemed like I always had huge objects in my way."

"Like what, if you don't mind."

"Catholic guilt, for the most part. But don't get me started on that. Look, I'm no Pollyanna when it comes to what we're up against. It's crystal clear to me that if these honchos decide to blast through 176th Street and destroy Tremont, that's what's going to happen."

We sat on the blanket, looking out towards the single-engine planes practicing takeoffs and landings. After a few minutes of not talking, she turned to me and said, "What if we can make the lives of the people who're shit-out-of-luck a little bit better?"

"How? If we go around telling them what's going to happen, no one will believe us. We're just a couple of Joe Shmoes who can't tell anyone how we found out, with the illegal wiretap and all that," I said.

"Yeah, well, here's where my brother can help."

"Hey there," Leo said, approaching us with a brown bag and a six-pack of soda. "How can I help? With what? Fill me in? Any more calls?"

"No more calls," Francesca said. "Thanks for lunch." She continued to talk as she took everything out of the bag and set the items down on the blanket, filling her brother in on what we were talking about.

"I agree. You two can't make any headway on your own. What were you thinking, Francesca?" Leo asked.

"This is a longshot, but that's all we have, so here goes." She looked at me and said, "When Leo was at Fordham, he worked on the newspaper."

"Managing Editor," Leo said proudly to me.

"Impressive," I said, giving Leo a thumb's up.

Francesca said, "We can't go to the people on 176th Street, but student reporters can—after we fill them in on what we know."

"But they can't take the information from the wiretaps and use it," Leo offered.

"No, they can't quote anything we've heard, but we can sure give them the gist of what's going on. You better believe they'll be intrigued. Who doesn't want to be in a big story, or to break it? What they *can* do is ask questions in such a way that they don't seem like questions." Francesca said.

"Like you know they're going to ban canoes on the Bronx River, don't you?" I said.

"Really?" Leo said.

I gave him a look.

"Oh my God, I fell for it," Leo said.

"That's what everyone will do if we guide these college reporters correctly," Francesca said.

I said, "It's basically what Nicky Shark does when he jams the microphone up to someone's mouth. He steers them to the answer that he wants."

Francesca sat up straighter, getting into it. "We give them the basics. Then I can see them asking folks in the neighborhood something such as, 'You wouldn't mind moving to another part of Tremont close by if the new expressway they're talking about were to come right through this street, would you?' Or, 'You'd put up with a year of inconvenience while they bury the new expressway under 176th Street, wouldn't you?' Or, how about asking someone, 'Where would *you* put the new expressway instead of through 176th Street?'"

"Wow, that's perfect," Leo said admiringly.

"So we find someone at the student newspaper—

"*The Ram,*" Leo said.

"—and tell them a lot of what we know, but without the details of how we found out," I added.

"On deep background," Leo added for authenticity.

Now standing and walking around the blanket, Francesca said, "We'll work with whoever it is at *The Ram* to come up with questions that sound like he knows something he can't reveal to the people he interviews on 176th Street. We can send him out with a cameraman and a sound engineer. It'll look professional, one guy taking photos—everyone wants to have his picture in the paper, even if it's a Bronx school paper—while another guy records everything, street noise and all."

"Very convincing and realistic," Leo said.

"You know what'll happen next," I said. "I see where you're going. Anyone who's interviewed will start blabbing to everyone he knows, over the phone, to his customers, in the apartments, to bus drivers. And then, they'll all want to buy the paper, read it aloud, cut out the article, post it on bulletin boards and lampposts outside the store, wherever."

"See, Leo, the paper will be a battering ram for us, and if we're lucky, the story will be picked up by the papers in Manhattan, maybe even the *Trib* or the *Times*," Francesca said.

"Okay, so let's say everyone in Tremont gets riled up. I get that. But how does that help? What difference can that make?" Leo asked.

"Here's an idea, off the top of my head," Francesca said. "Maybe if we expose what Liam Sweeney said, you know, that the guys at the Department of Buildings were in favor of the route that went through Crotona Park East along with what we just heard—that the head of the department is going to create a phony commission to overrule it, there'll be so much heat they have to revise the plan."

"I agree that this is something we should tell a reporter from *The Ram*, and it'll create a lot of smoke, but it's hard to see how a commission would change their view. I don't see a fire. Too much pressure from Robert Moses."

"I wish you weren't so fucking logical," she said.

"Well," Leo said, "we could organize the shop and apartment owners, get them together, a rally. The renters could come, too, and have speakers demand they don't destroy Tremont. It'd get a lot of news coverage—papers, radio, TV. The mayor needs votes, after all. He doesn't want the whole of The Bronx against him, saying he's in the pocket of Robert Moses, that kind of thing."

Francesca and I gave each other a knowing look, the kind couples can decode without speaking.

Francesca said, "Look, 2-Cig's going to offer everyone money to leave their homes and businesses in Tremont. Some people will want to take it. Cash in hand. But *we* can put cash into their pockets as well."

"No way. Where are we going to come up with cash?" Leo asked.

"We're not going to give them anything," Francesca said excitedly. "Rent strike. We'll get them all riled up to not pay their rent—that's cash that's going to stay in their pockets—and you'd better believe that's going to hit hard at the absentee landlords who own buildings, stores, and apartment houses. Those guys will go nuts, bananas. They'll threaten to cut off electricity and gas and pressure the phone companies to cut off service. That'll create a real brouhaha. That's where the rallies will come from, Leo. Demonstrations, people holding up big signs, 'No Way Expressway,' things like that."

"And we could get kids to make poster boards," I added, "with pictures of lions on them that say 'Lying Lyons'—you know, for the Bronx Borough

President, Jimmy Lyons. Trust me, he probably doesn't know a Goddamned thing about what's going on, but that doesn't matter. With this kind of pressure, he might even begin to stand up for his people."

Francesca said, "Wouldn't it be great to see a shot of a group of Tremonters at a rally giving Robert Moses the Bronx cheer."

With that, we simultaneously demonstrated our best version of our home borough's famous cheer by blowing through our extended tongues, placing a thumb underneath our noses, and waving our fingers—an acceptable alternative to giving the finger.

"I like it, a rent strike," Leo said enthusiastically. "A lot. This is great, but the whole thing depends on getting *The Ram* newspaper behind it."

Francesca said, "Why don't you give a call to the guy who gave you that nice commendation, the certificate that's on your wall. Have him introduce you to the current managing editor."

"Terrific idea," Leo said. "I'll do it tomorrow, first thing."

I turned to Francesca and said, "I love your ideas. They're fabulous."

"So are you," she said, grazing her palm against my face.

"Ahem!" Leo exclaimed, and we all laughed.

We finally felt that we were doing something, although none of us could've imagined where this was going to end up.

We heard a voice from one of the other receivers.

"Hello."

"Chub, it's Horace."

I looked to Francesca and Leo and whispered, "Stoneham, the owner of the Giants. He's calling Chub Feeney, the general manager."

Leo gave me a look that I interpreted as *how would you possibly know that?*

I knew everything about the Giants: that Willie Mays's over-the-shoulder catch of Vic Wertz's 425-foot blast in the 1954 World Series on September 29 was the greatest defensive play in the history of the game; that Bobby Thompson's three-run homer off of Ralph Branca on October 3, 1951 won the pennant against the Dodgers in what Red Smith of the *Herald Tribune* called the Miracle of Coogan's Bluff; and that Fred Merkle's blunder by not touching second base in a game against the Cubs on September 23, 1908 cost the Giants a chance to win the pennant. For sure I was a Bronx boy, but I somehow rooted for the team across-the-river that you could see from Yankee Stadium.

"How's it going?" Chub asked.

"As good as can be imagined," Stoneham responded. "Listen, Chub, they're going to offer us two different parcels on the cheap—the deals are so good I can hardly believe my ears—and we've got to make a decision within a month between the one in Claremont and the other near Fort Tryon Park."

"Bad idea to go to Claremont, boss. There's more room there if they tear down everything they say they will, but you don't want to be the second team in The Bronx. Bad enough we're in the shadow of Yankee Stadium as it is. Stay in Manhattan. More expensive, but it's worth it. Besides, you're going to get the *bustarella* from Giaquinto, which'll go a long way towards reducing the premium for the Manhattan site."

"Don't kid yourself, Chub. What 2-Cig gives with one hand, he takes away with the other."

This was undoubtedly true. I could only imagine the overbilling and non-itemized expenses 2-Cig would charge Horace Stoneham for the dismantling of the Polo Grounds. It would surely end up being many times more than the bribe he was going to pay Stoneham to be the prime contractor on the job of reducing the Polo Grounds to rubble for whatever new project would take its place.

Leo said, "So the Giants are going to move north, up near the new expressway, close to the Bridge! That's a whole lot better for us fans than if they were to move to Los Angeles or San Francisco."

"Hold your excitement, my dear brother, until you find out how many hundreds of people are going to have to look for new places to live and how many stores and small shops are going to go out of business up near Fort Tryon Park," Francesca said. "In the end, you know the little people are going to have a stick shoved up their asses."

My Francesca had a way with words.

An hour went by with no further calls.

"You think it's over?" Leo asked.

"Let's give it more time," I said. "I'd hate to miss something important just because we left early. We've only got this one chance."

In the middle of the afternoon, a call came through.

"Hello?"

"Rebekah, it's Ike."

With that, Francesca and Leo stood up and walked to the car, not wanting to eavesdrop on a conversation between my mother and father. I wasn't 100 percent sure I wanted to listen in either. I stayed, maybe because this was one time that I could hear what actually transpired between them without having to decipher what one told me later about a conversation with the other, and I could never be sure of how something was slanted. It was also helpful to hear the forcefulness, the sarcasm, and the empty spaces between words that are critically important to understanding the real meanings that can be misinterpreted when getting it from only one side or reading a transcript.

"Where are you? Up on Arthur Avenue with your Italian friends?" my mother asked.

"I suppose you were home alone all morning?"

What did that mean? My father wasn't exactly inscrutable, so this had to be something that my mother would interpret instantly. Not that I could.

"What do you want?"

"Do I have to want something to speak to my wife?"

"I'm busy. Out with it."

"Busy little beaver," he said

It was painful for me to listen to him emphasize the word beaver.

After a pause, he continued, "I need Gavi Yudakov's number."

"I don't have it."

"How could you not have it?"

"It's not in my book. What can I tell you?"

"How could it not be in your book?"

"There are a lot of people not in my book. The other Big Ike, for instance."

This was the first time I'd ever heard my mother stick it to my father hard, and I thought the rapid response of the reference to President Eisenhower was perfect.

"I'll bet the rabbi is in your book."

Rabbi Leviev?

"Ike, call my mother. She'll give you Gavi's number."

"You call her."

"Listen to me. Here's what you do: dial HAvemeyer 3, 9767. When a woman answers the phone, ask her for the number."

"That's more like it. Who is this woman?"

"My mother."

I heard the click of my mother's phone and my father hiss, "God damn son of a bitch."

After a minute:

"Hello?"

"D'vorah, this is Ike."

"Yes, Ike."

"Can you get Gavi Yudakov's telephone number for me?"

"Hold a minute." I heard the rustling of paper. "Are you still there?"

"Still here."

"Do you have a pen or pencil?"

"Yes, uh huh."

"Here it is: VAnderbilt 4, 6684. Did you get it?"

"Yes, thank you."

Click.

A few seconds later:

"Hello?"

"Gavi, this is Ike. How you doing?"

"Your son's doing a great job for me at Spins. Nice boy. Smart and trustworthy."

That was good to hear.

"You ever see Bobby Albanese at your place? Spins I'm talking about."

"Bobby Albanese? Who?"

"Bootsie."

"Oh, Bootsie, yeah. That *schmuck* comes in from time to time, always through back door, goes into my private room in the back, makes a big mess. He must think I'm a maid. Never stays more than half an hour. On the phone."

"Listen, Gavi, keep an eye on him for me, will you?"

"For what?"

"I don't know. See if he acts funny. Talks to anyone in the store. Gets a visitor . . . That kind of thing."

"You want me to spy on one of 2-Cig's guys? Not up my alley. Live and let live, I say."

"There's a grand in it for you," my father said.

"You could've led with that, Ike."

"Are we okay?" Ike asked.

"Yeah. But I want it up front. Give it to your son."

"Sure. Bud will hand it to you personally."

Click.

I called out to Francesca and Leo, who were leaning up against the other side of the car and told them to come over to the blanket. I filled them in on the call from my father to Gavi.

"What's going on? Any idea?" Leo asked.

"Specifically? No. But something's up. A grand is a lot of dough to spy on someone in your own organization. It's pretty clear that 2-Cig doesn't trust Bootsie."

In the next two hours, there were phone calls from Mayor Wagner and Carmine DeSapio that had nothing to do with Tremont, then nothing from any others in attendance. We drove back to the City. I thanked Leo for all he had done, including taking the risk of planting the bugs. Francesca stayed at my place. We were up late, replaying what we'd heard. She took notes on everything including our speculations. When she was finished, I put them into Alanphant.

15

DID SHE EVER SAY ANYTHING TO YOU ABOUT THE MONEY?

Bobby Albanese was an overweight, hard-edged kid who came from a second-generation family in Tremont, where hand-me-downs were as commonplace as trips to the principal's office, both of which were perceived as slights that would eventually have to be revenged. His enmity, however, wasn't limited to family members or school officials. He kept a list of everyone he believed had it in for him tucked away on scraps of paper held together by a rubber band. Bobby had hidden them in a slit he made in the underside of his mattress on the lower bunk bed that he shared with the brother closest to him in age. That's what he'd turn to, late at night while his brother slept. He used a small Pez-like flashlight to arrange and sort the list and employed mnemonics to recall his enemies during the day. He'd whisper them in alphabetical order, his parents thinking he was practicing his devotions. It didn't take much for a new name to be added to Bobby's list. A slur: "You fat *dago!*" A rebuff: "Sorry, Bobby, you're just *not right* for a part in the school play." A snub: "Don't let the bottle stop on Bobby! How disgusting!" Being at the bottom of the barrel was a potent motivator for his quest for vengeance when he was sixteen and able to leave school. He got a driver's license and began to put some money into his pocket as a member of the lowest rung on the Giaquinto ladder. He served first as a runner—someone whose job was to literally go as fast as he could to fetch a cup of coffee, get the latest edition of the afternoon paper, or retrieve a shovel from the back of the club to clear the sidewalk. No matter how hard he ran, 2-Cig's men made fun of him, egged on by Donatella. To turn insult to injury, they chipped in to buy him a pair of thick-soled, high-topped engineer boots, which made it even more difficult for him to run, while making it easier for them to mock him unmercifully. Bobby's smile was a mask that hid his determination for retribution, which he noted each night on the pieces of paper he'd read in bed.

At first, he struck back with little reprisals, telling the guys that he'd tipped the folks that he bought the cigarettes or newspaper or sandwiches from, but in reality, he pocketed the small change from each transaction, a minor satisfaction that began to turn into a haul after a year. More than a hundred bucks—a not insignificant amount for a kid—which enabled him to buy a small Luger pistol from a former GI who'd set up shop in The Bronx selling German weapons he'd stolen prior to his return to the US. In the dank basement of his house, Bobby practiced how he'd approach, taunt, and kill his tormentors, mimicking lines he'd heard from Detective Ross Dolan, the star of ABC Radio's *I Deal in Crime*.

February 14, 1947, was the first time one of 2-Cigs guys called him Bootsie, which caused all the others to laugh uproariously. That night, Bobby's basement fantasies had him mowing them all down—St. Valentine's Day Massacre style—his Luger aimed at each of his tormentors. They cowered and begged for their lives, which had no effect on Bobby. He repeated: *Take that, you bastard* seven times to his great satisfaction. Then, something strange happened: in a change as stunning as the transformation of a caterpillar into a butterfly, Bobby adopted the pejorative nickname as his own and began referring to himself in the third person as Bootsie. And wouldn't you know, the taunting ceased, and Bobby disappeared into history, replaced by Bootsie, an accepted—if not loved—member of 2-Cig's gang. His duties as a runner stopped and were replaced by assignments to collect points and vig from 2-Cig's loan sharking activities. Here again, he reprised the role from his running days, pocketing some of the vig, telling Donatella, for example, that he'd collected $40 in vig when he actually got

$50 after using his Luger to tell the sucker—in perfect Detective Ross Dolan style—that if he was ever asked, the vig was $40 not $50. No one was going to rat him out for chump change. Every once in a while, he had to use force. Typically, this meant using the flat side of the pistol as a hammer to the side of the head. Only rarely was he called upon to shoot—never at someone—preferring to pull a silencer out of his pocket theatrically and aim over the poor guy's head, leaving a permanent hole in the wall. It would serve as a reminder of worse things to come if the guy didn't pay up in time.

Within two years, Bootsie was at the top of the list of collectors and a key underling, reporting directly to Donatella. He was making good dough—enough for him to rent a fancy place on the Grand Concourse. It didn't matter to him that he was surrounded by Jews. He was a regular at the Masada Deli on Morris Avenue. He'd arrive just after they opened, and his lox and onion omelet would be waiting for him underneath a heat lamp. On his way out, he'd leave a generous tip for Manny Ginzburg, having noticed the numbers on Manny's arm on his first visit. My brother told me that this was the only occasion anyone could recall Bootsie showing empathy for another person.

He never put in that much time at his apartment. He preferred hanging out at the Italian social clubs, the bar at the Hibernians building on Crotona Park East, and sometimes one of the Irish pubs, where he'd down a half a dozen Guinness draughts, then call Carlos to escort him to a Puerto Rican whorehouse near the Bronx River—a safe haven for a tough-guy hood whose outward appearance belied his innermost insecurities when it came to members of the opposite sex.

By 1954, as a top earner, Bootsie had become indispensable to Donatella, who began to give him other assignments, including taking charge of the younger guys and whipping them into shape, which is how he came to manage the affairs of my brother Eric, Nate, Sean, and Carlos. While Bootsie played tough guy with Eric, Nate, and Sean, he hovered over Carlos as if he were a younger brother, allowing him to tag along on assignments to collect debts from those that Donatella wanted taken down a peg. Being short and slight, the marks never perceived a threat from Carlos, which made his lighting swift boxing moves all the more surprising to them, a delight that would set Bootsie off in a mocking howl, an added degradation to Bootsie's physical blows. After a collection accompanied by some swaggering and posturing over a cowering victim, Bootsie and Carlos would feel invigorated and show signs of euphoria, one speaking Italian and the other Spanish, rapidly, back and forth, neither understanding the other's words but perfectly comprehending the exchange of messages. What initially surprised me was that Carlos wasn't a mean-spirited guy, yet he went along with Bootsie as his concealed muscle. Eric told me that for Carlos, it was a job, a pretty good paying one at that, so while he played a little Stepin Fetchit to Bootsie, he knew right from wrong, and therefore never crossed the line, always letting Bootsie engage in a beat down by himself.

AT AN APPOINTED HOUR, Bootsie would enter the back door of Spins, go directly to the conference room, and wait for a sign from Eric, who knew to hustle a kid out of Booth 18 to make sure that he wasn't late. If he was, Bootsie would hold back some payments from Eric and Nate, shakedowns they could only avoid by being on time at this and other meetings.

The day after the meeting in Purchase, Bootsie entered Spins at noon; Eric called out to him as the clock struck the hour.

"Yo, Bootsie, Bud here."

"And Nate," he chimed in, hoping Bootsie wouldn't refer to him as Nappy, a nickname that he despised hearing from anyone but my brother. He was born Nathaniel Washington Carver Jr. but was referred to as "Nate" as a kid by his family to distinguish him from his father. To Eric, the nickname "Nappy" wasn't meant in a derogatory way, only as a descriptive. Although to others, such as Bootsie, it was an intentional put-down. And to the best of my knowledge, Eric didn't use it in public, the way Nate wouldn't call Bud "Jewboy" if anyone else was around.

"So's nows ya know what's goin' on," Bootsie answered.

"You mean what we heard in Purchase?" Nate said.

"Yeah, numb nuts," Bootsie said. "What the fuck ya think I'm talkin' about?"

"Okay, Bootsie," my brother said.

Bootsie continued. "Now listen up, jackasses. Yuse gonna go 'round, ya know, ta the folks on 176th Street, startin' tomorra, bright and early, both of yuse. Bud, ya make the pitch, all friendly and all, tell 'em like was discussed yesterday. Be like Joe Friday: 'Just the facts, ma'am.' Got it?"

"Yeah, sure, Bootsie, but you gotta know I went to all these folks with my old man. That's how we got all this information in the first place, so if I show up now, the cat's out of the bag. It's gotta be Nate by himself. Okay?"

"What the fuck, shit for brains, ya can't send some colored guy," Bootsie said as if Nate wasn't there in the booth, "except maybe to the Jews. And how many Heebs live there, huh?"

Nate was apoplectic. He cupped his hand around Eric's ear and whispered, "If that asshole wasn't packing, I'd go back there right quick and strangle him with the fucking telephone cord, then drag him out back to rot in his shit and piss."

Bootsie continued, "Maybe a spic, ya know, I could get Carlos to do it."

"Listen, Bootsie," Eric said, putting his hand on Nate's shoulder, rubbing it softly to both calm him down as well as to show him that he was going to take care of it. "Carlos went with me to the Puerto Rican places to get all the information, so he can't be the one to go now. Anyway, you got it all wrong about Nate. It's *better* if it's Nate. See, they'd never suspect who was behind all of this if it was a colored guy talking to them." He continued, winking at Nate, "Colored people shop on the street too. And it's not as if Nate is a pimp or a drug dealer or carries heat. He even knows a few *dago* words, okay?"

There was silence for about ten seconds.

"You still there, Bootsie?" my brother asked.

"Jesus fuckin' Christ," he finally replied. "Nate, I'm tellin' ya, if ya fuck this up, *boy*, I'm gonna carve three k's inta ya cheeks that no nappy beard can hide."

Eric took his finger and traced a *k* on Nate's cheek. Nate mouthed, *I'm gonna off him after this is over*. Eric gave him a thumb's up.

Calmly, Nate asked Bootsie, "Am I supposed to bring up how much, or what do I tell 'em if they ask first? And do I mention that I'm there on behalf of Alberto Giaquinto, because no one would believe that *a colored guy* would have this kind of cash for their place." Eric enjoyed that Nate was indicating two could play.

"Smart thinkin.' Maybe ya not so dumb afta all, ha ha. Lookit, ya gotta give 'em a number, so check out the graph paper where everything's written down, but don't bring the paper in witchya. Memorize it before ya go in, got it? So listen up numbskull: whatever's on the paper? Lower it by a coupla grand. Two thousand smackers. Got it?"

"So's if it says to give'm thirty Gs, I tell the owner he's gonna get twenty-eight?" Nate asked.

"Whoa, an arithmetic genius," Bootsie said.

"Then there'd be two grand missing," my brother said.

"Let's just say it gets found," Bootsie said. "And keep this between us, knuckleheads. If ya do, ya gonna get more than a lump a coal in ya stocking at Christmas. *Capisce?*"

"Got it," Nate said.

"So's we're clear."

"We're clear, Bootsie."

"All right. And no sayin' the money's from Alberto. 'Cause if ya, do, it'll get 'round to everyone, and then they'll know it's just one guy and that's kinda suspicious. So's all ya gotta say if they ask is something like 'It's confidential.' That'll sound official. And if someone mentions Alberto, play dumb; that shouldn't be hard, heh, heh."

Nate jabbed the middle fingers of both hands towards the wall—something I noticed from the other side of Spins, which signaled something interesting on the tapes I was going to listen to after closing time.

I called Francesca and Leo and asked them to meet me at Coogan's around seven. That would give me enough time to go home and listen to the tapes on the small recorder Leo had given to me. When I walked into Coogan's I was greeted by a chorus of "Hey Joogan," from a lot of my buddies, who gathered around and pummeled me with questions as to why I hadn't spent much time at the bar of late. I knew if I made up some bullshit excuse it'd be seen as hollow, insulting even, so I told them the truth. Pointing to Francesca, who was sitting with her brother at a café table near the back, I said, "Francesca Casterella, boys," which elicited pats on the back and howls like wolves. I stayed with the guys for a bit, drinking a beer and holding up a few fingers to signal to Francesca that I'd be there in about two minutes. She nodded.

When I took my seat, I told them what I'd heard on the tape.

"Holy shit," Leo said, "I can't fucking believe that Bootsie would skim off the top. What an idiot. Imagine if he gets caught. They'll kill him," Leo said.

"No shit, and it won't be as simple as a shot in the back of the head. Torture time," I said, knowing enough about what went on in 2-Cig's world to imagine the horrific death that was going to befall Bootsie, because no matter what he'd do to hide his theft, it wouldn't work. Eventually, 2-Cig would find out.

"Crunch time for us, boys," Francesca said, bringing me out of my gruesome daydream of a dead Bootsie. "This is the point of no return for us. There's no going back."

"I'm in," Leo said. "You can count on me. It's not just about buildings and money. It's people and communities. A way of life. I don't think I'd be able to live with myself if I walked away because it was going to be personally difficult for me. Certain wars are worth fighting. Yeah. I'll drink to that if I say so myself." With that, he finished his beer in one slug.

"YOU WERE ABOUT TO GO up against your father and brother," Dr. S. said. "I assume you knew it could get ugly. For you. For them. You had to think it could end up a permanent break."

"Given what I'd been through, it was a trade I was willing to make. I wasn't concerned about a confrontation with my father or brother. I was worried for my mother. I didn't want her to go down one more circle of hell."

"Did you tell her what you were going to do?"

"Here's what I had to wrestle with: If I told her, it would expose her to my father, who could make it—shall I say—very uncomfortable for her."

"Would he threaten her to get information?"

"Threaten, yeah. But beyond that? I'm not sure. But if I didn't tell her *something*, she'd have no warning and wouldn't be prepared for an explosion," I said.

"So, how did you resolve this conundrum?" Dr. S. asked.

"I told her a storm was brewing, and she should take a lot of her clothes to my grandmother's place just in case. She wavered and wondered if I was overreacting. She only relented after Francesca got on the line and told her if she were in my mother's position, she'd hightail it out of there. I got back on the phone and asked my mother to have someone drive her and her stuff by car to Pelham Bay."

"She took your advice?"

"It was made easier by the money."

"What money?" Dr. S. asked.

"The money I'd stolen from the duffel bag out beyond the backyard that night as a kid. The dough I stashed in Alanphant. I put a twenty, sometimes two, and occasionally a hundred in an envelope in the mailbox. No note, no stamp. Since I didn't see an uptick in her spending—no new appliances, or splurging on clothes or furniture—I knew she was saving it. I had no idea when or how she'd use it. Except for the three years I was in the army, she got that money every couple of weeks. My guess? At least ten grand. Plus any interest she got from the savings and loan.

"So I wasn't only a thief, I was a bagman."

"And, importantly, an enabler," Dr. S. said.

"A liar, a thief, a secret bagman, a facilitator of his parents' breakup, and an illegal wire tapper. Quite a rap sheet."

"Things you were proud of?"

"It all worked out, didn't it?"

"I wouldn't be so flip," Dr. S. said. "This is ends-justifying-the-means reasoning. I agree the outcomes were favorable. That attenuates the sense of wrongdoing. But let's face it, these aren't five things generally thought of as virtuous. Not sure this is something you would tell others to do. That's really the key test, don't you think?"

"It's easy to say I'd never do these things again. Lying? It depends on the circumstances is all I can say. Okay, I'll give you stealing. Isn't a bagman a tough-guy term for a secret Santa? That's kind of how I think of it. With regard to the facilitator, you're right; it was meddling. That's a tough call. It was my mother, after all. Let me think more about this; I get what you're saying." I neglected to comment on the wiretapping.

Dr. S. paused, then asked, "Did she ever say anything to you about the money?"

"No. But when the envelopes didn't come for the three years I was in the army and then started up again the week I was discharged, I assumed she put it all together. Anyway, she moved out. She took everything, lock, stock, and barrel. Clothes, pots and pans, pictures, knickknacks, you name it. It was time to 'get out of Dodge,' as they say."

"How did your father react?"

"If you can believe it, he actually called me. First time in how long I can't remember. Gavi came out of the office in the back of Spins and told me Ike was on the phone. It was a few days after my mother took off to stay at her mother's place. Ike assumed I knew. I didn't lie. He asked me to come for dinner at the house. Maybe he was baiting me and thought I wouldn't agree. He had calzones, pies, salad, and beer from Pirozzi's. He was relaxed. Eric was friendly. We talked about the Giants—nothing concerning the stadium, mind you. Scores, players, games. Guy talk. How was I doing at Spins? Eric heard I had a girlfriend who was a real hipster. What my apartment looked like; those kinds of things. I reciprocated. Did Eric like being a chauffeur? Was he still entertaining the girls at Connor Quinn's bar? Did my old man have any funny busts he could tell us about? The usual to keep the conversation going. As I left, Ike said we should do it again. I said sure. You want to know the strange thing? Not one mention of my mother. It was as if she didn't exist. The closest he came was to ask how Gavi was as a boss. I didn't know if this was his way of probing if I knew that Gavi was one of the people who helped my mother move her stuff to grandma's home. I stuck to anecdotes about how he ran the record store. And I for sure didn't mention that Rabbi Leviev was the other guy who assisted my mother with the move."

"It actually sounds nice."

"Yeah, well, the whole time I was there, I was thinking there had to be an ulterior motive."

"Like what? she asked.

"Like they were keeping me there long enough to have someone jimmy the lock in my apartment door and ransack the place. Or maybe they would've had someone lying in wait, you know, to beat the crap out of me. It was too soon for them to know anything about the fact that we'd bugged them at the Aronheimer mansion or that we were plotting to foil Robert Moses's plan to destroy Tremont. But I have to tell you that I was leery."

"Rest assured that paranoia can invade your territory like a foreign army cruising across at the border. And try as you might, you never have enough power to prevent it from taking over," she said.

Bullseye.

"When I got back to my apartment, I checked everything. No signs of anything being disturbed. Nothing. I still wasn't satisfied. I had Leo come over to check the phone for a bug. Oh, and he brought a brand new gadget that could detect hidden bugs *anywhere*, like in a wall. When he was finished, it was funny, he gave a pretty good imitation of the fifteen-second CONELRAD signal: you know, the one that's supposed to tell us that the Russians are coming."

"Did you ever go back?"

"To my father's place? You mean for dinner? No. He never called again. And Eric never brought it up when he saw me at Spins," I said.

"Maybe it was genuine. His way of reaching out to you, trying to reconnect. It's possible" Dr. Silverman said.

"That's the conclusion I came to then. How fucking naïve."

16

WE'LL NOODLE IT OUT

It'd been more than five years since Leo had been to Fordham—one of the jewels of The Bronx, which had other gems nearby, such as the University Heights campus of NYU, New York Botanical Garden, the Bronx Zoo, Montefiore Hospital, Van Cortlandt Park, Crotona Park, Claremont Park, Tremont Park, and Yankee Stadium. He'd first visited Fordham as a kid on a bike. It was one of the destinations that he and his pals would explore as they'd pedal around the borough. They'd swim illegally at night at the Jerome Park Reservoir, watch the girls sunbathe at Orchard Beach, and go over the bridge to get to City Island. They'd stand on the rocks and cast lines, earnestly striving to haul in a catch, which they never seemed to do, not that it deterred them from trying again and again. Invariably, they'd end up digging for clams to take back to their homes, where, in Leo's case, *Nonna Ebrea* would make the best baked clams oreganata. One of Leo's favorite things was to pedal over to the tidal pools—more than two hundred acres of marsh and salt water and one of the few areas where kids from all backgrounds could hunt for tadpoles, skim stones, make reed horns, or just pretend to be Huck Finn for a few hours. With sneakers tied around their necks by the shoelaces and their pants rolled up to their knees, Casterellas interacted with Goldbergs, O'Tools, Espinozas, Novaks, Kozlowskis, and Robinsons without parents, without rules, without fears.

In the late 1940s, The Bronx was divvied up into fiefdoms based on religion, regardless of economic class. The Jews held ground along the Grand Concourse, the north-south route that bisected several enclaves of Irish, Italian, and eastern-European Catholics and snaked around a shrinking German Lutheran territory near Van Cortlandt Park, an area that had been strictly off limits to Jews just a generation before. Though, rumor had it that the father of one of Rabbi Leviev's other bar mitzvah boys would sneak into the Edelweis bakery on the way home from Alexander's department store, making sure to ask Herr Haller to put his Lebkuchen or Berliner in a brown paper bag. Heaven forbid he should be spotted on the street advertising that he'd patronized a shopkeeper in a community that many still thought had unrequited love for a certain unmentionable Reich.

Leo approached Fordham with reverence, gazing at the beautiful Gothic-inspired stone buildings, acres of green, and hundreds of guys milling around, which brought back enjoyable memories of the time when he was a BMOC. The office of *The Ram* was tucked away in the same area of Keating Hall where he'd spent many hours putting the paper to bed. He made his way to the Managing Editor, telling the young man that he'd had that position when he was a student. After a little chit-chat, Leo got down to business.

"Kieran, I want to tell you a story. But it's not like one you heard as a kid at bedtime with a happy ending. In fact, this one has no ending. It's got a beginning; that I'm going to tell you. And there's a middle which we're still in."

Leo took Kieran Quigley through most of what was going on with an exaggeration here and there to get the kid's juices going. As we'd agreed, he left out the most confidential parts such as our illegal wire-tapping but hinted that 'there were people in the know' who'd be mighty embarrassed if their private conversations ever leaked out. A good salesman always has a close in mind, so Leo told Kieran that if he wasn't interested—no offense taken—he'd take a ride over to the University Heights campus of NYU and pitch it to them. That sealed the deal. So much so that Kieran said he'd head up the investigation as the lead reporter, something he could add to his resumé to bolster his chances of landing a job after graduation with *The New York Times* or the *Herald Tribune*.

Everything was now set in motion. Francesca invited me to dinner, and it was that evening that we told the Casterellas what was likely going to happen to their community unless we got their neighbors involved and forced the powers that be to change their plans. Mr. Casterella wanted to know how we came to know all of this. Leo had prepared for his father's question.

"Dad, when I was little and you told me things that caused me to say 'why?' or to ask questions that you clearly didn't want to answer, you'd put me off with a 'That's something for when you're older,' and if you remember, I didn't fight back. Not that you ever *did* tell me." Leo paused and then went on, barely able to suppress a smile and stifle a laugh. He reached into his pocket, pulled out and held up two folded-over stapled sheets, and continued rather dramatically: "So, Dad, here's the list of questions I asked at bedtime that you never answered." Sophia, Francesca's mother, was in a state of shock. Francesca, her younger brother Enzo, and little sister Kara erupted in wild laughter. When everyone calmed down, Leo continued. "There are only sixty-two of them, Dad. After you give me answers to all of these, I'm happy to give you answers to any of your questions." Mr. Casterella nodded his head up and down and side to side, pursed his lips, and then said, "That's fair. *Mangiamo.*"

Everyone clapped, even Sophia. *Nonna Ebrea* asked to see the sheets of paper. Leo handed them to her. She spent a minute or so, scanning both pages intently. When she finished, she said to Leo, "These are good questions, sweetheart. You're a good boy, Leo, and a terrific grandson. On Judgment Day, you'll get your answers. God will shine his light on you."

Of course, the pages were blank.

Leo, Francesca, and I spent the next few days memorizing a few speech points so we'd be consistent and not go off script with any of the store owners or apartment renters we'd meet. The plan was to engage as many people as possible with two pieces of news: that the City's plan for the new expressway would tear up 176th Street and dislodge every store and apartment house; and that if someone came around and offered cash to buy their store or get them out of a lease, it would be a low offer, even if it seemed generous. The messages were clear: If we could stand together and make a lot of noise, the politicians would have to take notice and reject the 176th Street route. And if by some chance our voices weren't loud enough to have them change the route, at least the City would be shamed into giving everyone a fair price to move, which might be twice as much or more than private interests would offer.

We practiced our pitches with Mr. and Mrs. Casterella. After they thought we were smooth in our delivery and could answer questions that might come out of the blue, Francesca's father offered to have some of his closest friends over to gauge their reactions. The next night, we greeted Rocco Scattennato, the tailor and his wife, Stella, as well as Paulo Pirozzi, the restauranteur and his wife Vittoria. Mr. Pirozzi asked, "May I speak in my native tongue? It's much easier for me to express my feelings."

Mr. Casterella said, "By all means, Paulo."

Looking squarely at me, Mr. Pirozzi said in English, "I apologize. They'll translate for you, I'm sure."

I pointed both hands at my chest and in Italian said, "*Mi chiamo deVenezia*," with a broad smile.

I assumed the incredulous look on Mr. Pirozzi's face reflected the shock that Francesca's Jewish boyfriend was Italian.

The rest of the discussion was conducted in Italian.

"deVenezia," he said. "Are you related to the big cop?"

"If you're referring to Ike, yes. He's my father."

"And you have a brother, also a policeman?" he asked.

I remembered what my mother told me about a uniform in Eric's room. I decided to ignore the second part of the question.

"Eric. Have you met him?" I asked.

"Both of them came into my restaurant recently. In uniform. They were looking for information," Mr. Pirozzi said. "For the census."

"The census? That's once every ten years," Francesca said. "The next one's not until 1960. What kind of information?"

"Did we own the store, the apartments above, how many people lived there, what kind of rent they paid, you know. It was for the City. To make sure we all get counted and get our due here in The Bronx, so they don't screw us. They went to everyone on the street. You met them, no?" he asked of Mr. Casterella.

At this point, Enzo piped up from the hall where he'd been lingering, unsure if he was invited to the meeting but interested in hearing what was going on.

"Dad, they came in a few days ago and asked the same kinds of questions that they asked Mr. Pirozzi. You were in the back. I answered them. I didn't want to bother you."

"That's okay, son," Mr. Casterella said.

I couldn't hold back any longer. "Mr. Pirozzi, my brother isn't a cop," I said.

"I knew it!" Rocco Scattennato exclaimed, turning to his wife. "The kid's uniform didn't look right."

"And he and my father weren't collecting information for the census," I added.

At that point, Francesca took charge and explained that *this* deVenezia—pointing to me—wasn't associated in any way with his father and brother.

"Ike and Eric deVenezia are working, how do you say . . . 'off the books,' for the *private interests* that want to buy up all the properties on 176th Street. We," she continued, pointing to Leo and me, "have a plan to foil them. We'd like to share it with you and, if you like it, join us in preventing this community tragedy."

The four of them—the Pirozzis and Scattennatos—inched forward in their chairs, a signal for Francesca to continue. "We want to speak to everyone on the street, every person that Ike and Eric visited. Everyone's got to know what's going on. All of you on this street are going to be scammed. And we won't let them do it to us."

When she finished telling them what was going on, there was silence. Mrs. Casterella filled it by offering the guests more espresso and gelato to go with the cannolis that the Pirozzis brought. Francesca and I gave each other the failure look—easily interpreted by close friends, siblings, and lovers. We weren't sure if the Pirozzis and Scattennatos understood the implications of what we were telling them. I'd been confident that when we told them what was going to happen, they'd be on board. If they weren't interested in joining with us, we were prepared to go back to the drawing board to reorient our pitch. I'd mentioned to Leo and Francesca that if we couldn't make headway, it was our fault for not presenting it in a compelling manner.

"THE ARROGANCE OF YOUTH," Dr. Silverman would remark to me later. It was an observation but not said in a dismissive manner.

"It was," I said to her, "but without it, I'm not sure we would've proceeded."

"SO," FRANCESCA CONTINUED in the conversation with the Pirozzis and Scattennatos, "here's what we're thinking. If you're okay with it. We'd like each of you to speak to your neighbors and tell them you've heard rumors—what we're telling you now—and ask them, in turn, to speak to their friends and neighbors until everyone on 176th Street knows the real story of what's happening."

"Then," I said, picking up the verbal baton from my girlfriend, "there'll be a call for a community meeting where everyone can raise their voices to the rooftops about how criminal it is to destroy Tremont."

"At the meeting—it'll actually be more of a rally—there's going to be newspaper coverage. There'll be a reporter, a cameraman to take pictures, and a guy with a tape recorder. Everything's going to be captured," Leo explained.

"In order to make sure everyone knows, we're going to have poster boards splashed up and down the street, tacked onto telephone poles, taped to the insides of store windows, and strung up on fire escapes, indicating that there's going to be a 'Save Tremont' meeting and where and when it's going to happen," Francesca said.

"Just think," Leo added, "how the politicians are going to react, reading about it in the paper or waking up to hear crowds on the radio shouting down the new expressway."

"Voices mean votes," I said, "and believe me, your voices will be heard by others who don't want to be in the same predicament, especially if they live in Manhattan, where mister big shot Robert Moses wants to build another expressway that would connect the Manhattan and Williamsburg

Bridges to the Holland Tunnel, destroying SoHo and Little Italy in one fell swoop."

Once again there was silence. Then, Vittoria Pirozzi and Stella Scattennato both looked to their husbands and gave them a nod of approval.

"If everyone's in, then it's okay for me," Paulo Pirozzi said, "but I have to say, Francesca, that if those 'private interests' as you called them are who I think they are, we've got to have hundreds—everyone in the community—together, otherwise, you know what could happen."

We did.

Francesca's father asked, "Okay, so if we get everyone, where are we going to have the meeting? If we do get hundreds, there's no store big enough to hold everyone."

Vittoria Scattennato said, "We could go to the Hibernians house on Crotona Park East. They've got one of those rooms that has sliding dividers. You can open it up, which they do for weddings."

"While that would normally be a great idea, Mrs. Scattennato, I'm afraid we can't use that space because, well, Crotona Park East is the alternative route for the new expressway. The Hibernians building is right in the middle of it."

"What about the movie theater next to the clothing store?" Mrs. Pirozzi said. "It's got at least 500 seats. Perfect."

"Who owns it?" Mrs. Casterella asked.

"The Jews," *Nonna Ebrea* interjected.

"All of them?" Mr. Scattennato asked incredulously.

"All eight of the Benjamins," *Nonna Ebrea* answered. "Jay," she said to me, "you and I will go to see the Benjamins." And that settled that.

The Scattennatos and the Pirozzis said their goodbyes, acknowledging that they would start calling their neighbors. Being an aspiring artist, Francesca's sister Kara was tagged with the responsibility for the design and creation of the posters. Her younger brother Enzo was drilled with the talking points and assigned to go along the street and scare the crap out of the kids by saying they wouldn't be able to play ringalevio, stickball, stoopball, or ride their bikes because the street was going to be torn down. This was Leo's clever idea, as he knew that a kid's panic would translate to his or her parents with lightning speed and would prime the pump for when the grownups would be contacted.

We had three major tasks to accomplish: Kieran Quigley of *The Fordham Ram* had to select a photographer and sound guy, give them a replay of what we told him, and swear them to secrecy; I had to go with *Nonna Ebrea* to the Benjamins to bring them in on what was happening and to secure their permission to use the RKO theater for a meeting; and Francesca had to prepare her remarks, as she was going to be the main speaker at the rally.

We left the Casterellas' home and went to Coogan's. I suggested that we needed a name for our cause because it would add authenticity, both for the news coverage and also for 2-Cig and his cronies, who wouldn't know who they were up against. "We need something with oomph, like the Uncle Sam 'I Want You' posters from World War Two," I said. We tossed around many ideas. Most had too many words and weren't impactful enough. Leo suggested Tremont Neighborhood Together, with exaggerated first letters that looked like sticks of dynamite with fuses. We got excited about this until Francesca said that it looked like *we* were the ones who wanted to blow up Tremont. After another bottle or two of Knickerbocker beer, Francesca blurted out "Don't Tread on Tremont!" She then snatched a napkin and drew a circle with the words 'Don't Tread' on the top, a coiled snake in the center and 'On Tremont' along the bottom of the circle. The alliterative ring sounded just right to Leo and me, not to mention its historical antecedent.

"I'll take this to Kara, who'll draw it up and create a stencil that can be applied to the posters," she said, waving the napkin wildly from side-to-side with a smile to match.

"And to polo shirts," Leo said. Front and back. Kids will wear it like a sandwich board."

"How do we get that done?" I asked.

"I don't have a fucking clue," Francesca said. "I'm exhausted. Let's go home," by which she meant to my apartment. "We're not going to be stymied by how to make a shirt with a message. We'll noodle it out," the Beat Generation girl said.

17

YOU'VE GOT TO ADMIRE THEIR *CHUTZPAH*.

I parked my car in front of the Casterellas' hardware store. *Nonna Ebrea* was waiting for me, wearing a housedress with an oversized collar and topped off by a brimmed hat bedecked with artificial flowers. She looked every bit the part of Ernest Borgnine's mother, Mrs. Piletti, in the film *Marty*, the lone exception that she wasn't wearing a large cross around her neck. I opened the car door for her, but she demurred, preferring to walk despite my protest that it was quite a distance to the Benjamins. It was six o'clock in the evening, but given the east-west nature of 176th Street, the light streamed in uninterrupted from Manhattan, which the residents joked was the only worthwhile thing they got from the island that everyone outside of The Bronx called New York. She'd picked this particular time of day, she said, because it reminded her of the evening strolls her family used to take in Naples, when the entire community seemed to exit their homes and strut around a square, engaging in little more than waves and formal greetings, rarely breaking stride.

Kids were out in droves: boys in shorts, mostly on bikes and scooters, many of which were on the street, there being little car traffic at this hour; girls wearing pedal pushers (the girls on City Island referred to them as clam diggers) were playing games on the sidewalk, which Mrs. Lagana stepped around with ease, usually commenting on something about the games and knowing most of the girls by name. When women my age walked by, I could see the influence of Eva Marie Saint from *On the Waterfront*, as some wore a simple pullover tucked into a long skirt, much as the occasional young man struck the Marlon Brando pose from *The Wild One*—black motorcycle jacket, dungarees belted with a big buckle, and a soft cap with leather brim, a look favored by the likes of my brother and his crowd. It all made me a bit self-conscious, what with my chinos, short sleeve shirt, and sneakers.

No one on East 176th Street could've picked out Jimmy Lyons, the Bronx Borough President, in a lineup, and I'd bet that shown a picture of Mayor Robert Wagner, many people would've identified him as either Nikita Khrushchev or Herbert Hoover. But as we passed stoops and upper floor opened windows, I heard a repetitive "*Ciao*, Daniela!" which was met by a hand or head acknowledgment from *Nonna Ebrea*. Daniela Lagana might not've been wearing a crown, but she was the queen of Tremont.

"Everyone seems to know you," I remarked.

"I've been here a long time."

"They know you from the hardware store, too, I guess."

As we strolled, some of the older people who didn't shout out saluted or tapped the fingers of their right hand to the heart or pointed to an American flag decal in their window as she came into view.

"And the camp thing," she said.

"What do you mean? I'm not familiar with that."

"During the War. In 1942."

She didn't elaborate.

"Can you tell me what you mean by that, Mrs. Lagana?"

"Daniela."

"Daniela."

"After Pearl Harbor. They rounded up the Japs in California. Put them in camps."

"Yes, I know," I said. "The government wasn't sure of their loyalty. They thought they might be fifth columnists. Have you heard that term?"

"Yes, of course. The same here."

"The same here what, Daniela?"

"Italy was with Germany. Mussolini with Hitler. Many of us were born over there. Same as with the Japs. They wanted to put us in camps."

I was astounded. "The Italians? Here in The Bronx? Into camps? Are you sure? I've never heard that."

"They wanted to. Yes. That's what we were told."

"By whom?" I wanted to know. I wondered if this was some fanciful tale she'd concocted or had been the recipient of an unseemly story.

"By the young men who wore suits and trench coats."

"These men said they wanted to put you in camps?"

"They told us that if we paid them, they'd make sure we wouldn't be rounded up. Those of us who were born in Italy. So we gave them money."

"You gave some people—"

"Men, they were Italians, too, but younger. They were born here."

"You gave money to some young Italian men in suits and trench coats—"

"I collected it. From all of us who weren't born here."

"After you collected money from a lot of people here in Tremont, you gave it to these men so you wouldn't be put into the camps like the Japanese people in California?"

"Yes," she said, looking up at me and smiling with pride. "And you see, none of us were taken away. We're proud Americans, Jay, and there was no cause for concern about us. So," she pointed to a couple on the stoop as we passed by, "they appreciate when they see me with their shouts, taps, and pointing. It's their way of saying, 'Thank you. Thank you for your part in making sure we weren't sent to camps.'"

Part of me thought she was clever as a fox, concocting this tale to find out if I was a gullible idiot. But I have to tell you, a larger part of me simply thought that this reflected a delusional personality. Especially taking into consideration the *Ebrea* thing.

There was nothing more said about the cash or the young Italian men to whom she gave it. We walked in silence for a whole block.

As we waited for a light to turn green, she turned to me and asked, "What's it like to be a Jew?" in the same tone she would've used to inquire about my job or apartment. It was quite a transition. There was no more talk of the camps.

"Do you mean how do I feel about it? Or are you asking about the religion, what we practice, what we believe in?" I responded.

"In a land of gentiles," she said.

"A little like a Protestant at the Vatican, I'd guess," I said. "They believe in Jesus, just in another way. So I imagine they're looked at a little funny. Not ha-ha funny. Unusual. People look at us the same way. Maybe because we've got some unfamiliar customs and foods and holidays that they can't comprehend. But you know what? We pray to the same God. Just differently."

"Is it hard?" she asked.

"You mean is it a burden being a Jew?"

"Yes."

"No," I said. "Pride can override feelings of isolation or discrimination. Too much pride—well, that's a problem. You know we're called a stiff-necked people. We're nothing, if not resilient. That's why we say, 'Next Year in Jerusalem' at the end of the Passover *seder*. Optimism has to be one of our defining values, as you can imagine, considering what we've gone through."

"You know they call me *Nonna Ebrea*," she said.

"I do."

We walked the next block in silence. I didn't know if she was going to give me a history of how this moniker came about or why she felt she had Jewish blood. I didn't think it was within my purview to pry.

"My daughter didn't want to have anything to do with it," she said. "The things my mother and my grandmother told me? Poof, gone, out the window. Sophia, Francesca's mother, wasn't interested. She'd stick her fingers in her ears and run away. I was always surprised she didn't become a nun. But Francesca, ah, that's a different story. When she was little, she'd come into my bathroom in the morning, sit on the mat with a toy or a doll when I was getting ready, and let me ramble on with my stories, my history, occasionally asking 'why?' or 'what do you mean?' I'd take the time. To explain. I didn't use baby language. I'd go on and on. For me, it was . . . what do you call it when you're saying something and you might be the only one that's hearing?"

"Do you mean a soliloquy?"

"Yes, that's it. I forget sometimes. Some words. I wasn't sure she fully understood then. But it turns out it wasn't in vain. She'd take books out of the library and ask me questions. So inquisitive! She read the *World Book*. And the papers. She was eager to learn. And a good student. Oh my. A's. I thought she was going to go to college and be a professor. But it wasn't to be. Money. We didn't have enough," she said wistfully. "But you know," she added quickly, "she wasn't, isn't resentful. About that. She's good at whatever she does. Gives it her all. I can imagine her at work soaking up everything, asking questions, learning, then trying to make things better."

Her granddaughter at work must've been a carbon copy of what she'd been like as a kid with *Nonna Ebrea*. Francesca had told me about the risks she took at work to create programs that made her department more efficient, which were conducted in a clever manner that avoided antagonizing her complacent boss and had resulted in a recent promotion.

"She adores you," I said.

"As I do her. She's special, that one."

What I didn't say was that there wasn't a ledge she avoided for fear of falling.

"All your grandchildren are terrific," I did say, and although that may have sounded to be excessively flattering, I meant it. After all, I came from a dysfunctional family, so seeing how siblings could maintain their individuality while being part of a cohesive group was something to treasure.

"She loves you," *Nonna Ebrea* said. "And I can see why."

I stopped, bent down, and gently kissed her cheek.

In about twenty minutes, when we reached the front door of Benjamins clothing store, one of the Mrs. Benjamins came up to *Nonna Ebrea* with open arms and said, "Mrs. Lagana, how wonderful to see you!" They engaged in some small talk before Mrs. Benjamin looked up at me and said, "Oh, how rude of me. Are you one of Mrs. Lagana's grandsons?'

"No, ma'am. Jay deVenezia, nice to meet you."

"deVenezia? Your father the policeman?"

"Yes, ma'am."

"What a special treat: Just recently, your father and brother came to visit us."

I couldn't admit I knew about their motive for visiting the Benjamins, so I made a few pleasantries and told her we had two purposes in coming to the store: the first, I informed her, was to buy a present for Leo, whose birthday was coming up. This was the *give* part of our visit. The *ask* would come later.

"He's going to be twenty-eight," Mrs. Lagana said, "and will be going to his tenth high school reunion, so we wanted him to look as spiffy as possible." Then to cement this fib with conversational glue, she added, "And Jay here has become close to Leo, through his relationship with my Francesca."

Nonna Ebrea took charge, taking the lead in picking out a shirt for her grandson. As I took some bills out of my wallet, I was pleased that Mrs. Benjamin said, "You mentioned you had two reasons for coming here today, Jay."

At that point, I asked Mrs. Benjamin if we could talk in the back with as many of the other Benjamins as were there. Within a few minutes, we were in an office that was vacated by a few people who gave us the opportunity to speak in private. After introductions (Harry, Sidney, and Mendy were joined by Rose, Ida, and Dora—Irving and Helen were absent), I gave a fairly extensive overview of what was going on and how it could affect the Benjamins, both in terms of their store, the apartments above, which housed all four families, and the RKO theater next door—all properties that the family owned.

"No mortgages. No debts. Free and clear," Harry said, rather emphatically.

It was clear that the Benjamins understood the implications of what they were hearing.

"Is there a Chinaman's chance that City Hall will override that *putz*—excuse my French—Robert Moses and put the expressway on Crotona Park East?" Mendy asked.

"Not unless we organize, Mr. Benjamin," I said. "That's really why we're here. To see if we can rally the community and upset the applecart."

"Rally, shmally," Sidney said. "It's all about money, cash on the line. You're not going to suggest that we bribe someone, are you? I don't want to take it up the *tuchas*"—this time there was no *pardonnez-moi* for his language—"for stuffing some bills into some *shmendrick's* pocket, because they always find out, and I'm not going to jail."

"No, Mr. Benjamin, no bribes. And even if we wanted to, there's no way we could ever get enough money to make that kind of a scheme work. Uh, uh."

"Anyway, if they're going to bulldoze the street, they'd have to pay us a pretty penny. Now, no one wants to move," Mendy said, then looked around to see if there was disagreement. When he got no protest, he went on, "But if they can give us our due and then some for a move and all, it'd be disruptive, sure, but maybe not too terrible. There are vacant properties and empty stores a couple of blocks north."

"We're not moving one single Goddamned inch, Mendy." That came from Ida Benjamin, Mendy's wife, given the way he bristled, but he didn't go on. "Forget about the store and the apartments," she continued acidly, "it's the movie theater. Where you going to move that to, Yemensville?"

"That's why Jay and I came here today, to talk about the RKO," Mrs. Lagana interjected in an attempt to restore some calm.

"It's the only place big enough to hold a rally," I offered.

"Where my Francesca will have a microphone to speak. Everyone from 176th Street will come."

"And the press will be there," I said, hoping they wouldn't ask from which newspaper.

"So, you're asking for permission from us to open it up for what, one night? No shows, just a rally?" Rose Benjamin asked.

"Yes. It's a start," I said.

She looked around at her family then said, "Look, we do things by unanimous vote, but I can't see Helen and Irving objecting. I'll speak to them. So for now, assume it's okay. Okay?"

"You're too kind," Mrs. Lagana said.

"I'll round them up, then get back to you," Harry said.

"All well and good," Mendy said, "but let's face it, you can't fight the big shots and win. They're going to put the expressway wherever it suits them, and if you ask me, there's plenty of dough for bribes from the *shmegegges* at the Hibernians building. They want it here on our street? It'll be here, simple, like two cents plain. So what we have to do is make sure we get a goodly piece of the pie. If they're going to kill us, at least let's pick their pockets on the way to our graves. We got rights. Eminent domain."

"Now, before we go any further," I said, "I've got to tell you that there are private interests who're going to descend on everybody up and down the street and offer you money for your properties. Soon."

"How do you know this, son?" Harry asked.

"He can't say," Mrs. Lagana said.

"But what I can tell you is that they're very clever, these guys. They're not going to come in low-ball. It'll be better than that. All cash, by the way."

"Sons of bitches. They'll clear out the suckers and then flip it all to the City after they've inflated the amounts, which they'll make sure of by handing out bribes," Sidney said.

"Sidney's an accountant," Rose said.

"You've got to admire their *chutzpah*. The folks who need every nickel, our neighbors? They'll get *bupkes*," Harry said.

"That's their plan, in a nutshell," I said. "So the rally—"

"Isn't really for the route to be changed," Dora interrupted—politely, I must add. "It's to make sure we all hold out for as long as we can and get the City riled up so they'll pay top dollar when they throw us out. Yes?"

"We're going to try to get the route changed, Mrs. Benjamin, but in the end, you may be right," I said.

"Don't tell me the people behind this *mishegas* are Jews, Jay."

"*Oi vey*," one of the Mrs. Benjamins said.

"*Gott in himmel*," another one said.

"No, not Jews." I didn't include my father and brother in the accounting, as they were merely foot soldiers. The generals were the Italians aligned with the Irish and a former Jew who, according to our customs, doesn't count anymore since he left the tribe: a *shanda*.

There was nothing more to say. We thanked the Benjamins and bid them goodbye. Out on the sidewalk I said to Daniela, "Leo's birthday isn't coming up, is it? And when it does, won't he be twenty-six, not twenty-eight? And wouldn't that mean it's only been eight years since his high school graduation, instead of ten?"

Without breaking her stride she gave me what I'd describe as a shit-eating grin.

18

THAT *BASTARDO* IS FREELANCING.

The start button having been pushed at the Aronheimer mansion, the gears began to mesh. Billy O'Boyle, the head of the Department of Buildings, dutifully created the Advisory Committee—based on recommendations from Robert Moses and the mayor—which began the inexorable march to the conclusion that 176th Street was the preferred route for the expressway.

Billy spent Saturday mornings washing and waxing his new 2-door, 2-tone Plymouth Belvedere.

Horace Stoneham was offered property for a new stadium—and a twenty-year tax abatement—next to Fort Tryon Park just north of the George Washington Bridge on a hill with a magnificent view of the Palisades. He secretly gave the rights to both tear down the Polo Grounds and build the new ballpark to Giaquinto Brothers.

2-Cig collected fifty thousand dollars from Tom Collins for the bribe to make sure the expressway didn't go through Crotona Park East, the site of the Hibernians building, knowing full well that the decision had already been made to avoid this route.

The fifty grand was delivered in small bills inside a garment bag to Robert Moses by a chauffeur driving a four-door Lincoln Cosmopolitan.

The superintendent in the building adjacent to Nicky Shark's apartment house received a package with a "Give to Nicky" note handwritten on it. Inside the box was a Mamiya-6 IV B—a just-issued, state-of-the-art camera with a silver nameplate embossed with the words 'Inquisitive Foto.' Inside one of the boxes of film was a rolled-up wad of bills totaling ten grand.

The sales manager of the Brooks Brothers Madison Avenue store was on-call to bring Egyptian cotton shirts, French silk ties, Italian leather shoes, and bespoke English suits to Carmine DeSapio's apartment in Washington Square, neither carrying an invoice nor returning with any payments. Despite being on one of the most prime pieces of real estate in midtown Manhattan, the store received a reduced property tax rate, courtesy of a special law enacted by the New York City Council, quietly buried in a bill at the request of Carmine DeSapio.

Bootsie was given the go-ahead to have Nate start making the rounds of the stores and apartment houses on 176th Street.

Ike came up with the idea that Nate should lay a hundred dollar bill on the palm of each owner, regardless of that person's level of enthusiasm for the offer to buy them out.

"Think of it, Alberto," Ike said, "a Negro giving big bucks to a white person; that's gonna spread like wildfire. I mean, who wouldn't take it?"

2-Cig was so thrilled with the idea that he had one of his best crews come to my father's house during the day to paint it, fix the porch, clean the debris out of the backyard, and landscape the property. When my father got home from work that evening, he'd thought he'd gone to the wrong house.

At this point, Ike was ready to put in his papers. He'd been on the force for more than thirty years, the last seven of which were at the 46th Precinct, sandwiched in between the Grand Concourse and Webster Avenue. He was proud of his three stripes, but being a desk sergeant had grown tiresome. His moonlighting for 2-Cig gave him the thrills that sustained him during the workday. He made the decision to quit the force and to join Giaquinto Brothers as the head of security, effective at the end of 1955. By then, the timing would be perfect: the decision to put the expressway through the heart of Tremont would be made, the plans for the Giants to move next to Fort Tryon Park would be revealed, his divorce would be final, and his pension would qualify him for more than 100 percent of his salary if he stayed through December 31. And then Bud could go on 2-Cig's payroll.

KARA CASTERELLA MADE dozens of poster boards and designed the stencil for the "Don't Tread on Tremont" polo shirts. She and *Nonna Ebrea* went to see the Benjamins to ask if they could silkscreen the designs. Dora Benjamin told them she had a cousin on West 36th Street, between 8th and 9th Avenues in the Garment Center, who could do the job. Kara recruited her brother Enzo to hop on the D train at 174th Street, get off at 59th Street-Columbus Circle in Manhattan, and transfer to the Number 1 Broadway-Seventh Avenue Local to 34th Street Penn Station. From there, they walked to a nondescript building with dozens of clothing companies listed on the directory. When they stepped off the elevator at the twelfth floor, the elegant sounding Murray's Fashion was seen to be a beehive buzzing with the activities of row upon row of sewing machines, dozens of racks filled with clothing being pushed or pulled on squeaking wheels, hundreds of bobbing spools of threads, innumerable presses and irons hissing, a handful of foremen shouting, and one receptionist trying to get the attention of these two teenagers staring into the factory, seeing how clothes are actually made for the first time. They were introduced to Murray's son Arnold, whose interest in assisting them perked up when he realized the two were siblings. Kara was what they used to call a "head turner." People said she looked like Natalie Wood—Leo said they should call her "Natalie Wouldn't"—particularly when she wore a short, tartan plaid skirt that showed her perfectly shaped legs. She was shorter than Francesca, which made her less intimidating than her older sister to young men, especially as she seemed to have no awareness of her extraordinary looks.

She told Arnold that they needed two hundred silkscreened polo shirts made in two sizes by the end of the week. He told her that she could save some money by using 100 percent cotton T-shirts and that he would drive the truck up to The Bronx personally. I'd like to say that this was the start of a budding relationship, but the truth is that Kara didn't reciprocate Arnold's interest. She simply said "thank you" and waved goodbye to a disconsolate young man after he delivered the order at the loading dock in the back of Benjamins on Wednesday afternoon.

Leo paid a visit to Kieran Quigley at Fordham, who introduced him to Brendan McCarthy, who'd handle the cameras, and Casey O'Donnell, who'd be responsible for the tape recorders. "The Irish mafia, I see," Leo said with a big smile. With that, Brendan pointed to the green and white decal of the Irish Rugby Football Union on the wall, mentioning that his father had been a scrum-half during the twenties. Not to be outdone, Casey stood up as if there was a musician playing a fiddle and did a few awkward step dance moves, which caused all of them to convulse in laughter. The boys' already pumped-up excitement went into overdrive when they were given state-of-the-art equipment, courtesy of Leo's manipulation of inventory at Westchester Electronics. The three of them were told to start by strolling down 176th Street and speaking randomly to people of all ages while taking pictures and recording sounds, a "before" tableau that would serve as an introduction if we later determined it would be beneficial to create a movie in addition to the photographic stills of what happened to this section of Tremont. Leo told them to meet him a few days later at the RKO theater, where they could get a lay of the land to be better prepared for the rally that would take place on Saturday night.

The dress rehearsals were finished. It was time to open the play.

The Pirozzis, Scattennatos, and Casterellas got the ball rolling by beginning to spread the word about the possibility of the neighborhood being torn to shreds. It would start with a simple, "Did you hear anything about . . . ?" or, "Do you know what Robert Moses and the mayor are up to when it comes to the new expressway?" These questions would invariably elicit a startled, anxiety-filled response, which the Priozzi, Scattennato, or Casterella family member knew would be relayed with lightning speed around the neighborhood. Gossip is the fuel that ignites uncertainty, which can explode into havoc. And it did. From the drug store counter to the barbershop to the hairdresser to the grocery store to the mailrooms of apartment houses, the buzz was: "How could they do this to us?" and "Why is it always folks like us who get screwed?" and "Enough is enough, we're not going to take it anymore!"

By early Wednesday evening, Kara and Enzo had recruited dozens of their friends and classmates to don the new T-shirts, which created sensations when they walked down the street and went home for dinner. By Thursday, the second wave had spread, the disquiet having turned to anger after Nate's first interactions with shop owners. While no one was displeased at having a C-note deposited into their hand, the pitch to sell their business was met by hostility based on the conviction that the hundred bucks was a bribe and that the folks behind the offers were up to no good. 2-Cig and Ike's belief that it would grease the skids towards a positive outcome for them had the opposite effect. It was a horrendous miscalculation, aided and abetted, of course, by the community gossip that was making the rounds, something that wasn't part of the calculus when 2-Cig's plan was being prepared.

After the first day out on 176th Street, Nate reported on his activities to Bootsie from Booth 18 at Spins.

"I gotta tell ya, Bootsie, I got *niente*. Zero bites. Maybe a coupla 'we'll sees' and 'could bes' but not one single person said 'yeah, that's a good idea.' But everyone was real happy about the hundred. Oh yeah."

Bootsie was silent for a bit. Nate thought that maybe the line was dead.

"You don't want me to be the one to tell Donatella that you fucked up," Bootsie said. Then he hung up.

Nate said to Eric, "The you is *me*, Bud. If he hangs this on me, I'm gonna tell Donatella about the two grand he's skimmin'. Then he won't be able to hang up on anyone else, ever."

FRANCESCA, LEO, AND I were sitting at Leo's dining room table listening to a prototype of a stereo player and record, which was being worked on at Westchester Electronics. We were exhilarated and astounded to hear one part of an orchestra coming from the left speaker while other sounds came through the right.

"By the time everyone gets to the RKO on Saturday night, they're going to be pretty hopped up. All the kids are wearing the shirts, the word is out that someone's trying to buy them out at a cheap price, no one wants to move, and a lot of people think that the honchos downtown know that when they squash a little guy, there's no political price to pay," I said. "That's why your speech has to be a humdinger. You've got to grab them by the you-know-whats at the beginning, squeeze harder in the middle, and only release them at the end when the pain's so bad they can hardly stand it. Short and sweet. The last thing you want is to drone on and sap the energy out of the room."

"I'm so Goddamned nervous," Francesca said. "I've never spoken in front of a crowd. What if I stammer or get so tongue-tied it all comes out as gibberish?"

"Did you say Yiddish?" I asked with a straight face.

"Very funny. Why don't you give it?"

"Movements need symbols, Francesca," her brother said. "And a shot of you—a young woman—standing in front of five hundred people with placards and fists raised is news. Man bites dog. That's what we need, a front-page story."

What I didn't add was that she was so telegenic.

"Will you at least introduce me?" she asked. "And also write me a speech?"

"Let's get started," I said.

THAT VERY NIGHT, Mr. Pappalardo knocked on the door of my father's house and asked to come in. He was thrilled to see how spiffy the house looked after all the work had been done on the outside. As a renter, Ike had no obligation to undertake the recent work and Mr. Pappalardo began the conversation by expressing his great appreciation. My father did not disabuse him of the fact that he'd done none of it himself.

Over a cup of coffee and a doughnut, Mr. Pappalardo told Ike that he wanted to report something strange and unsettling. "I could go to the stationhouse, but what would I tell them? What happened wasn't a crime, but it sure felt like there might be something illegal going on. So I'm coming to you, Ike, off-the-record as the big shots say. To get your view as a professional." Ike encouraged him to continue and told him that until he said otherwise, Ike would keep the conversation confidential. This had the immediate effect of calming Mr. Pappalardo down.

"It happened this morning, Ike. I was in the beauty parlor, as usual, bright and early, and around 8:00 a.m., a young colored man comes in, nice-looking, energetic and pleasant. He tells me he's there on behalf of someone else. He wouldn't give me the name. I thought it was strange that someone wouldn't come himself, that he'd send another guy instead. My first instinct was that he's either drunk or going to rob me. I used to have a pistol in the shop before the War during the Depression, but now, I don't see the need. Anyway, he hands me a hundred smackers. Can you believe it? Here I thought maybe this guy was going to hold me up, and what does he do? Gives me a hundred-dollar bill! I couldn't believe it. I asked him to come sit on this little loveseat I have so that when the lady comes out from under the hair dryer, one of my girls can give her a manicure, nice and comfy."

"Mr. Pappalardo, I don't understand how this is possibly a crime," my father said.

"Okay, I'll get straight to the point. This kid says someone was interested in buying my store. It's not even for sale. It's how I make a living. I mean, if I sold it, what would I do? I was about to tell him that the store isn't for sale when he says this someone will pay me twenty-eight thousand dollars for the store. In cash. I put ten, sometimes fifteen dollars a week into an account at the savings and loan, and it's up to almost six grand since the end of the War. Pretty good, huh? But not twenty-eight thousand. Oh my God."

"You've done well, Mr. Pappalardo. I want to make sure I understand. You said he offered you twenty-eight thousand dollars in cash for the store?"

"Twenty-eight smackers. I could probably retire on that, but I'm too young. What am I going to do? Play checkers in Tremont Park with the gangsters? Ha, ha, not for me. Anyway, this young man wouldn't give me his name, and as I said, he wouldn't tell me who he was fronting for, so I thanked him, handed him back the hundred—which he wouldn't take—and told him I'd think about it. Sounds pretty fishy to me. Doesn't it to you?"

"It certainly does," said Ike, "and I'm going to look into it first thing in the morning. I'll check the records to see if this is something anyone else has reported and call a couple other stationhouses to see if they know if someone's working a scam. You've done the right thing, Mr. Pappalardo. I appreciate you coming here to tell me, and I'll get back to you if I find anything else."

Within a minute of the door closing, Ike called Donatella, and told her there was an issue and that he'd come right over to the social club on Arthur Avenue. He called Eric and told him to bring all his graph papers and notes on everyone on 176th Street and then to hustle up and meet with him and Donatella. As soon as Eric walked in, Ike said, "Bud, what was the price for single-door and one-window stores?"

"Thirty grand."

"Is that what's here for Pappalardo's beauty parlor?" They spread all of Eric's papers on a table top. They found the entry and confirmed that it indicated the amount offered would be thirty thousand.

"Bud," Ike said, "Pappalardo came to see me and said a colored guy—it had to be Nate—offered him twenty-eight grand for his store."

"Yeah, that's right."

"How could that be right? It's supposed to be thirty for a small store."

"Yeah, but Bootsie told us to subtract two Gs from the number to the store owners."

"What?" Donatella exclaimed so loudly that the guys playing cards in the back all reached into their pockets at the same time and didn't stop staring at Donatella until she waved them off.

"He told you to take out two grand?"

"Yeah. And to keep our mouths shut," Eric said nervously.

"That *bastardo* is freelancing. Jesus Christ. We give that prick thirty Gs to give to a shop owner, and Bootsie tells the guy he's gonna get twenty-eight. Skims two grand right under our noses." Donatella addressed my old man. "Are you sure Pappalardo said twenty-eight? I'm not doubting you, Ike, he could've been nervous, you know, telling this to a cop and all."

"He said twenty-eight a number of times."

"Alberto's gonna shit a brick. We've heard stuff about Bootsie. A little piece here and a tidbit there, nothing big, maybe someone he leaned on said something out of anger, who the fuck knows. But this?"

"Donatella, I've got an idea," Ike said. "I'll call Pappalardo tomorrow and tell him to ask around and find out what others have been offered to make sure this wasn't a one-off kind of thing. You're better off going to Alberto with this if Bootsie's done it with a couple of folks."

"Please, call him first thing."

The next day, my father told Mr. Pappalardo that there were rumors of such a scam and asked him to talk to other store owners to find out if this same young man had visited with them, and if so, what kind of an offer he made. That night, Mr. Pappalardo called Ike and told him that his neighbors had all been offered twenty-eight grand for their stores. What's more, Mr. Pappalardo said everyone on the street was really angry about the news that the City was going to condemn the buildings on the street and put the new expressway there. No one wanted to sell now, that's for sure.

"We got three fucking problems, Ike," Donatella said when my father called with this news. "Bootsie's one. And how in Jesus's name did it get out that the expressway is gonna be built on that street? Okay three, we've gotta own all the buildings on 176th Street in order to cover the low bid on the construction of the road. Shit."

There was a pause and then Donatella continued, "One thing at a time. We'll take care of first things first."

19

JUST LIKE THE CASH
I COLLECTED IN 1942

"Let's get together on Saturday morning at the RKO to get you acclimated and to go over things," I said to Francesca.

"Make it early afternoon, I'm busy in the morning," she said.

"Okay, I'll start with Leo and the kids from Fordham."

I met Kieran Quigley at the back of the theater where he introduced me to his two classmates, who were so excited they could barely contain themselves. Leo showed up a few minutes later with coffee and bagels for everyone.

"It's going good," Kieran said. "We've been interviewing people up and down the street, going into stores, lobbies of apartment houses, sticking our necks into parked cars and trucks stopped at lights, filming the kids in their T-shirts ringing the bells on their bikes when they pass another kid wearing the same shirt. And you should hear what they're saying."

"Oh my God," Casey O'Donnell, the kid with the tape recorder interjected. "It's like they've got speeches prepared, and as soon as the camera light goes on and they see the tape moving reel to reel, they start blasting away at Mayor Wagner and Robert Moses. I mean, they're so pissed off. The older folks can't contain themselves. They start in English, but the angrier they get, their voices become shrill and they switch into Italian. They don't care if we don't understand. And you can't stop them. No way. Even when you start to walk away, they follow us, gesticulating wildly. It makes for great film."

"At first," the camera man, Brendan McCarthy, said, "we thought they were hostile to us. But it's not like that. It's as if no one's ever listened to them or even asked their opinion before."

Leo found the panel of switches and turned on the lights that illuminated the stage and the aisles. He found a podium and a microphone in a storeroom and set them up on the stage. Brendan McCarthy set his camera up on a tripod that peeked through a large opening in the back that customarily housed the projector, where he'd have an unobstructed view of the stage. Casey O'Donnell placed the tape recorder near one of the speakers on the side of the stage. That way, it could capture whatever was said from the podium as well as from the audience, where microphones were set up, one in each aisle, halfway up the rows of seats. One of the mister Benjamins walked in and introduced himself, telling all of us we could call him Sidney, but please, not Sid. "It sounds too much like *yid*," he said rather dramatically, and we all laughed. I knew it was Sidney's way of saying *I'm a Jew, so no anti-Jew jokes or comments.*

The Benjamins' maintenance crew showed up to sweep the carpets and pick up any junk underneath the seats. Francesca appeared a little after 1:00 p.m. with Kara and Enzo, who immediately began to tack up posters on the walls—"Don't Tread on Tremont" was accompanied by newer ones made up by the kids. They weren't as professional-looking, but their homemade touches made it all so personal and caused a buzz before the meeting started, as scores of parents and friends made the circle around the theater to gawk and comment on the art. You could tell when a family discovered a poster made by one of their kids—suddenly a squeal of delight would echo through the theater, giving a bit of a festive feeling to what was otherwise going to be a cantankerous affair. By seven fifteen, the place was half filled. Each of the thirty rows held twenty seats, ten on both sides of the center aisle. The lights were on, so when someone came in or recognized a friend, there were greetings in English and Italian mixed with some hale and hearty exclamations from the few Irish that also lived in the neighborhood. The meeting was called for seven thirty but since people were still streaming in, we decided to wait until everyone had been seated. At seven forty, it was packed, and kids sat in the aisles. There were about seven hundred people in attendance. I nodded to Leo. He turned down the lights, the universal signal to be quiet.

I strode to the podium. There were a few claps, which generated some laughter.

"Good evening," I started out, paused and said, "*Buona serata*," which drew hoots and whistles. "My name is Jay deVenezia, although some of you may know me as Joogan." I heard a "Yo, Joogan!" which was followed by more laughter. "Because some of you aren't Italian—oh, wow, I see two guys from high school," I gave a salute that looked more like a tip of the cap, "Bob and Paul, hey, it's been a while—I'm going to speak English tonight. I grew up a few blocks from here. I've had the privilege of meeting more than a few of you and have shopped in many of your stores." More scattered applause. "Most of you both live and work here. You may reside in a house or in an apartment, but Tremont is your home." Sustained applause, with some folks rising to their feet. "They say 'home is where the heart is,' and the heart of The Bronx beats strongest in Tremont." The applause, whistles, and foot stomping were picked up and amplified by the microphones that we'd neglected to turn off. There was as much noise as a crowd made at the Polo Grounds. "So I don't have to tell you that there's a group of politicians who must be heartless themselves, to want to rip the heart out of this community. You have to ask yourselves, '*Why would they want to do this? What's their motivation? What's in it for them?*' Simple questions, yes? I think so. And I believe there are simple answers." I scanned the faces in the crowd to see that they were paying close attention. I said the following slowly, for maximum impact. "They want to do this *because they can. Because they've done it in the past. Because they can get away with it. You* don't contribute hundreds of thousands of dollars to their campaigns. *You've* only got enough money to buy groceries, to pay rent, to go to the dentist, to buy a new shirt, to have a slice." I could see smiles but no laughter. "*You* don't hobnob with them at their friends' golf clubs or on their yachts. *You* take the bus to Orchard Beach. *You* don't sit next to them at the opera or the symphony. *You* listen to records.

"You. Let. Them. *Tread.* On. You!"

Standing ovation. I motioned for them to sit, acknowledging their appreciation with a smile. "Their motivation? To get a notch in their belts so they can say at the next election, 'See what I did for New York!' *New York.* Not The Bronx. Not Tremont. Not 176th Street. New York." A lot of boos and hisses. "What's in it for them? Well, you know what they say: Follow the money trail. By the way, it's not a path in Van Cortlandt Park." That got a big laugh. "And you can't find it on a subway or bus map either. The truth is, you can never find it because it's in the form of bloated contracts, kickbacks, campaign contributions, no-show jobs, sweetheart deals, jacked-up invoices, and secret slush funds." I could see a lot of heads turning and whispering to others nearby. "You know what Harry Truman used to say—"

Before I could say it, someone shouted out "The buck stops here!" Lots of applause.

"You've got that right. It's time to stop this merry-go-round. And the person who's going to tell you how to do that is one of your own—Francesca Casterella. Francesca?" Thundering applause, partially for me, I assumed, but mostly for this well-known daughter of 176th Street, whose confidence seemed to increase with each step toward the podium. I retreated from the microphone and touched her shoulder gently, guiding her to where I'd stood. All this had been decided in advance, recognizing that a kiss was inappropriate and a handshake too stiff and formal. I winked at her as I took my leave.

"Thank you, Jay," she said, looking over at me in the wings, then turned to the audience and added, "Let's show our appreciation to this adoptee of 176th Street."

I got a nice round, walked a few feet out of the shadows and applauded in her direction before stepping back. She looked down at the pages of her speech. I wasn't sure if she was going to read it or keep it close like a kind of security blanket.

"We're here tonight to stand . . . or should I say sit . . ." that got a laugh, "as a community, together, many hundreds strong." She nodded for a few seconds to let that sink in. "To lift voices that are rarely heard by the men who call the shots in this city. We may not have the money, as Jay said, but we have a lot to say about what's right and wrong, and I'm here to tell you that what they're going to do is wrong, wrong, *wrong*."

She was off script, and these extemporaneous remarks showed her passion, which I could tell was going to be contagious, as the people were echoing her by chanting, "Wrong, wrong, wrong."

"I understand the need for a road connecting the George Washington Bridge to the east, allowing access to New England. You and I aren't against progress. But is progress defined as running a highway through the middle of our community?"

Shouts of "No!" and "Stop them!" were heard from all sections of the audience.

"A community isn't just defined by the boundaries on a map. It's made up of people living and working together, walking the street, visiting neighbors, shopping. I say to Robert Moses and Mayor Wagner: You want to build an expressway through The Bronx? I've got two options for you: You smart guys who created the tunnels that lead from Manhattan to Jersey, Brooklyn, and Queens, build a tunnel *under* Tremont. Get your sandhogs digging and come up for air near Long Island Sound and *leave us be*!"

That got a standing ovation and chants of "Leave us be! Leave us be!"

"Oh, but I can hear the politicians now: 'That'll cost too much money and take too long.' Cost too much money? Well why don't you roll back some of the tax giveaways to big businesses? You'll find a lot of money when you retrieve those gifts to your friends. Take too long? The Bridge has been there since 1931, and New England has been there since 1620, if I remember my history correctly."

She was completely adlibbing at this point, much to the audience's and my delight.

"So what's another couple of years in the great scheme of things, huh? Okay, you don't want to do that because it's too *complicated*. Well, fellas, I've got a simple solution for you: Horace Greeley said 'Go west'; I say go *south*. Two blocks south. Build your road along the edge of Crotona Park. You all know what's there: oh, about a dozen homes and the Hibernians building. Now, I've got nothing against those folks, *but no one lives there*! It's empty most of the time. And you know what? There are plenty of big, vacant houses in The Bronx where they can move to. Yes, but then I'm being a hypocrite, they'll say. What about those dozen homes that will have to come down. Here's how I answer that. First, it's a *dozen* frickin homes! Not *hundreds* of homes and stores. And there's something else."

At that moment, from the other side of the stage, *Nonna Ebrea*—Daniela Lagana—walked out, holding what appeared to be a bucket of some sort. I had no idea what was going on. The audience applauded. Many shouts of "*Ciao*, Daniela!" were heard. *Nonna Ebrea* approached her granddaughter with a glittering smile. Each held one side of the bucket and faced the audience. Francesca said, "Twelve houses would have to be torn down on the route two blocks south. I'm sorry for those people. Truly. But these are not just some words. I'm ready to help them out." With that, Leo, Kara, and Enzo came on stage and stood behind Francesca and *Nonna Ebrea*. "The people in those twelve houses need to be fairly compensated. I'm going to start helping them out." She stuck her hand inside her pocket, pulled out her purse, held it up so everyone could see, then reached in and took all the bills out and deposited them in the bucket. Immediately after that, in succession, her grandmother and siblings did the same. The audience erupted.

"Who wants to help those twelve homeowners? Who wants to show how unselfish we are? Who wants to pitch in as a community to show Robert Moses and Robert Wagner the right thing to do?"

Francesca's younger brother took the bucket, walked down the steps to the audience and handed it to the first person who had outstretched arms.

"We may not be able to come up with all the money that should go to these people as fair compensation," Francesca continued, "but it'll be a big help in case the City doesn't give them enough, that's for sure."

I was impressed. Francesca had planned this stunt in exquisite detail, and it was working to perfection. People were dropping bills and coins into the bucket that was being snaked around each row and then on to the one in back of it. "I'm going to take all of your generous offerings and deposit them in the bank."

Sustained applause. When it died down, Francesca lowered her voice to make sure that everyone was close to straining to hear her. "You all know that someone's been coming around to ask us if we want to sell our shops, houses, and apartment buildings. He's even giving every one of us a hundred dollars. That's right, a hundred bucks that's ours to keep regardless if we sell out to whoever it is that he represents. You know what I say to that hundred smackers? Here's what I say." She pulled the hundred-dollar bill that her family had received out of a slit pocket in her skirt and said, "Here's the one *we* got!" She leaned down and gave it to a young woman in the first row. "Go find the bucket and put this in it too."

There was so much noise, I thought the roof was going to cave in. I could see others getting out of their seats to drop their hundred-dollar bills into the bucket.

"Now, the young man who's handing out those hundred-dollar bills isn't a rich guy himself. He's a hired hand. He's fronting for some wealthy guys who want you to sell out to them at what you may think is a decent price, but believe me, once these guys own your property, they'll get top dollar from the City, which has to buy them out in order to have the right to build the new expressway. That's right. The City will pay maybe double what you'd get from these guys now. I know for some of you it may be tempting. Twenty-eight thousand or more may be more than you've ever dreamed of. But if you take it now, you'll be hastening the death of Tremont, I'm sad to say. Don't give in! Stand together." With that, most everyone stood up and chanted, "Don't give in! Don't give in!"

When the commotion died down, Francesca said, "Friends, tonight is just the start. Thank you for being so generous. And thanks to the kids for wearing those T-shirts." Lots of applause to the kids, most of whom were still wearing them. "And special thanks to the reporter, cameraman, and sound engineer who've spent days with you this week and will interview many of you afterwards. Your stories will be heard throughout The Bronx and the whole City. But we need more than your money. We need you to show up at our councilman's office, the office of the borough president, our assemblyman's office, our state senator's office, the open hearings of the Department of Buildings . . . any place where we can register our concern. If you see someone on the street with a microphone, make sure you tell him what's on your mind. Be polite but persistent. Show them what the little people of The Bronx are really like. If there's a camera, look into it and say, 'Don't Tread on Tremont!'"

There was pandemonium. When the buzz settled down, she continued. "I know you think we're just the little people. The folks without any money. And you know that money talks. Well, we actually have a lot of money, right here in Tremont. I'm not kidding. Here's a little arithmetic for you: Add up how much rent those of us pay to absentee landlords on a monthly basis. Every month, you send that money out. Gone. Do you know how much we send away? Even if our rent is a hundred bucks a month, multiply that by a thousand families and then by twelve. Over a million dollars. A million. And you know what? The average isn't a hundred. Nope. It's more than two hundred. Two hundred dollars a month is two and a half million a year."

Francesca paused, knowing the effect of what she was going to say next would be more dramatic coming through silence. "So I say, keep your rent money in your pocket. Don't send that check. Don't give those dollars to the guys who come around to collect. You know what they call this? Huh? A rent strike. I can hear you say, 'But wait, Francesca, if we don't pay rent, they'll throw us out.' Really? Well think again. A rent strike is front-page news for the papers in this town, and tell me what landlord wants to have his photo on the front page of the newspaper kicking a family to the curb. And not just one family. Hundreds of families. Ladies and gentlemen, friends and neighbors, it's not going to happen. Close your wallets. Keep your checkbooks hidden. Let's show the world that by keeping our money, we've got power too. Rent strike! Rent strike!" she said, and the crowd echoed her, rising to their feet, pumping their arms in the air.

Francesca thanked everyone for coming, flashed a radiant smile, and walked off the stage. She was astounded to see Rocco Scattennato slowly walking past her towards the microphone. She mouthed, *What's going on?* to me.

I'd secretly arranged for the tailor to make an appearance after Francesca was finished. He was unbelievably nervous. He grabbed the microphone so hard it almost tipped over. You could see the strain on his face. He started to speak. He wiped the sweat off his brow, looked around as if to say *can someone rescue me, please.* He had every member of the audience silently urging him to speak, some with tears in their eyes, seeing his humanity when he finally opened his mouth and told those in the theater—and the others who saw him in the paper and on the TV news the next day—that his life was being turned upside down by the likes of Robert Moses, Mayor Wagner, and Carmine DeSapio. After a few sentences, he got so completely flustered that he picked up the pages of the speech I'd written for him, held them up for everyone to see, and in dramatic fashion, ripped them into shreds. As the pieces of paper floated to the ground, he started again, from memory, in a full-throated voice, only this time it was in Italian. He spoke from the heart, and it was clear that it was breaking. He told of coming to America as a boy before the Great War and raising a family in a tight-knit Italian community where crime was practically non-existent.

"This is my home," he cried as his voice cracked. "Outside my tailor shop, you see the flag, the flag of The Bronx. Some of you fly it too. We can all describe it by the three stripes of orange, white, and blue. But I bet few of you know the three words inside the crest in the middle." He paused and looked around the room. There was silence. "Three Latin words." There was no reaction. "Three little words that form the motto of The Bronx. Can you picture them? If you can't, I'm going to tell you what they are." He paused, scanned the room twice, flicked the fingers of his right hand from under his chin out towards the audience, and said in a strong voice, "*Ne cede malis.* You know what that means?" As soon as he said it, someone yelled out *Non cedere!* and the crowd went wild.

If there was more he was going to say, he never got the chance. The crowd surged towards the stage, chanting, "Never give up, never give up, never give up!" He had tears in his eyes.

Off to the side, Francesca asked me, "How'd you get him to do this?"

"I went to Stella."

"You wily Jew," Francesca said. "Using his wife to get to him. *Molto bene, fantastico!*"

I'D USED A SIMILAR TRICK a year earlier when I was in charge of the *mama-lukes*. Although getting them to speak pidgin English was what I'd been ordered to do, the thought that this assignment would simply lead to their becoming kitchen helpers or trashmen left me feeling complicit in a scheme for the army to take advantage of these young men. So behind the scenes,

I made other arrangements. I took some instruction manuals from the motor pool, quartermaster, engineering, and signal corps. I studied along with my charges, and my active participation next to them spurred them to take this seriously, as I was 'in it' with them. The upshot? They all reached a level of proficiency in at least one area, and could leave the military with the capability to speak English and practice a trade. And, not surprisingly, half of them re-upped for an additional three years. But what really got to me emotionally was the ceremony I organized not just for the platoon, but for the whole company. One of their own acted as the squad leader and in strong, confident English, called up each of the boys to say a few words in front of our commanding officer, Major Hughes, whose look was a combination of astonishment and pride.

LEO TURNED THE LIGHTS ON, and the four Casterella children and Mr. Scattennato came down from the stage and descended the steps. *Nonna Ebrea* stood next to me. She pointed to the bucket with the cash and said, "Just like the cash I collected in 1942 to keep us out of the camps." I remembered the wacky story she'd told me. I wanted to be respectful so I simply nodded my head and smiled. "Only the money wasn't in a bucket." Not wanting to be rude, I gave her a smile, the kind that could be decoded by someone such as Dr. S. as being sympathetic to a person who's lost her mind.

Groups of people had formed in the aisles and were engaged in animated conversations. Kieran Quigley was interviewing people who'd lined up to get a chance to speak their mind, knowing that there was a possibility they'd be quoted in a newspaper or even recorded for a news radio show. I sought out the Benjamins—all eight of them were there—and thanked them for allowing us to use the RKO. Each of them expressed delight at how it turned out. Sidney gently pulled me aside and gave me eight one-hundred-dollar bills for the bucket. "One from each of us," he said.

I spent some time glad-handing with Val Calandro, Susie Iarrabino, and Eugenio Marrone, three school friends who'd overcome the hardships of growing up in homes broken from alcohol (Val), abuse (Susie), and abandonment (Eugenio) by dint of perseverance and a will to break out of a mold. I last saw them just before I enlisted and often wondered how they'd turn out. The three years I was away gave me the perspective to digest the milieu from which I emerged, a luxury my neighborhood friends didn't enjoy, so their appearance as kind, thoughtful young adults was greatly admired. We didn't reminisce about the good old days, a recognition that even a few years of distance couldn't smooth over the terribly rough edges of adolescence that all of us had endured. Val and Eugenio parted with shakes, Susie with a cheek kiss and a wink as she turned to face Francesca, herself holding court with neighbors. I nodded; Susie smiled.

Leo went to retrieve the bucket, which was now near the back of the theater. I watched Leo make his way through the jangle of people, being stopped by friends who said a few words, shook his hand, and patted him on the shoulder. My eyes darted from Leo to where I presumed the bucket was when I noticed a young man in a black leather jacket over a white T-shirt tucked into dungarees. *Eric?* I wasn't sure. If it was, maybe he was there to report back to Bootsie what was going on.

Francesca made her way to my side. She saw me staring at the back of the theater.

"What's going on?" she asked.

"Eric," I said, nodding my head in his direction. "Well, now he knows that we're aware that Tremont's in their crosshairs."

"Yeah, and that the cat's out of the bag as far as your involvement's concerned," she said.

"It was bound to come out sooner or later."

While I was ruminating about that, I had to admit that my primary concern was that Eric would make off with the bucket. I was relieved when I saw that Leo had his hands on it.

We all walked back to the Casterellas', reliving the events, laughing lightheartedly at one another, and taking up a few of the chants from the evening.

I was supremely pleased about everything. Well, almost everything. I couldn't stop thinking about what Francesca had told me: "I'm busy in the morning."

20

BACK OFF, SCHMACK OFF

The reporter dialed the main number at Keating Hall and asked to speak with Kieran Quigley, the managing editor of *The Ram*.

"Kieran, this is Steve Speigel of the *Herald Tribune*. I wanted to let you know that I was impressed with your reports on the activities surrounding the Tremont demonstrations and would like to know if you'd take the time to meet with me."

They arranged to get together at the bar of JJM's, a hangout for well-heeled Bronxites, on Jerome Avenue off of Fordham Road. Steve Speigel cut a dashing figure in his dark blue double-breasted, pinstriped suit, white-on-white button-down shirt and red challis tie. He was tall, filled the suit as if he were poured into a mold, and had his black hair slicked into a perfect Cary Grant-type style. He plied Kieran with accounts of the underworld oddballs that he'd written about when he started out, a mélange of Damon Runyonesque characters whose stories propelled byline status. It was a pitch to lure Kieran to the paper after he graduated.

"Say, Kieran, all of us at the *Trib* were impressed that you got the scoop, but what we really want to know is how *you* were at the rally . . . and we weren't!" he said light-heartedly. "Just asking, you know, because it was a real coup for a college newspaper."

"Well, thanks for the compliment, it's really appreciated," Kieran gushed. "I was contacted by a former head of the *The Ram*, a guy who had my job about five years ago. He gave me all the inside dope."

"Wow, sounds like a guy in the know, as we like to say. A newspaper fellow?"

"No, not at all. He's the older brother of the girl who stole the show that night. Leo. Leo Casterella."

"Well, I can tell you that Leo did a good deed for the community and for his sister, that's for sure. He's the one who tipped you off about what was going on in Tremont, I'm guessing."

"Yeah. He wasn't specific. Couldn't reveal his source. I respected that. Gave me enough to figure out what was going on, you know, generally speaking. Then we hit the streets—I had two guys with me, one with cameras, the other with a tape recorder—so by Saturday evening, we knew what was going on. And then, at the rally, we talked to dozens more people, and I think we pretty much got the whole story."

A minute or so later, a young man in a chauffeur's uniform whispered in Steve's ear then took his leave. Steve Speigel apologized that he'd have to cut the meeting short but offered Kieran a ride back to the campus in his four-door Lincoln Cosmopolitan.

"One of the perks of getting star billing on a column," Steve said, seeing Kieran's eyes pop out when the limo pulled up to the front of the restaurant.

When the chauffeur opened the door at the Fordham campus for Kieran to get out, Steve said, "We'll be in touch!"

On their way to Manhattan, Eric loosened his tie and thanked Nate for approaching him at the bar at precisely the right time.

"I have to admit that speaking like that was an effort," Eric said. "It's so unnatural. Like being in eighth grade English; diagramming sentences, enunciating like the teachers, pausing for effect, all of it."

"Those duds from Benjamins look great on you," Nate said. "2-Cig gonna let you keep 'em?"

"They're not gonna be returned, although to tell you the truth, I'm not sure when I'll ever get the chance to wear 'em again. Maybe at a funeral." They both laughed. "You know how to get to Leo Casterella's?"

"Yeah. The guy your father paid to track your brother found out where he lives."

"Okay, Jeeves," he said playfully, "find a spot near his apartment."

In about an hour, Nate spotted Leo walking on the street.

"Ready, set, go," Eric said.

"No problem," Nate answered, having slid over to the right front seat.

In the instant that Leo was next to the passenger's-side door, Nate opened it with such force that you could hear the crack as it smacked against one of Leo's knees.

"Oh my God, I'm so sorry," Nate said, scrambling out of the car. "Here, let me help you. I hope you're okay," he added. It had all been choreographed to suggest to any onlookers that it was an accident. Leo was dazed and lying on his back, moaning, his knee throbbing. Nate helped Leo to his feet; he was groggy and couldn't support himself. The back door opened. He continued his mumbling charade to no one in particular—"I've gotta get him to the emergency room, they gotta check him out"—as he gently hefted Leo inside, closed the door, then got back in the car, and pulled away from the curb.

"Nice to meet you, Mister Casterella," Eric said to a woozy Leo. "I hope you're not hurt too bad. Not because I care, mind you, but because I want you to be alert. Can you? Be alert?" He slapped Leo's cheek. Leo's forehead jerked into the door handle. "Up, up and at 'em, Leo boy."

Leo was nauseous and couldn't open his eyes. The pain was excruciating. His face burned. He needed air. He fumbled for the knob to open the window.

"Not so fast, my friend," Eric said, smacking Leo's hand violently. "Let's just get comfy back here."

Spittle came out of Leo's mouth.

"I think you'll be just fine, Leo. Yessir. I'm glad we're gonna have a chance to talk, the two of us."

Leo was short of breath. He managed to speak in a labored whisper. "My . . . name. How . . . do . . . you . . . know?"

"See, Leo, normally, that would be a good question. Legit. But not today. I'm gonna do all the asking. And here's the thing: If I don't like an answer, I'm gonna give you a beating. You don't want that, I'm guessing. So here's the first question. Are you ready? How the fuck did you and your sister know what's going on over in Tremont?"

With his eyes closed, he wheezed, "My . . . parents . . . live . . . in . . . Tremont. Grew . . . up . . . there."

Eric hit Leo's neck with the back of his hand. Leo yelped. Tears flowed.

"Lemme go a round with him," Nate said, looking at Eric through the rearview mirror.

"Leo, let me give it to you straight. I don't give a shit about your family history. Don't fuck with me. Answer my Goddamned questions or else those parents of yours aren't gonna recognize that handsome face. Cut the bullshit. Who told you about Tremont?"

Leo managed to say one word. "Overheard."

"Overheard?" Eric looked at Nate. "He says he overheard." To Leo: "What the fuck did you overhear, smarty-pants?"

Leo was in agony at this point. He didn't respond. Eric cuffed him in the back of the head.

Leo groaned softly. Eric leaned in to within a few inches of Leo's lips.

"What was that again, Leo?"

"Boot."

"Boot? Boot what?" Eric shouted, losing his patience.

"Boots . . ." was all Leo could manage.

Eric smashed his fist into Leo's abdomen. Leo slumped over, out cold.

"What'd he say," Nate asked.

"Something about boots. What about boots? Who talks about footwear when he's getting the crap beat out of him?"

"Maybe he was talking about Bootsie," Nate said.

"Oh, shit, boots is Bootsie? This son of a bitch was talking about Bootsie? Bootsie must've run his mouth. Jesus. When I tell 2-Cig, that's gonna be the nail in Bootsie's coffin."

It was.

Nate drove north on Amsterdam Avenue, took Leo out of the back seat, and dropped him on a bench in Highbridge Park, looking for all the world like a stumblebum sleeping off a bender. Around dawn, a guy walking his dog in the park saw Leo and tried to rouse him. When Leo didn't move, the guy went to a payphone and called the cops, who brought him to Columbia Presbyterian. They stitched his cuts, set his broken nose, put his knee in a brace, gave him painkillers and drugs to reduce the swelling around bruises on his face, neck, knee, back, and stomach. Through the hospital grapevine, Francesca heard Leo was there for treatment and hurried to be with him. He was heavily sedated. Francesca took the opportunity to call me. I said I'd open Spins later and went to the hospital. In a few hours, a resident told us that Leo was able to whisper, and we could visit with him for a few minutes. Francesca gasped when she saw him. We'd heard from the cops that his wallet was in his back pocket, filled with bills, when he was picked up, so we knew it wasn't a robbery.

I put my hand on his shoulder and kept it there so he could feel the warmth while Francesca held his hand, both of us slightly rubbing him. He tried to speak several times. Francesca put her finger to her lips, a signal to rest. There'd be time enough later when he felt better to talk to us. I called Gavi and asked if he could open the store, telling him that Leo was in the hospital with non-life-threatening injuries and that I'd give him a full report later.

By early evening, Leo was conscious. I adjusted his bed so he was in more of a sitting position. Francesca lifted a glass filled with water and held the straw close to Leo's lips. He thanked us by touching our hands. His face was puffy.

"You look like you've gone a round or two with Floyd Patterson!" I exclaimed. He gave a small laugh that ended up in a wince as his lips and cheeks were still badly swollen.

"What happened? Can you tell us? Do you remember?"

One of the physicians had informed Francesca that Leo's bruises were consistent with a beating, not a fall or a traffic accident. We both leaned in close, not wanting to miss a word.

"They asked about . . . Tremont," he said slowly.

"What about Tremont?" Francesca asked.

"Who, who wanted to know?" I asked before he could answer.

"How we, us, knew. What was going on."

"Someone knew that we knew? Is that what you're saying?" His sister looked at me with concern.

"Two guys."

"Two guys beat you up to find out how you knew about 2-Cig's plans? Is that it?" I asked.

"Yeah," he said softly.

"Did you say anything to them?" Francesca asked.

"I told them I overheard . . ."

"Overheard who?"

"Bootsie."

"Bootsie?" Francesca and I both said simultaneously.

"Did they ask if you knew him?" I asked.

"No."

"So they think you just, what, heard him talking to someone, like out on the street or something?" Francesca asked.

"I . . . guess."

"Who was it? Could you see them?" Francesca asked.

"No. Hit me. Fell down. Eyes closed. Blacked out."

We could see how swollen his face and forehead were; it looked like he wouldn't be able to open his eyes for a while.

"But . . . I know."

"You said you couldn't see them, Leo," Francesca said.

"Voices," he replied.

"You can identify them by their voices? Who was it?" I asked.

"Brother."

"Whose brother."

"Yours."

"Eric?" I practically shouted. "You're saying it was Eric?"

"And Nate."

I was in a rage.

"You knew it was them. You're sure?" I quizzed him.

"Yeah, from the tapes," he said, through coughs that made him wince.

It was time to let Leo rest.

We knew the game had now changed.

Turning to Francesca, I said, "Look, Leo got it first, physically, and they're sending a message to us through intimidation and fear. It's a threat to back off."

"Back off, schmack off," my girlfriend said in a manner that closely resembled how my mother would say something like this, both in phrase and tone. "It's war."

I knew it was the wrong time to say anything in opposition to this.

"We've got to step it up a notch, Jay. If we don't, they're going to stick it up our tushes."

I agreed that if we stood still, the odds of anything turning out in our favor would be reduced to zero.

"Why don't we get word to them that we've got tapes. That'll get them shit-scared. They may back down," she said.

"Wait a minute. What we did is illegal. Bugs are against the law unless you've got a warrant. I don't fancy orange jump suits."

"Why don't we play it one step at a time?" she said. "See how they react."

"What's your idea of the first step?"

"Call Ike," she said.

"You want me to call my father? Are you crazy?"

"As a loon. Hear me out. Let's wait a week or so. See what happens. You call your father. Say it's been a while; you know the drill. Tell him whatever you want, that you'd like to get together. Meet him at a public place. Like Coogan's. When Leo's sight is better, and he's feeling up to it, he'll get into your father's house and bug the place when you're with him. Like he did at the Aronheimer mansion in Purchase. Like you did at Spins."

"I still have a key," I said.

"Do it on a night when he's at the social club."

"He plays poker on Thursday nights."

I PARKED GAVI'S 1951 four door black Chevrolet Fleetline sedan opposite Ike's house. Leo and I each put on a surgical mask and head covering that Francesca had swiped from the hospital where she worked.

Leo handed me a bug.

"Do the same with the bug as I did at the mansion. Here's something else. Put it in your pocket."

"What's this?" I asked.

"A garage door opener. It sends a radio signal to a receiver that's mounted on a garage door. When it's raining or snowing, all you have to do is hit this button and presto! the door opens. You don't ever have to get out of the car."

"Wow. You sell a lot of them?"

"They're still being tested. I gave one to your Uncle Gavi."

"I'm going in the front door."

"Look, if I see someone coming, I'll press the button. It'll vibrate. When you feel it, get the fuck out by the back, fast."

I hesitated before opening the door, then looked back at Leo, who motioned for me to go in. I bumped into a stool in the kitchen, which sent it toppling over. I peeked out the window to see if anyone passing by heard the noise in the darkened house. I took the phone off the hook. It was so dark I couldn't see what I was supposed to do. I took the phone under the table to shine a small flashlight attached to my key ring. I placed the bug in it. Then I felt my pocket vibrate. I thought I was going to wet my pants. I bumped my head underneath the table when I tried to stand up, straightened out my headgear that had brushed against the underside of the table, then stumbled a few feet, righted myself, saw headlights swerving into the driveway, then beat it to the back window.

"Shit, shit, shit."

I had trouble opening it and heard the key in the front door. I strained to push on the upper part of the sill. After a few seconds, it finally opened. I tumbled out, smacking my elbow against the window just as Ike entered the house. Ike heard the sound and rushed through the living room, poking his head out the window. My old man went out the window and landed on his feet. He chased the figure I hoped he didn't recognize around the neighbor's house onto 176th Street.

Thank God Leo saw me being chased by Ike. He slid over to the driver's seat, put the car in reverse, leaned over and opened the door just enough for me to slither through. He pumped the brake when he saw I hadn't closed the passenger side door. Ike was running furiously on the driver's side in the manner that many do when chasing a car, hoping that the car would stall so that a door handle could be yanked open and the driver pulled out. I didn't want to shout, which would give my identity away, so I smacked Leo's leg, and he hit the gas pedal hard, which snapped my head back, then forward. As we turned the corner, we heard my old man scream.

"You're a dead man, you son of a bitch. Dead man. Anyone who fucks with me, goddammit."

I could sense the rage, even from a hundred feet or so, only this time, I burst out laughing, spittle dribbling out of the edge of my mask, a euphoria that took more than an hour to subside.

"YOU'LL TELL IKE THAT there's tapes of all the shenanigans," Francesca said. "He'll go crazy. That's why you've got to meet him in a public place. The first thing he's going to do is go home and call 2-Cig. We'll have it all on tape. I'll have Enzo listen in from a car on the street with a recorder going. Like we did at the airport parking lot."

"Wouldn't Ike just go directly to the social club and tell 2-Cig in person?"

"When you tell your father you've got tapes, he's going to think the social club's been bugged. Ike'll call 2-Cig at home, I bet. Neither of them would think his home is bugged. We'll have it all."

My father was surprised when I called to invite him out for a drink. He wasn't particularly amiable, likely knowing by that time I was aware Eric had beaten up my girlfriend's brother. Reluctantly, he agreed to meet me. I approached him when he came through the door at Coogan's.

"Hey, Ike," I said, not wanting anyone to know he was my father. It'd be unlikely from a physical point of view—given how much I didn't resemble him—but I was taking no chances. We went to the back, away from the noisy crowd at the bar. "Look," I said, getting right into it without any pleasantries, "you know that we know what's going on behind the scenes. I saw Eric at the rally at the RKO."

He didn't flinch.

"To make it clear, we know Bootsie had Nate make lowball offers to buy out everyone on 176th Street."

He didn't move a muscle.

"We know Bootsie is skimming off the top for himself."

He didn't blink.

"And make no mistake, my girlfriend's brother ID'd Eric as the one who beat him up. He looked like a fighter whose eyes were closed up from one too many to the face, but he recognized Eric's voice." I paused.

With this revelation, my father craned his neck to one side and then the other, the first sign that I'd gotten his attention.

"You don't know shit," he said acidly. In the past, his icy stare and seething tone would've intimidated me.

"From listening to tapes," I said. "Eric's voice."

Ike stared at me.

"Yeah, you heard me. Tapes. And not just Eric. I can imagine what the press would do with this information. Can you? Oh, by the way, I'm not talking about *The Fordham Ram*. I'm talking *The New York Times*, *Herald Tribune*, *New York Mirror*. After a good listening, I doubt they'd say 'we don't know shit.'"

"You don't have any fucking tapes. If you had them, you wouldn't be sitting here with me. You'd have given them to the papers already."

When my father said this, I realized he hadn't yet thought it through—that if we released the tapes, we'd be admitting to a criminal act.

"All I'm saying is that if the new expressway goes through Crotona Park East, the tapes will never see the light of day."

With that, I stood up, walked to the bar, put my arm on the shoulder of a guy I knew and started a conversation with him. I made a sign to the bartender for a beer and never looked back to see when my father left.

As soon as Ike got home, he called the private number that rang on the phone in 2-Cig's den. Enzo had the tape running. When the conversation ended, he drove to Leo's apartment and we listened.

"MY BASTARD SON says he's got tapes of everything."

"Bud?"

"No, not Bud, the other one. Jay."

"You're fuckin' kiddin' me."

"I didn't believe him at first. Thought he was bluffing. I'm not so sure now. He says he knows about everything. Mentioned Nate's offers. Bootsie's skimming. And that Eric beat up his girlfriend's brother."

"What the fuck? Tapes? How does he have tapes?"

"I don't know. Maybe the club's bugged."

"Are ya shittin' me? I got a turncoat? No fuckin' way."

"I'm just telling you what he said."

"What's he want?" 2-Cig asked.

"For the expressway not to go through 176th Street.

"A big problem, Ike. A big fuckin' problem."

"I'll talk to him tomorrow, Alberto. I'll get this straightened out."

"Ya better."

The line went dead.

"Round two tomorrow," Francesca said when the tape of this conversation ended.

I couldn't help thinking about Ike's response to 2-Cig: "my bastard son."

21

HE DIED WITH HIS BOOTS ON.

Starting Monday morning and going through the week, groups of people from Tremont descended upon the offices of their councilman, borough president, assemblyman, and state senator. They requested meetings and were persistent, not accepting being brushed off when they were told the official would be pleased to take any written material but didn't have time to meet with them. They staged sit-ins, politely taking up every seat in a reception area and waiting to ambush the official on his way out of the office. On several occasions, they were able to entrap the official for a short period of time as he tried to get outside, never breaking stride, until he finally got into a car that whisked him away.

The Fordham Ram ran the story on its front page, highlighted by multiple pictures taken on 176th Street and from the Saturday night rally at the RKO. This caused quite a sensation, and the three students from Fordham who participated were themselves sought out for interviews by major newspapers and radio stations. The *New York Mirror*, with a circulation of more than one million, ran multiple stories with photos of Francesca standing on the stage with her outstretched hands on the bucket under a headline reading: "Bronx Bucket Babe." By the end of the week, the Tremont protest was front and center in the news, as evidenced by it being the first question asked of the mayor at his weekly press conference.

The "Don't Tread on Tremont" movement had "legs," as they say, in that it emboldened other local citizen groups to band together to make their voices heard. By the end of that week, when Horace Stoneham, Chub Feeney, and Leo Durocher went to inspect the property promised to them for the new baseball stadium near Fort Tryon Park, they were met by hordes of people from Inwood and Washington Heights, who booed and heckled the men, holding signs that said "Giants Go Home, Don't Tread On Us." They voiced their concerns about destruction of a part of the park, excessive noise, disruption from the construction, traffic bottlenecks on the local roads, subway congestion at the Dyckman Street local of the IRT red line, and a loss in housing property values. Stoneham got so angry he had to be restrained by Leo Durocher, who found himself in the unusual role of peacemaker, far from his customary charging and screaming at umpires over what he perceived as missed calls.

In Little Italy and SoHo, similar community organizations sprung up to protest the possible building of the Cross-Manhattan Expressway through their neighborhoods. There were even offshoots of these movements in the ritzy towns of Rye in Westchester County and Oyster Bay in Nassau County. Local residents wanted to make office holders aware that if Robert Moses was going to propose a bridge between these two towns across Long Island Sound, he'd be met by fierce opposition from deep-pocketed and well-connected residents.

2-Cig was pissed off. Donatella had told him about Bootsie trying to skim payments from the residents of 176th Street, that no one had accepted any of Nate's offers, that the community was in an uproar and was prepared to fight to get the expressway moved two blocks south, and that Ike's other son was a ringleader of the opposition. Furthermore, 2-Cig had taken a call from Tom Collins of the Ancient Order of Hibernians, worried that his fifty-thousand-dollar payment to ensure that the route would go through 176th Street was going to be money down the drain. "So's you know, if it doesn't come out the way it's supposed to," Tom Collins told 2-Cig, "you owe me the full fifty with a twice over vig, yeah."

2-Cig met with Donatella and Ike at the social club. His anger was palpable.

"How the fuck does he know anythin'?" he asked, referring to me.

"I don't see how he can," Donatella replied. "Everything's private through the booth at Spins where Bud and Nate speak to Bootsie."

"Ya think he listens in, like puttin' an ear against a wall?" 2-Cig said.

"Unlikely," Donatella responded. "It's got to be that the colored kid fucked up, maybe said something wrong."

"That's on Bootsie," 2-Cig replied. "Ike, have Bud see what he can find out from his brother. Put a tail on ya other son too. Find out where he goes and who he talks ta. Ya gave the dough to the guy who owns Spins, what's his name?"

"Gavi. The grand you gave me to turn over to him to keep an eye on Bootsie."

"Anythin' come of it?"

"No. Says Bootsie's an asshole. A slob. And he's nasty to Bud and Nate. Pushes them around. Yells, plays big shot."

"Push him a little. He owes us."

"THIS WAS AROUND the time I started to get worried," I said to Dr. S. "I'd see this guy in the lobby of my apartment building, hanging out near the mailboxes and spending too much time just lingering. An average-looking guy, medium height, probably my age. The only thing I found odd was that he was wearing gloves when it was maybe 55 or 60 degrees. I had the feeling he was waiting for me to leave so he could hightail it up to my apartment, sneak in, look around."

"To find the tapes?" she asked.

"That and more. Your mind starts to play tricks on you. That maybe you left a message on a scratch pad or put something incriminating down in your address book, that kind of thing. It got to the point that I did little things, like arranging my stuff on the bathroom counter in such a way as to spell out a word, upside down. Same thing in the fridge. Towels in the linen closet were lined up in a pattern. One day I had a conniption and was sure someone had been snooping around when I noticed the suitcases under the bed were in a different position. I was about to tell Francesca what I thought was going on when I found her reaching under the bed for her sneakers. That's where she kept her shoes so we wouldn't trip all over them."

"So in the end, it was all in your mind?" she asked.

"I assumed so. Then, one night, I saw this same guy at Coogan's."

"It's the neighborhood bar."

"Sure. I almost went over to introduce myself. Maybe he was just a new neighbor. Or if he was a plant, then maybe I could smoke him out."

"What happened?"

"At Coogan's? Nothing. He left before I did. Francesca joined me. After a few beers, we walked to Leo's. The opposite way from my place. I wasn't thinking about the guy anymore, had dismissed him completely, figuring I was imagining all this. Then, you know what? I see him on one of the side streets, same guy, wearing those gloves, by himself, doing nothing. That's when I knew something was up. He must've followed me to Leo's before and was out there lurking to make sure where I was going, then he'd double back to my place."

Dr. Silverman said, "I can see you pivoting one way and a second later another way. You'd probably call that being jumpy. To me, it's something else. It's what happens when you can't process diametrically opposed positions at the same time. You think one thing and then, just like that, you think another, and each thought may have equal value on its own. It's a fifty-fifty game you can't win. It causes agitation. That can result in reckless decisions."

"Are you sure you weren't on that street with me that night?"

"Were you out of control?"

"You tell me: I bolted towards this guy, took off without saying anything to Francesca, shouted out something like: 'Who the fuck are you? Why are you following me, asshole? Who sent you to spy on me?'

"He ran into what he must've thought was a side street, but it turns out it was an alleyway that gave access to back entrances of two buildings. The doors were locked. There was no place for him to go. I stopped and opened my palms as if to say, *what gives*. I walked towards him, picked up the handle of a trash can and a two-by-four leaning against it—maybe subconsciously becoming a Roman soldier. After all, we'd just seen *The*

Robe—and became Bootsie. Or maybe I channeled the son-of-a-bitch drill sergeant at Fort Dix, who delighted in intimidating us by showing neither fear nor reluctance to do harm as he got into our faces in a way that was disproportionate to our perceived offenses.

"I approached this guy, telling him I'd beat the crap outta him. 'Start talkin', I said, emulating how Bootsie would do it, having heard him on so many tapes. 'Take it easy,' he said, 'I don't got a weapon, I'm just supposed to tail ya to find out where ya go, who ya see, that sort of shit. Okay?' 'Who, who the fuck is behind this?' I said. 'Who's payin' ya, huh?' I came towards him with the trashcan cover as my shield in case he's lying and had a knife or something. He held his hand up and I stopped. 'Some cop,' he said. 'Which cop? Got a name?' I asked. 'I don't know, he's a big fuck and works for the guys at the social club up on Arthur Avenue in The Bronx. Fifty bucks to tail ya. That's it.' My father. Can you believe it? Dad of the year."

Dr. S. collected her thoughts; this was a new me I'd presented to her, and she needed to process what she was hearing. Calmly, she asked, "And then what?"

"I backed out. I pointed my fingers at him in the form of a gun. 'Next time,' I said, and the implication was clear. Francesca was at the entrance to the alleyway. 'Let's go,' she said, loudly enough for the guy to hear. 'Leave this rat here to play in the garbage.' When we got to Leo's, I threw up. We stayed at his place that night. We weren't going to walk back home in the dark."

"You'd crossed the line," Dr. S. said. "Were you aware of that at the time?"

"I think so."

"Did you understand the implications?" she asked.

"Generally, yes. But specifically? No. I was filled with a little bravado, you know, the success of the rally, my relationship with Francesca, the independence from my father. It goes to your head. I didn't know what was ahead."

"We think we live by calendars and maps," she said, "but the truth is, they're just props. They give us a false sense of organization. Most people deviate from plans at the drop of a hat and go off in a new direction without understanding the consequences. So your behavior, Jay, was commonplace. And you're to be congratulated."

"For what?" I asked.

"For pretending to be a tough guy, then walking away. You earned self-respect because of your restraint. That's much more valuable than if you'd charged and hit him with the two-by-four."

"The truth is, I wasn't pissed at him. He was doing what he was paid to do. I reserved my enmity for Ike."

"Interesting. You said 'Ike,' not 'my father.'"

"At that point, he was only Ike to me."

GAVI WAS WAITING for Ike at the back entrance to Spins. They greeted each other in a business-like manner, reflecting the thousand dollars Ike had given Gavi to keep an eye on Bootsie. Since my mother had decamped to Pelham Bay, Gavi was no longer *mishpucha* to Ike.

"So what's the deal, Gavi? Anything to report?"

"He's the same schmuck he always was. Treats your son like shit. Lords it over him and his friend. I don't know how they take that crap from this guy. He acts like I'm his maid, leaves wrappers, cups, napkins all over the table. And takes drinks from my refrigerator. It's not the money, but you'd think he'd once say thanks or bring some cans to restock. The only thing I got that may or may not be useful is this wrapper from a sandwich. See, here, it's kind of blotted out from the tuna fish—by the way, he's a disgusting slob when he eats—some numbers. A thirty, a minus twenty-eight, and an equal sign followed by a two."

Ike took the wrapper and gave it to Donatella.

Later that day, Eric walked into Spins. He glided by Booth 18 and approached me.

"Can we talk?" he asked civilly.

I was apprehensive but managed a "Sure."

We went to the front of the store near the window.

"I was there, you know, at the RKO on Saturday," he said.

"I was pretty sure I saw you at the back."

"What the fuck are you doing? Is it all about the girl?"

"Eric, please. It's about what's right . . . and what's wrong."

"What's right for those people is wrong for everyone else. And everyone else includes some guys who'll stop at nothing until they get what they want. You understand? You know who you're up against?"

"We all do. You probably thought it was a clever move to have Nate make the approaches, that people wouldn't think 2-Cig was behind this. I have to give you guys credit. That was a brilliant plan. But it fell apart because 'those people,' as you called them, don't want any part of selling out. It's not about money. It's about home. Community. A way of life. Oh, and don't underestimate them; they're willing to go to battle."

"Nice speech, little brother. Romantic notions and all that. You've got a way with words. But words don't mean shit in the game you're playing. It's a money game, and all the dough's on the other side. Oh, sure, you can stuff a garbage pail with a few thousand bucks—that was actually a nice touch, very smart, the girl's idea, I presume—but it's chickenshit compared to what's lined up against you. And don't think that because our old man's a cop that you've got some sort of protection. Let me tell you that if *that* doesn't bother you, this should: Dad could go down a fucking rat hole for the crap you're pulling."

"That doesn't cut it with me, Eric, especially since it was Ike who sent that kid to spy on me. So don't make him out to be Robert Young."

I was going to add that I knew he'd beat up Leo, but I was hesitant to say anything about that. I decided to bide my time for a better opportunity.

"It helps to have 2-Cig on your side," Eric said.

"I'll take my chances," I said.

"Suit yourself. All's I'm saying is don't come bellyaching to me when he's holding your bloody balls in his hands."

We nodded at each other. He actually said "Take care" when he left. The next time I saw him was the following Monday, noon, as usual, in Booth 18 along with Nate. Around closing time, Gavi came up to me and said, "No Bootsie today."

"That's odd," I said, "because they were just in 18, talking, so I assumed it was Bootsie."

"Nope. It was Donatella."

Something was up. I couldn't wait for Gavi to leave so I could get the tape. I called Francesca and told her to meet me at Leo's. I tucked the tape securely to the back of my knee. By the time I got to Leo's apartment, he was there, ready with the recorder.

"HEY DONATELLA."

"You by yourself?" she asked.

"Yeah."

That must've been when I saw Eric through the glass putting his finger to his lips to make sure Nate didn't say anything.

"It's on."

"Okay."

"Don't fuck it up."

"No problem."

The line went dead.

"YOU THINKING WHAT I'm thinking?" I said.

"Whoa, maybe we just heard an order for a hit," Leo replied.

"Maybe they'll just take him down a bit," Francesca said.

"Down under is more like it, out past the Lower Bay" I said.

DONATELLA'S NEXT CALL was to Bootsie.

"Hey Bootsie, it's Donatella."

"Yeah, Donatella."

"Listen up, we got good news."

"I'm all ears."

"I think the Jews are gonna cave. One of the Benjamins called Ike. You know, Jew to Jew and all. Anyway, they've seen the handwriting on the wall. They've got the most to lose. Big store and the theater. They want to meet."

"With Nate?"

"Bootsie, wake the fuck up. I'm calling you; if I wanted to speak ta Nate, I'd call Nate. They want to meet with you, not some messenger boy."

"Okay, okay. When?"

"Tonight. Late. Midnight. They don't want to be seen with you. It's got to be secret."

"Where?"

"The best place is the RKO. They'll have the lights out. Go up to the projection room. No windows. Real private. Don't mention anything to anyone else."

BOOTSIE PARKED his car on the side of the theater a little before midnight. He was packing, just in case. The big double doors were unlocked. He took out a flashlight and walked up the stairs to the projection room. Good sign: He could see a light on underneath the door crack. He opened the door slowly.

A voice said, "Bobby, I assume that's you, please, come in."

He walked in, saw 2-Cig standing next to Donatella, and said, "Oh, shit." He was jumped from behind by two guys who twisted his arms behind his back and removed the small gun tucked into his waistband.

"Have a seat, Bootsie," 2-Cig said, motioning the two guys to place Bootsie in it. They tied his arms and legs. "Bootsie, I don't wanna hear no bullshit from ya. That'll make things tougher on ya. Ya know we're gonna beat the crap outta ya, so's ya can save us from doin' real harm and all by just telling us the fuckin' truth. Now, I've been good to ya, wountcha say? Treated ya real good. Ya make a lot of dough, run the kids, I even play cards witchya, right, and ya never hafta pay for drinks or nothin' at the club. Am I right?"

"Yeah, Alberto, ya treat me fair and square, and I do good for ya, so's what this all about, huh? And where's the Jews, anyways? Donatella, you says they want out. So's the plan's workin'. That's good."

2-Cig said, "Yeah, well, the thing is Bootsie, the Jews ain't breakin' ranks with the *paesans* or the micks or even the spics on this street. They're all in it together." He paused for a few seconds and said, "I hear you like tuna fish sandwiches." 2-Cig pulled out a couple of scraps of paper from his pocket. "I do, too, Bootsie, I do. But ya know what? I don't write on no wrappers. Looks like ya do, yeah? See, here's ya writin', from notes ya took when ya was talkin' to Bud and the colored kid about how ya was gonna skim two grand offa me with each transaction."

"I'll kill those little fuckers," Bootsie said.

"So's should I warn Bud and Nate ya gonna come afta 'em, huh?" At this point, 2-Cig looked at one of the *goombah*s who'd tied Bootsie up and said, "I think ya better call them and warn them that Bootsie's gonna kill 'em." Both the *goombahs* gave a hearty false laugh. "That's a good one, Bootsie, because afta wes get finished witchya, ya not gonna be in any shape ta get ya revenge."

"It wasn't my idea. Nate's."

2-Cig nodded to one of the guys standing next to Bootsie who slammed his fist into Bootsie's face so hard you could hear a bone crack. Bootsie screamed. Blood poured out of his nose.

"Bootsie, ya deaf? Dincha just hear me say, 'Bootsie, I don't wanna hear no bullshit from ya?'"

With great difficulty, Bootsie said, "Alberto, okay, Jesus, I went along with it. I shunt've. It was wrong. I thought the kid was showin' promise."

2-Cig nodded and this time the fist slammed into Bootsie's stomach so violently that the chair was knocked to the ground and Bootsie's head smacked into the floor. No one made a move to get him up. Bootsie started to whimper. 2-Cig said, "What's that, Bootsie? Whaddya tryin' ta tell me, huh? Ya gonna tell me the truth? That ya been skimming offa me for years, a little cut here, a little nip there, no one'll notice, no one'll talk, yeah? And now, ya thought ya'd hit the big time, hundreds of people and thousands more from each of 'em. There's gonna be a couple a hundred thousand for ya, whoa, ya hit the jackpot. I'm gonna be nice to ya, Bootsie. After all, ya been around a long time. So once more, tell me the fuckin' truth."

Bootsie's breath came in wet, ragged gasps, and a pitiful, broken moan came from his mouth. His eyes were closed. Softly, he labored to say, "Sorry, Alberto, so sorry. Won't happen again. No way."

"Okay, Bootsie," 2-Cig said jovially in a loud voice. "That's my boy. Fellas, help Bootsie up. Let's get a coupla hankies and wash around."

They righted him. 2-Cig patted him on his shoulders. "Ya coulda saved yaself a lotta pain if ya'd just said that to start, Bootsie."

Wearily, Bootsie said, "So sorry, boss."

Bootsie began whimpering.

2-Cig said, "Ya think Bootsie learned his lesson? I don't think Bootsie's gonna skim offa me anymore. So maybe we should be nice ta Bootsie."

Donatella smiled, then sat in a chair opposite Bootsie.

"Yes, I agree," she said. "That's the right thing to do."

Bootsie exhaled, tried to talk, but nothing came out.

"Okay, Bootsie, that's my boy. Let's get a coupla hankies and wash around."

Donatella started to wipe the blood off of Bootsie's face.

"Looking much better," she said.

Donatella continued to clean Bootie's face.

"To show there's no hard feelings, I'm going to do you a special," she continued.

"Thank you," Bootsie whispered.

Donatella looked to the two henchmen and her uncle.

"Fellas, please turn around," she said.

The three men did as she asked. Donatella then unzipped Bootsie's fly. Bootsie's eyes were closed. A broad smile emerged. Donatella started to caress Bootsie's private parts with her left hand. He began to moan. Her right hand pulled Bootsie's head between her breasts. Then, her right hand reached into her pocket to take out a clean hankie. She kept her left hand inside his pants. She hovered over Bootsie, cooed gently into his left ear. Bootsie was highly aroused. Suddenly, Donatella jammed the clean hankie into Bootsie's mouth. She took her hand out of his pants. Bootsie started to gag and kicked his legs violently. She called out to the two goons.

"Okay, boys, the party's over. Time to clean up the mess."

One of the two goons kneed Bootsie in his balls, which elicited an agonized groan. 2-Cig held up a fist, a signal for the other goon to knock Bootsie out with a roundhouse right to his temple. They dragged him up the stairs. Donatella followed them. On the roof, they removed the hanky from his mouth and hustled him to the edge. Down below, a man on the street gave them the all-clear signal. Donatella patted Bootsie's shoulder.

"Fly away, little birdie."

The two goons threw Bootsie down.

The man on the street leaned over the body, taking pictures. Donatella and the two henchmen came back downstairs. 2-Cig was gone, having slipped out by the back exit door, where he met Nicky Shark, who was standing a few feet from where the body was lying on the sidewalk. 2-Cig handed an envelope to Nicky Shark, who drove off to make sure the photos of the suicide of Bobby 'Bootsie' Albanese made it into the morning edition of the *New York Mirror*.

ERIC HADN'T FUCKED IT UP. His presence at the rally at the RKO hadn't been to steal the bucket full of cash. Instead, he'd been asked to make sure he could jimmy the front lock of the theater. On the night Bootsie was lured to the RKO, Eric brought a coat hanger, a thin metal nail file, and a set of four blood-stained pick tools he'd gotten from Carlos, which he used to ratfuck the door. He'd also gotten in touch with Ike, who called Nicky Shark with the details of where to be and when. And when my brother saw Bootsie nosediving, he went to the payphone on the other side of the street, covered his mouth with a bandana, and called the cops, telling them that there was a body on the sidewalk near the RKO theater in Tremont.

Nicky Shark helped the night editor shape the story that Bootsie had stolen cash from the RKO, had been caught by the accountants, felt extreme remorse, and made the fateful decision to end it all, as opposed to getting six to twelve years at Attica for larceny. There was no mention of Alberto Giaquinto, Donatella, or the social club on Arthur Avenue. Nothing about the rally. No backstory about the plans for the expressway.

There was no police investigation. No one checked the front door of the theater to find the scratch marks that evidenced a picked lock. The blood from Bootsie's wounds on the projection floor, stairs, and roof had been cleaned up by the two guys who'd worked him over.

Nate celebrated Bootsie's death by singing the opening verse of Fats Domino's *Ain't That A Shame* over and over again in the most sarcastic manner he could muster, thumbing through the stacks at Spins, smiling wide each time a teenager joined in with him, having no idea why such a song about loss could make Nate so ecstatic.

The next morning, Donatella took the wrapper from the tuna fish sandwich on which Bootsie had written the numbers that attested to his skimming and showed it to everyone at the social club, a not-so-subtle reminder to the "fellas" of what would befall them if they didn't toe the line.

One of Nicky Shark's photos from the paper was tacked up on the wall opposite the bar. Someone scribbled, "*He died with his boots on.*" over it.

22

THERE'S STILL A LITTLE LEFT IN ALANPHANT

My mother invited me to bring Francesca to her mother's house on Friday night for a Shabbat dinner. Francesca was eager to go. Gavi Yudakov was there with his wife, Yudit, along with Uncle Mickey, his wife, Ruti, and Rabbi Leviev. The rabbi brought transliterations as well as English translations of the Hebrew prayers for Francesca. My grandma lit the two candles and covered her face while we all recited the Shabbat blessing. I was concerned Francesca would find this too foreign and possibly distasteful, but when I glanced at her, she was reading the transliteration with ease, caught my gaze, and winked at me. I was relieved. We sang the kiddush, then sipped the wine. We chanted the short blessing over the bread. My mother uncovered a beautiful challah that she'd baked herself. She passed it to Uncle Mickey who tore a small chunk out. I explained to Francesca that this wasn't crude, it was the way we share the bread—slicing it into pieces just wasn't done. I was impressed that Rabbi Leviev was simply a participant and hadn't assumed the role of leader; he was just an invited guest.

Grandma asked how I liked working at the store. Before I could answer, Gavi expounded on how I'd organized it to be the go-to place for teenagers and young adults interested in all different forms of music: rhythm and blues, country, pop, jazz, and rock. Francesca asked if the store now sold folk music. When Gavi said it did, Francesca said, "Cool, man."

Uncle Mickey entertained everyone with tales from when I was a kid. "I'd arrange to meet him up at a pre-determined hour in my pickup. He preferred to sit in the open-air flatbed, nestling in between endless coils of wires, stacks of tubes, specialty equipment to measure various aspects of electricity, and boxes with exotic tools. I'd drive to all corners of The Bronx. It didn't matter where I was going. Sometimes it was just to the bakery or the drugstore where I'd buy him an egg cream and a comic book."

I told everyone, "I used to imagine all the stuff in the back was designed to crack locks on safes, which gave rise to my friends' speculation that you weren't an electrician, Uncle Mickey, but a criminal—a *nogoodnik*. So I asked you, Ma, about it one day. You were indignant. Do you remember what you said?"

She smiled and shook her head from side to side.

I assumed my mother's voice and said, "How could you possibly ask that? My God! What on earth are you thinking? My brother a criminal?"

We all laughed, perhaps at what my mother was reported to have said, but it was equally likely a result of my mimicry.

"Then Grandpa Yuri, of blessed memory, chimed in with, 'Mickey was the wire man for the Rosenbergs,' with a straight face. And with that, Ma, you rolled your eyes, frowned, picked up a cast-iron frying pan, and shooed us both out of the kitchen. Grandpa winked at me, then went into the bathroom to smoke a cigar . . . something he wasn't allowed to do."

Grandma offered us all coffee and my favorite apricot and marzipan rugelach, which Francesca dove into with abandon, a nice gesture on her part, as I remembered being quite hesitant poking around at the snails her mother served at one of our dinners at her parents' place.

Rabbi Leviev asked me if I was a baseball fan. I said, "Yes, I root for the Giants."

"Well, young man," he said in a jovial manner, "you might want to divorce that team and become a Dodgers fan. They just signed a Jew—a pitcher—and I hear he's quite something."

"I read about this guy, tough but wild."

"Sounds like my other son," my mother said, and we all laughed.

The rabbi's comment energized Uncle Mickey, who was probably thinking about how he'd been prowling around Yankee Stadium a generation ago when he met Ike and later introduced him to his sister. We talked about Jews in baseball—Hank Greenberg was everyone's favorite—then pivoted to Jews in prominent positions and in public office.

"Do you think there'll ever be a Jew as president?" my grandma asked.

"We've never even had a Jew as *Bronx Borough* president," I said. "And forget mayor of New York. I don't care how high a percentage of the population we are, the anti-Semites will come out of the woodwork to vote against a Jew. No Jew will ever sit in Gracie Mansion, trust me."

"Well, we're one out of two," Francesca said. "LaGuardia was good but the one we just got rid of, Impellitteri, was in bed with Robert Moses, so for all I know, there may never be a New York mayor again whose last name ends in a vowel!" I thought back to a dinner at the Casterellas' when someone else brought up the Little Flower—LaGuardia's nickname—and *Nonna Ebrea* said under her breath, "He's a Jew." I knew his mother was one, but he was raised a Christian, so he didn't count.

Francesca's ability to enter a conversation effortlessly and with ease charmed my family.

Gavi and Yudit Yudakov took their leave, along with Uncle Mickey and Aunt Ruti, hugs and kisses all around. Sweet *"Shabbat shaloms"* drifted into the cool night air. Shortly thereafter, Rabbi Leviev said goodbye, and grandma went into the kitchen, refusing all entreaties to assist her in cleaning up.

My mother was sitting in a hard, stiff chair—"good for my back"—while Francesca and I sat on the sofa.

Rabbi Leviev's use of the word divorce, albeit in a very different context, opened the door for me to ask my mother about the separation from my father.

"Has it been difficult?" I asked. As soon as I opened my mouth, I realized the question might be awkward for my mother. "If you'd rather not talk about it, I understand completely," I quickly offered.

My mother waved off my concern.

"It was hard pretending. He cast such a large shadow. It's much sunnier near the shore," she said, laughing, proud of her comeback. She was relaxed.

The words came out as if she were reading from an invisible script that she'd memorized many years earlier. "I knew about his temper before we were married. I hoped he'd calm down, that the very fact of being married would offset the demons he'd lived with since his childhood. Was it having been an orphan? Or the only Jew with a hundred Catholic boys? Or not knowing whether he should speak Italian or English? I don't know. The funny thing is that it was being a Jew that defined him as a kid, but once he grew up—other than marrying me—he had no interest in being a Jew. I wonder why he did marry a Jew. Things were different then, you know? Everybody pretty much stayed with their own. It was easier."

I tried to be delicate. "How was he, in the beginning?"

"He bled for the blue. All cop, 100 percent. At first, I didn't resent it. After all, it was his career, and he was dedicated to it. I respected that."

"Did you know about his association with the guys at the Italian social club on Arthur Avenue?"

"At first, no. Because his shifts were all over the place. He'd come home very late or early in the morning. I didn't question it. I figured that was a cop's life. And I was a cop's wife. But then, some neighbors said some things. They were friendly enough about it, just giving me tidbits of information in case I wasn't aware, that kind of thing. Like they'd seen him at a table outside the club with a girl. I brushed it off. It could've been innocent. Someone else's wife. A friend.

"I have to say that although he had a temper and could blow his top at the slightest thing—he never hit me or even threatened me. He was menacing, I'll give you that. But it was always about something trivial. And then he'd apologize and say he'd never do it again. But of course, those were empty words."

"Did you ever say anything to him? About his temper? Or not coming straight home? Or that he should start spending more time with you?" I said.

"Not until . . . the *event*."

She stopped. Neither Francesca nor I said anything. We could hear the water running in the kitchen, Grandma humming as she washed the dishes.

I was prepared to break the silence by changing the subject. I was about to when she started up again.

"It was in the fall. Eric was a baby. Around eight in the evening. It was a cold night. There was a knock on the door. I looked through the peephole and saw a young woman, coatless, shivering. She seemed to be in distress, mumbling to herself, not standing still, rubbing her arms. I opened the door a few inches and peeked over the chain. 'Yes?' I said. 'Are you okay? Do you need help?' I asked. I hadn't noticed the cigarette she was holding until she brought it to her lips, inhaled, and then blew the smoke right over my head. 'Yeah, I need help,' she said, 'that's why I'm calling on a cop.' I was about to unlatch the chain when she said, 'Who're you, the housekeeper?' That's when I realized that this floozy was the reason Ike spent so much of his time away from home."

My first thought was that the woman was Donatella Giaquinto.

"How did he react when you confronted him?"

"He denied it. Got angry at me. He actually had the nerve to ask me to apologize. I realized that if I continued to confront him, it might set him over the edge, so I backed off."

"Did he stop seeing her?" I asked.

"Her? Maybe. Probably. Actually, I don't know. He started coming home on time regularly, but this could've been a ruse. I never knew how he spent his day. There were the too-elaborate details about why he needed to be someplace and when he'd be coming back. Some of it might've been true, you know. Everyone in the neighborhood knew about his association with Alberto Giaquinto. So he wasn't necessarily always with a girl. But with the stress of being a cop and working off the books for 2-Cig,"—I was surprised she knew that nickname—"and his running around, it drove us apart. I spent more time with friends. Played canasta, bridge, read books with synagogue ladies, attended lectures, took a Jewish course, those kinds of things. That's how we cope."

"Things had to have gotten better at some point. I mean, you had me," I said cheerfully.

"Eric grew up to be just like your father," she said. "At an early age, he looked like Ike, aped his every move, mimicked him, used the same kind of language. It was as if I had nothing to do with him. I was tearing my hair out. Then, one day, I gave up. I sat in a kitchen chair and cried. I felt sorry for myself. I went to bed. I don't know what was hurting worse: my head or my *kishkes*. It took me a long time to fall asleep. It was pitiful. I had no self-respect. I got up several times and paced throughout the house. Finally, just before dawn—I remember this so clearly because the milkman came early that day—I heard the bottles being inserted into the metal box outside the front door. It was as if everything changed. Rabbi Leviev says I wrestled with an angel that night. Maybe. At any rate, when Eric got up, the first thing I said to him was, 'You don't want to go to Hebrew school? Okay, don't go.' I followed this up with, 'You don't want to do your homework? I don't care. It doesn't reflect on me.' What I wouldn't do was be his maid. If he wanted to live in a pigsty, that was his problem. If he decided not to wash his hair or wore dirty clothes, I never said anything. He was loud, rude, and embarrassing. I was hoping he'd be drafted during the war. Maybe basic training would've cut him down to size. But he didn't turn eighteen until forty-six, and when he received his notice, the Giaquintos must've paid someone off, because he never even went for a physical."

I'd always wondered about that.

"You, oh you were different," she said, "you were a little Mountain Jew. Went to learn Hebrew from Rabbi Leviev without complaint, never a problem at school, captain of the basketball team, always eager to come to Pelham Bay to be with your grandmother, volunteered to go into the army. My good little boy." She turned to Francesca: "The best son a mother could have. Sweet, polite, loving, and generous."

She looked back at me. "Thank you, Jay."

"You're more than welcome, Ma," I said as I got up to give her a kiss on the cheek.

"You know," she said cheerfully, "I always thought it was Rabbi Leviev who was sending me the money."

Francesca gave me her *Oh my God* look.

"Until, of course, you went into the army and it stopped. Then it started again when you got out."

"I assumed that was when you figured it out."

"Where did it come from? I hope you didn't steal it," she said.

"I did," I replied, and my mother looked as if she was in a state of shock. I gave a thumbnail sketch of how I got the money and doled it out secretly to my mother for all those years.

"There's still a little left in Alanphant," I said. "It's mostly filled with old T-shirts, socks, and towels, you know, to keep its shape." I left out the part about the tapes and notes that were stuffed inside of Alanphant as well.

"Do you think the rest of the money's still in the backyard?" my mother asked.

"I don't know. A few times I thought about going back to dig up more, then decided against it. You know, my luck might run out; one of the guys who buried it would come back just as I was digging it up. I wouldn't take that risk. It's got to be Giaquinto dough. Burying it at the social club wouldn't have been a smart idea. A search warrant would allow the cops to crawl through the rafters, rip up the floorboards, and look for bodies out back. And if one of the lesser punks got his hands on it, you know he couldn't keep his mouth shut. Who'd suspect that it was buried near the tracks in back of a cop's house?"

Francesca asked my mother, "Mrs. deVenezia, why did you think Rabbi Leviev might've been the one sending you the money?"

"Please, call me Rebekah."

"Thank you, Rebekah."

"None of my girlfriends had any more money than I did. My brother Mickey would've just handed it to me. It wasn't coming from Ike, that's for sure. God knows, in the beginning I never suspected my boy. How would he have gotten that kind of money? The Rabbi wasn't married, lived modestly, and was always on the go. Busy. Hebrew lessons. Bar mitzvah lessons. He runs *Torah* classes, bible readings, conducts High Holiday Services at the nursing home and the hospital. He's even got a beautiful voice; you've heard him chant, Jay, don't you agree?"

I nodded affirmatively.

"He's called on to be a cantor when someone's ill. He officiates at marriages and funerals. You see, with all that activity, it would be possible for him to have saved some money."

While that all made sense, I was left with the nagging question: Why would she think the rabbi would've sent the money *to her*?

23

LET BYGONES BE BYGONES.

The attempt to scare residents and shop owners into selling out quickly and cheaply had failed completely. Francesca Casterella had become a household name in newspapers, which didn't have to gussy her up to be seen as sharp and glamorous. She was photographed or drawn with her ever-present beret and was occasionally referred to as an "east coast cool Beat cat." 2-Cig had gotten word that Horace Stoneham was getting cold feet with regard to a new stadium for the Giants near Fort Tryon Park. The rally at the RKO theater had caused a ruckus within political offices throughout the city. Momentum was building to locate the expressway through Crotona Park East. Word was that Robert Moses was looking for an *inducement* to put out a press release and to hold a press conference in which he'd lay out the rationale for the 176th Street route for the new road. The chairman of the Department of Buildings new advisory board—hand-picked by Billy O'Boyle himself based on a willingness to go along with Robert Moses's preferred route—was having second thoughts. He'd been considering a run for Bronx Borough president, a likely losing proposition given the highly charged atmosphere of most of the residents and shop owners of Tremont. Carmine DeSapio met with Robert Wagner and told him that the issue was becoming a political football, and the best way to handle it was to sit on the bench for a while and not get into the game—that coming down on one side or the other would hurt him in his bid for re-election—which he did, thus depriving Robert Moses and 2-Cig of some valuable public support.

2-CIG CALLED A MEETING at the social club to determine the next steps. He told Donatella and two other guys what Ike had told him about a wire. "If they've got one in here, we're gonna find it and rip it out," he whispered. "Then we're gonna find the stooges who put it here and rip their guts out."

They pulled the phones apart, aimed flashlights into the air ducts, unscrewed every wall outlet, removed all the lightbulbs and peered into the sockets, checked every piece of furniture, felt all around every radiator, inspected each panel in the ceiling, pulled out every bottle in the wine racks, went through each silverware, glass, and plate drawer, made sure nothing was hidden in piles of napkins, rolled up the shades, examined every article of clothing in the closets and even went so far as to inspect the taps on the kegs. Nothing.

"It's not here, uncle," Donatella said.

"The cars!" 2-Cig said, as if he'd finally figured it out. They went through everyone's car in great detail. It took them the better part of an hour. Nothing.

"The park?" 2-Cig asked. They walked down to Tremont Park and searched underneath the game boards and the chairs, then went further in, to the big boulders where they checked the crevasses. No trace of anything.

"They're lying," Donatella said to 2-Cig back at the social hall. "They don't have any tapes."

"The kid told Ike they got ya orderin' the hit on Bootsie," 2-Cig said in a barely audible voice to Donatella, as if to give lie to the statement that there was no bug in the club. "Now, how the fuck would they know that, huh?"

"Let me have a go with Jay," Donatella said.

"It's not gonna work with him," 2-Cig said, knowing what Donatella had in mind. "He's stuck on the Casterella girl."

"He's got a dick," she said, giving it one more try.

2-Cig ignored her, then took a long sip of his espresso, tapped his cigar into an ashtray, and sat quietly. No one else made a sound. He exhaled and said, "Let's say they got a tape. Why haven't they released it, huh? Tell me why not? If ya had a tape on someone, Donatella, which contained evidence, like of a crime, what's stoppin' ya from releasing it? Tell me. I gotta call Aye Aye."

2-Cig walked down the street to the candy store on the corner, dropped a nickel into the payphone, and dialed his lawyer's number. He recounted the story of the tape and asked Aye Aye if the tape existed, why they hadn't used it.

"It's simple, Alberto," Asher Andursky replied. "For argument's sake, say they have a tape. Forget for a moment from where. It's illegal to tape anyone without a warrant. Plain and simple. So the second they hand the tape over, they're admitting to a crime. There's no way they're going to go to prison to stop the expressway from going where Robert Moses wants it to go. End of story."

"What if they just put it inta the mail and it gets there without anyone knowin' who it came from?"

"I stand up and say to the judge, 'Your honor, the voice isn't Donatella's or Eric's. It's an impersonation. It's been spliced. There's no date on it. There's nothing specific. It's inadmissible. It's libelous. It's phony. Phony baloney'. You've got nothing to worry about, Alberto."

Still, 2-Cig knew he had to do something before there was so much momentum from the people in Tremont that they'd start to sway the politicians. Normally they wouldn't listen to these kinds of people, only to the folks who made large campaign contributions and lined their pockets.

"Okay, Aye Aye. It's time ta say it."

With that, his attorney said 2-Cig's favorite words: "Batten down the hatches, boys!" It was the phrase that Lieutenant Asher (Aye Aye) Andursky would shout to the crew of PT 88 when they were headed into battle in the South Pacific. Those words were the equivalent of what *"chaaaarge!"* meant to a group of soldiers—in this case, 2-Cig's soldiers from the army on Arthur Avenue.

"Listen to me," Andursky said after they enjoyed their laugh. "I've got a three-pronged approach to get the momentum back on your side. The first is that you send someone back to the Department of Buildings to speak to Billy O'Boyle. Get him to have his guys come up with a bigger amount the City will pay these folks under eminent domain. Grease him. Not enough to create any suspicion, mind you, just enough to make his wife happy. When he makes that ruling, you can offer more to the people on 176th Street. The higher the prices go up, the lower the resistance to not taking it. Money talks. Then, go see Carmine."

"DeSapio?"

"Yeah, Alberto, DeSapio. He owes you. Tell him to talk to the guys on the City Council. Warm them up to the higher costs for the City to get the people to move out. They'll bitch and moan, but at the end of the day, with O'Boyle's group behind it, they'll understand this'll reduce the tumult and make the issue go away. Got it?"

"Yeah, thanks. Time ta collect a debt. With interest."

2-Cig was about to hang up then added, "Ya said three things."

"Yeah. You need Ike to go after his other son. Have him meet him again. All nice and friendly. Let bygones be bygones. Get him to talk. About the tapes. You may finally get to know if he's telling the truth. This kid's a wild card."

Later, 2-Cig told Donatella about the plan.

"Those smart fucking Jews," Donatella said. "Who else would think of getting a Jew to turn on his son. Another Einstein."

24

IT MUST'VE BEEN SOMEONE ELSE WHO LOOKED LIKE ME

Ike called me. His tone was cordial. He asked to meet on Saturday morning at the bakery near the corner of the Grand Concourse and east 187th Street. I walked past the kosher stores all lined up in a row: butcher, grocery, deli, fish market, Chinese restaurant, liquor store, and bakery. They'd set up a few café tables outside under an awning, where we had bagels and coffee. My father was polite; he paid for me as well.

"I'm going to join Giaquinto Brothers as the head of security at the end of the year," he said. "The money's too good to pass up. I know you think they all wear black hats," he continued, somewhat defensively, "and, I admit, some of them are a little rough around the edges, but the list of things they've built is long and impressive. And, don't forget, they hire a lot of people who otherwise maybe wouldn't be able to get jobs. They've been great for The Bronx, you'd have to agree."

Sure, I could agree that the beautiful old Bronx County Courthouse in Melrose, the Bell Tower in Riverdale, and a few of the most iconic Art Deco apartment houses on the Grand Concourse were built by Giaquinto Brothers. If that was the only legacy of 2-Cig's operations, I'd tip my cap to him, wish him well, and probably not think twice about him or his company.

"You deserve a change of pace," was what I said, a neutral response that my father would hear as a compliment. My mother was the queen of such rejoinders intended to trick the other person into believing that she agreed, even if the statement was something she really couldn't swallow. Once, when a new mother held up her hideous infant and asked: "Isn't she beautiful?" my mother replied, "What a baby!" It's quite a talent. She would've been proud of the comeback to my father.

"Don't get me wrong, I'm glad you asked to get together, especially after our, well, *acrimonious* exchange at Coogan's, but I'm not sure if this is to sweep that under the rug or for some other reason," I said.

"Both," my father said. He took a deep breath, a signal to me that he wanted to blurt something out without pause. "Look, I'm sorry for how I behaved. I shouldn't have doubted you. I shouldn't have cursed at you either. I, you know, I just come unglued sometimes; out of control, I guess. And, also, we haven't had the best of relationships, that's for sure. Now this thing—the expressway—is coming between us. That's funny, huh? Between us, like a road comes between two sides of the street."

Or like an expressway divides two parts of a community, I said to myself.

I nodded but didn't say anything. My silence was designed for him to fill up the empty space.

This was the first time he'd ever apologized to me. If it was genuine, it would've been something special. And uncharacteristic. If, on the other hand, it turned out to be a ruse, it would confirm my worst feelings about him.

"We're on opposite sides," he continued. "I see your position. Maybe I'm the only one on my side who does. That doesn't mean I agree with you. I know you think what you're doing is right. I've got to learn to respect that. What you like to say: We can agree to disagree? That's it. That's where we are. Where we've come to."

I stared at him and tried not to show any expression of agreement or sympathy. I could sense that he was uncomfortable. He wasn't used to this from me.

"You said you had tapes," he said.

Aha, that's what this meeting is all about.

"I do."

"Is there any chance I can listen to them?"

"That wouldn't serve a useful purpose. Is the issue that you want to be able to verify that I have them? That they're not a figment of my imagination? I can assure you they're real. Have you ever known me to fabricate something?"

"Can't say I have."

"I told you at Coogan's the three things that are on the tapes: Nate making lowball offers to buy out everyone on 176th Street, Bootsie skimming off the top, and Donatella putting the hit out on Bootsie. You know all three of those things are true. How do you think I knew about them? Huh? From tapes. Don't ask how I got them. It's not important. Now, I'll give you one more you can take back to Alberto: Tom Collins is going to seek revenge. Remember, Bootsie was his wife's cousin. If I were Donatella, I'd keep a low profile."

"On the tapes?"

"Clear as crystal."

Another lie.

I'd bought my father off by planting false information about the head of the Ancient Order of Hibernians chapter on Crotona Park East. It was either that or going back and forth to Nowheresville, which is how Francesca would phrase it. He bought it. He didn't push me for anything else. I avoided a shakedown. Then I went in for the kill.

"Ike, why did you send the kid to follow me? Did he ever break into my apartment? What was the deal?"

"It was Donatella's idea."

"Okay, that's good for starters, thanks. But my questions deserve answers."

It was new territory for the tough guy to come clean; he didn't have a map for this. Especially to the son he'd enjoyed berating and humiliating for years. I stared at him intensely.

"Yeah, he was to follow you."

"Why?" I asked.

"To find out what you knew."

"Did he ever get into my place?"

"He did. Found nothing. Said your place was clean. The only thing he thought was strange was that you still had your stuffed animal, the elephant, on your bed. Thought it was odd, you know, you being in your twenties."

A small smile emerged as I thought about Alanphant. If Ike only knew.

"And the night I confronted him in the alley?"

"He was scared shitless. Thought you were going to beat the daylights out of him."

"He was tailing me to Leo's."

"He was."

I paused, then said, "You know, I do think they all wear black hats."

There was nothing more to say. I wondered what would happen next. Small talk? We sat in silence, finishing our coffee. To the other folks going in and out of the bakery, we were a father and son spending time together.

"Okay, then," he eventually said. "Thanks for the info." He stood up. I didn't know if he'd extend his hand, maybe tap me on the shoulder. Instead, he gave me a mini-salute, the kind where your index finger touches your forehead, then extends out a foot or so. I nodded and pointed my index finger at him, a gesture that I thought would be appropriate. Neither of us smiled. I stayed in my seat, enjoying the moment. It was ironic, I thought, that we were in the midst of a very Jewish neighborhood, kosher stores all around us, mostly Jews walking around, in a place where maybe Ike had his Jacob moment, wrestling with a spirit and coming away from it a changed man.

Maybe was the operative word.

I finished my coffee, caught the attention of the waiter by writing an invisible check in the air, then was startled to see Francesca crossing the street. I was hoping that she was coming to surprise me. I was primed for a lift. As the waiter came over, I saw Francesca enter a building on the corner. I paid the bill, waited for a minute to see if she came out, then hustled back to work, Saturdays being the busiest day of the week at Spins.

That night, I recounted the conversation I had with my father to Francesca and Leo at Coogan's. Leo wore a Giants' baseball cap and a pair of glasses he bought at the drug store, both of which did a fairly good job of hiding his bruises.

"I can't believe you told your father that Tom Collins intended to get back at Donatella," he said. "How the hell did you come up with that?"

"It was spontaneous. I wouldn't be surprised if Tom does do something to 2-Cig's operation. Vendetta didn't become an English word out of the blue, you know. Anyway, I had to give him something. He wasn't there on his own. He was sent."

"You think that's the end of it? With you and your father?"

"I don't think he'll come back to me for more. He's a real son-of-a-bitch, but he's not going to stand for them torturing me or anything like that."

"You've got to pull the bugs," Leo said.

I said, "First thing in the morning."

"Tonight. On the way home. You'll kill yourself if you wait and they break in late tonight or just before dawn. Do it now. I'll help you."

We spent the next hour or debating what our next move would be after removing the telltale evidence.

Another rally? A sit-in at the Department of Buildings or the City Council? A press release from *The Ram* with interviews and photos? Or something darker, such as a tip to the *New York Mirror* about Bootsie's death and the lack of a police investigation? We didn't reach a resolution. Getting up to go, I casually remarked to Francesca that I'd seen her on 187th Street earlier that day.

"It must've been someone else who looked like me," she said. "I guess I have . . . what do you call it when someone looks exactly like you?"

"A *doppelgänger*."

She gave me a kiss on the cheek. "Let me know if you see her again," she said playfully. "And get her address, so I can let her know person-to-person to stay away from my boyfriend!"

25

IT HIT ME LIKE A TON OF BRICKS

"He's not talking through his ass," Ike said to 2-Cig. "I can tell you, there's no way he could've known about what's going on unless he heard it. I asked, but he wouldn't let me listen to any of the tapes. Oh, he told me one more thing: that Tom Collins's got it in for Donatella on account of Bootsie's swan dive off the roof."

"That motherfucker. I shoulda gotten five hundred grand from him, not fifty. Donatella's gotta lay low. Oh, by the way, I talked with Aye Aye. He wants me ta get ta Billy O'Boyle at the Department of Buildings. Ta get him ta recommend higher take-out costs. In writing. Then ta send them over ta the City Council, so's they can put it inta law."

"It's a good idea, Alberto. You've got to sweeten the pot on your end, too, otherwise these folks aren't going to get out. It'll be years of litigation. And they'll end up deciding to go through Crotona Park East anyway."

"Ain't that somethin'? The only consolation is that I'd get ta drive a stake inta Tom Collins's fat ass."

"He'd come after you for the fifty G's he gave to you."

"Big fuckin' deal. It'd be worth it ta see his buildin' all rubble. Ya know what? I'd lowball the bid ta cart it all away."

They both shared a laugh.

"I'm gonna send Nicky Shark ta get ta O'Boyle. I don't want no one seein' me goin' inta or outta his office."

"Good move."

"And he can pay a visit to DeSapio too. I gotta stay under the weather."

"Radar," Ike said. "Under the radar."

"Give Nicky a call for me, willya, Ike?"

"Sure thing, Alberto."

NICKY SHARK SHOWED up at the office of the head of the Department of Buildings with photos of Billy's new two-tone Plymouth Belvedere, the spanking new screened-in porch on the back of his house, and the newly painted shingles on his modest home in Queens. Nicky didn't have to say anything else as he laid these pictures on Billy's desk. He suggested that Billy revise the value of the properties on 176th Street that the City would claim under eminent domain. From Billy's office, Nicky called Carmine DeSapio to set in motion the approval of the new recommendations by the City Council.

AT HIS HOUSE IN TREMONT, Ike told Eric what I'd said about having the hit ordered on Bootsie.

"Jesus Christ, Dad, you know what that means? I'm fucked."

"What are you talking about?"

"Donatella told *me* to get Bootsie to the RKO that night. I jimmied the door so he could get in."

"Big deal. You weren't there when it happened. What's got into your underwear?"

"The tapes, that's what. I'm involved. Who the fuck would believe me if I said I didn't have anything to do with it. And even if I didn't, which I didn't, I knew something was gonna happen. I didn't think they'd kill him, you know? Rough him up, something like that. Hey cop Dad, sounds like I'm an accomplice, right? Pretty incriminating, don't you think?"

"Where were you when Donatella told you to get Bootsie to go to the movie theater?"

"Where we always are. At Spins. Booth 18. We never see Bootsie or Donatella. They come in through the back door, and we talk over the wire that was rigged up."

They stared at each other for a few seconds.

"Wait a minute. You think Gavi or Jay knew about the wire so they set up a tape recorder to capture the conversations?" my brother asked.

"How else would Jay know?"

"You're kidding me. Holy shit."

"That's gotta be it," Ike said. "We ripped the social club and all our cars apart, looking for bugs. Nothing. It was Spins. I can't fucking believe it. Here we were thinking we were so clever, and look what they did. Made us out to be amateurs. Talk about being sucker punched. By my kid, no less. And my wife's cousin. Outdone by two Mountain Jews."

Eric winced. He'd never seen his father so frantic.

"Hold your horses," Ike said. "There's more."

"More what? Tapes?"

"Maybe. Jay told me Tom Collins was gonna take it out on Donatella, for Bootsie. He's related to Tom's wife. Where'd *that* tape come from?"

"You're fucking kidding me. A tape in the phone at the Hibernians? I don't know, Dad. I'm getting spooked by all this. They killed Bootsie. I'm an accomplice to a murder. It's one thing to be involved in a shakedown, smacking a guy around, listening in on some political back-scratching, or knowing about a payoff here and there. Okay. I'm good with that. But they've got me on tape as a participant in a murder rap. I'm done if that tape gets out. Finished. Goddammit."

"Hold your fucking horses, Bud. Take it easy. Let's get to the bottom of this. Can you get us into Spins?"

"You mean tonight? I guess so. I mean, I haven't looked at the lock, but I'm pretty sure it's nothing fancy. What are you thinking?"

"Go through every nook and cranny to find the tapes. My guess is that they're stored there. The kid I sent to Jay's found nothing at his apartment. Leo wouldn't have them. Too obvious with all his electronic equipment."

"What about Gavi?" Eric asked.

"That's a real possibility," Ike said. "I've got to be careful there."

BY MIDNIGHT, Leo and I had removed the tape-recording equipment at Spins, having made sure that we covered the flashlight with a handkerchief and kept it narrowly focused so no one on the street would suspect anyone was in the store. We knew if we got rid of the wire, 2-Cigs' guys would realize we'd been onto them. We paid careful attention to make sure we didn't leave any trails. We vacuumed the floor and stuck the hose into each opening where we'd removed equipment. We left via the back.

Fifteen minutes later Eric broke into Spins. *Through the back door.* I still think about what would've happened if we'd run into each other that night.

"Nothing. No bugs," Eric said to Ike the next morning.

"I'm starting to think there's a turncoat," Ike said. "You know, Jay tells us he's got tapes, but maybe he's being fed stuff from one of 2-Cig's guys."

"If that's the case, no one can be trusted."

"If you're right, I can't look at anyone the same. I have to suspect everyone."

"I can't live like this," Eric said.

"I'm gonna pay a visit to Gavi," Ike said.

"On neutral territory," Eric warned.

"Yeah."

IKE ASKED GAVI to meet him in The Bronx at the same kosher bakery where he'd met me. After a few pleasantries Ike said, "Here's the thing, Gavi. My last request for the grand I gave you."

"Promise?" he asked with a smile.

"I'll try."

They both gave a little laugh.

"Do you know what's going on at Spins? I'm not talking about the record business."

"Other than Bootsie, of somewhat blessed memory, and Donatella coming in, no. They arrive by the back door. Eric and his friend come through the front. As far as I know, they never meet."

"Strange, isn't it?" Ike said.

"That whole crowd is. Your son excepted, of course," Gavi added quickly.

"Look, Gavi. There's a wire from Booth 18 to the room in the back. That's how they communicate."

"You're kidding me. Why don't they just meet face-to-face? Why all the rigamarole?"

"So no one could ever say they saw them together. That they even talked to one another."

"I get it."

"You didn't know anything about the wire, did you?"

"Ike, if I did, I would've told you. You gave me a thousand bucks. I owe you for that."

"Well, Jay told me that in addition to a wire, the line was recorded."

"Why would they tape what they were saying? That seems like it would defeat the purpose of the whole thing. You know, the secrecy of it." Gavi said.

"They didn't tape *themselves*."

"Who did then?"

"Jay."

"Whoa! Jay recorded the conversations that Bootsie and Donatella had with Eric and his friend?"

"That's what he claims," Ike said. "But he may be bluffing. We couldn't find any tapes."

"Assume he did record things. Why would he do that?"

"Jay's on the opposite side of the expressway issue. This would keep him one step ahead. Make that two steps. Jay says he's got a tape of Tom Collins—the guy who heads up the Hibernians on Crotona Park East—saying he's gonna get back at 2-Cig on account of Bootsie being his wife's cousin. We can't figure out how he managed to bug the Hibernians building."

"Man, Ike, this sounds like a war I'm not prepared to fight in."

"As long as you've told me the truth, you're not gonna get drafted."

GAVI CAME INTO SPINS early the next morning. "I've got to talk with you," he said. "About the wire."

"How'd you find out?"

"From your father."

"And the tapes?" I asked.

"Ah, so you weren't bluffing," Gavi said.

"He thinks I was?" I asked.

"They're not sure. They didn't find any tapes."

"We took them out last night."

"Make sure they're in a safe place."

"They are."

As he was leaving, I said, "Hey Gavi, do me a favor."

He turned around, looked squarely at me and said, "You don't have to say anything, Jay. I won't tell your father about this conversation."

THE NEXT NIGHT I had dinner at the Casterella's. Francesca's father told us that Mr. Pirozzi had been approached by a different young man and had been offered forty thousand dollars for his business. Mr. Pirozzi told him that he was inclined to accept. That others were too. That it was very tempting. And that they were offering more cash to apartment renters in the hope that they'd move out too.

"That'll put pressure on the owners to settle. They're not going to get replacement tenants with all this noise about eminent domain," Leo said.

"I guess the enthusiasm of fighting this is fading in the light of cold, hard cash," Francesca said. "What about the Benjamins? They've got the most to lose."

"The Jews know all about getting kicked out of places," *Nonna Ebrea* said. "They've had enough of being displaced." We all looked at her. She said, "I spoke with Mr. Sidney."

I guessed that meant they were going to stay. Or sue.

"They have the most to gain if they hold out. The longer they do, the more they're going to be offered. That's the way this works," I said. I turned to Mr. Casterella. "Do you think the Pirozzis and the others who want the cash now understand how this could be better for them if they decide to hold out?"

Leo stepped in to answer for his father. "My guess is they don't think that way, Jay. They're being offered a lot now, and their fear will be that if they turn it down, they'll get less."

"It's all come crashing down so fast," Francesca said. "The little guys always get stomped on. Is there anything else we can do?"

"I don't know," I said. "We never had a backup plan. We lobbed a couple of grenades, and now the other side opened up with artillery."

I WAS SURPRISED when I stepped outside my apartment the next morning to find Eric waiting for me with two cups of coffee. "Can we talk?" he said. We walked to Spins and went to the back room. This was the first time I'd ever seen him nervous. His usual bluster and superiority had been preempted to reveal an altogether new persona—one with faltering speech, an inability to sustain eye contact for more than a second or two, tics such as tapping his fingers against the table, and exaggerated exhalations. I was prepared for him to tell me of a serious health issue.

He opened with, "I'm fucked, Jay." He gave me a rundown of what he'd learned from Ike. He was despondent. Within a short span of time, I'd witnessed transformations from my father and brother. I was wary. Given all the history and years of abuse and cruelty, I wasn't sure what to make of it. When he finished, I said nothing. I reached for my cup and drank.

"I could end up in the slammer," he said.

I didn't respond.

In an exasperated tone, he blurted out, "Did you hear any of this? Are you gonna say anything?"

"Why are you here?" I asked.

He didn't expect that response.

"I . . . I thought . . . maybe, you know . . . we could talk," he stammered as if he'd been punched in the face and was trying to regain his composure.

"Look, Eric, we don't have much, maybe anything, to talk about. We chose different lots. The only thing I can tell you is that you don't have to fear retribution from Tom Collins, if that's any comfort to you."

"I don't know how you can say that. You've got him on tape saying he's gonna get revenge for Bootsie."

"It's not going to happen, Eric, I can guarantee it."

"You got some influence with Tom Collins, I see."

It was then and there that I decided to change the nature of the relationship with my brother to see if it would have an impact.

"Eric, listen to me. For all I know, Tom Collins fell for the story Nicky Shark put out in the *New York Mirror* about Bootsie going over the railing by himself."

"But—"

"There's no 'but,'" I said cutting him off. "There's no tape of Tom Collins. Kiss that concern goodbye. The other thing? Your involvement in Bootsie's death, however tangential, is another story. I can't help you there."

"There's no tape?"

"No tape of Tom Collins."

"You told Dad there was."

"I made it up."

"Did you make up the other tapes too?"

"No. They're all stored in a safe place. But I do agree with one thing that you said."

"What's that?" he asked.

"You're fucked."

He bolted out of his chair and began to circle around the room. It was pretty obvious to me that he was nervous and scared. He didn't say anything I could distinguish, just some mumbling and running his hand through his hair.

"Look," I continued, "I've got no idea how all this with the expressway is going to end up, but I can tell you that if there's a hiccup with anything in 2-Cig's operation, it's not him or Donatella who's going to take the fall. They'll throw you, Nate, and even Ike to the wolves, lickety-split."

"Can you help me?" he asked, turning towards me and gasping for breath.

"The only thing I can give you is advice."

"Do you have any?" he asked, regaining some of his breath and composure, coming back to his seat once again.

"Make up a story that's believable. That you're going to do something different. Like go to college. Or join the army. Or that you're moving to Arizona, you know, for the weather. But here's the thing, Eric. Whatever you say, you've got to do. No bullshit. And you've got to sound enthusiastic. You're excited. Don't ask for anything. If they owe you money, forget about it. Play it the same with Ike. The last thing you want is for them to have Ike put the squeeze on you because they suspect something."

"Like what? What would they suspect?"

"That you're a rat."

"Oh, shit."

"You've got to think about this. Hard. And fast."

"Yeah, yeah, okay." He looked despondent. No eye contact with me. After a few seconds, he met my gaze and said softly, "Thanks, Jay, I owe you one."

You owe me way more than one, I said to myself.

He stood up. Started to walk to the door. But then he stopped, turned to me and said, "Okay. Here's one you didn't hear from me: if things are looking dicey, they're gonna resort to force."

I never expected he'd start to repay his debt to me right there and then.

"They're going to rough more people up?" I asked.

"No. Do things that will look like an accident."

"Like what?"

"All I know is that the first one has something to do with setting off a propane tank. To destroy a building. But really to send a message."

"I never thought it would come to this," I said.

We looked at each other with a *Well, that's all I've got to say* expression.

"Can I speak to you again?" he asked.

"I don't think it's a good idea for us to be seen together. Even at Spins. If you want to talk to someone, I can give you the number for a guy named Leviev."

"The rabbi? How can he help?"

"He's a good place for you to start," I said. I couldn't tell if the shock on his face was that he'd been summarily dismissed by his kid brother or that I'd told him to speak with a rabbi.

As soon as he was out the front door, it hit me like a ton of bricks:

The propane tanks must've been the ones stored in the basement of the Casterella's house, underneath the hardware store.

26

I HAD SO MANY MISGIVINGS.

It was still early, so I locked up at Spins and drove to Tremont. When I rang the bell at the Casterellas, *Nonna Ebrea* came down to open the door for me. I asked if her son-in-law was home.

"He's already in the store. I can let you in."

I told Mr. Casterella I was concerned that if someone wanted to do damage to his property on account of Francesca, they might throw a Molotov cocktail through his front window or blow up a propane tank in the basement, that kind of thing. I could tell he was extremely upset. He stammered; it was difficult for him to verbalize what he what thinking. He was talking to himself. Little bursts, some in Italian, others in English. It was as if he couldn't believe that someone would do such a thing.

I wanted him to take action, so I suggested he install steel window covers and move the tanks out into the locked metal shed in the backyard. I told him I'd help him. He didn't say anything but nodded assent. I went down the stairs into the basement and began the process of bringing the tanks up. I expected that he'd assist me, but he never made his way downstairs. My guess was that he was traumatized. After a half an hour, when I finished, I reminded him about the steel window covers. He nodded, then shook my hand and placed his left hand on my other arm. I smiled and told him he'd be safe. Then I said goodbye.

Nonna Ebrea met me outside the front door.

"What are your intentions?" she asked.

"I'll probably make visits to your neighbors to give them the heads up so that they can prepare." But for what, I couldn't specifically say. I was going to give them notice to be on the lookout for anything suspicious. Honestly, after I said what I did to *Nonna Ebrea*, I thought my generic warnings might not be helpful; they'd raise the level of anxiety and uncertainty without a commensurate dose of practicality, and this wasn't going to be helpful. Unless I heard about any explicit threats, I decided not to say anything to anyone. I must've been in a reverie because *Nonna Ebrea* again asked me about my intentions.

This time, she added, "With regard to my granddaughter."

"Oh, well, sorry, I thought you were referring to safety precautions. Uhm, why do you ask? Has she said anything to you?"

"Other than she loves you? No. I asked her about the religion thing. Catholic and Jew. She said she's not concerned about that. Are you?"

"Honestly, Daniela"—I remembered not to say Mrs. Lagana—"with all that's been going on, we've never talked about it."

"It's okay with me, Jay," she said, putting her hand on mine.

I wasn't sure if the "okay" part was the fact that Francesca and I hadn't talked about it or if Daniela was giving me her blessing for her granddaughter to marry a Jew.

We were startled by the ring of a bell and turned to see a Cub Scout wearing his uniform, riding a bike, signaling his approach. We stepped aside and waved to him. Rigged up to the back of the bike was a red Roadmaster wagon, weighed down by a large blue duffel bag, which I assumed contained all the equipment necessary for a camping outing in one of the parks. As he passed us, *Nonna Ebrea* said, "Why, that's exactly the same color and size of the duffel bag stuffed with cash that I gave to the young Italian men to keep us out of the camps in 1942!"

"A duffel bag?" I gasped.

"Yes, a big blue duffel bag. It was filled with bills. We could hardly get the zipper closed there were so many bills in it."

Oh my God.

The duffel bag buried near the tracks in back of our house. The duffel bag out of which I stole as many bills as I could grab and hid them in Alanphant. Those bastards had created a ruse to steal from the Italians in Tremont. They'd been suckered into thinking these payments were so they wouldn't end up in camps like the Japanese in California. *Nonna Ebrea* wasn't delusional. She'd told me precisely what had happened. Because the story was so outlandish, my reaction had been disbelief. It dawned on me that the buried duffel bag full of money must've been the source of the bribes that 2-Cig's men handed out to win contracts. My only consolation was that I'd reduced the amount they could use. The more I thought about it, though, it was blood money that I'd given to my mother, taken from her neighbors for whom these dollars were likely to have been the sum total of their life savings.

I had so many misgivings. Not just about this stash of money. What made me dizzy was the constellation of things around my head, including Bootsie's murder and the bribes, payoffs, and sweetheart deals with City officials. All of this aided and abetted by 2-Cig's pulling of the strings, Nicky Shark's photos, my brother and Nate serving as unwitting dupes, and my father at the epicenter of it all.

I didn't know which burden I was carrying was heavier: that I now knew how the world really works or that the expressway was going to tear through Tremont and there was nothing I could do about it.

27

I MIGHT'VE BEEN THE REASON HE BECAME A PUNK.

Francesca and I met with Leo at his apartment that night. I told them about my conversation with *Nonna Ebrea*. I also mentioned what Eric had said about firebombing one of the businesses.

"With you having been beaten up," I said to Leo, "and with your family being threatened," I said to both of them, "it's time to reconsider what to do. The jig is up, I'm afraid. There doesn't seem to be an alternative. Any ideas?"

They both shook their heads.

"Maybe it's time to go to the DA. It's not going to stop the expressway, but it could end up as front-page news and might put a crimp in all this self-dealing and enrichment of a few at the expense of the great unwashed."

"It's a big step," Leo said. "And you could end up being charged even though you're the one blowing the whistle."

"I know. But better I come clean on my own than to have them find out, in which case I'd be lumped in with all the hoods."

"I'm in with you on that one," Leo said.

"No way. If I do go to the DA, I'm leaving you out of it."

"Jay, they're not stupid. They'll know you had to get the equipment from someone, and with my job, the cat's out of the bag, as they say."

"I won't give you up. That'll be the deal, if they want to know what I have to say."

"Before you do anything, why don't you talk to Rabbi Leviev," Francesca suggested.

"That's funny. It's exactly what I told my brother to do this morning."

"Really? You said that to him? I can't see him unburdening himself to anyone, let alone a rabbi. Do you think he'll do it?" she asked.

"I've got no idea."

I CALLED MY MOTHER and asked if Francesca and I could come to dinner on Saturday night. She was delighted. I said it would be a good idea if Rabbi Leviev were there as well. She was agreeable, though she did inquire as to why I wanted him there. I told her it would all come out when we were together. She didn't push.

On Saturday morning, I went to the kosher bakery on 187th Street by myself. I sat outside, having bought a copy of the *Herald Tribune*, ostensibly to find out if there was any news on Tremont. The real reason, of course, was to use the paper as a shield if I saw Francesca—or her *doppelgänger*—enter the building above the bakery. I lingered for more than an hour and was about to give up when I saw her briskly enter the same doorway as she had the morning when I was with my father. I waited a few minutes, paid the check, and went into the vestibule of the entrance. I scanned the names next to the buzzers. Not surprisingly, the last names were all Ashkenazic. Except for the very last one. It was written in Hebrew: *Beit Midrash*.

MY MOTHER AND GRANDMOTHER clucked over Francesca like mother hens as soon as we came through the door. Rabbi Leviev stood and greeted us warmly. He conducted a brief *Havdalah* service, then we all sat down at the dining room table. Immediately after saying a blessing, I began to unravel the mystery of why I wanted to have this dinner.

"You always compliment me and tell me what a good boy I am, Ma, and I thank you for your love and support. There are things you don't know—that I hope won't change your view of me—that I need to tell you. And in doing so, Rabbi Leviev, I'm also seeking your advice, which will mean a lot to me."

"Of course," the rabbi said.

"It's no secret that Ike's involved with Alberto '2-Cig' Giaquinto and his crew and that he drew Eric into that world. I'm not going to give you the litany of things they're involved in. Suffice it to say, there are a lot of shady deals that involve bribery, shakedowns, rigged bidding on contracts, those kinds of things. They're not relevant to what I want to tell you about. And, by the way, I can say that to the best of my knowledge, neither Ike nor Eric was the recipient of any kickbacks. As far as money is concerned, it's my belief that they've got clean hands. This 2-Cig runs a legitimate construction business, albeit with some illegitimate activities. Francesca, her brother, and I found out about them by illegal means."

"Are you in trouble, Jay?" my mother asked, her eyes begging me to answer in the negative.

"Not yet," I said.

"Whew, that's a relief," she responded quickly, focusing on the "not" as opposed to the "yet."

"Not so fast, Ma. We wiretapped these guys: 2-Cig, his key lieutenant, and one of his foot soldiers." There was silence.

"Wiretapping is illegal," Francesca added. "Unless you have a warrant. Which, obviously, we didn't have."

"We have other people on tape as well."

"Like who?" my mother asked.

After each person I named, I paused to see the effect on my mother, my grandmother, and Rabbi Leviev. "The owner of the New York Giants baseball team, Carmine DeSapio, Mayor Wagner—"

"Mayor Wagner?" my mother exclaimed. "You bugged Robert Wagner?"

"Yes, Ma, the mayor. And there's more: Nicky Shark, the Inquisitive Fotographer of the *New York Mirror*, the guy who heads up the Department of Buildings, and Ike."

"Can't say I'm surprised with that one," my mother sneered.

"And you, Ma."

"What!" she practically jumped out of her seat.

"Ike called you from a private home in Westchester. He wanted Gavi's number."

"I remember. I was testy. I gave him your number, Mother."

"He called me. I gave it to him. Big deal."

"We got that call too."

"So I'm famous now, huh?" my grandmother said, with an air of irreverence.

"There's more," I said. "We got 2-Cig's key lieutenant telling Eric to 'get one of the hoods into the RKO on 176th Street.'"

"Are you're talking about the guy who fell from the roof?" Rabbi Leviev said.

"He didn't trip or commit suicide, which is what they reported in the papers. He was whacked."

"Someone was thrown from a roof? What? Murdered?" my mother asked, her voice cracking, her hand grasping her mother's. "How on earth do you know about this?" she asked Rabbi Leviev as she got up and began to pace around the dining room table.

"Eric told me," the rabbi said.

"What? Eric told you about a murder? Why would Eric talk to you, let alone about a murder?"

"I suggested it to him," I said.

Her voice rising, my mother said, "Is up down? Is left right? Will the sun come up in the west? This is Alice in Wonderland. I've got one son involved in illegal wiretapping. And the other son is a murderer. I'm going to stick my head in the oven."

"Hold it, Ma. Calm down."

"Calm down? The world's coming to an end, and you tell me to take it easy?"

"Rebekah, Eric's not a murderer," the rabbi quickly said.

Francesca said, "The extent of his involvement was to, you know, break into a theater, so when this guy Bootsie—"

"Bootsie? Who has a name like Bootsie?"

"That's not important, Ma. Listen to Francesca."

"Rebekah, Eric got the guy into the building. He thought Bootsie was going to be roughed up. Not killed," Francesca said.

"Oh, that's some consolation. A son who thought it was okay for another guy to get beat up."

"Eric came to talk to me, Ma. This may sound corny, but I think he wants to go straight."

"Straight to jail if he wanted some poor guy to be beaten up."

Rabbi Leviev said, "Rebekah, when Eric met with me, he gave me the lowdown on his involvement in a lot of illegal activities, the whole gamut. It started when he was a teenager and came under Ike's wing. Bottom line, he wants out. He's afraid that if he doesn't do anything, he'll be lumped in with all the others, and when they unravel how this guy Bootsie died, he'll be charged as an accessory."

"So you're telling me the only reason he wants to come clean is to save his own neck? Did he express any regrets? Does he have a conscience? I can't believe I have to ask that question of a son of mine."

"It's a process, Rebekah. You can't jump from one set of circumstances to another just like that," Rabbi Leviev said, snapping his fingers, "and change everything about your personality, behaviors, and understanding of how you fit into the world. It's going to take time. Maybe you're right. Perhaps it's only a pose. What I can tell you is that he stayed with me in the *Beit Midrash* for more than two hours, and we've set up a second meeting in a few days. I told him in the interim to keep a low profile and say he's not feeling well. He's going to hang around his apartment so he can answer the phone. The last thing he needs is for someone to think he's conflicted or worse, is going to go to the DA to be a snitch."

"And what about you, Mister Wiretapper?" my mother asked, holding on to the back of one of the dining room chairs.

"I wanted to lay the whole thing out for the two of you and get your views on what I should do. It's odd, isn't it—two brothers, estranged—both coming to the same rabbi for advice—"

My mother interrupted, "One who's been a good Jew and the other who probably doesn't know how to spell *Torah*."

Rabbi Leviev said, "From my vantage point, you've both got to come clean. You're like Jacob and Esau, crossing paths after many years, both leery of the other, not knowing if you'll get into a confrontation that will cause one or the other to revert to the very ways that triggered the alienation years earlier. And certainly not knowing what the future holds for either of you. One thing's for sure."

"What's that?" I inquired.

"In order for this to work out for both of you, there's no going down memory lane to dredge up hurts, slights, and animosities to try to convince the other of his wrongs. As hard as it may seem, you need to divorce yourselves from your history," the rabbi said.

"It's good advice, Jay." Francesca said.

"It's almost word for word what I told your brother," the rabbi said.

"What was his reaction?" I wanted to know.

"Same as yours."

"But I haven't reacted yet," I said with a light tone.

"Neither has he," the rabbi said.

The plates were cleared and coffee and dessert was served amid chitchat on lighter topics.

Rabbi Leviev silently motioned for me to follow him into the living room. He put his hand on my shoulder. "Atonement," he said softly. "Do you remember?"

I did. He said it was his most important teaching: There can be no atonement without forgiveness, reparation, and repentance.

I nodded. He squeezed my shoulder.

The others followed us and settled on the sofa and chairs. I sensed that my mother was unsettled.

"What's bothering me," she said, trying to regain her composure "is a lot, I can tell you, so let me start with this: If Eric goes to the authorities and gives them all the stuff you've told us, he's likely to strike a deal and get off with a slap on the wrist."

"You're probably right, Ma," I said. "You shouldn't be upset with that. I mean, shutting down criminal activities is good in so many ways."

"I don't disagree. But from what you've told us, *you* going to the powers that be with all your information won't get you off the hook. The only way you can have an impact is to admit to serious wrongdoing."

"Wiretapping," I said.

"Even I know that's illegal," she said.

My mother looked to Rabbi Leviev and said, "Eric didn't push the guy off the roof. So his crime is pretty minor, don't you think?"

He nodded.

My mother said to me, "Oh, I agree that it looks a lot worse if Eric doesn't say anything and gets arrested because of what you reveal. Do you see what's at stake? You coming clean means your brother is going to get off scot-free. And you're going to be the one to go to jail. I can't believe I'm putting you and jail in the same sentence."

"That's the thing, Rebekah," the rabbi said. "They have to do this together. One corroborates the other. That's what's important. And who knows? Jay may get leniency." He turned to me and said, "I'm going to get together with your brother in a day or two. Why don't you take that time to think all of this through. If he comes around, the next step is for the two of you to meet again. In the end, the most important thing for Eric to consider will be his relationship with his father. He's got as big an issue to wrestle with as you do: Either he brings Ike in on what he's willing to say to the DA, or he doesn't, in which case he's leaving his father to twist in the wind. It's a tough call. The repercussions from either approach are difficult to assess. It's possible that Ike could turn on Eric."

We sat in silence for about half a minute.

Then my mother said, "For most fathers, it wouldn't be a difficult decision. Blood over livelihood."

"You'd think so. Especially since he's already lost his wife and his second son. Eric's the only thing he's got left," Francesca said.

"Okay," I said, then stood up, kissed my mother and grandmother, thanked Rabbi Leviev for his observations and suggestions, and walked out to the car.

Francesca said, "What were you saying 'okay' to just before we left? Okay that Ike wouldn't turn on Eric? Okay that you and Eric would get together?"

"It was just a general okay, nothing specific. Kind of a conversation stopper. There wasn't much more that could be said."

"I beg to differ," Francesca said. "I'm bursting at the seams."

"If you had more to say, how come you didn't speak up? That's not like you."

"Well," she said, staring at me with a face that that looked like it'd been illuminated from within, "the first thing is that your mother and Rabbi Leviev are a twosome. A couple."

"*What?*" I said.

"It's so obvious," she said. "The glances, the head tics, the way they never step on each other's lines. The warmth between them is quite apparent. To me, anyway."

"They've known each other a long time. Perhaps what you're seeing is affection, but it's not necessarily romantic."

"If I were in your shoes, I might find it difficult to accept as well. After all, he was the rabbi at your bar mitzvah and the one who's been close to you and your mother for all these years. I also know it's hard to imagine a parent in a relationship with someone else. It's the kind of thing one pushes off to the side."

"Like the fact that I'm around because my parents had sex," I said. "I see closeness, for sure. I just never thought about it. And don't get me wrong. I wouldn't be against it. At all. He's a wonderful man—thoughtful, smart, a good teacher; he seems to know what, when, and how to say important things, and he's always there in the difficult times—he's a *mensch*."

"A real *heymishe* guy," Francesca said.

"Did you learn that at the *Beit Midrash*? I asked. "Or was it your *doppelgänger*?"

"Were you following me?" she asked playfully.

"I was curious. I saw the last name on the directory. *Beit midrash*. I knew my mother went to classes in a house of learning with the rabbi up on the Grand Concourse, so I figured this must be the place where Rabbi Leviev hangs his hat. Or maybe I should say hangs his *kippa*."

She laughed.

"So, what's a good Catholic girl like you doing in a Jewish study hall on Saturday mornings?"

"Maybe I'm not such a good Catholic girl," she said.

"What do you mean?"

"It's a study hall, Jay."

"Yeah, I know."

"What do you think I'm studying?"

"This may sound stupid," I said.

"Coming from you? I'm not so sure."

"I thought you were there to ask him, Rabbi Leviev, what it's like for a Catholic girl to be married to a Jew."

"Are you proposing to me?"

"Are you changing the subject?" I asked.

"Well, are you?" she asked.

"I would, except that I wouldn't want my prison sentence to interfere with a honeymoon."

"Okay, Joogan deVenezia. First, I accept. Even though you used the conditional 'would.' Boy, would my English teacher be proud of me for remembering that one. Anyway, you're not going to be sent up the river unless it's on a Circle Line cruise up the Hudson to West Point. Hey, come here, at least you can give me a kiss. I'll settle for a ring later."

The fast-paced back-and-forth reminded me of the dialogue in *Bringing Up Baby*, one of my favorite movies starring Katharine Hepburn and Cary Grant.

Let's just say it was the best kiss ever.

"And if you haven't figured it out by now, knucklehead, it'll be Rabbi Leviev performing the service," she said.

"He'll do interfaith?" I asked.

"No."

It was only then that I realized what Francesca was doing with Rabbi Leviev in the *Beit Midrash*.

"YOU REALLY SUSPECTED nothing of the kind?" Dr. S. commented.

"Honestly, it never occurred to me. I loved everything about Francesca: her originality, cleverness, decisiveness, passion. But with all that was going on, the idea of marriage wasn't top of mind. And the idea that she'd convert? Well, honestly, that was a shocker."

"Did you ask her how she came to that decision?"

"In a roundabout way."

"How so?"

"I asked my mother. She said that Francesca gravitated to her more than her own mother. It was nothing negative about her mother. Let's just say she had a preference for mine. There was a warmth there, a feeling; she said it's hard to explain. She told my mother that she absorbed a lot of *Nonna Ebrea*'s ramblings when she would make her morning trek to see her grandmother getting ready for the day. Stories about her family history, which oftentimes included tales of Jews. She's not sure if her grandmother actually has ancestors who are Jews. Francesca became—I know this sounds strange—a bit acculturated through these early morning tales."

Dr. S. said, "Did you ever think this was merely a fascination? A passing phase? New, shiny objects are attractive because they're so different from what we're accustomed to. Then, over time, they begin to fade. The novelty wears off. I'm not being cynical; it's the way of the world."

"If she'd gone to see Rabbi Leviev once or twice, that might've been the case. Or if her main takeaway from being with my mother was to learn how to bake a *challah*. I was pretty sure her sincerity was built upon a foundation of excitement with the basic tenets and the culture."

"I'm going to push you a little here. Did you ever consider—somewhere in the back of your mind—that your comment about not wanting to get married because you might go to jail stemmed from a subconscious thought that you needed more time to determine if her conversion was going to hold?"

"I can't answer that any more than I could know if Eric's conversion to being a good guy and a helpful brother was solely related to his desire to avoid jail time. Strange, isn't it? How the contemplations of incarceration from two siblings might've shaped the way both of us approached the world?"

I paused. Dr. S. stared at me. It was her way of urging me to go on.

"I've had dreams. About Eric."

"Tell me," Dr. S. said.

"The snowball, the one with a stone in it, hit him and not the other kid. He was all bloody."

"Did you help him?"

"No. I gloated. From behind the house. I didn't want him to know I threw it."

"What happened? Were you punished?" she asked.

"No one knew I threw it. I went into the house as if nothing happened. A few seconds later, Eric came in. His face was red, and there was blood streaming out of his nose."

"Did your mother's maternal instincts take over?"

"She wasn't there," I said.

"Ah, so you erased your mother such that she couldn't minister to him. That would've diminished your standing. Eric was competition for your mother's affection. No mother, no loss of station for you. Did you do anything?"

"No. I went upstairs to do my homework. He was in the kitchen with a paper towel with ice pressed against his face."

"And then?" she pressed me.

"Another dream. I was sneaking back around the house with the stone snowball, peeked around the front expecting see Eric in a fight. He wasn't there. I never threw the snowball."

"Were you disappointed?" she asked.

"You know, strangely, I was relieved."

"Now that's a surprise," she said. "You erased your mother in the first dream and Eric in the second. Maybe on account of the fact that you were going to see him the next morning. It was almost as if not throwing the snowball in a dream was going to make your meeting in the *Beit Midrash* less confrontational." She paused. "Guilt; you'd suppressed it all these years. Did you feel shame?"

I nodded. "I was morose." I sighed. "Then, you know, I had a third dream: I missed him with the snowball and hit the other kid in the face like it really happened, but when I came into the house, I never said anything to my mother."

"No tricking her into thinking Eric had done it to the other kid?" Dr. S. asked.

"No."

"An equally important admission that the wrong wasn't just to Eric."

I sat quietly, reliving the three dreams.

She met my eyes and said, "Is there more you want to say?"

"About the dreams? No. I remember waking up and being nervous about the upcoming meeting with my brother in the *Beit Midrash* because

I might've been the reason he became a punk. You know, the police coming and hauling him off to Juvie Hall for something I did. Eric was a shit to me for sure, but this put a mark on him in the neighborhood, the kind of stain that might've shamed someone else, but not my brother. He wore it with pride. It became part of his greaser persona. Maybe, just maybe, I was the one who sent him down a path that he didn't choose. What if it was chosen for him by me, a kid who'd had it up to here and did something he couldn't have known would have such repercussions."

28

WHAT ARE YOU, BACKWARDS NOSTRADAMUS?

Who knew if Eric's guilt over his participation in Bootsie's death and his behavior towards me for all those years, or my guilt over framing him for my actions and never coming clean were hanging over us. I'd been wracked by my dreams. What about Eric? Neither of us knew what the outcome of our meeting was going to be. We each came with an agenda that'd been created without input from the other, so we wouldn't be able to predict how it would all turn out. I knew that there had to be no posturing; I hoped my brother recognized this as well. We were both in trouble and needed each other. It would be a marriage of convenience. What we didn't know was whether it would lead to a quickie divorce in a few days or if we'd be able to celebrate a golden anniversary fifty years hence.

Uncharacteristically, he stood up when I entered and offered his hand. I shook it. As soon as he settled into his chair, I asked him to stand.

"Take off your clothes," I said.

"What?" he said as if I'd swatted him across the face and challenged him to a duel.

"Take them off, let me see you're not wearing a wire."

"You too," he said. "Fair's fair."

We both disrobed simultaneously, demonstrated that we were clean, and put our clothes back on.

"Any other surprises for me?" he asked.

"I'm going to keep you guessing," I said, cognizant of Francesca's reminder to assert myself and keep the edge on him so he'd know he was playing the game according to my rules in my home territory.

"Have you decided what you're going to do?" I asked.

"The only way to save my ass is to turn myself in," he said. "But I'll tell you this right now. No fucking way I'm gonna wear a wire and go back to the social club. If these sons-of-bitches at the DA's office tell me to do that, I'm gonna walk."

"Actually, that's an excellent strategy," I said. "You have to be able to call their bluff. If you weasel around and say you have to think about it, you're dead in the water. They've got to be convinced you'll only do things on your terms. So—and this is critical—don't say anything until you've got a deal. On the table. Written down."

"I'm gonna need a lawyer, don't you think?"

"Agreed. I've already thought about that. I spoke with Sidney Benjamin. You know, the oldest of the Benjamin brothers. His family has agreed to pay for lawyers for both of us."

"Not because I went to the prom with his daughter, I'm guessing," he said, laughing.

"That would be a good one. No. Because he and his brothers and their wives know that their future—and everyone else's on the street—is going to become topsy-turvy, all on account of the dirty dealing by the likes of 2-Cig and the heavy hitters in government in Manhattan. The Benjamins want them exposed. To Sidney, what we're going to do is a *mitzvah*. Do you know what that is?"

My brother gave me a sheepish look.

"A 'good deed.'"

"Time for the first one," he said.

"Yup. Time to call the lawyer," I said. I took the note with the attorney's name and number. He answered it himself. I told Eric to lean in close so he could hear the lawyer as well.

After a few introductory remarks, I explained what had gone on in detail to the attorney Jonas Levinthal.

"You've got work to do before you show up at the courthouse. Jay, your girlfriend's brother—"

"Leo."

"Leo should call the kid at the student newspaper—"

"Kieran Quigley of *The Fordham Ram*," I said.

"Tell him to meet with the two of you. Tell him what you're going to say to the DA. Have him write a story that positions the two of you in the best way possible. Remember, it's the first story that has legs, that resonates. Once it's out there, no one's going to remember anything else. Also, Kieran's a kid. He'll allow you to take a look at what he's written. Leo can help with that. He'll say it's necessary to make sure Kieran's got it right. But the truth is, it's your chance to put yourselves in the best light."

This guy was good.

"And, listen up, boys" he added. "Have the camera guy take pictures of the two of you. Together. And film also. Along 176th Street and at your mother's house. You should have your mother there with you. 'A family together.' The last thing you want is for the first photos to be of you guys on a perp walk taken by that *New York Mirror* photographer guy."

"Nicky Shark," Eric said.

"That'll sink you. If there's ever a trial, you want the image of two brothers with their mother trying to right wrongs in jurors' minds. The sound guy's got to be there as well. People need to hear you, not just see you."

The Benjamins had done us a huge favor by hiring Jonas Levinthal to represent us. I was impressed.

After we hung up, I said, "Okay, Eric. Let's get to work. Write down everything you want to tell the DA. Don't leave anything out. I don't care if you think it's an inconsequential point. Put it in. I'm going to do the same. We're going to stay here until it's finished. If we get hungry, I'll go get food and bring it back. And even when each of us has it all on paper, we're actually not finished."

"What do you mean?" he asked.

"We then have to compare notes. Your words and mine. They've got to be consistent. I'm not talking about making things up to get them to agree. We can't afford to do that. We can't lie about anything."

"That'll be a first."

"We're not going to leave until we have something that can stand up to intense grilling," I said.

We stayed until the sun went down. When we were satisfied with what we'd accomplished, I took what each of us had written and inserted the papers into one of Rabbi Leviev's file drawers marked 'Sermons.'

"No way we're leaving with these notes only to have them lost to one of 2-Cig's guys who's followed us here. That reminds me. You leave by the fire escape out back. You may have to lower the final rung. I'll go out the front door fifteen minutes later."

LEO CALLED KIERAN QUIGLEY, who assembled his crew. They met us the next day in the early part of the evening at my grandmother's house, where she'd set up plates of food for us buffet-style in the dining room. From the looks of the Fordham boys, we could tell it was the first time they'd ever tasted *kov roghan, kugel,* or *knishes.*

We laid out our plans for how we were going to stage the photos, the film, and the audio; right after everyone said they got it, we started. Francesca told me later that I was good, but after seeing and listening to my brother, she knew he was the star of the show. I could tell my mother and grandmother were seeing in Eric a son and grandson they'd never encountered before. There was an authenticity that stemmed not only from the highly detailed specifics of what he had to say, but also from the way he said it: his vocabulary, diction, and body language—how he moved his neck in semi-circles, used his hands as an appendage of his mouth, rotated his head a few inches off center. The last thing he said with the camera rolling, looking off to the side towards me with his eyes half shut, his plaintive voice barely above a whisper, was so heart-wrenching it was difficult not to shed a tear: "It didn't have to be this way," which I heard as the famous movie line Budd Schulberg wrote in *On The Waterfront*: "I couda been somebody, instead of a bum, which is what I am, let's face it."

My grandmother served rugelach and coffee to a silent group.

After a few minutes, Francesca told the Fordham boys that she'd arranged for us to be met the next day by people supposedly walking randomly down the street. I told them about '*Ciao* Daniela!' which got a laugh out of proportion to its humor, a not infrequent response when comedy is intended to interrupt melancholy. She mentioned that we were going to pop into stores extemporaneously. The reality was that each encounter was being set up to accommodate the best angles for capturing our conversations with the owners or proprietors. Kieran was accompanied by the same two students who'd been with him at the RKO theater the night of the rally, so there was no learning curve for these guys.

We hit the streets the next morning and captured it all. It was the perfect opportunity for the neighborhood residents to get their frustrations about the expressway off their chests. We let them talk, mostly without interruption. They didn't need scripts. It came from their hearts as if they were paying respects at a wake. A few directed their anger right into the camera, wanting their belligerence to be felt by those who'd later watch—a warning to others that this could happen to them too. We told the Fordham boys not to edit out the stumbles or hesitations or dabbing at the eyes of anyone on the film and that we needed all their work done by the end of the week. We took that time to write up the stories we wanted to convey to readers and asked Kieran to pull some quotes from the audio, which we'd sprinkle in liberally.

Eric and I were to meet again at the *Beit Midrash* the next morning, having spent the night turning over in our minds what we'd left behind in our notes. I was concerned that Eric would have second thoughts. It occurred to me that he might not even show up. After twenty minutes, I was convinced I'd been duped. No Eric. My mind raced through everything we'd said, written down, and filmed, to see if there was anything that he could use against me. *How could he do this to me? Once a punk, always a punk.*

"Hey, sorry I'm late," Eric's voice announced before he came into view. "The old me would've said I had car trouble, but being *here*," he swept his eyes around the *Beit Midrash*, "I'm not gonna lie. I overslept."

We shook hands.

I retrieved the notes from the file cabinet and displayed them on the table.

"I used the fire escape," he said proudly. I gave him a thumb's up. We worked for a while, making edits to our notes and exchanging comments quite civilly. After an hour or so, Rabbi Leviev and Francesca walked in with coffee and bagels. The rabbi asked if he could help. I suggested that he read our notes and then assume the posture of a confrontational ADA to ask us the most intimate details of what we *knew* as opposed to what we *suspected*. He played the part to such perfection that both Eric and I got rattled . . . which was the whole point of the exercise. He cautioned us against raising our voices or being defensive or pugnacious. "Respect!" he called out at certain times when he saw either one or both of us ready to blow our tops, especially when he continually intoned, "I don't believe you." This was a device, he noted, that was designed to make us dig deeper, to come up with additional corroborating evidence. It was infuriating to say the least. For a few moments, I forgot he was the man who'd guided my mother for so many years and had been a rock on the shore for her to throw a rope around when she thought she was drowning. By early afternoon, we were exhausted. It reminded me of him teaching me to read from the *Torah* with no punctuation—that might've been the real test of whether turning thirteen was the dividing line between child and adult. So, too, this exercise we were undertaking might turn out to be a dividing line which we might define as the point that separated our before from our after.

"We're ready," I said as we put our notes away.

"What's the next step?" Eric asked.

"I'll call our lawyer. Tell him we're ready for him to go to the DA."

"On the QT," Rabbi Leviev said. "No publicity, no fanfare. No one else can know about it. That's got to be part of the deal."

I was pumped. What I didn't say was: *We're going to blow the lid off more than one scandal.*

"And remember," the rabbi added, "they need you. You don't go in as supplicants. More like horse traders."

Eric left first, down the fire escape out back. Francesca and I left ten minutes later via the front door, after expressing sincere thanks to the rabbi.

We got stuck in traffic on the Grand Concourse. There must've been an accident. Cars were hardly moving. Francesca opened the window, turned off the radio and said, "I have to tell you something. It's going to be a shock."

By my rapid heartbeat, I assumed it had something to do with me. Or us. I barely managed an, "Okay," while rolling down my window to get a breeze, which would be good to cool me down if I got hot and sticky.

"I've been putting a puzzle together," she said, "and up until now, I couldn't finish it because I was missing a big, critical piece. I could make out the general outlines of what it was, but the hole in the center prevented me from knowing for sure what I was looking at."

I was a wreck.

"But now I'm pretty sure I've found what I was looking for. Do you remember a couple of nights ago when we were talking about your mother's relationship with Ike—all his running around? You said to her, 'Things had to have gotten better at some point. I mean, you had me.'"

"I do," I said, feeling so much better now that I knew the conversation wasn't going in a direction that would end up with an anvil dropping on my chest. "So, what's this all about?"

"Do you remember what your mother said in response?"

"No."

"She never answered your question."

"I'm sure she did."

"No, she didn't. What she said was, 'Eric grew up to be just like your father.'"

"Yeah, so what? He did. How's this your missing puzzle piece? And what's the puzzle supposed to look like, anyway?" I asked.

Francesca looked at me and touched my right shoulder.

"Jay, your mother didn't respond to your question because things never got better with your father. You know what I mean by the word *better*?"

I turned my head towards her.

"I think so," I said uncomfortably.

"Don't you recall how testy their conversation was when you overheard them on the wire at the Aronheimer mansion when your mother mentioned the rabbi?"

"What are you saying? That my parents stopped having sex and that my mother had an affair with Rabbi Leviev? Really? Isn't that a little far-fetched?"

"Jay, it's not just that your mother and Rabbi Leviev are a couple today. They've been a couple for more than twenty-three years."

"You know the specific date of all of this? What are you, backwards Nostradamus?"

She laughed. "That was a good one."

"You can tell *Nonna Ebrea* that his family was originally Jewish."

"Okay, you're funny and you know your history. Now, look at me. Square in the eye."

I turned to face her.

"Yoseph Leviev, your rabbi, the man you look up to, is your father. Your biological father. All these years, he's been a father to you, albeit at a distance. Hold the picture up of the rabbi in your mind. Now do it for Ike."

I didn't say anything.

"Jay, your sweetness, your way of looking at the world, your sense of right and wrong—it's from your mother and the rabbi. Not Ike. I can't find a single trace of Ike in you. Not your demeanor, your behavior, your outlook, your sense of duty. Why do you think your mother first thought the money that was sent to her came from Rabbi Leviev? Why don't you have the thick black hair that Eric and Ike have? Yours is closer to the thin sandy brown hair of the rabbi. You have the same blue eyes and slim build. And what about what we heard on the tape when Ike called 2-Cig? Huh? 'My bastard son says he's got tapes of everything.' He didn't say my conniving or asshole or piece-of-shit son. He said *bastard* son. It wasn't just a turn of phrase. Jay, sweetheart, the puzzle's completed, and you have to be able to recognize it."

My father wasn't my father. My rabbi was my father. My mother had an affair. Sure, in response to Ike's infidelities, I could understand that. I raced through dozens—hundreds—of interactions I'd had with Rabbi Leviev. I know how I never caught on: I wasn't looking for it. He was a wonderful teacher—a man who appreciated my family. I never suspected anything. Oh, now that Francesca gathered her clues so she could put the puzzle pieces together, I could see it. It made sense. When were they going to tell me? Why hadn't they? What would happen the next time I saw him? How would I approach him? Or my mother? Should I tell them I knew the truth?

Now I could understand Ike's contempt for me, his bastard son. It was his way of rebuking my mother.

29

YOU *SCHMUCK*, YOU JUST GOT CONVICTED BY A DIFFERENT COURT.

Francesca came back from Benjamins with a trench coat, fedora, tartan scarf, blue blazer, gray flannel slacks, and wing-tipped shoes. It was the costume that I wore when I arrived at the DA's office in the Bronx County Courthouse, looking like any young lawyer going to work. As an extra touch, she bought a pair of wire-rimmed glasses with no magnification. When I approached the large glass front door, I had difficulty imagining that the person staring back at me was me.

Eric and our attorney had arrived a few minutes before. As unusual as I looked, I was rocked back on my heels when I saw my brother's greatly shortened hair, neatly parted on the left. He, too, had on a pair of phony glasses, black and thick-framed, that made him look like one of the guys in school who used to walk around with slide rules in their shirt pockets. Speaking of which, he was wearing a blue button-down shirt tucked into pleated wool slacks with bright shiny pennies in the half-moon cut-outs on top of his loafers. He looked like he'd strolled over from the campus at Fordham or NYU.

He moved his hands from the top of his head down his body and said, "Francesca."

"Me too," I said.

Jonas Levinthal told us that he'd gone to the DA's office and informed an ADA that he represented two men who could blow the whistle on a scheme that reached into City government and included kickbacks and payoffs that affected hundreds if not thousands of people here in The Bronx. The ADA was unimpressed. Our attorney mentioned that his clients could name names, including politicians as well as owners of big businesses. The ADA perked up a bit at that. Our attorney told him that his clients were themselves in the thick of it and could provide first-hand information. That got the conversation rolling. Our attorney let it be known that a near-death beating and a murder covered up as a suicide would be exposed. The ADA left the room and came back with the DA himself. Our attorney then mentioned that each of his clients would confess to a crime connected to what had occurred, but only if the DA would agree to plea deals for each of them. The DA said that, in concept, he could agree to it, but he could only make an offer once he determined the value of the information we'd provide. It was on that basis that we were in the room that day.

Everything had been arranged in advance. The conference room had a portable screen set up in front of one wall. A projector was on the table. After a few minutes, the DA, accompanied by a young ADA, walked in and introduced themselves. After the exchange of names, the lights were shut off and the projector was turned on.

What they watched first was an edited version of the Saturday night rally at the RKO theater. Leo had Kieran Quigley's boys compress forty-five minutes into ten, hitting highlights of the speeches Francesca and I made. Next, we saw the interviews of the shopkeepers and residents of East 176th Street; this segment was cut down to five minutes in length. Last, we sat uncomfortably as my brother spoke to the camera at my grandmother's house. That segment was a little more than four unedited minutes. When the reel was finished, the lights were turned on and our attorney handed a ten page summary of what they'd just watched to the DA, with new background information included.

It'd been Rabbi Leviev's suggestion that we start with the films. "The impressions linger in your mind and can't be easily dislodged. That's why

I start out with colorful pictures of biblical events when teaching children about Jewish history. Do you remember, Jay?"

I did. I couldn't necessarily recall either the spoken or written words that accompanied them in books, but even now, at twenty-three, I could easily recall images of Abraham breaking his father's idols, of the Egyptian taskmaster beating a Hebrew slave, of Nachshon ben Aminadav, the first Hebrew to jump into the Red Sea, of Moses holding the Tablets, and so many more.

"These films will form the context of what you're going to tell the DA. Even if they have questions about the details, they'll keep coming back to the films."

He was right.

Our attorney had told us not to spill our guts at once. "Dribble it out, slowly. If you're not sure you're ready to dive into a new area, call for a recess and ask me. Now, here's the hardest part. There are going to be times when they ask you a question and after you answer it, they won't respond. Don't interrupt their silence! It's an age-old trick to get you to keep talking. I know how hard this can be. Most people are so uncomfortable with silence that they get verbal diarrhea. Trust me, silence is your best friend. Make them work for their answers. If they ask you a narrow question, give them a narrow answer. Don't introduce new subjects. Let them ask you about it."

He worked with us in the manner that Rabbi Leviev had done in the *Beit Midrash*.

He prepared us well.

I knew the overall strategy was working because their questions seemed to be taken from the notes they wrote down as they watched the films. We spent three hours with them before we broke for lunch. We'd gone over the basic outline of the scandal, mentioned each of the participants, explained how we knew what we told them—whether it was first or second hand—and if it was information gathered indirectly, why we were convinced of its reliability. We were very matter-of-fact. There was no emotion when we mentioned a specific person. Had we done otherwise, that might've suggested we had a motivation to color our statements, and we wanted them to get each piece of information without any bias.

It was during the afternoon session that we told them of the crimes we'd committed. Eric started with his beating of Leo. He recounted the story of how he'd lured Kieran Quigley into believing he was the made-up Steve Speigel of the *Herald Tribune*, which led to Nate smashing the car door into Leo, incapacitating him to become an easy mark for Eric. The look of chagrin on my brother's face cemented his sincerity in this process for me. He told them that he'd jimmied the lock on the door of the RKO so Bootsie could get in to meet Donatella. He insisted that he knew nothing of what they were going to do to him. "I figured, you know, a workover, like I gave Leo, that's all." I'm not sure they bought it, but it didn't matter very much as Eric could finger Donatella as the person who issued the death warrant. Eric was small potatoes, and his insight into everything else was good enough to inoculate him even if they didn't fully believe his story.

When it was my turn, I told them about the wiretapping, first at Spins, then at the Aronheimer mansion, and finally at Ike's home. They wanted to know who assisted me. I said I wouldn't tell them even off the record, and if they insisted to know more, I'd clam up and take my chances at a trial. They hemmed and hawed for a while, playing their best blustering approaches, but I never wavered. At one point, our attorney told them that if they persisted, I was walking out. He made this statement more dramatic by closing his notebook and slipping it into his briefcase, as if to say, *we're done here*. The other side backed off, knowing it was less important to find out who was on the technical side of the bugs than to get at the heart of what was on the tapes of those we'd wiretapped. Once they stood down, I began to tell them what I'd heard on the tapes. I was amazed at my ability to recall so much of what was said. It was as if I were reading from a script. Pages and pages of conversations came tumbling out. I could see the ADAs suck in their breath as I went beyond Alberto Giaquinto, Donatella, Nate, and Bootsie to Nicky Shark and Billy O'Boyle of the Department of Buildings, and then to the really big fish: Mayor Wagner, Carmine DeSapio, Horace Stoneham, and finally Robert Moses, whose name generated a pencil drop, looks of incredulity, and one "Holy shit." Rabbi Leviev had also given me the idea to use the blackboard to illustrate the names and connections between the men. So I did.

When I was finished, the DA asked me to hand over the tapes to corroborate what I told them.

"Not before we have an agreement," our attorney said.

"Then we'll get a warrant and go in on our own. We have enough here to take to a judge. And not just for your place. Your girlfriend's. Her brother's. Their parents. You name it; we'll find those tapes."

We'd anticipated this request, so at precisely the right time, I chimed in with, "Forget the warrant. I'll give you permission, right now, in writing. I'll go with you—get your overcoats on—and open the door to my place for you. You can have a swipe at every floorboard, unbolt the toilets, look to see if the mattresses have been scissored, tap against the soffits to listen if there's anything hidden within them, peek behind the medicine cabinet, do what you want. You won't find anything. And then we can go to any other places you want. Don't believe me?" I stood up. "Come on, let's go."

When I was finished with my histrionics, our attorney said, "Why don't we draw up the outline of a deal tomorrow, fill in the details in a day or two, and when we both sign, my client will turn over the tapes. Gentlemen?"

They looked at each other knowing they'd been boxed in, so they did what most everyone does in that position. They repeated the offer that our attorney had stated as if it were the first time those words had been used.

We knew how to play the game. "We agree," our attorney said.

They started to get up out of their seats.

"Oh, there's one more person I need to tell you about," I said.

"Can it wait?" the DA asked.

"I don't think so," I said. "There's a cop who's about to retire from the force. He's been working for Giaquinto Brothers on the side for more than thirty years. His reach into the PD is deep, and he's trusted by everyone on both sides, so the information he gets and then leaks to 2-Cig hits the yellow circle in the middle of the target. He knows everything about everybody. All roads lead to him. My brother here's going to try to get him to come speak with you."

The DA looked at Eric. "What's your angle, Bud? What makes you think you can turn him? And just as important, how do you keep him from blabbing to Alberto Giaquinto such that they don't put that yellow bullseye on *your* back?"

"He's our old man," Eric said.

"Jesus fucking Christ," the DA exclaimed. "Are you serious? What kind of dumbass dysfunctional family do you have? Are there any more perp relatives you want to tell us about?"

"No. That's it. Old man Ike," I said.

"When are you going to tell him what's up?" the DA asked Eric in an exasperated way.

"Saturday night."

"Christmas Eve? You're going to rain on his parade on the 24th? You two are some pair."

"Yeah, well, it's not a big day in the deVenezia family," our attorney said, telling the truth but side-stepping the fact that we didn't celebrate Christmas.

"Suit yourself," the DA said, standing up, the signal that the meeting was over. "See you chumps on Monday," he said to us, avoiding eye contact with our attorney, his message that we were the chumps he was referring to.

Eric and I walked out of the courthouse separately and with our heads down to prevent as much rain as possible from hitting our faces. We scampered to our cars parked near the intersection of 161st Street and Morris Avenue. As I turned north on Melrose, flashing headlights behind me indicated that Eric wanted to talk. I pulled over. He got out of his car and slipped into the passenger seat of mine. He looked like a frightened animal.

"Holy shit, Jay, you're not gonna believe this, but I think Sean saw me," he said, shifting his head around like a periscope.

"Where?"

"A few blocks back, walking to my car," he said, unconsciously rubbing a fist into a palm. "Oh fuck," he moaned.

"Are you sure?" I inquired. "I mean, through the rain and all, you might've *thought* you saw him, but it's not likely. Probably someone who looks like him."

"Bird's nest hair?"

I was amazed that my brother would use the same description as I did.

"White T-shirt? Red jacket with the collar up?" he continued. He fidgeted, then started up again. "Maybe, I don't know, I'm not 100 percent. Maybe seeing things, you know. Didn't want eye contact."

"Smart move," I said.

"Not smart enough. You know that Graciela the Gorgeous lives nearby?"

Sean had finally got the nerve to ask Carlos if it was okay to date his sister.

"Shit." I gathered my thoughts. "Listen," I said, trying to get him to focus. "Nothing we can do about it. Look, even if it was Sean, it doesn't mean he knows you were talking to the DA."

"Why else would we be at the courthouse, huh?"

"A traffic ticket, a permit, jury duty? Come on. Calm down. And for shit's sake, don't do anything stupid. If he does suspect something, he may try to call you to see if you're home. Get there as fast as you can. Go with the traffic ticket story. In any case, stick to the plan. Call Ike. Where're you going to suggest you meet with him?"

"Coogan's," he said, appearing to unwind a bit.

"Good choice. Let me know how it goes. And Eric?" I said, tapping his arm. "Relax. It's almost over. You're doing the right thing."

He nodded, exhaled in an exaggerated fashion, and got out of my car.

ON SATURDAY NIGHT the 24th, around eight o'clock, Ike walked into Coogan's. Eric got there a few minutes earlier. Both were soaked. A torrential rainstorm had started a few hours earlier that wouldn't let up until the next day. It was a good conversation starter.

"You're drenched," Eric said.

"It's like a hurricane out there. In December. What's next, a drought? Can you imagine, a drought in a city surrounded by water. What are you drinking?"

"Draught."

"Feeling better?"

Eric was waiting for this, the so-called excuse that had kept him away from Ike and the social club for a few days while he prepared for and then met with the DA.

"Yeah, much."

Throughout this warmup banter, Eric tried to assess whether Ike knew he'd been at the courthouse. He couldn't tell. Ike only showed his cards when he knew he had a winning hand.

Eric started out with a roundhouse right: that he'd been to the DA and was turning state's evidence on account of the fact that he'd been pulled into Bootsie's murder.

At first blush, Ike didn't seem fazed. "Better to come clean to get a reduced sentence. Otherwise, they'd jack you up if they ever found out."

"It's not just about that," Eric said. "I'm gonna tell them about beating up Leo. Better to admit that, too, and express remorse than have them come after me for that as well, don't you think?"

"Yeah, that makes sense," Ike said. Then silence. Eric remembered the attorney's advice to not fill the conversational void, so he drank sips from his stein and scanned the crowd, noticing girls he'd like to talk to later.

Ike finally said, "So that's it?"

"No, there's more. They want more."

"More what?"

"More about, you know, what goes on up on Arthur Avenue," Eric replied without mentioning 2-Cig or Donatella's names.

Ike now understood that Eric's going to the DA was not just about getting ahead of the issue of being linked to Bootsie's death. He seethed. He lowered his head, leaned in towards Eric and said, "You *schmuck*, you just got convicted by a different court. And now I'm involved. You dragged me into this shit? What the fuck happened? It's like I'm talking to Jay, for chrissakes. Better to not go back to the courthouse. You get what I'm saying?"

Eric reflected Ike's posture and spat back at him that he should consider speaking to the DA as well. "It's all gonna unravel—killing Bootsie, paying off Robert Moses and Nicky Shark, buying the stores and apartments on 176th Street at lowball prices and flipping them to the City under eminent domain, bribing Horace Stoneham. When it does, you'd be better off not standing next to this deluge when it comes crashing down on your head. And it will."

Ike didn't respond. He was probably shell-shocked. Eric got up to leave. There were no goodbyes, no bills dropped on the table. Eric put his coat and hat on and walked out. Ike followed him. As soon as they got outside, Ike blew his top. He screamed at Eric through the wind and rain, the two of them hurling insults at each other as they approached their cars. Ike pointed his finger at Eric and yelled that he was up shit's creek without a paddle. Eric smiled and said a paddle might be nice because it looked like the parking lot had turned into a river. Ike gave him the finger and got into his car. Eric saw him turn the key, but there was no response. Ike was fulminating that his car wouldn't start, despite repeated attempts to push the clutch to different levels while pumping the gas pedal. Eric made note of his rage—that it resembled what he'd seen when Ike would go after me. My brother walked back to Ike's car, held up his own key, and yelled that Ike could take his car. That he'd get a ride from one of his friends at Coogan's, and that he'd find someone later who had jumper cables. Ike wouldn't look at Eric.

"Listen, Dad, take the fucking key, drive home, get some rest, and I'll call you tomorrow." He stood still next to Ike's car, completely soaked, the key in his outstretched hand. When Ike didn't respond, he put the key on the hood of Ike's car and walked back into Coogan's. He assumed that, after a while, practicality would overcome Ike's pride and he'd drive Eric's car home. Which is what he did. Ike got into Eric's 1937 brown Dodge coupe. It started up just fine. He drove out of the parking lot, down past Coogan's Bluff and the Polo Grounds, across the Macombs Dam Bridge into The Bronx, traveling on East 161st Street—his old haunts as a patrolman—wended his way up Webster Avenue, then the Claremont Parkway, and finally turned left onto Crotona Avenue. The rain was as strong as it'd been in the parking lot at Coogan's. He stopped when he saw a woman trying to change a tire on the other side of the road, yelled over the top of the partially opened window that he was going to give her assistance, opened the door, swiveled his body out and then, well, he was crushed by a car speeding by, ripping the door clear off the hinges and dragging him underneath.

30

I TRIED MY BEST TO GIVE IT ALL IN CHRONOLOGICAL ORDER

Eric called as soon as he got home from Coogan's. It was after midnight. He told me about his conversation with Ike and gave me a graphic picture of Ike's stubbornness and anger in the parking lot.

"I don't think he's gonna come around, Jay. I'll let him sleep on it and give him a call in the morning. I've got to recharge his battery and get his car back to the house. I'll let you know."

A little before noon, Eric called again.

"Ike wasn't at his house. Neither was my car. I drove past the social club on Arthur Avenue to see if I could spot his car. No dice. He's MIA."

FRANCESCA AND I went for a late afternoon Christmas meal at her family's house in Tremont. Leo was there, along with Francesca's younger brother and sister. *Nonna Ebrea* was excited to see us all together. I'd decided not to discuss the visit to the DA's office. It was a family holiday, and I didn't want to overshadow the festivities. There'd be time enough in the next day or so to fill them in.

We were still having pre-meal drinks when Mrs. Casterella came over to tell me that my brother was on the line.

Eric was breathless. "Jay, I got a call from the cops."

"Oh no, did Ike rat us out?"

He was hyped up. "No. Listen. They found my car. Smashed. On Crotona Avenue. They called after finding my registration in the glove box."

"What about Ike?" I asked.

"He's dead, Jay." Eric's voice was trembling.

"He's dead? Was there blood in the car?" My first thought was suicide.

Eric was talking so fast it was hard to keep up. "What? No. No blood. There was a guy walking home, last night, he sees this girl, pretty girl in white, with blonde hair, standing in the rain, waving frantically, thinks she's Marilyn Monroe, with all the wind, her skirt is blowing up to her face, had a few too many for sure, anyway, this fella thinks it's a movie he tells the cops, so he starts to cross the street, waits for a car to pass, sees it stop, he steps off the curb, then *wham*! another car goes whizzing by and slams right into the guy getting out of the first car, opened the door, he guesses, to see if she's all right, the girl, Marilyn Monroe, the wind and rain as bad as it ever, and this second car comes out of nowhere and plows into the guy, and takes the door off the hinge, he's dead, Ike's dead, it was Ike who was going to help the girl, driving my car."

I told Eric to drive over to our mother's place in Riverdale. I said I'd meet him there. Francesca and I left a raucous, celebratory holiday party to attend a subdued get-together with family members who, although they didn't speak ill of the dead, didn't mention Ike much at all. I called Rabbi Leviev, who was kind enough to make the arrangements. The funeral would be held the following day. He joined us, as did Uncle Mickey along with his wife Ruti, and Gadi Yudakov with his wife Yudit. In a most desultory manner, my grandmother said we should recite *Kaddish*, which was the sole acknowledgment of the recently departed Ike. There were no fond remembrances. Even Eric refrained from conjuring up a story or two that would put Ike in the limelight in a manner that's typical at such family gatherings. We hadn't assembled by tradition. It was rather as if an autonomous behavior had kicked in, requiring us to meet simply because that was the way things were supposed to be done.

After the short prayer, my grandmother asked how it had gone at the DA's office. She was clearly amazed that Eric and I were getting along and that we'd managed to pull together—clearly out of self-interest—but in her eyes, she hoped this might be part of an earnest rapprochement. We gave them the lowdown. When we were all talked out, the doorbell rang, and we welcomed Leo. He asked if it was all right if he came to the *shiva* without bringing something for the host. My mother smiled—she was clearly touched—and never brought up the fact that the *shiva* would be after the funeral. Leo put his coat on a rack and set his umbrella and afternoon newspaper on the floor near the door. As soon as he walked into the living room, Eric approached him and gave a truly heartfelt apology. It happened so fast that at the outset, I could sense that Leo was dumbfounded and momentarily didn't realize who Eric was. Then, after honing in on his voice, he realized it was the guy who'd assaulted him. Leo accepted the apology in a reserved manner. There was no doubt in my mind that if the setting had been different, he might not've been so polite.

My grandmother served coffee and Entenmann's cakes (an ever-present staple at her house), after which Leo excused himself, wanting to get back to his family's celebration. I walked him to the door and reached down to collect his umbrella and newspaper. I unfolded the *New York Mirror* and was shocked to see a picture on the front page of Eric's 1937 brown Dodge coupe with a missing front door on Crotona Avenue. The headline said, "Cop KO'd By Hit And Run." Under the photo it said, "Two Witnesses, No Suspect" and "Turn to page 4." There were other photos there, with credits to Nicky Shark. The story said, in part, "According to Piero Cutrupi, he saw the man who we now know as Ike deVenezia, a cop who worked out of the 46th precinct in The Bronx, get sideswiped by a passing car as he was trying to come to the aid of Veronica DeGiglio, who'd suffered the misfortune of a flat tire during the tumultuous rainstorm that hit the City on Saturday night."

I mouthed, *Say good fucking farewell to Ike deVenezia.*

"Francesca, Leo, Eric, come with me, outside, please," I said urgently.

I closed the front door and read the report in the paper to them. There was astonishment on all their faces.

Leo: "How the fuck did Nicky Shark just happen to be there in a storm to take pictures on that particular street on Christmas Eve?"

Eric: "Piero Cutrupi is one of 2-Cig's runners. An old dimwit. Would've been hit by the car himself if 2-Cig asked him to stand in the street. Jesus Christ."

Francesca: "You're not going to believe this. Do you know who Veronica DeGiglio is? Huh? Get this: She's 2-Cig's granddaughter. Donatella's daughter! A Giaquinto. DeGiglio's her married name. She was in my class. She wasn't there by chance, boys. And, oh, the paper may have called her a Marilyn Monroe type, but to everyone at school, she was the second coming of Veronica Lake. What guy wouldn't slow down or stop to lend her a hand?"

Me: "Eric, you know what this all means, don't you?"

Eric: "That they *intended* to kill Ike?" We didn't answer, preferring for him to let the conclusion sink in. "Not an accident? Murder? Oh, man. You're not serious. I can't believe 2-Cig's that big of a scumbag. Bootsie's one thing. But Ike?"

None of us moved a muscle.

"Hey, what's with the looks? You're saying it was payback for us, me, going to the DA? They *trailed* him from Coogan's? They knew the route he'd take home? Could count on him, of all people, being the Good Samaritan? Un-fucking-believable."

I spoke up.

Me: "Eric, they had no intention of killing Ike."

Eric: "There's too many coincidences, Jay, for it to be anything else but murder."

Me: "Oh, it was murder all right. But they got the wrong guy."

Eric: "Who? Who were they going after?"

We stared at him. He looked at each of us. We didn't say a word. After a few seconds, Eric said, "No way. Come on. They were gonna kill me? *Me? What?*"

Leo: "Nicky Shark was *there* with a camera?"

Francesca: "The damsel in distress just *happened* to be 2-Cig's granddaughter?"

Leo: Piero Cutrupi *coincidentally* was on the scene to tell the cops what happened?

Me: "*Your* car?"

Eric: "They were after *me*? Oh my God. Holy shit. Me! They wanted *me* dead. Those bastards. Bootsie I get. But *me*?" With each outburst, his voice got louder. He went from morose to manic in a second. The old Eric then appeared in a flash: "It must've been that prick Sean who saw me leave the Court building. I'll kill that son-of-a-bitch."

I put a hand on each of Eric's arms and told him he had to get it together. "Take a deep breath . . . or two," I said. "When you come back inside and everyone sees you on fire, it's going to scare them. Okay?"

I suggested that Francesca go back to her parents' house with Leo.

As soon as Eric and I re-entered the living room Gavi said, "What's up, Jay?"

"Are you all in trouble?" Uncle Mickey asked.

"It's in your faces, your eyes," my mother said.

"Those bastards were trying to *kill* me," Eric shouted.

So much for my influence.

Everyone gasped.

What's the expression? The horse has left the barn? The ship has sailed? I knew asking Eric to sit wouldn't work. He was fidgety, walking around the room, not making eye contact, craning his neck, blowing air out of his cheeks, pounding his right fist into his left palm. It was time to tell the family what was going on. I needed to take control before Eric blurted out something that would frighten them even more. I wanted to tell them the truth, to be sure, but in a way that was orderly and logical, and delivered in a manner that would convey a feeling that not all was lost.

I gave them the play-by-play as if I were imitating Russ Hodges calling the Giants' games over WMCA. It went on for more than an hour. Occasionally, Eric would chime in with a comment or a correction like a one-person Greek chorus. Uncle Mickey asked for clarification here and there, Gavi corroborated a few of my anecdotes about what was going on at Spins, and my mother made a few statements that were in the guise of questions, such as, "You're not in trouble because of that, are you?" I tried my best to give it all in chronological order and spent a considerable amount of time explaining what went on at the DA's office before hitting them over the head with the near-certain view that Ike's death was not only not an accident, but it was a murder and Eric was the intended victim.

To say there was consternation was an understatement. My mother bounced up from her chair, walked around the room, and repeated several of the things that I'd said. My grandmother was shaking. She kept asking my mother to sit. My mother ignored her. Gavi offered to assist us in any way he could, which we interpreted to mean with a contribution for legal expenses. I was touched and told him so. Uncle Mickey said he rued the day he'd introduced Ike to his sister, only to be admonished by Aunt Ruti to apologize to Eric and me, which he quickly did: "I didn't mean I wished you two wouldn't have been born." We both went up to him and put our arms around his shoulders.

Rabbi Leviev stood and got our attention. "Boys," he said, which made us both smile as we were usually referred to as *young men* or *fellas*, "you're in a tough spot, and how you deal with this tricky issue may have a disproportionate impact on your lives. I'm not just thinking about how a legal case can wind its way through the courts and how you'll be treated. It's also about the two of you. Together. Or apart. How you interact with each other in the coming days may define your relationship forever. Think about one another each time you have to make a decision. Think about how you'll view what you say or do now from the vantage point of ten or twenty years from now. Be careful not to divulge something you'll later regret. That can break a link in the chain, and trying to repair it is, well, nearly impossible."

It was based on these wise words that I decided it wasn't the time to tell Eric either about the snowball fight or the fact that we were half-brothers. Those things would have to wait.

31

SHE BECAME SULLEN WITHIN A SHORT PERIOD OF TIME

The City Council agreed to offer a substantial amount of money under eminent domain for the people on 176th Street under the proviso that there'd be no announcement for a few months. There was no formal resolution. It was kept hush-hush so that 2-Cig could acquire the properties on the cheap. The Department of Buildings approved the plans for the route of the new road to go through that street. When the time came, Mayor Wagner and Robert Moses held a press conference announcing the approval of the route for the Cross Bronx Expressway. The Bronx Borough President, Jimmy Lyons, was given the task of finding alternative opportunities in The Bronx for the stores and apartment buildings that would be razed. Photos of 2-Cig and his cronies taken by Nicky Shark at the social club on Arthur Avenue appeared in the *New York Mirror* under the headline, "Jobs to Spring Up in Bronx Building Boom by Spring!" Horace Stoneham signed a contract with Giaquinto Brothers to demolish the Polo Grounds and erect a new stadium for the Giants near Fort Tryon Park. The announcement caused Walter O'Malley, owner of the Dodgers, to threaten to sue the City unless he also got a prime location within Brooklyn for a new stadium.

Owners of stores and buildings on 176th Street began to sell their properties to 2-Cig's agents. The Pirozzis found a vacant store a half dozen blocks away. It was on a side street with little foot traffic. Their restaurant suffered. The Scattennatos were excited at first because they found a bigger place where the rent was cheaper, but because they weren't known in their new neighborhood, few people frequented their store. The Casterellas didn't find a place that could accommodate their hardware store as well as separate apartments for themselves and *Nonna Ebrea*. Mr. Casterella managed to find an apartment with an extra room for *Nonna Ebrea* a block away. With neither friends nor the occasional "*Ciao*, Daniela" shouted her way, she became sullen within a short period of time. Unable to find a suitable location for his business, Mr. Casterella took a job managing a hardware store in the Eastchester section of The Bronx thirty blocks away, which was nearly an hour commute by bus. The Benjamins established a new clothing store on Centre Avenue in New Rochelle. It was smaller and catered to a very different crowd. They did well financially but missed the interactions of their neighbors from The Bronx. They gave the proceeds from the sale of the theater to a foundation they created to help those displaced by the expressway.

Even before the last tenants vacated their apartments on 176th Street, Giaquinto Brothers' construction workers—along with their dump and cement trucks, excavators, backhoes, cranes with attached wrecking balls, and pneumatic drills—showed up to begin the process of tearing down buildings to make way for the Cross Bronx Expressway. There was no fanfare. No ceremony. No speeches. No city officials wearing hardhats with their hands on shovels, bending down for the obligatory photo that customarily makes its way into the papers and scrapbooks.

There was, however, a cocktail reception at Robert Moses's brownstone on East 92nd Street, where he was joined by Mayor Wagner, Carmine DeSapio, Horace Stoneham, Alberto Giaquinto, and Tom Collins. They indulged on canapés and drank 1945 Veuve Clicquot Ponsardin Vintage Brut champagne brought up by servants from the cellar underneath the first floor. Nicky Shark recorded the festivities with photos of the attendees and the label of the champagne bottles which appeared the next day in the *New York Mirror*.

32

...HE COULDN'T PICK HIM OUT OF A LINEUP

The trial of Donatella Giaquinto and the two goons for the murder of Bobby (Bootsie) Albanese attracted the attention of every newspaper, radio station, and TV channel in and around New York City. The scrum around the courthouse steps was populated by dozens of jostling photographers and news reporters with microphones and tape recorders, each one screaming to snag a snippet of conversation that he or she could feed to the hundreds of thousands of subway strap-hangers, train commuters, store owners, shoe-shine stand sitters, waitresses on break, and stay-at-home news junkies, eager to watch the parade of the City's high rollers, a favorite pastime of the other half, whose interest was in seeing them all fall.

Because of the information that my brother and I supplied to the DA, the people parade included Alberto Giaquinto, Robert Moses, Horace Stoneham, Nicky Shark, Carmine DeSapio, Billy O'Boyle, Tom Collins, and Nate.

I agreed to testify knowing my fate in advance. My plea deal was granted under the condition that my testimony wouldn't differ from what I'd previously told the court. I made a point of making eye contact with each of the defendants and other witnesses who'd be called to testify. Rabbi Leviev's advice was to show strength through resolve, which would find favor with the jury when they went into deliberations regarding the defendants' crimes.

I was raked over the coals by the various defense counsels. Well coached by Jonas Levinthal, I kept my cool. When they brought up my "sweetheart deal" and used it to imply that I could lie without consequences, I simply admitted my guilt and expressed remorse. My attorney told me to hold my head high when I stepped down from the chair. "Walk with an air of confidence, it'll support the court beat writers who're more likely to give you a favorable report in the court of public opinion." That was the easy part. What no one could see was what had me churning inside—the fear of retribution from 2-Cig or one of his cronies. I was sure it was going to happen; I just didn't know when or how it could come.

My brother had a tougher time. He was ratting on men with whom he'd worked for many years. He squirmed uncomfortably, looking like Harry Houdini trying to get out of his suit and tie before drowning in a glass booth filled with water. The perspiration that soaked through his collar caused him to make ungainly neck movements which the jurors could've viewed as a guilty tic. But he pulled through, giving extraordinary details of conversations that illustrated the bribery schemes, kickbacks, loan sharking, and beatings that led up to Bootsie's murder. His takedowns were countered by the defense as fantasies to cover up his own participation in Bootsie's death. Eric's admission that he jimmied the door to the RKO theater placed him near the scene of the crime, but unlike Donatella and the two goons, his fingerprints weren't found inside the theater or on the roof. He also got into the record that Ike's death was likely a murder and that it was he who was the intended target for turning state's evidence.

Nate's dark blue suit and tie, absent his ever-present porkpie hat, and nearly shaved head startled even Eric as he approached the witness chair. He was calm, confident, and contrite. He explained that his time at Spins was related to his love of music. He paid tribute to Gavi for featuring what the white kids called "race tunes." Nate knew he couldn't lie on the witness stand about being Bootsie's agent in the scheme to buy properties from the people on 176th Street, especially since he could easily be identified as the person who gave out the hundred-dollar bills. But he denied knowing anything about what happened to Bootsie and was saved by Eric's insistence that he made Nate keep quiet so Donatella wouldn't know he was with my brother in Booth 18 the day he got the instructions. Nate insisted politely to the DA that he wasn't there with Eric, so it came down to a "he said, he said" confrontation in which the DA was sure Nate was lying but had no third-party evidence to press charges. In any event, the DA was looking for the big fish, so he wasn't pressed beyond establishing that Bootsie was skimming from 2-Cig—the motive for his murder. After Nate stepped down from the chair, he walked back to the gallery, where Gavi motioned for him to come over. When he bent down, Gavi whispered to him, which was reciprocated by a nod. Then the two of them shook hands. I found out later that Nate asked Paddy Sean to get a message to 2-Cig that Nate was through being part of Eric's crew but would keep everything he knew under wraps. 2-Cig never made a move on Nate, fearing a race war if he did.

Nicky Shark explained his presence on Crotona Avenue the night Ike was killed by claiming he'd given a ride to Piero Cutrupi who lived in the neighborhood. Being captured on the wrong side of the camera was an uncomfortable circumstance for Nicky, and he told anyone who'd listen afterwards that the photographs of him coming and going to the courthouse caught him in unflattering lights, single shots where his mouth was caught in a snarl, his eyes were partially closed, or his body was slouched in such a way as to make him look ape-like. Unsurprisingly, this had no impact on how he went about his job photographing others. Although he was intimately involved as a messenger that connected the dots between Robert Moses, Billy O'Boyle, and Alberto Giaquinto, he wasn't charged with any crimes. No one was going to rat him out given his vast trove of photographs that no one wanted to see the light of day.

Billy O'Boyle, the head of the Department of Buildings, was asked by the mayor to take early retirement after he testified that he couldn't recall meetings with Nicky Shark despite his secretary's logs that indicated they met in his office a half a dozen times.

On redirect, Nicky Shark said that if the meetings did occur—which he couldn't swear to—they were simply about photographing new construction for the Department of Buildings. Nobody believed him. Of course, the *New York Mirror* renewed his contract.

2-Cig acknowledged that Donatella was a frequent guest at the social club on Arthur Avenue, but insisted he knew nothing of Donatella's activities outside of the club. His testimony was riddled with inconsistencies. He claimed he didn't understand English very well and insisted on having an Italian translator in court. Despite constant battering by the DA, there was no evidence to link him directly to Bootsie's murder. Fortunately for him, despite enormous pressure, Donatella didn't squeal.

Donatella didn't do herself any good by saying she'd never been to Spins (in direct contrast to the testimonies Eric, Gavi, and I gave) and saying she was out of town on the night that Bootsie was killed without providing any corroborating evidence. Her testiness didn't sit well with the jury. The press turned her into a caricature of a mafia queen.

Carmine DeSapio testified that he was barely acquainted with Alberto Giaquinto and knew nothing of 2-Cig's activities regarding the Cross Bronx Expressway or the Polo Grounds projects. No one from the City Council was called to discuss interactions with him. He came to court each day in a different, handsome Brooks Brothers outfit. He was not charged with any crimes.

Tom Collins erupted with indignation when asked about a fifty-thousand-dollar payment to Alberto Giaquinto, shouting at the DA to show him the proof. Because it'd been a cash payment made in small bills from what he'd skimmed off of the Hibernians dues over the years, it couldn't be traced. "I swear to the Holy Virgin that I've done nothing illegal in all my life," he said, and accused the DA of creating trumped-up charges against law-abiding Irish men. No honest person in the courtroom believed anything he said, but in the absence of paper trails, his testimony stood the test of time.

When Robert Moses was called to the witness stand, he made no eye contact with the judge, the DA, or the jury. He seemed to be staring at an invisible mirror in front of him when he answered questions, as if he was assuring that his expression sent a clear message that the whole affair was beneath his dignity. His responses to the DA often began with, "To your question regarding . . ." a dismissive tactic that all but infuriated the interrogator. Robert Moses knew, however, that Ike's death buried the only trace of the fifty grand he'd received. He left the stand, didn't acknowledge his attorney's motion to resume his seat in the gallery, and walked out the courtroom door, never breaking stride or turning his head. Neither his proposed Rye-Oyster Bay Bridge nor the Cross Manhattan Expressway was ever built.

"SMALL CONSOLATION," I said wearily to my mother and Rabbi Leviev on a phone call when I heard the news that the City Council nixed the Cross Manhattan Expressway before I headed off to jail, knowing that at that very moment, a scar was being ripped through the heart of Tremont.

"Actually, it's a big win," the rabbi said. "You, Francesca, her siblings, the boys from Fordham—and don't forget Eric, regardless of his motives—all of you can take pride in what you did. You put a chink into the automatic machine that's fueled by money—payoffs, bribes—that heretofore would've rolled over other neighborhoods, consequences for the residents be damned. Stand tall, young man, and give a hearty cheer."

When I hung up, Francesca asked, "What did he say?"

I recounted the conversation.

"Well," she said, rising to her feet, "I think we should."

"Should what?"

"Give a hearty cheer. Come on, hepcat," she said, extending a hand to me, urging me to stand up. "Now, instead of holding our thumbs under our noses and blowing through our tongues like over-tired dogs, do this." She raised both of her arms straight up in the air, splayed her fingers, waved them, and moved about in a jouncy manner. My first impression was that she was simulating a St. Vitus dance. Although it did look a bit deranged, it was offset by her incandescent smile that was so infectious I began to imitate her. Excited that I'd dropped my guard, she exclaimed louder and louder "Yeahs!" in which I joined, allowing myself to express some of our triumph.

Laughing uncontrollably, she pushed against my shoulders and we fell to the sofa, her kisses interspersed with some words I couldn't decipher.

"What?" I struggled to say.

She mumbled something that was impossible to understand with her tongue inside my mouth. She said it again. Nothing. Finally, I moved my head back and said, "What are you trying to say?"

"A new cheer," she said. "Only for us."

"What will we call it?" I asked playfully.

"The *new* Bronx cheer," she said. "For the good times." She looked down at me with a changed expression. "But listen to me Joogan deVenezia: We keep the old one too."

HORACE STONEHAM INFORMED Mayor Wagner before the trial that the Giants wouldn't consider building a new stadium near Fort Tryon Park, since the maelstrom created by local community activists in northern Manhattan—emboldened by the actions of the residents of 176th Street in The Bronx—caused the City Council to reject subsidies and work permits for any construction that abutted the park. On the stand, Stoneham acknowledged that he met Alberto Giaquinto "once or twice" at the Polo Grounds and noted that he couldn't pick him out of a lineup—an unfortunate turn of phrase that gossip said cost him a large donation to 2-Cig's social club on Arthur Avenue.

Donatella and the two goons were convicted of murder. They were given life sentences and were transferred to the prison at Attica.

My brother wasn't charged with any crimes.

Mayor Wagner wasn't called to testify.

Within a week after the conclusion of the trial in April of 1956, I was sent to Alden. Upon my release in July, I began to see Dr. Silverman and the parole officer on a weekly basis.

I SERVED AS BEST MAN at the wedding of my mother and Rabbi Yoseph Leviev on Tuesday, September 18, 1956.

33

I'D LIKE TO MEET THE GUY SOMETIME, TO SHOW HIM MY GRATITUDE

"We have to talk," I said to my mother over the phone. "And the 'we' includes Rabbi Leviev." We arranged to meet for dinner at her apartment in Riverdale. As soon as Francesca and I walked in, the rabbi handed me a photo of a young boy about eight or nine years old—the same age I was when I stole the money from the blue duffel bag. He looked like me but with clothes I imagined street urchins from the Lower East Side wore during the years before the Great War. I tried to recall wearing something similar in a school play or as a costume for Purim or Halloween but drew a blank. As I was examining the picture, my mother handed me another. This one was clearly of me from 1942. I held the two photos side-by-side.

"So now you know," my mother said.

I embraced my father. We all cried softly, the kind of emotional response that invariably ends in sniffles, then in laughter. During dinner, I said that I was going to talk to Eric about my biological father, sooner rather than later. My mother asked if I wanted to do it alone or if she should be there as well. At first, I thought it would be best to talk to him without an audience or an entourage but then reconsidered. She might be able to answer questions that I couldn't. She was pleased. It was then that I told her about what really happened during the snowball incident and expressed a sincere apology, which I wasn't sure Eric would accept.

My mother was startled by this revelation. "You lied to me," she said. "Tricked me. Put your brother in the worst light."

"I'm ashamed of myself," I said.

"It's a *shanda*," my grandmother said.

"I've been trying to make it up to him," I said.

"I'm not sure anything you do now can offset the harm," my mother said.

She was right.

In leading up to what I was going to say to Eric, I pondered how I'd react if the roles had been reversed. I was pretty sure I would've had mixed emotions: pleased to find out the details of a shattering event, but also vexed by how my life might've turned out differently if the truth had been revealed at the time. The more distance I had between the snowball incident and the present, the more shame I felt.

A week later, my mother, brother, and I met at the *Beit Midrash*. We didn't tell Eric the reason for the get-together. I had coffee and Danish spread on the table. After a minute or so of chit-chat, my mother told him that I was his half-brother, and I revealed the ugly truth about the snowball fight. It was difficult to say which overwhelmed him more. There was no belligerence on his part. He said both pieces of news came as a shock. He was considerate to both of us, asked a number of key questions, and thanked us for telling him the truth. He gave my mother the first hug she'd received from him in so many years she couldn't remember. I told Eric that I was surprised that he wasn't outwardly angry with me.

"For you to have had such venom towards me, means I must've been so nasty to you. I can't imagine . . ."

We knew we'd failed one another and were humiliated with our behavior. We both apologized. Our mother cried.

Although these exchanges had taken only about a half hour, we were spent. I told Eric that I'd like to have some time with him in the coming months to get a better feel for what went on with Ike and 2-Cig. He offered to talk without preconditions. We agreed to start within a few days. I felt it was necessary to end on an upbeat note, so I asked them to save the next

Saturday night for a celebration, ostensibly to mark the end of my obligations to meet with the parole officer. What I didn't say, not wanting to pre-empt myself, was that it'd be the night Francesca and I would announce our engagement.

AFTER A SHORT *HAVDALAH* service on Saturday evening, we asked everyone to clear their calendars for Sunday, January 6, 1957, for our wedding. What we didn't tell them was that shortly after the ceremony, we were going to move away from New York. I was concerned that 2-Cig would seek retribution. I had no specific inklings; it was a hunch, knowing he might simply be waiting for the right opportunity. My fear wasn't without foundation. After all, I'd seen what had been done to Leo and Bootsie, and what had been planned for my brother. I was on edge. I took extra precautions, including making sure I left Spins with others, varying my comings and goings, and eventually packing heat. That'd been Gavi's idea. Where would I get one? Surely Nate or Sean would be good sources, but with loose lips, 2-Cig might find out, and that would've defeated the whole purpose.

"Why don't you ask Carlos?" Francesca suggested. "He was Bootsie's apprentice, and after they killed him, Carlos lost all loyalty to 2-Cig, that's for sure."

Carlos gave me a derringer, some .45 ACP rounds, and the address of a shooting gallery in the basement underneath a bodega not too far from where I lived. Each time I walked in, I was Corporal deVenezia, back on the firing range, snapping off rounds at imaginary reds, winning the Cold War single-handedly.

Of course, I told none of this to my mother. It was hard enough to deliver the news that we were moving away; mentioning that I felt the need to carry a concealed weapon would've destroyed the illusion that the affairs that had resulted in me being sent to jail had been buried in the past. She put up a brave front when Francesca and I told her we'd be leaving the City.

"I understand. It's for the best, you need to live your own lives," she said gamely, a façade that came naturally to her. Having lived with so many disappointments, she'd perfected the art of masking her true feelings.

While we were excited about planning new beginnings, we weren't immune to sadness about leaving our families behind. I called Dr. S.

"Moving away is really hard," I said, soon after introducing Francesca.

"My parents say everything's fine," Francesca said, "but I can tell it isn't. They weren't in favor of me moving to Manhattan a few years ago, let alone miles away to another city. It'll be equally hard on us too."

"Decisions have consequences that impact both sides of the ledger," Dr. S. said.

"It's tough to quantify the pluses and the minuses," I said.

"It's not an arithmetic exercise that leads to a definitive answer," Dr. S. replied. "It's about feelings and emotional well-being. For them," by which she meant our parents, "and the two of you. I suggest you evaluate your feelings every day. At some point, you'll come to the realization that you're either comfortable with the move . . . or you're not. In either case, you'll then know what's the best thing for you to do. If you leave New York, you'll figure out how to accommodate your families as best you can. And you know what? They'll be fine. Disappointed that they won't be able to see you at the drop of a hat? Of course. But they'll be happy for you. Genuinely."

THE DECISION WAS MADE easier when Gavi told us that he'd been contacted by a law firm that represented music companies to see if he wanted to go into a music store partnership with organizations in Detroit, Nashville, or San Francisco, where rhythm and blues, country, and folk music centers were beginning to develop as alternatives to the New York Tin Pan Alley scene.

Francesca enthusiastically opted for San Francisco. "It'll be a gas," she said.

"We have to swear everyone to secrecy," I said.

I bought a two-tone green and white 1955 DeSoto Firedome station wagon which could accommodate all of our clothes when the back seat was folded down. The only other items we brought were Alanphant and the derringer, along with some ammo.

At the outset, we took a circuitous route, driving north towards Albany, frequently pulling over on the Taconic Parkway, watching carefully to see if we recognized any cars or noticed anyone slowing down to stare at us. For the most part, we talked of the future. Although outwardly confident, I was apprehensive, and suspected that Francesca was as well, despite her mask of self-assuredness. During one of those interminably long stretches across the Plains on Route 66, I fixated on what my brother had said when the Fordham boys were filming us: *It didn't have to be this way.*

"It didn't," I said to her, "in no small part because of what I'd set in motion as a result of the snowball fight when I was a kid."

She brought me back to the here and now. "You know, your mother told me that when Eric said that, it overwhelmed her. Truly. Motherly instinct may be the strongest force in the world. And it took her oldest son's lament to bring it out."

AS SOON AS I SPOTTED the sign on the 101 that indicated we were in San Francisco, I looked over to Francesca and said what I'd been thinking about since we crossed over the George Washington Bridge, "No more Joogan. It's time. Jay. Only." She raised her left hand and let it drop on my shoulder, keeping it there until we parked.

Gavi arranged for us to open a small music store in North Beach, in the same area as the hungry i, The Purple Onion nightclub, and City Lights Bookstore. We needed a name. We thought Alanphant would've made for some interesting press, but it was too cutesy. Spins SF meant nothing to people in the Bay Area, and adding the SF made it seem to be an appendage of something else, so we discarded that idea as well.

"A name has to have meaning to both the proprietors and the public, although it can say different things to each," Francesca said late at night when we were discussing every aspect of how we'd set up and run the place. We attempted to find a word or phrase that would resonate with us and be understandable to the public. During the back and forth, Francesca said that since we were in the same neighborhood as other club venues, we might call our place Hop, Skip, and Jump. "There's movement, excitement, it'll draw folks in." I liked the originality and musicality of it, but it didn't seem to have a connection to us.

"True that we're only a stone's throw away from those other places—"

"That's it!" She shot up in bed. "A Stone's Throw. The 'o' in Stone will be a black rock and the 'o' in Throw should be a pure-as-white snowball."

We established individual booths just like at Spins and catered to the new folk sound exemplified by the Kingston Trio, who frequently performed in the area, along with our favorite comedians and social commentators like Mort Sahl, Lenny Bruce, and Tom Lehrer. Posters on our walls were signed by Allen Ginsberg, Elise Cowen, Lawrence Ferlinghetti, Joyce Johnson, Jack Kerouac, Carolyn Cassady, and Neal Cassady. It was the Beat Generation, and we were drum-rolled into it.

Within a year, A Stone's Throw expanded to include an intimate performance area in the basement, where Francesca introduced acts with a special élan that helped to create a group of regular attendees, such that it became a kind of club for the 'in crowd.'

Leo gave us the idea of projecting images onto screens that we could hang on the walls during performances, which created a sensation in the press when a critic came to review a star headliner. Leo had shipped out two improved versions of the Eastman Kodak 8 mm movie projector. Francesca convinced Tom Lehrer to open the first show with associated images, and when he sang "I Wanna Go Back to Dixie," it was accompanied by scenes from *The Birth of the Nation*—of Klansmen and white actors playing African Americans in caricature. Rather than just being a clever and witty song, it brought Lehrer's acid social commentary to the fore, which was the start of turning a disparate group of performers into a community of activists who would use the stage to educate as well as entertain audiences.

The contrast with my life in New York was stark. It was as if I'd shed the skin of young adulthood and watched a new covering emerge—a representation of a reinvention that could mask the emotional baggage that might've plagued me if I hadn't moved away. That can happen. Seeing the same people and places can cue reactions that are difficult to suppress. It's easy to fall into patterns and never find an alternative path to enjoy new experiences. It can be debilitating.

We experienced New York through Sunday long-distance phone calls with our families. The only outward manifestation of traces of New York for both Francesca and me were in our accents and desires to be part of a community that wouldn't be torn apart. Towards that end, we created a *chavurah* that met on Saturday mornings in the performance venue in the basement. Some initially thought the invitation to be part of a Jewish group from a deVenezia and a Casterella was an extension of Francesca's popular humorous introductions of performers. It took some cajoling to convince a few that this wasn't an act. We started out with a few obviously Jewish neighbors. As word expanded throughout the immediate vicinity and to the local performers, it grew to become a close-knit group of almost thirty people. As the first High Holy Days approached, we sought out a student rabbi from the Reform movement's Los Angeles campus to conduct services for our eclectic group ranging from those brought up in Orthodox homes to those whose Judaism was a fossilized relic that needed to be unearthed from decades of neglect.

I CALLED LEO ON APRIL 15, 1958, after Francesca and I went to a baseball game at Seals Stadium. "It was hard to believe we were watching the *San Francisco* Giants play the *Los Angeles* Dodgers. It took some getting used to seeing the Giants without the distinctive NY logo on their uniforms. But I have to tell you, I was pleased that I could watch the game concentrating only on baseball and not the comings and goings of who was sitting in the stands with the owner."

In the late spring, Gavi came to visit. He told us that Nate was doing an excellent job as the manager of Spins. I'd spoken to Nate after he first learned he got the offer, and could hear the enthusiasm in his voice as he talked about his new responsibilities. He also mentioned that he'd called Leo and apologized profusely for his part in the assault. Leo said it sounded genuine, so he accepted his apology, and told me they'd even seen each other at Coogan's, where they'd shared a few beers and reminiscences.

Gavi asked if I'd had any communication with Eric.

"No," I said. "We'd spent a lot of time together in New York after I got out of jail, during which he gave me the lowdown on conversations he'd been part of and others that he'd heard secondhand. In great detail. I took copious notes. We said goodbye. Good luck and all that. I reached out via letter when I moved out here."

"How did he respond?" Gavi asked.

"I never heard back. It was returned with no forwarding address, and his phone was disconnected.

"Were you surprised?"

"That he flew the coop? Not really. If you think *I* was concerned about payback from 2-Cig, imagine what was going through Eric's mind, considering they'd tried to kill him once already. I doubt he's in New York. He's probably as far away as I am and using an alias. I have no idea if we'll ever see each other again. Maybe it was unrealistic to expect anything else. We were estranged practically our whole lives and came together out of mutual self-interest. You remove that catalyst and there's nothing to grab onto to establish a relationship. You know what? You can ask me again in ten or twenty years. Who knows what could happen. We may run into each other. Accidentally or on purpose. And if not? Well, at least I can take solace in remembering our last interactions."

"Ending with a good thought," he said.

What bothered me was that it was indeed likely to be the end. He wouldn't have the opportunity to read my 'Dear Bud' letter. I've kept it in the top drawer of my desk. Every once in a while, I take it out and read it, as if my brother were beside me, imagining he can hear my words. It gives me comfort.

It started out as a short, intimate apology, coupled with a plea to stay connected, somehow, even if not face-to-face. I also wanted to tell him about the last time I was at Coogans before I moved out west. As soon as I walked through the door, the bartender made a beeline for me, his hug a pretense to whisper to me that Paddy Sean was in the men's room, and it would be best if he didn't see me. I'd always had suspicions that Sean really had spotted Eric coming out of the DA's office and had ratted out my brother to 2-Cig. And, given our testimony at the trial, Sean would be a hero to the guys at the Arthur Avenue social club if he managed to whack either one of us. As the bartender walked me towards the door, he told me Sean had been asking around, trying to pin down Eric's whereabouts. According to the bartender, he'd fended Sean off by saying, in his musical lilt, "I've missed the oul' chum. It's been a while. He seems to have dropped out of sight, he has."

I THOUGHT ABOUT WHAT *I'd* missed, *my* old chums at Coogan's, the kids at Spins, the many people I'd gotten to know from 176th Street, the interactions with Leo and the Fordham boys, and my sessions with Dr. Silverman. Memory flashes burst every few seconds that brought feelings of warmth and comfort. Yet, interspersed with these fleeting images were visions of Leo's pummeled face at the hospital, photos of Bootsie's hideously bruised body on the sidewalk, snippets of my encounter with the punk in the alley who'd been following me, and the picture in the *New York Mirror* of my brother's car with the door cleaved off and Ike's lifeless form on the wet pavement.

A jumble of polar opposites.

And then, the canvas reflecting these conflicting impressions went blank. I imagined Dr. S. would've interpreted this as representing my missing brother.

Following Rabbi Leviev's advice, the letter to Eric didn't rehash any of our ancient history; it focused instead on our recent rapprochement, and the hope for a genuine reconciliation in the future.

THREE THOUSAND MILES was distance enough for Francesca to shed her fears, but mine were ever-present to the point where my fiancée thought I was becoming paranoid. I told her I'd been walking on Pacific heading towards The Embarcadero and saw a reflection on the window of The Tavern of someone on the other side of the street who hightailed it away when I turned to look at him. I mentioned that I saw a guy on the corner of Columbus and Broadway leaning against a lamppost reading a newspaper that I swore was upside down. She didn't seem concerned when I said a guy bumped into me at night in Portsmouth Plaza. What I didn't tell her was that I instinctively leaned down to grab the derringer, which I kept hidden between my shin and the sock on my right leg.

"No one knows we're here," Francesca would say sweetly, trying to dismiss my angst in a most rational manner.

That didn't work for me. I imagined a telephone number with a 415 area code scribbled on a tuna sandwich wrapper that one of 2-Cig's guys would fish out of the garbage can out back of Spins. I envisioned a scene in which Nate was strapped to a chair in the back room with 2-Cig grilling him to find out our location, and stuffing a handkerchief into his mouth even after he spilled his guts about where we were now living.

Perhaps Francesca was right.

After the last act at A Stone's Throw on a preternaturally warm post-midnight, I stayed late to take care of the books so I wouldn't have to come in on Monday, our one day off. We were doing well. Making a nice profit. I felt a great sense of pride. With a bounce to my step, I left the club and approached Washington Square to get to our apartment on Filbert. It was quiet. There was no one on the street. No one in the park. I walked up to pass the statue of Benjamin Franklin. Suddenly, a figure jumped out from behind the statue and pointed a gun at me. As I reached down to get the derringer, he shouted "Joogan," which startled me. I jerked the gun from my sock. As I raised my arm to shoot, he came down with a blow from his gun that cracked against my wrist so viciously that my gun fell to the ground, and I screamed in agony. Then, suddenly, a sparkle of light. I couldn't tell if this was something I imagined or a headlight from a car driving down Stockton or the muzzle flash from the gasses that are ignited when a bullet is fired, something I was familiar with from practicing in the dim light of the shooting range underneath the bodega in Manhattan with Carlos. I expected the impact of the bullet, which I wouldn't be able to ward off, given my helpless position on the ground. "Joogan, Joogan," the figure said loudly. Were these to be the last words I'd ever hear? My affectionate New York nickname, screamed at me in a taunting manner? How pathetic. They say your life appears in a speeded up movie when you're about to breathe your last, in this case, a big bang that would lead to nothingness. This was 2-Cig's revenge. My body would be found as a victim of a robbery gone bad or maybe as the result of an exchange of drugs, since I was in a park with a gun. That's what the cops would speculate to the beat reporters of the *San Francisco Chronicle*—my life condensed into a short paragraph that would read like the one that was reported the day before and would be the day after. Not really news, just something that filled the page between ads.

"Get up, Joogan," the figure commanded, and I imagined he wanted to look me in the eye before he put a bullet in my brain. I felt the hot dribble down my leg. He pulled me up by putting his hands underneath my shoulders. "Can you stand?" he asked. The pain from my shattered wrist was excruciating. "Look at me, Joogan," he ordered. Ah, an execution, I thought. He didn't move. It's hard to explain that I did, indeed, look at him. Dr. S. would probably have described it as my innate desire to please. The first thing I noticed through blurry eyes was that he was wearing gloves. On a warm night. How ridiculous, I thought. His gun was large and clunky. It didn't even look like it had a barrel.

"Joogan, can you hear me? Hello?"

I nodded.

"I'm sorry I smashed you," he said. "I didn't expect you to be packing, so I did the only thing I could think of. Are you okay?"

I certainly wasn't. I ached and thought I was going to throw up. My piss settled into both of my socks. I smelled my own stink. On the other hand, I felt that the worst might be over; maybe this guy wasn't going to kill me after all. "How the fuck do you know my nickname?" I asked, breathing heavily, each word coming out like when they run a movie in slow motion and the sounds have an exaggerated elongation.

"Yeah, well, that's a long story," he said. "For now, I want you to lie down, close your eyes, and don't move a fuckin' muscle. And let me take some photos with this fake blood shit I'm gonna paste onto your body and clothes."

"What the fuck?" It was then that I realized his gun was a camera.

"Just do it, c'mon. Get down. It'll do us both good."

"What good's in it for me?" I asked as I first knelt, remembering to lower myself with my left hand.

"The thing of it is, you'll be dead as far as the goons who sent me, and that's all that counts." He positioned himself over me, pulled my shirt up to expose my belly and chest, then dipped his gloved hand into a jar and smeared this red stuff that actually looked like blood on me—the kind my brother would get at Halloween and come screaming into the house to tell my mother hysterically that he'd been knifed by the only D'Onofrio boy who wasn't in Juvie Hall.

"What's with the fucking gloves?" I asked, as if I were the reporter who was going after the human interest part of the story to give to the night editor. Before he could answer, I looked at his face and gloves and said, "Holy shit, I know you! You're the asshole who followed me from Coogan's that night. I almost beat the crap out of you. You said you'd been sent by the big fuck who works for the guys at the social club." My voice was beginning to return to normal.

"Yeah, genius, that's me."

"My old man was the cop who hired you."

"You gotta be fuckin' kidding me," he said. "Anyways, he wasn't the one who sent me now."

"Yeah, I know. He's dead."

"Whacked?"

"That's *my* long story."

"Stories are for bedtime, so here's one you can tell your lady friend. It was two grand to kill you. Two thousand fuckin' dollars, plus expenses. From an Arthur Avenue social club guy. Plus, I got this nice camera from the guy who takes photos for the *Mirror*. I can keep it. For real. Nice, no? This is big money for a punk like me. Half down, and half when I showed them proof. And lemme tell you, I had no guilt. You pissed me off."

This wasn't the time to apologize for intimidating him in the alley. "So why'd you decide *not* to kill me? I asked.

"Money," he said.

"Wait, I don't understand. You were going to get another thousand and you're turning it down?"

"No, dumbass. They gave me a thousand, I'll get another grand with the photos, and I get another for *pretending* to kill you, so's I'm gonna come out with three."

"Someone else paid you *not* to kill me?"

"Yeah. A grand. I'm gonna collect the second thousand from the guys at the social club by showing them photos of your dead body, then the last grand from the other guy, once he gets a call from you. Not bad, huh? Maybe I'm not such a dipshit punk, you know?"

"Who's the guy giving you dough *not* to take me out?"

"I don't know his name. I just have his number."

"What is it?"

"Lemme take a few more shots, then drag you on the ground. I gotta make it look like I pulled you along and dumped your body in the trunk of the car. Then I'm supposed to bury you in this desolate part of Nevada on my way back to New York. They gave me a map."

We practiced a few times, making sure there were marks in the soft grass, mud on my shoes, and green stains on my pant legs. He positioned me in the trunk of his car with my head dangling off to the side, the fake blood surrounding the hole he cut in my shirt. "Piss a little more in your pants, will ya" he ordered, and I complied, wanting to make this look as authentic as possible. He took shots of it all. Then he gave me the phone number. I immediately recognized it as belonging to Carlos.

The next morning, I asked Carlos how they found out I was in San Francisco. "Something you said to the bartender at Coogan's the last time you saw him."

"I'm pretty sure I didn't mention San Francisco."

"You didn't."

"Then what was it?"

"You were excited that you'd be seeing the Giants again."

Shit. After thanking the bartender for steering me out of harm's way before Sean came out of the bathroom, I did mention something about looking forward to seeing the Giants . . . who had just moved to San Francisco. I'm such a moron.

"Listen, do yourself a favor. No news about you. Nothing in the papers. No publicity. Remember, you're dead to them, amigo."

When I told all this to Francesca, she trembled and cried. Then she composed herself, took a deep breath, and said, "Keep the derringer." I did. It took four full months for my wrist to heal and, during that period of time, I practiced pulling the gun from my left leg with my other hand.

GAVI WAS IMPRESSED with what Francesca and I had accomplished. He presented us a check for five thousand dollars as a bonus. We thanked him for his confidence in us and for backing us with a significant investment to start the store and launch the business.

"I appreciate you thanking me," he said, "but I can't take the credit. The money came from someone else." He hesitated, as if he didn't want to tell us anything about an anonymous investor.

"Well, I'd like to meet the guy sometime, to show him my gratitude," I said. "At some point, can you introduce us?"

"He's dead," Gavi said.

"I'm so sorry to hear that," I said. "It must've been recent. I mean, with him entering into an arrangement with you to open up out here."

Gavi looked at me, at Francesca, and then back at me.

"It was Ike's money," he said.

"*What?*" I was thunderstruck. I had to catch my breath. "*Ike?* Ike didn't have two nickels to rub together. Did he rob a bank?"

"Not a bank." He paused. "But he was a thief."

Francesca and I exchanged *Oh my God* looks. I turned to Gavi.

"Tell me he didn't steal money from the duffel bag buried near the train tracks," I said.

"He never knew you'd taken any. When he told me what he did, I didn't disclose *your* theft, hiding the cash in your stuffed elephant or sending dough surreptitiously to your mother. None of that. He told me about it the night he and I went for a walk during your welcome home from the army party. He'd given Donatella permission to hide a duffel bag on the other side of the chain link fence in your backyard. He didn't know what was inside, but he was convinced it was something of value. He said his curiosity got the better of him after a few days—"

"Holy shit," I interrupted. "I held out for only three nights. Can you imagine if we'd both snuck out on the same night?"

It was a question no one bothered to answer.

"Do you know how much he took?" Francesca asked.

"He said about twenty grand. He put it into the bank and never touched it. With interest, it added up over thirteen years. When I told him I needed someone to manage Spins, he suggested you and told me he'd withdraw the money and give it to me on the condition I'd only use it for Spins or to help you in the future. That was it."

"Did he ever say why?"

"No. But when I told all this to Rabbi Leviev—I should now say your father—he said simply, 'atonement.'"

"Just like your letter to Bud," Francesca said softly. "Add to it. Turn it into a story. Or a memoir."

"I thought those were generally written when you're older, looking back on so many earlier years with a different outlook. Can I have poetic license to change some things?"

"Just don't let invention get in the way of truth."

EACH MORNING, I'd get up early and sit in front of my Smith Corona. I was encouraged by several of the more prominent Beats who read my early drafts and made helpful suggestions.

On April 8, immediately prior to opening day of the 1960 baseball season, I stood outside of City Lights Bookstore and took a photo of my recently released novel featured prominently in the window, titled *Atonement*, dedicated to my unnamed brother, written under my pseudonym—Jacob deIsaac—with an artist's rendering of me: a profile obscured by a shadow.

34

YEAH, I GOT A BROTHER.

Francesca's cheery "Hello" was followed by a sigh and thirty seconds of silence. At first, I thought she was staring at the Coit Tower, but as she lowered the receiver back into the cradle, I realized she was staring at me through a reflection in the window.

"Jay, my *nonna* just died."

"Oh my god, I'm so sorry. I know how close you were and how much she meant to you."

I leaned over and kissed Francesca's forehead. She leaned into me.

"We should go back for the funeral," I said softly.

"It's too risky, Jay. The church'll be mobbed. Everyone who's ever called out, 'Ciao Daniela!' will be there. It's the perfect place to send a few capos who'd blend into the crowd and then report back to 2-Cig that you're alive." She sniffled.

"I'm so sad." I held her, motionless, for a few minutes.

When she gently pulled away, she said, "I'd like to find a way to memorialize her life."

I said, "Let's celebrate here in her honor."

"What are you thinking?"

"A wedding."

"Got anyone in mind?" She asked, turning around to face me.

"A couple of dago Jews."

"I've got an eye on one," she said blithely.

"And the other eye?"

"Smart ass."

"I'll give you a ring later," I said ambiguously.

"A call?" she said playfully.

"Smart ass."

"Daniela Lagana will be here in spirit. *Ciao*, Daniela," she said, smiling.

THE BASEMENT OF A Stone's Throw was transformed into a cozy chapel. A makeshift *chuppa* was installed on the stage with enough room for a small band of musicians on the side. Francesca wore a black silk dress with a wide white belt that Mr. Scattennato swore was the one he created for Lauren Bacall in *To Have and to Have Not*, an indulgence we were only too happy not to protest. After our vows, Rabbi Leviev took out a glass and placed it in a cloth napkin on the floor. I smashed it with my foot to a chorus of *Mazel tov* from the fifty guests, including my mother, Uncle Mickey and his wife Ruti, as well as cousin Gavi Yudakov with his wife Yudit. They all made a big fuss about taking the train from The Bronx to Boston for a week, telling folks they were visiting recently arrived Azerbaijani relatives in Dorchester, but then hightailed it to Logan Airport immediately after arriving at South Station, a ruse to make sure no one suspected where Francesca and I were actually living. Mr. and Mrs. Casterella informed us that they weren't feeling well enough for a cross-country trip. We suspected this was not about physical ailments so much as malaise, so we made sure to include them with an open long-distance phone line so they could listen to the ceremony. As the band played *Hava Nagila*, Francesca and I were hoisted on separate chairs, held aloft by Leo, Kara, Enzo, Uncle Mickey, and Gavi Yudakov, while our guests danced the *hora*.

A week later, coming home from a book talk and signing at Congregation Emanu-El just south of the Presidio, I was surprised to see Francesca sitting on the steps with a large manila envelope and a newspaper on her lap.

"This arrived today," she said, handing me the envelope.

"The newspaper? It came in the mail?" I asked incredulously.

"Yup."

"Who'd mail us the *Chronicle*? It's in every newsstand and drug store."

"It's the *Mirror*. New York. Take a look. Page four. Read it," she said.

I read the headline out loud. "Construction Executive Killed in Car Crash."

"Go on."

"Alberto Giaquinto, owner of Giaquinto Brothers Construction Company was killed in the crash. According to police, his car was forced off the road and into a concrete barrier as it was exiting onto the Cross Bronx Expressway in Tremont during last night's violent rainstorm."

"Holy shit, you've got to be kidding."

"No joke, I'm deadly serious."

I paused to let it sink in.

"No return address?" I asked.

"Nope."

"Do you think it was an accident?"

"Who knows?" she said.

I noticed handwriting on the first page of the paper.

"Did you see this? Handwritten scribble."

"No. What's it say?"

I read it out loud: "God has granted me happiness."

"That was Alberto Giaquinto's pet phrase, wasn't it?"

"Yeah."

"Are you thinking what I'm thinking?" she asked.

"Maybe. Eric?"

"He's back in The Bronx."

"It looks like he was, anyway," I said.

"Know what this means, don't you?"

"What?"

"We can go home again."

WE SETTLED INTO the spare bedroom of my mother's apartment, my grandmother having been moved into a nursing home. We didn't have enough for a place of our own because neither of our jobs—Francesca's at Columbia Presbyterian or mine at the *New York Mirror*—would be starting for at least a month. On the afternoon of our second day, I turned on the TV in the living room to watch the news. Francesca was reading a book on the easy chair next to the sofa where I'd stretched out to get comfy. My mother was puttering in the kitchen. After the first commercial, there was a story about a drowning in Eastchester Bay near the City Island Bridge.

Francesca perked up.

"Did somebody jump?"

"They didn't say."

The live camera captured a group of firemen and police lifting a body out of the surf, placing it on a gurney, then gently pushing it into the back of the ambulance. I was transfixed. Seeing this live as opposed to reading about it in the newspapers created an intensity of emotion, much as I used to feel when watching *You Are There* with Walter Cronkite, where reporters interviewed famous people in history; you knew it was a re-creation, but you were transported to a time when a major event in the past had been taking place and, well, you were there.

"What the fuck! There's Nicky Shark." Snapping pictures as rapidly as he could change bulbs, Nicky was the only person there not in a uniform. I knew what that meant—he was back with 2-Cig's crew. And then I saw it—a gold chain with boxing glove pendants so tightly wound around his neck that it had cut into his skin. It had been used as a garrote.

"It's Carlos. Jesus Christ," I shouted.

My mother hurried in from the kitchen.

"Carlos Colón? The young man who gave you the derringer?" she asked, in a way that people query you hoping all along that the answer would be in the negative. "Are you sure? Could it be someone else with the same necklace?" my mother added.

"They got him," Francesca said with authority.

"They? There's no *they* anymore. Alberto, Bootsie, and Ike are six feet under. Donatella's holed up in Attica. The music's stopped, and the only chair left is for Sean," I said.

"He must've found out Carlos paid the kid to save you in San Francisco," Francesca said.

"There's no one who can help me, us, now," I said.

"What about Eric?" Francesca asked.

"Good luck finding him."

"Go to Quinn's on Hoffman Street. Connor was his pal and seemed to know all the goings on with the regulars," she said.

◆

I WAS OUT OF BREATH when I walked into the bar. I might have looked a bit crazed. Connor was pulling a tap handle for Knickerbocker Beer.

"Hey, Connor. Jay. deVenezia."

"Long time. What can I getcha?"

"Rheingold."

"What brings you in?"

"Eric. Seen him lately?"

Pointing to a girl at the end of the bar, he said, "Not the one to ask. Over there."

I took my beer and sat next to the girl.

"Listen, I'm not trying to pick you up or anything. Looking for someone."

She sized me up like I was a slab hanging from a meat hook in a cold storage room at the Hunt's Point market.

"You're Eric's brother."

"How'd you know?"

"I was with him a coupla times when he went to the music store in Manhattan."

"Spins."

"He used to steal records, you know. Well, he'd pick one out, and when he'd go into a booth, that was the signal for me to grab a record and shove it into my pocketbook."

I smirked.

"You didn't know?"

"Um, yeah. So, Janet is it, now that it's coming back to me," I said remembering her as the one that every boy ogled when she came in with my brother.

"Janice. Janice Byrne."

"See, Janice, I've lost track of my brother. You still in touch?"

"So I'm a carrier pigeon?"

"It's not like that," I said, lowering my voice to a whisper. "It's kind of urgent that I speak to him. I don't know how to locate him. You may be my last hope."

"What's with the hush-hush?"

"Maybe life and death."

"Ooooh. Okay."

I wrote my mother's address on a napkin and pushed it in front of her.

"Thanks, Janice." I clicked my glass with hers, nodded to Connor and walked out.

"THAT WAS A REALLY GOOD IDEA, Francesca. I ran into Janice Byrne at Quinn's and gave her our address."

"Whoa, hold on. *The* Janice Byrne?"

"She used to date Eric."

"Forgetting something? Also Sean."

"Oh, shit."

"Did she say she was gonna speak to Eric?"

"Not exactly."

"Jay, we're fucked. You gotta get your mother outta this place. Now. Have Gavi come and take her away."

"A little melodramatic?"

Francesca turned to my mother.

"Rebekah, listen to me. I don't want to alarm you, but I'm going to anyway. It's possible that Sean McMenamin is gonna come after us, here, so you gotta leave. Jay's on the phone with Gavi. He's gonna take you to his place.

"Sean's the one who had Jay tailed to San Francisco, yes?" my mother said.

"Yeah. And probably the one who killed Carlos."

"Heaven help us," my mother said, looking upwards for an angel to come to our aid.

I took out my derringer.

"If he comes here, we ambush him."

My mother put her face in her hands. She couldn't speak.

"Jay, listen to me, no hero shit. We're outta here with your mother," Francesca said.

"Ma, pack up. Gavi'll be here soon," I said to my mother. Then I turned to Francesca. "Look, I know it sounds crazy—"

"Loony bin stuff, if you ask me," Francesca said.

"Hear me out, listen. I'd rather take my chances with Sean on my own terms, in my own place, rather than spending my life looking over my shoulder, around every corner, at each face in the crowd, wondering if I'll be attacked without warning. I can't live my life that way. Sorry. But, and this is an important but, you should leave with my mother and Gavi. I've got the upper hand here and the element of surprise. No way Sean will think I'm lying in wait with a gun."

Francesca's eyes were wide with fright. She hesitated for a few seconds and then grabbed both of my arms.

"You're not gonna do this alone," she said.

I drew her into me, then kissed her on the cheek.

We were all frantic. My mother went into her room to pack a small suitcase. I pulled the sofa to the middle of the room facing the door and turned the marble coffee table on its side. Gavi came and quickly left with my mother, his arm around her back, surely for comfort and support but also as a restraint to prevent her from remaining in the apartment. Francesca stacked pots and pans on the floor in the apartment's entryway. I did the same with wine glasses. Francesca locked the windows and the doors to the fire escape, then turned off all the lights. We both knelt behind the sofa. I held a hand over my mouth to deaden the sound of heavy breathing. Francesca did the same. After a few minutes, she whispered to me, "I have to go to the bathroom."

"Pee in your pants for all I care, but don't even think of getting up," I said softly but forcefully. She gave me the finger.

After a couple of hours, we heard the lock on the door being picked. I gently pushed Francesca down so there was no way she would be exposed. I had the derringer in my right hand and bullets in my left. The door opened slowly. I could see from the light in the hall that it was a man. He tripped over the pots and pans and crashed against the wine glasses. I shot twice in rapid fashion.

"Goddammit!" the man screamed.

I reloaded and shot twice again in the direction of where the man had ended up on the floor.

"For Christ's sake, stop fucking shooting me!"

"Eric? Eric Is that you?"

Francesca's hand crept up on the end table and pulled the chain on a lamp.

"You were expecting someone else, dipshit?" Eric said.

"Why didn't you ring the fucking bell?" I said as I stood up and moved towards my brother, who was cursing and picking pieces of glass out of his hands.

"In the middle of the night? It would've frightened Ma to death."

"I thought you were Sean."

"Sean's dead. Goddammit. Help me up. It's a damn good thing you're a piss-poor shot."

"You're bleeding," Francesca said, standing next to me.

"From my hand. From this broken glass. I'll live," Eric said.

Francesca went into the kitchen, got paper towels and soap, then rushed back and began to clean up Eric's hand.

"How'd Sean die?"

"Janice Byrne called. Said you were back here in The Bronx. I knew about Carlos and put two and two together. I realized Sean had both of us in his crosshairs."

I looked to Francesca. "Janice came through for me."

"Carlos had told me about the attempted hit on you in San Francisco. That Sean was behind it," Eric said. "I made a call. Then Nate and I went to his place over on East 181st Street near Valentine Avenue. Nate rang the bell. Sean hit the buzzer. Nate went inside, while I stayed across the street in the shadows in case things went south. When Sean opened the door and saw it was Nate, he said, 'What the fuck do you want, boy?' Nate said it was all he could do to not cock him right there. 'Heat, man,' Nate said. 'I need a piece.' Sean took him up to the roof and opened the door to the pigeon coop. 'Two hundred smackers, buddy,' Sean said, holding out his hand. Nate took his wallet out and give him the money. Sean bent down, opened a hidden box underneath the coop, and reached in for a revolver. Nate pulled a metal wedge out of his jacket pocket and smacked him hard on the back of his head. Out cold. Nate took one of Sean's guns, wrapped a towel he found next to the coop around the barrel, and put it next to Sean's temple. That was it. Nate came down and let Nicky Shark climb up to the roof to take pictures. They'll be in the *Mirror* tomorrow. Suicide."

I turned to Francesca and exhaled dramatically.

"First, he made a call."

"To Nicky Shark," Francesca said knowingly.

Eric nodded.

I pivoted toward Eric.

"I owe you," I said.

"We're even."

ON THE FRIDAY AFTER THANKSGIVING, I parked next to the railing that overlooked the Cross Bronx Expressway that had cut through the heart of Tremont. Francesca and I watched the cars and trucks slowly make their way through the season's first snowstorm. Our grim faces must have looked like they'd been carved out of stone. Neither of us spoke. We looked over the expressway at the other half of Tremont, then walked silently to the car.

We drove to lower Manhattan and parked on Hester Street. Half a dozen boys were engaged in a playful snowball fight. One kid was being pelted as he ran toward us, most likely to seek cover and deter the others from throwing near a couple of adults. An older boy came running after the kid, laughing and shouting at the top of his lungs.

"Hey, Joey, come back, I got a stash next to the hydrant."

"Is that your brother?" I said to the kid.

"Mister, I don't got a brother. You?"

"Yeah, I got a brother." I paused, then said, "I do."

I turned to Francesca. She nodded, then gently touched my arm.

The older boy caught up with us, smiled, and said, "I gotta teach him not to be a pussy." He looked at Francesca and said, "Sorry."

Francesca waved him off.

We crossed the street and made our way towards a coffee shop with a sign above the door that read: ~~Cross~~ Manhattan ~~Expressway~~ Café.

ACKNOWLEDGMENTS

I'm immensely grateful to Ann Streger Price, who read every word of each draft, pushed me relentlessly to raise my standards, and offered words of encouragement when I needed them most. In this regard, she is, as they say, a "tough cookie," which is exactly what this author needs as he attempts to perfect his craft. I wouldn't have it any other way.

Heartfelt thanks to:

Howard Jay Smith, a talented novelist and screenwriter who guided me to incorporate screenplay techniques, settings, and dialogues into the novel to amplify tension, anxiety, and feints, such that the reader can have a greater sense of being a current observer of the action.

DJ Schuette, for extraordinary editorial and copyediting skills. His unusual ability to understand what an author wants to do enables him to provide the most insightful and helpful critiques.

Asha Hossain of Asha Hossain Design, LLC for the elegant cover and jacket design, which exquisitely captured the essence of the book.

Pauline Neuwirth, Beth Metrick, Jeff Farr, and Beth Kessler of Neuwirth & Associates, Inc., for the highest quality production values as well as the classy interior look of the book.

Rachel Tarlow Gul of Over the River Public Relations, for excellence in publicity.

Peter DeGiglio of St. Lawrence Publishing Consultants and Dan Kohan of Sensical.design for superb assistance in navigating the book world.

Matthew Price of Design by Price, for first-class website designs and IT wisdom.

Alison Sheehy of Alison Sheehy Photography, for distinctive photographic gifts.

All authors should be so fortunate to be surrounded by such skilled, unselfish people with whom it is a delight to work.

Finally, a special thank-you to those gifted authors who read this novel before publication and were generous enough to write reviews and blurbs. I recognize the value of your time and greatly appreciate your willingness to take some of it to give insight to future readers as to what they may find interesting and enjoyable:

Meryl Ain, author of *Remember to Eat and Other Stories*; Esther Amini, author of *Concealed*; Jacqueline Friedland, author of *Counting Backwards, The Stockwell Letters*, and *He Gets That from Me*; Michael Gold, author of *Horror House Detective*; Barbara Josselsohn, author of *The Secret Orphanage* and *The Forgotten Italian Restaurant*; Howard Langer, author of *The Last Dekrepitzer*; Michael Lavigne, author of *Not Me, The Wanting*, and the upcoming *A Song at the Edge of World*; Haya Molnar, author of *Under A Red Sky*; Abigail Pogrebin, author of *My Jewish Year, Stars of David*, and co-author of *It Takes Two to Torah*; Alan Swyer, author of *The Beard*; Jeff Wallach, author of *Mr. Wizard* and *Everyone Here Is From Somewhere Else*.

AUTHOR'S NOTE

This book is a work of complete fiction; no characters or settings are remotely related to anything that deals with me, my family, friends, or acquaintances. To avoid any misconceptions, no fictional character is based on any real person.

Although appearances are made by Mayor Robert Wagner, Horace Stoneham (the owner of the New York Giants baseball team), Carmine DeSapio (the head of Tammany Hall), and Robert Moses (the master builder of New York), the actions and dialogues associated with these people are fictional and do not represent any attempt to link them to any actual illegal activities.

For the avoidance of doubt, I have had no interactions (i.e., verbal, electronic, or written) with any person who was involved in the planning or construction of the Cross Bronx Expressway or with any third party who has written about this subject.

The anti-Semitism noted in the novel is of the familiar kind that existed in the US in the 1950s and '60s, which consisted mainly of occasional slurs, exclusions, and off-camera slights, and reflects conversational language that was typical of the times. Today, these almost seem quaint when compared to the anti-Semitism and anti-Zionism from those whose physical assaults, ignorance, calumnies, and blasphemies are directed at Jews in general and the State of Israel in particular.

ABOUT THE AUTHOR

DAVID HIRSHBERG is the pseudonym for a biotech executive who prefers to keep his business activities separate from his writing endeavors. He adopted the first name of his father-in-law and the last name of his maternal grandfather as a tribute to their impact on his life. He is the author of two previous novels: *My Mother's Son* and *Jacobo's Rainbow*, each of which has won multiple awards. In addition, he has published four short stories and written the introduction for a nonfiction book. Hirshberg holds an undergraduate degree from Dartmouth College and a master's degree from the University of Pennsylvania. He lives with his wife and two sporting dogs in Westchester County, New York. Visit his website at www.DavidHirshberg.com.

www.ingramcontent.com/pod-product-compliance
Lightning Source LLC
LaVergne TN
LVHW041657060526
838201LV00043B/472